THE GETAWAY

NICOLA MARTIN

RAVEN BOOKS
LONDON · OXFORD · NEW YORK · NEW DELHI · SYDNEY

RAVEN BOOKS
Bloomsbury Publishing Plc
50 Bedford Square, London, WC1B 3DP, UK
29 Earlsfort Terrace, Dublin 2, Ireland

BLOOMSBURY, RAVEN BOOKS and the Raven Books logo
are trademarks of Bloomsbury Publishing Plc

First published in Great Britain 2024

A catalogue record for this book is available from the British Library

ISBN: HB: 978-1-5266-7242-1; EBOOK: 978-1-5266-7241-4; EPDF: 978-1-5266-7238-4

2 4 6 8 10 9 7 5 3 1

Typeset by Integra Software Services Pvt. Ltd.
Printed and bound in Great Britain by CPI Group (UK) Ltd, Croydon CR0 4YY

To find out more about our authors and books visit www.bloomsbury.com
and sign up for our newsletters

THE
GETAWAY

1

I set off for the island by boat, knocking against crates of champagne and cool boxes full of black truffles. Just another import.

It had taken three planes and two ferries to reach this remote corner of the Caribbean. I hadn't slept during the thirty-two-hour journey, but I'd pushed through exhaustion into a jumpy alertness and now I leaned against the bow, searching out details of my new home. I had to squint against the early-morning sun, blazing from a cloudless sky.

Keeper Island was an emerald, small enough at this distance to seize in the hollow of my hand. A central peak rose up, covered in green forest. As the boat motored closer, I caught sight of a sandy shore; palm trees waving to me.

This was my safe haven. This was my escape.

I touched my cheekbone instinctively, then glanced at my fingernails. I couldn't stop checking them, imagining there was blood underneath them. No. They were clean now. Everything was fine.

We were approaching a long wooden pier, but the man driving the boat showed no sign of slowing down. He was animated, head thrown back, telling a story ('and she say, you too damn rude, ya sick, man'). The other three passengers were all muscular men, all Virgin Islanders, I presumed. They'd been polite as they'd ushered me on board, but there was a guarded quality to their expressions.

My hands tightened around the salt-sticky railing. The pier was rushing to meet us. With a whoosh of wake, the skipper slammed the boat into reverse. I stumbled against the railing, but my companions retained their balance. One of them kicked a couple of fenders off the boat and we bumped against the side of the pier.

As soon as the motorboat was tied up, the men jumped into action, unloading provisions. They lifted out my overstuffed purple suitcase and wheeled it away to a procession of waiting golf carts, along with the brie and Bluefin tuna. 'It's fine, you don't need to,' I called, but the suitcase had already gone.

The skipper extended a hand to help me off. He had springy hair and sleepy eyes.

'Thanks.' I stepped ashore. 'Know where I can find Moxham?'

Mike Moxham. My new boss. The reason I was here – in more ways than one.

'He around here somewhere.' The skipper heaved a crate into his arms. He was already jogging after his companions.

I felt a reflexive need to help, but the provisions were gone from the pier. The men had disappeared, God-knows-where. I was alone. When I sought out the neighbouring island, I was surprised at how far away it looked. A rumble-and-splash out on the water caught my attention. Fifty metres from shore, a pair of red jet skis were skimming the waves. Now that looked like fun. Refreshing, on a scorcher of a day like today.

Jetlag was hitting me. I needed a shower and a meal and a bed and a brain transplant. I hoped this island could rustle up a cheese sandwich for me, at least. I scuffed along the worn wooden boards of the pier, inland towards a biscuit-coloured, paved path, edged with palms and spiky green foliage.

'Hello, hello!' A voice rang out.

Another golf cart had arrived. A slender woman, glamorous yet understated in a pink floral maxi-dress, glided over to me. I felt wrung-out, but gave my hospitality-smile. She looked ready to step into the Keeper Island brochure, her long black hair falling like silk and her lips a beachy coral. I presumed she was one of the people who paid thousands of dollars a night to be pampered on this private island.

'You're Lola,' she said.

'Uh, that's the rumour.'

'I'm Fizzy.' She offered a limp handshake, almost like she didn't want to touch me. 'I'll get you situated.'

Oh. So, she wasn't a guest. Looking closer, I spotted a two-way radio clipped to her belt, along with a raft of keys. The radio crackled with distant voices, the volume turned low.

'I was expecting Moxham?' I said.

'He's busy-busy, like always.'

She flipped open a cooler in the back of the golf buggy and presented me with a rolled hand towel. It was ice-cold and smelled of eucalyptus. I passed it gratefully over my face, rubbing away the sweat, and then regretted it when my thumb hit my cheekbone. The concealer I'd reapplied an hour ago would have disappeared, revealing the bruise underneath.

When Fizzy's gaze darted over my face, I produced a smile, hoping to distract her. 'Thanks.'

'You know, this is somewhat of a surprise.' She had the shifting accent of a jet-setter, with straying vowels that mostly rounded down to American. Sometimes I could hear my own accent heading in a similar direction, but I normally managed to re-route it back to London, where I'd grown up.

'Moxham only told me you were arriving an hour ago,' she said. 'I didn't know we required a deputy manager.'

I tried not to wince. 'Snap decision, I s'pose.' I was feeling faint and it wasn't just the jetlag.

'Mox… I'm fucking terrified.'

'Showgirl…'

Two nights ago, I'd been slumped on the bathroom floor, phone to my ear, begging for help.

'You need to fix this, Mox. You're the fucking fixer, so fix it.'
'How about a new job? A fresh start.'
'Where?'
'Paradise.'

Out on the water, there was another roar of engines. The jet skis were back, closer to shore this time.

'On behalf of us all… you're very welcome.' It didn't ring true. Fizzy had the air of someone who used a fake-nice voice so often, she'd lost the ability to speak normally. It was a hazard of working in hospitality.

'Thanks,' I said again, but my eyes were on the jet-ski riders.

Two men, both bare-chested. One was dark-haired, one ginger. They were doing tricks. One cut a sharp turn left, then right, a cowboy on a bucking bronco. The other man leaned back, pulling the jet ski's nose upwards, a plume of white water gushing out of the back like a rocket ship.

For a second, it was impressive. Then it was calamitous. The jet ski turned into a Catherine wheel, spinning out of control, and the dark-haired man was flung from his steed, hitting the water with a splash.

'Oh, my God!'

The engine died, but the jet ski was still spiralling. The man hadn't surfaced.

'Shit… are they OK?' I took an instinctive step towards the shore. Belatedly, I realised neither of the men were wearing life vests.

There'd been too much death this week. I couldn't handle any more.

'They're just playing.' Fizzy wasn't even looking, concentrating instead on tidying away my balled-up towel.

A familiar hyena laugh drifted across the water. I'd know that laugh anywhere. Moxham. He'd surfaced and was swimming a lazy loop around his jet ski, which lay on its side in the water.

I pressed my lips together, a sharp breath escaping my nose. Of course he was fine. I didn't want him to know he'd made me sweat, so I waved, but either he didn't see me or he ignored me. Seconds later, Moxham had climbed back on the jet ski and he and the other man zipped away, out of sight.

'You and Moxham know each other?' Fizzy asked.

'We used to work together. Before he came here, to manage this place.'

'Then I assume you already know all about Keeper Island?'

'A bit.'

Who didn't recognise the name, even if most people couldn't locate it on a map?

This private island, part of the British Virgin Islands, was owned by billionaire Kip Clement and he'd lived here since the 90s. When I was growing up, magazine spreads of him and his wife were a familiar sight. *Our lavish life in the tropics.*

Of course, since Kip had made his money in the hospitality industry, he couldn't resist transforming his home into an exclusive resort, with a handful of guests on the island at any given time and staff to cater to their every whim.

'I'm Kip's assistant,' Fizzy was saying, in a tone of voice reserved for *I'm related to the Royal Family.* 'Not as easy as it looks, corralling a great man like that.'

'Bet you know where the bodies are buried.'

'Ha,' she said in lieu of a laugh. 'Well, in you get.' She gestured to the golf cart. There were half a dozen bracelets on each of her wrists that jangled as she moved. Along with the keys at her waist, the sound reminded me of a jailer.

'First night on Keeper,' she said as she settled herself in the driving seat, 'we like to give new staff the rock star treatment. Stay in a villa, feel like a guest.'

'I'll take anything with indoor plumbing,' I said.

Fizzy frowned; my response hadn't been the right one. 'Kip wants everyone to understand the ethos of the place. Luxury but laid back. Like the model who's so gorgeous she doesn't have to try.' She pulled at her cheeks, imitating a face lift. 'Don't I wish that were me?'

Earlier, I'd pegged Fizzy for my age, but now I noticed the laughter lines at her eyes. Forties, maybe, with expert make-up to conceal any blemishes. I rubbed at my own face and winced when I aggravated my bruise.

In some weird twist of fate, I'd missed my thirtieth birthday. The date had been swallowed up by time zone shifts and delayed flights. I'd set out from Hong Kong aged twenty-nine, now I was thirty and one day.

'Yes, it's a resort,' Fizzy was saying, 'but it's our little home away from home.'

We set off in the golf cart, barrelling along a paved path that followed the shoreline. Part of the inland forest had been cut back and I craned my neck to the right to see tennis courts and a putting green, perfect and artificial, nestled within the chaos of nature.

'How long have you been on the island?' I asked Fizzy.

'Ohhh...' She paused to think. 'Fifteen years, for my sins. I keep thinking someone will tell me the world's ended and we never noticed, out here in paradise.' Her fingers twitched around the word 'paradise', brows arching. 'The worst thing that will ever happen to you here is boredom.'

After the week I'd had, boredom sounded heavenly.

Another golf buggy approached from the opposite direction. The driver slammed on the brakes and motioned for Fizzy to do the same.

'Big problem,' he said. It was the guy with the springy hair who'd ferried me to the island. Fizzy introduced him as Reggie, but he only waved a distracted hello.

'No Beluga caviar in today's provisions.' He pulled at his wispy moustache, clearly agitated.

'Shhh-sugar,' Fizzy said. 'Did you call them?'

'They say tomorrow.'

'Not good enough. See if they can bring it in by jet to Beef Island.'

'Yeah… OK, yeah.' Reggie looked relieved. His golf cart jumped forward and he was off again.

'We've got a party tonight,' Fizzy said to me. 'No caviar, all hell will break loose.'

I nodded, trying, and probably failing, to hide my surprise. Sure, sure, it was totally normal to send a private jet to pick up caviar because you needed it for a party. We continued to roll along in silence. The rocky outcrop to my left turned into white sands, deserted except for one stooped man. It took me a few seconds to figure out what he was doing: raking the sand in smooth arcs, getting rid of footprints and making it pristine again, before the guests rose for the day.

'I forgot to ask,' Fizzy spoke up, 'where are you joining us from? England, I presume?'

'Originally, yeah, but I've been in Hong Kong the last couple of years.'

'We have a guest staying with us right now. Eddie Yiu. Does something terribly fascinating with finance in Honkers. The two of you must talk.'

I gave a noncommittal nod. I didn't want to chit-chat about 'Honkers' with a stranger.

Before catching a taxi to the airport, I'd left a note for my boyfriend, Nathan, saying I was going away for a couple of days, a mini-break to Vietnam. That ruse wouldn't stand for long. When my lease ran out at the end of the month, my white box of an apartment in Wan Chai wouldn't be mine anymore. My hotel name badge would be binned, my office drawers cleared out by a janitor. I tried to remember what I'd left in there: coconut candy and a half-finished thriller. I guess I'd never find out how it ended.

I felt a stab of remorse. I'd left my colleagues at the Clement Hong Kong in the lurch. Nathan would probably punch a wall when he realised I was gone for good. The thought sent a shiver up my spine, despite the heat of the day.

I let Fizzy ramble on about all the 'terribly fascinating' billionaires who stayed on the island, while I concentrated on taking deep breaths. Onward we went, past what had to be the main complex: sloping thatched roofs overhanging the beach and a man-made pool that merged with the sea. It took less than ten minutes for us to arrive outside a white cube, built on the rocks above the sea.

'You'll be in Villa Queen Conch.' Fizzy drew the buggy to a smooth stop. 'One of my favourites, next door to Kip. You're probably exhausted, poor thing, flying cattle class. Anyway, get some rest. Join us at the party tonight. Keeper Island does full-moon parties like nowhere else on Earth.'

I thanked her and shambled inside my five-star home for the night. It was air-conditioned cool, smelling of jasmine. From an outsider's perspective, I'd landed a dream job. As long as everything from Hong Kong stayed in the past, I was safe.

2

I was so exhausted I would have accepted a piss-dribble shower and a sleeping bag on the floor. Instead, Villa Queen Conch was pure luxury.

The colour palette was pale hues of sand and stone and everything had a curved edge, as if sharp corners were unbecoming. The fixtures and fittings were understated, but I was seasoned enough to know the value of everything in Villa Queen Conch. There was Italian marble in the bathroom, Scandinavian designer chairs in the living room, bespoke light fixtures everywhere, glass shimmering as it cascaded from the ceiling.

After a long, hot shower, I collapsed onto one of the white sofas and shovelled Iberico ham into my mouth like it was a Big Mac. I'd ordered room service via the villa tablet and it had arrived so quickly that the island was either overstaffed or run with military precision.

Mid-morning, there was a light tap at the door. My head snapped up. Moxham?

'Come in!' I lumbered to the door, feeling the ache of every hour of my long-haul travel.

The door opened to reveal a small, curvy woman with satin-dark skin. When she introduced herself as the masseuse, I let out a whimper of gratitude. 'Yes, please.'

She gave a wry smile and began setting up her table. I complimented her dangly earrings, which were shaped like birds, but she didn't seem in the mood to chat, so I went into the bathroom to strip off.

Minutes later, I was stretched out on my front, closing my eyes and breathing in the lavender scent of the oils. The moment the woman dug her thumbs into my shoulders, I began to weep.

Once I started, I couldn't stop. I was crying for Nathan, for everything I'd lost. I was crying because here, now, I was safe, wasn't I? In paradise, I could be safe.

The masseuse pretended not to notice at first, but when my entire body was racked with sobs, it was difficult to ignore. She drew the sheet up over me and murmured, 'Would you prefer I leave you?'

'Yes,' I choked out, too humiliated to look at her.

After she'd left, I consoled myself by mentally listing all the weirdest guest encounters I'd had during my career. Snotty crying didn't crack the top 100. I was comforted by the memory of the guests who referred to their toy poodle as their son and required a twenty-four-hour dog-nanny. With any luck, it wouldn't have cracked the masseuse's weirdest guest encounters either. But unfortunately, I wasn't a guest, and I'd have to see her again.

I went out onto the veranda to clear my head. The sun was inching to its apex, but a strong breeze whipped off the water. The vast decking, which protruded over the rocky shoreline, was bigger than my old apartment. Wicker chairs were arranged around the oversized bowl of a fire pit. There was an outdoor shower, a pair of hammocks and a Jacuzzi.

I looked down over the railing. Five metres below, a shelf of rock stretched out to sea. It must have been low tide when I'd arrived, but now the sea was creeping in. At high tide, there'd be nothing but water beneath the veranda.

Then I saw her. A woman was laid out on the rocks. She was clinging on for dear life.

'Jesus Christ…'

What was she doing out there? She was going to drown.

I had a mad urge to jump over the railing and help her. But when I blinked, the scene resolved itself.

The woman was a statue, alabaster pale. She reclined across the rocks, her back arched, her head thrown back, orgasmic. As the tide drew in, the waves would crash over her. Was she drowning or surrendering to the sea? I drew back from the railing, unnerved. I didn't want to watch the sea claim her.

I'd planned to sleep for a few hours before the party, but I was wide awake. The indolence of pretending to be a guest didn't suit me. I wanted to get out there and see what working on Keeper Island really meant. More than that, I wanted to find Moxham.

He was the only person in the world I could talk to about what had happened. *Everything is fine.* I kept repeating the words to myself, but until I heard them from Moxham's lips, I wasn't sure I'd believe them.

*

'Hello?' The restaurant, when I ducked inside, was empty. It was a Balinese-inspired structure, all natural wood and bamboo, with vented sides open to the elements. I wandered through to the neighbouring kitchen, which wafted garlic and something meaty sizzling in a pan.

'Excuse me?' The only person I could see was a muscular man with a buzz cut, elbow-deep in soapy dishes and wearing headphones.

I'd followed the coast road on foot, back the way I'd come with Fizzy. A ten-minute walk had taken me to the resort's main complex, replete with swimming pools and tiki bars.

On my way, I'd flagged down a golf cart that was being driven by a woman, whose appearance was half-concealed by the piles of laundry she was ferrying around. Her name was Shirley and she was polite but brisk when I asked where I could find Moxham.

'He bring me cakes at lunchtime sometimes.' A quick smile flashed across her face. 'Like to hear the gossip. But I haven't seen him today. Must be busy with the party.'

I'd sensed I was holding her up, so when she'd told me to speak to the chef, I hadn't pressed her for more details.

I took another step inside the kitchen. 'Excuse me,' I said again, and this time the dishwasher looked up. Before he could speak, a commotion erupted at the other end of the room.

'I can't! I can't! I just can't.'

It was a female voice, high-pitched. The dishwasher didn't move, but I was pulled instinctively towards the fallout.

The kitchen was generously sized, with gleaming expanses of stainless steel. I passed what must have been 100 tiny jam tarts, cooling on racks.

'He's a creep. I'm quitting, I'm quitting, I'm quitting.'

A young woman was on the floor in a heap, blonde hair covering her face, sunglasses askew on her head. She tried to say something more, but all that came out were moaning sounds, like she had a mortal wound.

'What's going on?' I asked.

Two men, both in chef's whites, stood over her.

'She is having a bad day,' one of them said.

It was such a wild understatement, delivered in a flat French accent, that I almost laughed, but his face remained solemn. The first thing I noticed about him was his eyebrows, which were perfectly angled. They fitted with the rest of his model good looks: olive skin and chestnut hair.

He scrutinised me. 'And you are...'

Before leaving the villa, I'd changed into a uniform that had been left for me. Black shorts, white T-shirt with a tiny key logo. 'New deputy manager.'

'Yeah, Moxham mentioned you this morning.' The other man, string bean-thin, a bandana holding back his black hair, narrowed his eyes at me. 'Lola. London.' He pointed finger guns. 'Young hospitality person of the year but not so young anymore.' His accent was South African.

They'd looked me up online. I would have done the same in their position. I smiled blandly. 'That's me.'

'Hobbies include hiking and squash. Foot fetish. Actually, maybe I made that last part up.' The South African bandana man smirked.

If a foot fetish was the worst thing they could conceive about me, well... thank fucking God.

'Pleased to meet you, Lola.' The model-chef dried his hand on a dish towel and shook mine in a portentous way. He introduced himself as Guillaume. Bandana man was Tyson.

'We are having a small situation,' Guillaume said. 'Excuse us.'

As if on cue, the woman on the floor let out another might-be-dying cry. 'It's not worth it! No amount of money is worth this...'

These men, for all their efforts, were doing no good at all. I crouched down, touching her gently on the arm. 'Sweets, let's get you up off the floor.' I looked up at Tyson, 'Get her a chair. And a glass of water.'

'Coffee,' she sniffled, 'with oat milk.'

I suppressed a smile. Evidently, she wasn't actually at death's door.

'Get her a coffee.'

Over the next ten minutes, Tessa (Irish, twenty-one, humble beginnings, would-be model-influencer, but lately a host on Keeper Island – 'I quit!') emerged from behind her curtain of hair and told her story.

Tobias Ford, a tech bro with a cool billion in the bank and a moody trophy-girlfriend in tow, had arrived two days ago. The pair had stayed on the island a few months earlier and their reputation preceded them. Tyson had called them 'The Cunt and Cuntess of Silly-Cone Valley'. Tessa and the other two hosts, Maria and Alex, had drawn straws to decide who would be assigned to their villa. 'I lost,' she said, her lower lip wobbling.

During their most recent forty-eight-hour stay, Ford and his girlfriend, Carolina, had complained about the Wi-Fi (not fast enough), they'd complained about the golf carts (not fast enough), they'd complained about the sloths (not friendly enough) –

'There are sloths here?' I asked.

Guillaume nodded.

– they'd complained about the food (him: not gourmet enough; her: too gourmet). An hour ago, they'd complained about the water sports team.

'Mister was out on the jet ski and Missus was at a loose end' – Tessa took a slurp of her coffee – 'so we set her up with a paddleboard. Then Mister comes back and pitches a fit because the guys were looking at her in her bikini. I mean, they *were* looking. They were making sure she didn't drown. She kept falling in.'

Tessa, seated in a chair stolen from the restaurant, was pitched forwards, still on the verge of tears. Her coffee cup was nestled in her lap. I was rubbing her back in slow circles. It was a relief to be back at work, to have a catastrophe to focus on that was so easily rectified.

A small crowd had assembled, skiving kitchen assistants and a couple of waiters who had wandered in from the restaurant floor, but Guillaume shooed them away. 'Will lunch prepare itself?' His inflection was wrong, not sarcastic enough, only gloomy, but it had the desired effect. The crowd dispersed. Guillaume sighed. 'This bunny party...' he said under his breath.

Tyson banged a pan onto a burner and began flambéing something in a showy manner. 'Let her drown, teach 'em a lesson.' He raised his voice to be heard over the sizzle.

'Yeah, wish I had,' Tessa said. 'He screamed at me, said I was a useless bitch.' She covered her face. 'My head is in bits, I can't do this anymore. I was up at five because they tried to flush a banana down the toilet. This job is the pits.'

'How did you leave it with Ford?' I asked.

'He wanted to speak to the manager.'

Guillaume nodded. 'We should wait for Moxham. He will know what to do.'

'I radioed, but I can't find him,' Tessa said.

I tugged on my earlobe reflexively. 'We don't need to wait.'

I met Tessa's gaze. Her eyes were a washed-out grey, her eyelashes pale.

'If you want to quit tomorrow,' I said, 'you quit. Right now, we're fixing this situation. You're going to get the water sports team to apologise.'

Tyson spluttered. 'What?'

'They probably were getting an eyeful. Even if they weren't, he's upset. When you're upset, you get an apology.'

I stood up, snapping my fingers. 'We'll make it funny, in case she's embarrassed by his hissy fit. Blindfold the guys, write I'm Sorry across their foreheads in marker pen. Make them ham it up. Then deliver a magnum of champagne, along with… Guillaume, what's your fanciest dessert? Something chocolatey.'

Guillaume mumbled that the pastry chef quit last week and he was overburdened with food for 'the bunny party', but perhaps, possibly, at a stretch, he could make a triple-layer chocolate ganache cake.

'OK.' I clapped my hands. 'So, we have a plan.'

'You really think I should do all that?' Tessa was clasping her coffee cup like a stress ball.

'Yes' – I eased the cup from her grasp, placed it on the counter – 'and, in a few days, they'll leave and give you a big tip because weren't you so wonderful and understanding?'

'Uh huh.' Tessa put on her sunglasses. I noticed they were designer, Cartier. Must be getting good tips to afford those. Maybe Keeper's guests weren't that bad after all.

When she stood up, I steered her to the door. 'You'll be great. Just keep smiling.'

Tyson scratched his chin. 'Shit, my only suggestion was to cut the electrics in his villa. See how he likes paradise without air-conditioning.'

'We're here to solve problems, not create new ones,' I said.

Guillaume, whose brow was furrowed into an expression straight out of a moody editorial photo-shoot, snapped at Tyson to get back to work.

'Sorry to add to your workload,' I said to him.

He shrugged, staring into middle distance. 'It is only the job.'

I swallowed down a laugh. 'Any idea where I might find Moxham?'

'Try the control centre?'

*

I wouldn't tell Moxham this, because it would give him a big head (a bigger head), but I learned everything I know from him. After only a couple of months of working together, the two of us developed a code. During fraught situations at the hotel, I'd yank my earlobe once. That meant, *this guest is being particularly horrendous*. He'd meet my eye and yank his earlobe twice, meaning, *I know, they can go fuck themselves*.

Mox never let his irritation show. He charmed even the most impossible guest. He found a way to laugh on the most stressful days. We kept each other's morale up with gallows humour, pretending we'd pour cyanide in so-and-so's champagne, or toss a toaster in such-and-such's whirlpool bath.

Despite everything, I was looking forward to working with Moxham again. Yet I couldn't, for the life of me, locate him. He wasn't at the control centre, an insalubrious collection of buildings on the north side of the island, hidden from view of the guests, that encompassed the laundry, the desalination plant and the cess pit.

On my way back, past the guest villas, I glimpsed someone climbing a tree, shimmying up its slender trunk to cut down coconuts with a machete. But it wasn't Moxham.

He was also missing from Main Beach, where a small army was lighting tiki torches and setting up huge trellises of white roses dripping red paint.

Eventually, as the shadows lengthened and my jetlag crept back in, I trudged to Villa Queen Conch to get changed for the party.

*

The sun set early this close to the equator. From the villa's veranda, it was spectacular; oranges and reds reflected in the water. The marble statue had disappeared beneath the waves. In the distance, steel drums started up.

I was sweaty, after an afternoon of traipsing around. My eyes flicked to the Jacuzzi. A soak would feel good. What had Fizzy said? I should 'feel like a guest'. One last luxury wouldn't hurt. The bubbles felt heavenly as I slipped into the seething water.

*

I must have fallen asleep.

I sat up, water splashing as I clawed at the ceramic. My mother was always superstitious about drowning in the bathtub.

The music was louder now, reverberating across the sea. A scream made the hairs on the back of my neck stand on end.

It resolved itself as laughter. Only the party. The veranda was dark, but at the edge of my vision, there were dancing lights.

'Lola.'

I twisted my neck, not sure if I'd imagined the voice.

I shifted. The water had gone cold, the surface flat. I was buck naked.

'Lola…'

My knuckles turned white as I gripped the edge of the Jacuzzi.

A figure wavered out of the blackness.

3

'S cared the shit out of me.' I relaxed into a smile.
 'Nothin' scares you, Showgirl.'

Moxham collapsed to his knees at the edge of the Jacuzzi. He didn't bother to avert his eyes. I'd probably been naked in front of him before — skinny dipping in the hotel pool after-hours — but being nude came with a sense of vulnerability.

'How did you get in here?' Sleep was still clouding my mind. I'd locked the door to the villa (hadn't I?). Moxham must have a master key. 'What time is it?'

'Ten, still early.' When he shrugged, a top hat tumbled off his head. He raked a hand through his brown hair, making it stick up straight. 'Good to see you, darl.' A bottle of champagne sloshed in his other hand. He offered me a swig, but I shook my head.

'It's been too long.' My tone turned teasing. 'You got old.'

He snorted. I thought about telling him to turn his back, to make a palaver of retrieving my clothes from where I'd discarded them on the veranda. That would reveal my squeamishness, though, when I wanted to appear unruffled.

'Y'know, I got a blister looking for you today,' I said. 'Where have you been?'

I reached for the Jacuzzi's control panel, stirring the water to life. At least with the bubbles frothing I was partially covered.

He cracked a smile. 'Just like old times, eh? Me bludging and you doing the real work.' Moxham draped one arm over the ledge of the Jacuzzi. His breath smelled like sour wine and cigarettes. He was wearing a creased linen blazer in baby-blue, shirtless underneath.

I laughed. Moxham and I had always been our true selves around each other; there was a comfort in that.

'What's going on?' I asked.

'A lot.' He punctuated the words by tapping his bottle against the ceramic. 'A lot going on. I've missed you. Need your help.'

My amusement cooled. I shook my head.

'Earn some pocket money?' he asked.

'I don't want that.'

He dipped a hand below the surface of the water. My whole body tensed.

'Course you do.' He swirled his fingers and made a playful splash.

'I don't.'

I splashed back, but it wasn't playful; aggressive enough to drench the sleeve of his jacket. It got my point across. He removed his hand from the water.

'You and me, we're realists. And the realest thing there is...' He rubbed his fingers together, sending droplets flying. 'Cold, hard cash, Showgirl.'

Usually, his nickname for me, borrowed from the Barry Manilow song, made me smile, but today it was annoying.

'What kind of scheme are you running now?' I tried to lighten my voice, but the words came out tight.

'I got the devil on my back,' he muttered.

Sweat beads broke out across my forehead as the Jacuzzi water heated up. 'What?'

He didn't reply, only guzzled champagne. 'What happened in Hong Kong?' he said at last.

Earlier, I'd wanted to unburden myself, but Moxham's nihilism was unnerving me. My story came out in stilted, incomplete sentences. Finally, I faded away into silence. In the distance, there were drums; closer, only churning water.

'You fucked that one up, didn't you?' Moxham said.

His words were a gut-punch. No reassurance. No attempt to make me feel better. Pressure was building behind my eyes.

'Still' – he laughed, that distinctive hyena yelp – 'you're here now. Out of Dodge. Might come in useful.'

I couldn't find a response. It was taking all my effort not to cry.

He laboured to his feet, unsteady, dipping to retrieve his costume top hat.

'C'mon, get dressed, come to the party... don't be late, we got work to do.'

Moxham slipped away into the darkness. The glass door reverberated shut behind him.

*

An hour later, I was Alice in Wonderland. Barefoot on the sand, I weaved past a wooden sign, hand-painted with *We're All Mad Here*. A glittery black dress had been left for me by some anonymous hand in my villa, along with my work uniform. The hem was too long and I almost tripped.

I'd organised themed parties at the Clement Hong Kong, but nothing as elaborate as this one. In addition to the painted roses I'd seen earlier, there was a fairy-tale tree, like something from the English countryside, made of real wood but with its trunk sawn off at the base. Enormous pocket watches hung on chains from its branches. It was rendered all the more strange when juxtaposed with the dark, rippling Caribbean Sea and the sand glowing under the full moon.

A couple of dozen people milled around Main Beach, drinking, laughing, making unfortunate attempts at dancing to the DJ set. With everyone dressed in formal wear, it was hard to tell the difference between the guests and the staff.

'Hi, honey!' Fizzy gave an overhead wave. For unknown reasons, there was a plastic crown perched on her head. She swooped in to bestow air kisses, and then introduced me around to a bunch of high-fliers.

In addition to a condiments tycoon and a TV exec, there was an England footballer. A chic Italian woman, heiress to a beauty products fortune, was flirting extravagantly with him, despite the fact that his wife was standing right there. Perhaps she, like the rest of us, had heard of his extramarital affair, which had been in all the papers. None of the guests were particularly interested in me, so I was relieved when a blustering German man said, 'A drink, please, sweetheart?'

Glad of the excuse, I went to find him a champagne flute. He thanked me warmly ('*danke, merci*, thank you'), like I was an attentive friend. A friend who was paid to be here. A friend who always poured the drinks. He went back to ignoring me.

I wandered over to the food table, where the spread had been picked-over but there was still plenty left; more than would ever be eaten, surely? I had a vague thought that I should find a local charity and arrange to donate some of our excesses. I wasn't hungry, but jetlag was making me woozy, so I figured I should eat if I wanted to remain standing.

Guillaume had created a gourmet take on a tea party. The tarts I'd seen in the kitchen were here (strawberry jam with a kick of rum), along with tiny smoked salmon sandwiches, Earl Grey shortbread and mini lemon meringue pies.

I scanned the throng. I'd anticipated seeing the famous Kip Clement, but I heard in passing that he'd gone to bed early with a headache.

From the tiki bar, I grabbed one of the miniature glass bottles labelled Drink Me. It didn't make me grow or shrink, but the hibiscus-infused tequila it contained was delicious. I downed it before I had a chance to contemplate whether I was supposed to be drinking while working.

Moxham's earlier words kept circling in my head. What was he up to? Had I been wrong to come to Keeper Island? Or was I overreacting? Either way, I didn't want to leave our conversation hanging.

I sidled up to Fizzy. 'Seen Moxham?'

'No.' There was a snap to her voice, which she sweetened with a smile. 'But you must meet Eddie.' She pushed me in the direction of a man dressed head-to-toe in what looked like brand-new athleisure wear. 'Big in Hong Kong,' she said, sotto voce, before she began introductions.

Eddie Yiu produced a wide, artificially whitened smile that didn't meet his eyes. 'Ah, here's a familiar face,' he said in an American accent, nudging me.

I frowned but couldn't place him. Perhaps he'd been a guest at the Clement Hong Kong? Eddie Yiu was a few inches taller than me, puffed up with muscles turning to fat. Before I could ask what he meant, he launched into a long, boring story about 'his time away' and the spiritual quest he'd completed. (I guessed it involved ayahuasca and the desert.)

Fizzy floated off and I was trapped with Eddie. He, alone, among the one-percenters, seemed interested in me. Mainly because he was hitting on me, with all the subtlety of a man who's never heard the word 'no'.

Nearby, two women in jewel-toned dresses were playing croquet using plastic flamingos. I half-watched them, while Eddie launched into another anecdote about a recent big-game hunting trip ('took down a big bitch, I did'). As he spoke, a drop of something – wine? ink? blood? – rolled down his arm and landed in the sand.

Before I could figure out whether I'd imagined it, there was a tinkle of broken glass. One of the croquet women had swung her flamingo so extravagantly, she'd sent her companion's champagne flute flying.

'I must go and clean this up,' I said to Eddie. 'It's a hazard, really.'

Not a lie. Broken glass was the gremlin of beach resorts.

Without waiting for Eddie to respond, I scurried away, heading up the beach and along the paved path that led to the restaurant, with its Balinese sloping thatched roof. I gathered there were never more than twenty guests on the island at a time – often, far fewer – but the restaurant was large enough to accommodate twice that. It seemed further proof that Keeper Island was not a normal resort and operated according to the excesses of a kingdom.

With all the guests on the beach, the restaurant was dark, its vented sides shut. The door was locked. I was already failing at my new job, since I didn't know where to find something as simple as a dustpan and brush.

No one was around, but I could hear rap music in the distance, a contrast to the electro-pop favoured by the DJ on the beach. I followed a path edged with ferns that skirted the back of the restaurant.

A low moan filled the air, like a wild animal. What was that?

Round the corner, I reached one of the guest swimming pools, surrounded by patio. Striped sun loungers were scattered with plates and half-empty glasses. The smell of weed itched at my nostrils.

The 'wild animals' loomed into view. A pair of guys were wrestling. One of them was dressed in a rabbit onesie.

'Kneed me in the balls!' the bunny shouted, in a familiar South African accent. 'You dirty cheater.'

'Never said there was no rules,' came the reply. American.

The crowd assembled around them erupted into commentary about who was right and who was wrong. I got the sense there was some money riding on the outcome of the wrestling match. Everyone here was staff. They'd sneaked away to enjoy the facilities; to drink and smoke and skive and complain about the guests out of earshot.

That reminded me of my mission. 'Need to clean up some glass.' I said it even though everyone was caught up in settling bets. I was hoping I might find Moxham here, but when I craned my neck, there was no sign of him. I walked away down the path.

'You the new girl?' a voice said.

When I turned, I recognised the masseuse who'd come to my villa earlier. She'd been inscrutable then, but now she wore a rubbery grin, her dark skin sheened with sweat.

'You don't know what you got yourself in for.' She dissolved into giggles.

'What's that?' I assumed she meant long days and shit pay, but there was something disconcerting about her laughter.

'Come have a drink with us.' She lurched towards me, narrowly avoiding a fern, and clapped a hand on my shoulder. Her dangly earrings were red birds with open mouths and they jumped as she struggled to steady herself.

Now I was closer, I could smell the booze on her breath.

'Sounds good,' I said, 'but I need to clean up some glass on the beach…'

She was staring past me, not listening, so I said loudly, 'Hey, you seen Moxham?'

'Yeah.' Something flashed in her eyes. 'I seen him.'

She let go of me and took a step forward. Out came a great whoosh of laughter.

'Are you alright?'

Her legs crumpled. She crashed into a fern next to us.

'Shit!' I tried to catch her, but she was already on the ground.

I kneeled down beside her in the earth. I didn't know her name. 'Hey! Can you hear me?'

She didn't respond.

4

I shook her, but it was no good.

How much had she had to drink? Was she breathing?

'Help! I need help,' I called, but the wrestling match had resumed nearby. People were cheering and booing.

I pushed my fingers into her neck, feeling for a pulse. That was when she moaned and rolled over. There were leaves stuck to her braids, earth on her white T-shirt.

'You OK?' I asked.

Her face had a seasick slackness to it, but at least she was breathing.

'I want... I want...' She slurred something that sounded like Elvis.

'Oohman!' A man swooped down next to me. 'Party over.' His voice was jovial, made more so by the Caribbean inflection that stretched out the words into *pah-tee oh-vah*. 'Cinderella gotta get to her carriage.'

As he heaved up the woman under her armpits, I realised it was Reggie, the boat skipper. He gave me a nod.

'She fine, she gon' be fine.'

The woman was already coming back to life. She batted away Reggie's assistance. Only when she wobbled on her feet again did she allow him to support her.

I watched them go. I'd seen it all a thousand times — someone drunk and messy and on the verge of doing harm to themselves — but after the week I'd had, it was hard to find levity in the situation.

The bunny (Tyson) helped me locate a dustpan and brush. When I retraced my steps back to the beach, the official party felt staid compared to the raucous one I'd left behind.

Some of the guests seemed to have gone to bed, including Eddie, thank God. Among those that remained, a card game had sprung up. On one of the tables, which was topped with fake grass, a group was wielding oversized playing cards. A muscular man with rumpled blond hair lounged with his feet propped up like he owned the place. He hailed me – 'wanna play?' – but I waved my brush at him. 'Another time!'

I'd finished cleaning up the broken glass when Moxham finally appeared. He was glad-handing, leaning in to look at players' hands during the card game, acting like this was a party in his honour. I saw the blond man glower and mutter something under his breath. Maybe he had a bad hand.

It must be close to midnight by now. I stifled a yawn. Villa Queen Conch was beckoning me. Before I called it a night, though, I wanted to iron things out with Moxham.

'Mox, let's talk a minute.' I darted in close.

'You got a drink? Have a drink.' He was still holding his bottle of champagne, or perhaps it was a new one. His bleariness made it easy for me to guide him clear of the card game. Twenty metres away was a wooden beach hut, painted turquoise. I beckoned him inside and he followed. His phone pinged as he slumped onto a cushioned seat.

'Bloody oath, these people couldn't organise a piss up in a brewery.' He swiped clumsily. 'Stupid bitch. Needs me to do everything.'

I bristled. Who was the stupid bitch? 'Listen to me a minute.' I snapped my fingers and he looked at me.

'Showgirrrl… you're here now. My ace in the hole. You're good at this stuff.' He reached over and pulled on my earlobe twice. 'A little whisper in the ear… all his secrets come out. Fuck me, he has secrets that would curl your hair.'

'Who?'

Without replying, he levered himself up and bounded forward like he wanted to leave. I blocked his exit, filling the frame of the beach hut's door.

'Listen, I need this to be a clean slate.'

'Course, course,' he mumbled, eyes back on his phone.

I grabbed it from his hand. 'Everything above board, I'm serious.'

He let out a hyena laugh. 'But I got a nice big fish on the line.'

I shook my head. 'No.'

'Big fish. Enough to share. Sometimes that sucker thrashes around a while. They go quiet in the end though. Eyes almost popped out of my head when I found out. Drowned, my arse. More to that story, course, course. Don't they know? This is my island now.'

'Mox, you're not making sense.'

For the first time, I wondered if it wasn't drunkenness but actual madness.

His phone pinged again. I was still holding it. My eyes flashed automatically to the new message on the screen.

I'm sorry. I want to——

I didn't have a chance to read the rest of it before Moxham snatched the phone away from me. There was a Gollum-like sheen to his face as he read the message.

'I'm late, I'm late,' he said.

'What?'

He'd lost his top hat at some point during the evening, but he doffed an imaginary cap anyway. 'I'm late. For a very important date.'

It took me a second to realise he was quoting the rabbit from *Alice in Wonderland*. Moxham nudged me out the way and ducked out of the beach hut.

'Mox, please—'

'Whatever you do, don't trust these people, Lola.'

He was still grinning, but all lightness had vanished from his voice.

'Why not?'

My nails were digging into my palms. These people? Who? My new colleagues? The guests?

Moxham was racing away, but he looked back and shouted, 'They're all backstabbers. You'll see.'

Inside the beach hut, the smell of cigarettes and sweat lingered. I didn't know what Moxham was rambling about, but I realised a bigger truth now. It had been a mistake to come here. It had been a mistake to trust Moxham.

I dropped onto the seat, fighting a wave of despair. My eyelids were drooping when a whoop from outside woke me up again. Through the open door, I glimpsed a figure streaking down the beach. It was too dark to identify much about the person, but they were tall, and running like they were being chased.

A few more minutes passed and I summoned up the energy to drag myself out of the beach hut.

Boom.

An explosion split apart the sky. It took me a second to realise it was only fireworks and not the end of the world.

*

The next morning, I woke up in a bed that felt like a cloud. I burrowed down under the Egyptian cotton sheets, tempted to go back to sleep.

I'd slept fitfully last night. At one point, I was sure I'd shifted out of sleep and seen a distant light out on the water, too bright to be the moon. Perhaps it was a dream.

Reluctantly, I threw back the covers. No more sleep. A to-do list was already forming in my mind. It was my first real day of work and item one was to talk to my boss. Surely, sober, I could have a normal conversation with Moxham.

It was still early, not yet seven, and I was ravenous. I ordered breakfast on the villa tablet, even though it made me feel guilty to still be acting like a guest. Delivered to my door, I received fresh coffee, scrambled eggs, crispy bacon and pancakes with maple syrup. A side of papaya was carved into a leaf pattern.

After breakfast, I showered and dressed in my uniform. In the vast bathroom off the master suite, I glanced at myself in the mirror and toyed with my thick, dark hair. Back in Hong Kong, Nathan liked to run his hands through it as we lay in bed, making dreamy strokes. I fumbled a pair of nail scissors from the dish on the counter. Holding out a hank of hair, I hesitated. Nathan's warm brown eyes and broad smile filled my mind.

Snip.

I cut until the basin was full and my hair fell to my jaw. The nail scissors meant that the cuts were ragged, forming a staircase of sorts. I didn't care. The woman who stared back at me in the mirror looked different and I liked it.

New job. New life. Whole new person.

I poured myself another cup of coffee from the cafetière and strolled out onto the veranda for one last moment of peace before I started work. After the air-conditioning, the hot sun was invigorating. I breathed in the air's salt tang as I leaned against the railing.

Only the head and shoulders of the alabaster statue were visible this morning. Another wave lapped over the woman's face. What a bizarre statue. But then, if I knew one thing about rich people, it was that most of them were certifiable.

I'd half turned away when I saw it. Red in the water.

The statue was bleeding.

I stood on tiptoes, stretching out over the railing. I hadn't imagined it. The rocks were streaked with blood.

A wave crashed. A rag doll swirled in the current.

Another wave. More blood bloomed in the water.

The man floated face up, his eyes blank, a sting or welt across his cheek. His hairline was matted with gore. His jacket was wet-dark and bloodied, but I could tell it had once been baby-blue.

Moxham.

5

I ran from the villa.

Dead? Was he dead?

So much blood.

My eyes darted left to right. Spiky bushes, taller than I was, lined the path. Where the hell was I going?

'Help,' I gasped, even though there was no one to hear me. 'Help me, please.'

Should I have dived in? Tried to save him?

No, the rocks. If he was alive—

The memory of his blank eyes swooned in front of me, making me stumble.

He was dead.

My stomach churned. I'd brought death with me to Keeper Island. My fault. Everything I touched turned to shit.

What should I do? Call 999? Was that even the emergency number in the BVI?

I laughed, a shrill, helpless sound. I didn't have a phone with me. I didn't have friends on the island. I didn't know anyone.

Moxham's parting words returned to me. *They're all back-stabbers.*

I could see the neighbouring villa, but I couldn't figure out how to get there. I heard a noise. *Screech-screech-screeeeeeech.*

The tip of my toe caught on a jagged stone at the edge of the path. I wheezed out a scream. My legs buckled and I hit the ground, knees jolting against the paving.

'Fucking help me, someone!' I yelled at the sky.

A man loomed into sight. My vision was blurred with tears, but I recognised his tall, thin frame, his perfectly bald head.

'What's the matter, gorgeous girl?'

*

I lay on a striped sun lounger, with a Hermès cashmere blanket draped over me. Kip had brought me a glass bottle of water, frosty from the chiller, but each time I sipped at it, I imagined cold water closing over my head. I couldn't stop shaking.

Mr Christopher 'Kip' Clement, hotel tycoon, number forty-four on the Forbes Rich List, was perched on the edge of my sun lounger, playing nursemaid to me.

'A dreadful shock,' he said.

'Yes...'

'Deep breaths now.'

Kip had driven me to the main complex in a golf cart. We were sat in the patio area that I vaguely recognised from last night's staff party, although it was swept clean now. A few metres away, the bright blue of an oval swimming pool gleamed in the morning sunshine. Everything was too pristine; it didn't feel real.

I'd expected Kip would want to know all about Moxham, but instead we were chit-chatting about my family back in London.

'Tell me about Flora,' he said.

'I worry she's... too much like me,' I said of my niece.

'No bad thing, surely.' Kip's wrap-around sunglasses reflected my ashen face, but his upper-crust voice had a calming quality.

'I was a bit of a wild child.'

Kip chuckled. I estimated he was in his sixties, but his easy smile and foppish demeanour made him appear younger. He rubbed his neck, thumbing a yellowish bruise above his collar-bone. 'I know the type.'

A gangly, dark-haired man arrived, head bowed. 'The police are here,' he said to Kip in an undertone.

Kip patted my arm and stood up. I had to bite my lip to stop myself from grabbing his hand and crying out, *please stay*.

'Back soon.'

I watched him go, feeling abandoned. Pulling the navy-blue cashmere up to my neck, I let my eyes drift out of focus. I wanted to call my sister, hear a familiar voice, but I didn't have a phone.

God, the blood. So much blood.

Had it been quick? Had he suffered?

'Good morning.'

I started. 'Hello…'

Another man, not Kip but perhaps the same age as him, was ambling towards me, carrying a leather satchel and leaning on a walking stick.

'I'm Doctor Clarence Jeston, but everyone calls me Doc.'

He doffed his fedora and sat down on the neighbouring sun lounger.

I was so out of it, I forgot how to make small talk and instead stared at him.

His hand hovered over mine. 'May I?'

'OK.' I choked out a laugh, because it sounded like he was asking me to dance.

He lifted my wrist and took my pulse. Over the next ten minutes, he checked all my vital signs, tutting over my bruised knees. 'Took a bit of a tumble, eh?'

He had a baritone voice and there were deep laughter lines etched into his dark brown skin.

I gave a shaky nod. He dug around in his satchel and produced a red lollipop.

'I used to work in paediatrics, but I find everyone likes a sweet treat.' There was a plummy Britishness to Doc's voice that over-laid the Caribbean accent.

I didn't unwrap the lollipop, but I made an effort to echo his smile.

'Do you know… what happened?' I asked.

'Not a nice thing.' Doc settled himself on his sun lounger. 'I went to see the poor fellow. Fortunately, I was on the island attending to one of the guests. *Un*fortunately, I was too late for Mr Moxham. Did the necessary, signed the death certificate.'

'He was…' I was alarmed at how easily it had all been wrapped up.

'Friend of yours?'

'Yeah.'

'I'm sorry for your loss. It's a tragedy.'

I fidgeted with the blanket. I'd gone from being chilled to the bone to being too hot. The sun was beating down on us, the drone of a mosquito nearby. We were close enough to the restaurant that I expected a steady stream of foot traffic, but there was none. Where was everyone?

'How did he die?' I asked.

'Blunt force trauma. The speculation is that it was a jet-ski accident. Crashed into the rocks.'

My stomach roiled. An accident?

'The police are here?' I asked.

'They arrived a few minutes ago.'

I sat up straight. 'I should speak to them. Tell them—'

Tell them what? That something about this felt wrong to me? Should I tell them Moxham was a scam artist and he'd been hoping to make me his accomplice in whatever scheme he was running? For that matter, should I reveal everything that had happened in Hong Kong?

No, it wouldn't be smart to speak to the police.

'I'm sure they'll call you if needed,' Doc said.

He pressed his palms together in prayer for a couple of seconds. I wondered how many deaths he'd presided over, how many people went home from paradise in a box.

I didn't speak to the police. Perhaps because I was a new arrival, perhaps because they assumed I didn't know Moxham, perhaps because of whatever Kip said to them.

I did glimpse the group of police officers outside Villa Queen Conch, clad in identical grey and black uniforms, from a distance as Doc and I sped by in a golf cart. We looped around to the north of the island and turned inland, past the cess pit and the control centre. As the road got narrower, it became a dirt track. Green forest – Doc called it 'the bush' – flashed past, accompanied by the chatter and whistles of birds.

As we arrived at a clearing in the forest, Doc bumped to a stop and killed the buggy. The journey from the main complex had taken less than ten minutes, yet this was a different world. The buildings here were small, shabby and concrete, half a dozen of them arranged around what had the look of a makeshift town square. Although the bush had been hacked back to make this clearing, there was evidence of it creeping back in to reclaim the space.

Overhanging trees made the light muddy. If I had to guess, I'd assume most of the guests had no idea the staff village existed. The servants were non-player characters; we disappeared when we left your sight.

'Wha' you hangin' around here with that fool look on your face?' a voice rang out.

'Someone died, mehson.'

A knot of people were leaning against one of the buildings, smoke wafting upwards. The sunshine melody of soca blared from an open window, battling a hip-hop beat from another.

I slid out of the golf cart. I expected Doc to follow me, but he only gave a wave and manoeuvred the buggy back the way we'd come. Was he under the impression I knew where I was going? Keeper Island seemed to be built on that assumption.

There were no signposts. Either you already knew or you didn't belong.

A couple of heads turned as I shuffled across the clearing. It was sticky inland without the sea breeze. Insects itched against my bare legs and my knees throbbed where I'd fallen earlier.

'The boss. The boss is fucking dead.'

It was Reggie who'd spoken. His springy hair was dampened with sweat. The scent of weed tickled the back of my throat as he exhaled a cloud of smoke.

'Kip Clement is your boss and trust me, he still alive,' a woman said. Her brown eyes flicked up to meet mine. It was the masseuse, the one who'd collapsed at the party last night. She showed no signs of a hangover, dressed in a clean white T-shirt and jeans, with her braids neatly swirled on top of her head. She adjusted her speech, flattening her accent. 'Good morning.'

'Good morning,' I said.

'I'm Diara,' she said, giving me a strong handshake. As she pumped my hand, her dangly earrings, a pair of gold leaves, bounced up and down.

It was hard to reconcile this bustling, no-nonsense woman with the girl who'd drunkenly collapsed the night before. It seemed tactless to refer to it. For that matter, I didn't want to talk about how I'd turned into a snivelling snot-monster when she'd given me a massage. Better to pretend this was our first meeting.

'Oh, hey, it's Lo-la,' Reggie said, 'you picked a day to join us.' He offered me his joint, but Diara snatched it from his grasp and threw it on the ground.

'Get to work,' she said.

Reggie ignored her, peering at the ground as if contemplating retrieving his joint. 'I knew it would be a bad fuckin' day when the dead cow washed up.'

'Dead cow?' I said.

'Stinking up Windy Beach… those eyes… all white and staring.' He shuddered. 'Bad luck come in threes.' His accent was different to Diara's. Jamaican, perhaps.

'A dead cow is just a dead cow,' Diara said. 'You'll burn it and it'll be like it never happened.'

Apparently noticing my confusion, she explained that, in a freak occurrence, a cow had washed up on Windy Beach, presumably from a cargo ship transporting livestock.

There was a crackle and the two-way radio at Diara's hip came to life, echoed by the one on Reggie's belt. A garbled voice was speaking too fast for me to interpret.

'Stand by, Shirley, stand by,' Diara said into her mic, giving a tiny roll of her eyes.

She twirled the volume on the radio and said to Reggie, 'She saying someone messed with her cleaning supplies. I don't know why everyone lost the ability to deal with their own shit today.'

'Threeeees,' Reggie muttered darkly.

Diara gave him a light shove. 'Go burn a cow.'

He ambled away, calling over his shoulder, 'See you later.'

'I think I'm supposed to have a room somewhere…' I said to Diara, glancing around.

Through an open door, I could see a couple of people in what resembled a student common room, reclining on a faded-orange sofa.

'You'll be sharing with me.' Diara beckoned me to follow her and strode to a concrete building fronted with decking. 'Home, sweet home.'

The wooden railings were adorned with wet suits and bikinis, draped out to dry. There were flags too: the Union Jack and the shield of the BVI, alongside Jamaica, Philippines, South Africa. I climbed a couple of steps and the decking's boards creaked, haunted-house style, as we traipsed across them. The door, with black peeling paint, was unlocked.

'Bathroom at the end.' Diara led the way down a gloomy hall-way. 'Kitchen opposite, basically kettle and hot plate.'

There was a screech outside. I started, but Diara didn't react. She pushed at the door on the right with her shoulder. Inside, apricot walls clashed with terracotta tiles on the floor. The room was furnished with two single beds and shabby wooden furniture. My purple suitcase was parked at the end of one of the beds; it appeared to have wandered home like Lassie.

'It's nice,' I said blankly.

Diara snorted, though I hadn't meant to sound sarcastic. I'd lived in worse. In my experience, the fancier the resort, the scummier the staff quarters.

'Last girl only lasted a month,' she said.

'What happened to her?'

'They never found the body.'

Horror must have registered on my face, because Diara cracked a wan smile.

'I'm joking.' She leaned over and patted me on the shoulder. 'Went back to Idaho or wherever she wa' from.'

I laughed. It was a relief to do so.

I sat down on the bed I presumed to be mine, because the other was unmade, clothes tangled up with sheets. Diara remained standing. She grabbed a set of keys from the chest of drawers and tossed them to me. 'Yours.'

With both of us in the room, it felt cramped as a cupboard. Even when Diara flicked on the overhead fan, it remained stuffy.

Diara's side of the room was papered with pencil sketches (her own?), while above my bed, there was only an ugly painting. Two white men, on board a ship, one scrutinising us through a telescope.

'What are people saying about...' I hesitated. 'About Moxham?'

'All jus' chatter. We saw them dragging the jet ski out of the water. What was left of it. Now everyone sitting around, crying... or smoking... or wasting time. What that gonna achieve?'

Diara wrapped a silk scarf around her neck. It struck me as incongruous for the weather, but she was also wearing jeans, so she obviously didn't feel the heat the way I did.

'We here to work, so work,' she said.

I wished I could be as practical. 'You know, I found him,' I said in a small voice. 'On the rocks.'

Her face softened. 'You OK?'

I was struggling to feel anything at all. 'I have no idea.'

Diara hesitated. 'You need anything? I hafta get back to the spa, but I can send someone over. Food or something.'

'... A lie down, maybe.'

'I'll check on you later.'

The kindness in her voice made me want to cry, except my eyes were dry and scratchy. I was supposed to be grieving, but I was still expecting Moxham to pop his head round the door. ('Oi, oi, fancy a drink?') Each time I pictured him, I saw the froth of blood around his limp body.

Diara was at the door. I couldn't stop myself from blurting out one final question.

'Was it really an accident?' I asked.

'Yes.' In Diara's accent, the word stretched. 'It was an accident.'

She turned away, her leaf earrings bouncing. Her voice dropped.

'And if it wasn't an accident,' she said, 'they'll call it an accident anyway.'

She bustled out of the room before I could react. The door fell shut.

6

In my dream, I was swimming, but the sea had turned to blood. Moxham's body floated towards me, a bloated starfish in a sodden baby-blue jacket. There was a sting on his cheek. I could hear the *bzzzzzzzzz* of an insect. I tried to paddle away, but hot blood lapped into my mouth.

The corpse's eyes opened.

I'd been wrong.

It wasn't Moxham. It was Nathan.

I woke up drenched in sweat. The room was dark. What was the time?

Groping for the bedside lamp, I winced as it lit up the room. I expected Diara to wake up, but when I glanced at her bed, it was empty.

Outside, there was a screech. I tensed. I'd heard it earlier, but now it resolved as a strangled *cock-a-doodle-doo*. There must be wild chickens on the island. Not monsters stalking me, just roosters with a broken internal clock.

I pressed my face into the pillow. It smelled like synthetic flowers. I wished I were home.

I imagined Nathan pacing his apartment. His short black hair would be flattened from obsessively smoothing his hands through it. He wouldn't have bothered to shave, stubble showing up on his jaw, making him look even more like a male model.

In reality, his hand would still be too injured for boxing, but I pictured him in sweats, returned from training. In my mind, I curled my arms around him and inhaled his scent. Musk and pine-resin. I was the same height as him, but he was all muscle. A tattooed wave crashed across his chest.

My first impression of him was as a broad-shouldered, swaggering security guard, his physique bulked out by a bulletproof vest. There was high demand for security in Hong Kong, with everyone skittish about anti-government protests. God forbid anything as gauche as democracy prevented guests from having a peaceful stay.

Unlike the hotel's other security guards, who adopted a permanent glower as part of their tough-guy persona, Nathan was a smiler.

'Good morning, beautiful,' he'd said, the first time we met, opening the hotel's lobby door for me. The only hint of a Cantonese accent was the clipped quality to his speech.

How could I have known then what he was capable of?

I returned his smile, my eye contact deliberately hazy, and neglected to reply. Sorry, bud, not interested. I strode across the vast grey-flecked marble of the entrance hall, past the walls hung with enormous Chinese silk paintings of egrets and cherry blossom.

Nathan was too young for me, too handsome. I liked 'em with grit, with scars, both real and emotional.

(*That's the reason you're alone.*)

However, Nathan was persistent. Always there, always smiling.

'Pick a card,' he said, a few weeks later, fanning a deck in my face.

'No.'

In clippy heels and a black skirt suit, I was on my way somewhere, or back from somewhere; busy, busy, busy. I did not have time for magic.

'Don't you want to be amazed?' he asked.

I laughed in spite of myself. 'No.'

'I think you do.' His dimples deepened. 'Secretly.'

Here, now, in the cramped little room on Keeper Island, the memory of his smile twisted into a sneer.

I got out of bed and unzipped my suitcase. I'd packed in a fever, everything inside jumbled up. My phone had died during my journey, somewhere around San Juan, and it had been a relief to stop checking it. Now, I scrabbled around until I found my charger.

A few minutes later, days' worth of messages unfurled across the screen. Most of them were from Nathan.

I'm sorry, OK? I should've told you.
Let's talk. Tonight?
I know you're not in Vietnam. Where are you?
I checked at the hotel, no one knows where you are.
Please. Let me know you're OK.
Where are you???

I hunched over. The final message settled in my chest with a crushing weight.

I don't care where you've gone, I will find you.

My thumb jabbed at my phone screen. Block. Nathan vanished.

There were other messages of concern from friends in Hong Kong. If I told them where I was, Nathan would find out. Even to dash off an *I'm OK, don't worry* message risked Nathan tracking the send location.

I had run to the other side of the world. There was no way for Nathan to get me here. Yet I couldn't shake the feeling there was someone lurking behind me. What had Moxham called it? The devil on my back.

Delete, delete, delete. I turned Hong Kong into a black hole. Every friend, every colleague, every acquaintance – gone.

There was heat behind my eyes, but no tears would come.

My annihilation spree left Moxham as the most recent person to send me a message. The day of my arrival, he'd texted me a *Lord of the Rings* meme. *One does not simply walk into Keeper Island.*

Loneliness yawned inside me. I'd always prided myself on thriving in my own company, but now I felt stranded at sea. I calculated the time difference – London was four hours ahead – and scrolled through my phone until I found my sister.

'Hi.' The voice that answered was muffled.

'Allie!'

'It's *Flora*.' She emphasised her name hard and I imagined her small mouth sinking into a pout.

'Hi, baby. What are you up to?'

My six-year-old niece told me about a planned excursion to the river to feed the ducks. Not with bread, which 'made their tummies hurt'. They were taking them kale and pumpkin seeds because apparently these were bougie birds.

If Flora were with me, she would have hurled herself onto the bed like a puppy, her dark curls in my face, smelling of baby shampoo. I smelled it as strongly as if she were really here.

'There's a naughty pigeon at the park,' she was saying, 'his name is Charlie and he has one eye—'

The voice on the phone changed. 'Where have you been?' Allie asked. 'I tried calling you.'

'Sorry, I was… travelling.'

'Oh. You're on holiday?'

I rubbed a hand over my face. My skin was greasy with sweat, my cheekbone still throbbed.

'No, I… got a new job. New continent.'

Part of me wanted to tell Allie everything, about Nathan, about Moxham. I wanted to be soothed with platitudes, even if they weren't true.

'I thought you liked Hong Kong,' Allie said. Even from four thousand miles away, I could intuit the edginess in her voice.

'I did.'

I imagined her wafting around the flat on creaking floors. Her wild hair, the same dark brown as mine, would be tangled; a flush showing in her cheeks. Was she eating? I tried to picture her plump, but worry nagged at me. I could still remember the way her ribcage once poked out, the waxy look to her olive skin. I pushed the image away.

'This new job… it's a great opportunity.' I tried to make my voice enthusiastic. 'Really high-end resort. Caribbean island. It's beautiful.'

For Allie, I embroidered my picture-postcard lie. Obviously, I couldn't tell her the truth. I was the big sister. I protected her.

'Wow,' she said, her voice relaxing. 'Lolo, that's so cool.'

'Tell me what's going on with you.'

'There was a butterfly in the hallway this morning.'

I smiled in spite of myself. 'Oh, yeah?'

'I think it's a sign.'

'A sign you left a window open, sure.'

'Never seen one like it before, I'm going to paint it…'

I let her voice wash over me, her rapid speech, her overexcitement filling my heart. My sister and I couldn't be more different. Different mothers, different upbringings, different outlooks on life. But I loved her fiercely.

Allie was only a year younger than me, but I hadn't met her until I was nine. That was the year the phone call happened. I was the one who answered the landline. 'I know who you are,' the voice said, 'a slut, just like your mother. Put her on the phone. Put her on the phone!'

My dad had come clean. Or he'd been caught. Either way, the Real Wife had found out about us. Mum was jubilant, which made me think she'd left a trail of breadcrumbs. Mum thought Dad would divorce the other woman and we'd get him full time. The opposite happened. He decided to make it work with the Real Wife and ditch my mother, the mistress.

After the phone call, we had a strange period of détente, when everything was out in the open and Dad was interested in being a father to me for the first time. He'd take us on Saturday outings, me and the real children. There were two brothers, who were slouching, older, wary of me. They were both intent on going into the RAF, for reasons that escape me. Maybe they wanted to get the hell away. Then there was Allie. She was smaller than me, petite, with big eyes. Her mother must be beautiful too, I remember thinking, although I never met the Real Wife.

One Saturday, Allie dropped her teddy bear off an escalator. A teddy bear? At that age? I should have scoffed, but instead I ran down and got it for her. I didn't like to see her cry.

The year of the détente, we went to the aquarium, bowling, ice skating. I liked to begin sentences with 'my sister...' I'd do it at school with friends, sometimes even randomly, with sales assistants. I did it at home once and my mum scoffed. 'She's not your sister.'

Not long after, the détente ended.

I zombied across the room and flipped on the ceiling fan, though the air still felt heavy around me.

Allie broke off from her story about the butterfly. 'Flora, don't!'

Flora's voice was muffled. 'I'm feeding the ducks!'

'You're spilling everywhere.' There were sounds of a struggle. 'Baby, give me the cereal box. You can't do that. We're inside, bubs.' Then, to me, 'Sorry, I might need to go.'

'Where's Charlotte? Can't she help?'

'Charlotte couldn't come today.'

I drummed my fingers against my thigh, mentally berating Charlotte. I paid her well above market rate because Flora was so fond of her. What was she doing, skipping work?

Wait. Shit. Had I paid her this month?

I grimaced. No. With everything going on, I hadn't made the payment.

'Oh, God, Allie, I'm sorry. I'll sort it.'

'Don't worry, you don't need to—'

'I'll sort it. I want to make sure everything's good with you. You're getting the right treatment and everything.'

'Art is my treatment.'

'Yes… but you're still going to see Rowan, right?'

'Mmm.' Allie's voice was distant; there was a *flick-flick-flick* sound, like she was fiddling with something. Finally, her voice resolved. 'Why did you switch jobs?'

'It's a step up. You and Flora can come visit once I'm settled. You'll love it.'

In the background, Flora was singing. Something from Disney.

'Sorry, Lolo, I have to go, I said we were going to the park…'

She rang off before I could say goodbye. Whether it was because she was in a rush or because she was annoyed with me, I couldn't tell.

When I moved overseas in my late teens, it was easy to lose touch with my parents. My mum married a new bloke. I've met him a couple of times and he could cure insomnia. My dad finally divorced the Real Wife, but he never said sorry for any of it. Narcissist. Last I heard, he was living in Dubai. My family now was Allie and Flora, and that was it. The thought of anything bad happening to them made my insides shrivel.

I couldn't believe I'd forgotten to pay the babysitter. Tapping at my phone, I transferred money from savings and paid Charlotte's salary. It wasn't cheap, paying for Allie's therapy, paying for Flora's Montessori school, paying for their flat in London, the one with the 'great light' and the room for an art studio. These expenses stretched my wages, but they kept Allie's life on an even keel. I remembered too vividly what her life looked like without stability.

Maybe I should go back to London, see for myself how Allie was doing? The idea filled me with unease. London had never felt like home to me. It was also – and this thought snagged at me, like a fingernail scratch down my back – the first place Nathan would look for me.

Grey light was creeping into the room. It must be almost dawn. Time to start work. What was my job, without Moxham? Who was my boss?

I'd slept all last night and most of yesterday, but my limbs still ached with tiredness. I lay down and closed my eyes, tempted to go back to sleep. Another rooster squawked.

When I opened my eyes again, there was movement.

With a yelp, I scooted away, half-falling off the bed.

A rat! It was a rat.

Could rats really climb like that?

I grabbed one of my shoes to use as a weapon and saw the thing crawling up the wall wasn't a rat.

It was a lizard, speckled greenish-brown. The crest along its back and its darting feet reminded me of a tiny dinosaur. Though it was no longer than my handspan, it had a malevolent glint in its beady eyes.

I banged the wall with my shoe. The ugly painting of the men on a boat skewed sideways.

Whack.

The second time, the lizard got the message. It scurried down the wall and out of sight, behind the chest of drawers. Actually, now I thought about it, the idea of a lizard hiding in my room was more horrifying than a lizard in plain sight.

I was about to shift the furniture to try and find it when—

I saw it.

There was a tiny lens attached to the top of the picture frame.

I stood on tiptoes, lizard forgotten, and reached for the thumbnail-sized camera. A wire sprang loose, dangling a battery pack.

A camera. In my room. Above my bed.

I'd worked in hotels where you couldn't move for CCTV, but those cameras were fixed and obvious. This one was well-concealed. If I hadn't banged on the wall and dislodged the painting, I never would have found it. This had Moxham written all over it.

'Motherfucker,' I said out loud. *You're spying on me?*

I wanted to slap him – except he was dead.

I examined the spy-cam. My thumb flicked at the slot and a micro-SD card jumped out.

It took me a few minutes to retrieve my laptop from my luggage and power it up. Sitting cross-legged on the bed, I jammed the SD card into the laptop's card reader. A list of video files appeared, automatically labelled by date. There was only three days' worth of footage. Moxham must have installed the camera ready for my arrival.

I picked the most recent file and let it play. The footage showed the room empty, my bed made. I skipped through at random. Diara appeared and then disappeared. With a jolt, I saw myself, taking a seat on this very bed.

What a creep. Moxham wanted to keep tabs on me. He was gathering collateral. If he was harvesting footage of me, he could be secretly filming other people too. Was this how Moxham kept an iron rule over his staff?

I yanked the SD card from my laptop and took a deep breath. I was being paranoid. Moxham was the king of practical jokes. 'Wanna see something funny?' he'd asked me once, shoving his phone under my nose. It was a video of me snoring with my mouth open. He'd told me, in between sniggers, how he'd sneaked into my room while I was drunk.

The spy-cam could be one last prank. If he'd lived to tell the tale, he would have laughed it off.

I bundled clothes from my suitcase into an empty drawer. At the same time, I shoved the camera and the SD card into a sock and jammed the drawer shut.

I needed to get to work. Earn some money. Move on from the past.

7

Ford and Carolina, the Cunt and Cuntess of Silly-Cone Valley, were now my problem. Their host, Tessa, had not quit after all, but she was now 'sick'. The other two hosts, Maria and Alex, had also made themselves scarce. I noticed that, among the staff, yesterday's malaise lingered. ('We don't really have to work, do we, since the boss is dead?')

Through my brand-new, handheld radio, I was now plugged into the network of Keeper Island staff. I learned that Ford and Carolina had revved up their complaints to eleven. Guillaume's Michelin-star-quality food, made with the best ingredients, was pigswill. Nothing else about this paradise island was good, either.

There aren't enough towels.

The beach is too windy.

Where are the fresh flowers?

The water's too rough.

Oops, the vase is on the floor in pieces.

It was mid-afternoon and I was crawling on my hands and knees under the bed in Villa Mangrove, looking for an earring Carolina had misplaced.

'Don't worry about that.' Ford strode into the room. 'Turns out it was in her ear the whole time.'

I stood up and allowed myself a brief internal scream, before conjuring my best smile for him. 'That's great news.'

Despite the heat (which he'd complained about), Ford was dressed in a yellow hoodie and army fatigues which swamped his scrawny frame. He fixed me with beady eyes and rubbed a hand through his cropped red hair.

'Small matter,' he said. 'I've decided to propose.'

I bit back the inclination to make a joke. *But we just met! What a whirlwind. Yes, yes, a thousand times yes.*

'Excellent,' I said. 'I'll have the Dom Pérignon on standby. I hear Carolina likes the 2006 Rosé.'

'Yes… I'll need a few other things too. Red roses, make it two dozen. A ring.'

'You don't have a ring?'

'Whaddaya take me for, some cuck who carries around his grandmother's wedding ring in a velvet pouch, right along with his shrivelled balls? No, I don't have a ring. You can pick one out.'

What a lovely, romantic gesture, to have a stranger pick out your beloved's engagement ring.

'No problem at all.'

'Oh, and I need a plushie unicorn. Like, a soft toy. Caro's nuts about them.'

'Right.'

That was a completely normal gift for a grown woman. And it was definitely something I could buy on a rock in the middle of the ocean.

Perhaps Ford noticed my face had tightened, because he leaned in to squeeze my shoulder. He smelled like cheap ocean-splash body spray.

'I don't need them immediately,' he said. 'I'm not that much of an asshole. Tomorrow is fine.'

We weren't in London or Hong Kong, where I could get hothouse flowers at a moment's notice or drop $500k on a solitaire diamond. I was new to this part of the world, but as far as I could determine, the British Virgin Islands consisted of small towns, populated by regular people.

'Oh, and if I throw in an extra C-note, could you get a professional haircut, doll? You look like a scarecrow.'

My fake smile threatened to crack my face open. I burbled all the standard lines – yes, sir, three bags full, sir – and left the villa in a daze. I could see how these people might have driven Moxham over the edge.

*

No, believe it or not, it wasn't my childhood dream to grow up and cater to billionaires' whims.

At eighteen, I got a place studying physiotherapy at uni. I'd barely moved into the halls of residence before the problems started. My dad promised he would pay for everything. He paid for nothing. So, I did what anyone would do. I applied for a credit card. My application was denied. It turned out Dad had taken out credit cards and loans in my name and not paid them back. When I called him, he apologised and said he'd take care of it. He didn't. I borrowed money off friends, I took out payday loans, to get through till Christmas. At Christmas, Dad told me I was spoiled and should learn to look after myself. Later, I found the term 'financial abuse' online, next to a picture of a haunted-looking woman in a woollen green cardigan. I x'ed out of the tab without reading it.

I'd been invited on a girls' trip to Spain. Even though I couldn't afford it, I wanted to get away. That was where I met some women working as promoters. It looked like easy money. My friends returned to London; I stayed in Spain. What was the point in going back, when I was being turfed out of halls?

The life of a promoter was not as glamorous as it seemed. The money wasn't as free-flowing as promised and the apartment-share was borderline unsafe. Still, the drinks were free, the weather was hot and the beaches were beautiful.

It was day-to-day living; I didn't need to think about the past or the future. I got connected to a network of nomadic girls who moved countries the way other people changed clothes. I became a club rep for a while, a stewardess on a superyacht. I cleaned villas, worked night shifts on reception, practised my fake smile as a host.

If there was one thing I was good at, it was working in hospitality. Ford and Carolina would not defeat me. I would handle them with grace; I would prove myself outstanding at this job.

On my way out of Villa Mangrove, I scrabbled for my phone. Over the last few years, I'd built up a network of high-end forwarding agents who could source almost anything, at a price. Even they were stumped by the prospect of delivering everything Ford wanted within twenty-four hours.

Moxham would have known how to deal with this. He'd tug his earlobe twice, but he'd come up with a solution. He had to have a contact list of his own here in the BVI. One of his agents would know where to find this godforsaken plushie unicorn.

*

I crunched along the white shell path, the rocks and pebbles arranged at the edges echoing a zen garden. Guillaume had told me I would find Fizzy here, behind the pink door. The office, and its adjoining storeroom, was near the restaurant kitchen, tastefully shielded from the view of any guests ambling past. How terribly tacky, to imagine that work was required to keep everything on the island running smoothly.

'Knock, knock.' I peered through the open door. 'Hello?'

Instead of Fizzy, I found Kip, his tall frame folded into a desk chair. There was a nasty bruise on his neck. He was squinting at a laptop screen, but when he spotted me, he closed the lid. 'Hello!'

'Sir... I was looking for Fizzy.'

He pantomimed sadness. 'Ah, no one ever wants to talk to old Kipper.'

I laughed, taking a couple of steps into the small office. Its terracotta floor was an echo of my room at the staff village. There were two desks. The one where Kip was seated was strewn with chewed biros and half-crumpled Coke cans. Opposite, the other desk was regimented with rows of Post-its in pink, green and yellow. A mottled pink crystal the size of a fist sat beside a spider plant.

'I'm trying to get up to speed,' I said. 'With my job.'

'Want a job?' In an instant, Kip's expression went from cartoonish sorrow to joy. 'You're that lovely girl from Manchester, aren't you? Big in real estate. Quite a firecracker.'

'Uh… I'm Lola, the new deputy manager.' *Remember? Yesterday? The dead body?*

Kip's brow furrowed. 'Sure, sure.' A look of consternation passed across his face. 'Of course I remember, not senile yet.'

I didn't know how to reply, so I circled the desks and dropped into what had to be Fizzy's chair. Tacked to the wall, there was a series of inspirational statements. Cursive fonts, pastel backgrounds. *Kindness costs nothing. A smile can change the world. Put the 'I' in mindful.*

I cleared my throat. 'Have the police said anything?'

'The police?'

'Do they know what happened… exactly?'

'It was an accident, my girl.'

I wondered how the system worked, in this sleepy Caribbean nation. Technically, Keeper Island was private, which had to give Kip some kind of control. Diara's comment returned to me: *if it wasn't an accident, they'll call it an accident anyway.* Who were 'they'?

'Surely there'll be an investigation?' I said. 'Actually, I'm surprised you don't have private security.'

I'd half expected Kip to be trailed by a bunch of men in dark suits with holsters.

'No, no, never liked people buzzing around. Anyway, look where we are.' He gestured, although it was to a blank wall, not a beach scene. 'Never had a lick of trouble out here.'

'Right… but now there's the issue of…'

Kip looked at me like he didn't understand my meaning.

'We're a family here.' When he spoke, a querulous smile appeared on his lips, like a grandfather making a toast at Christmas. 'We deal with things like a family.'

Before I could wrap my mind around that one, there was the crunch of footsteps. Fizzy appeared, a plume of white smoke trailing her, as she wafted a lit bundle of leaves like an oversized joint.

'This young lady's working for us, don't you know?' Kip said to Fizzy.

She looked at me gauzily, as if she couldn't quite place me. 'And what a moment to step into the fray.'

I laughed awkwardly. 'I'm used to it. Constant chaos.'

'Hrm.'

She made another sweep of her arms, rattling her bracelets as she sent more smoke drifting across the room. I'd seen Allie use sage a few times; apparently it was good for psychic cleansing, whatever that meant.

'I'm happy to be acting general manager,' I said. 'Already doing it, really. Just need access to Moxham's devices and I can be up and running.'

'Right…' Fizzy frowned.

Belatedly, I remembered I was sitting at her desk, so I stood up. She brushed past me and dropped the sage into a pale-pink ceramic bowl. When she sat down and patted her hair, I flushed. Perhaps it was done unconsciously. Ford might be a dick, but he was right that I could do with an appointment at the hairdresser's.

'The main thing is making sure the guests are happy,' I said, sounding overly hearty.

'Yes!' Kip rose from his seat. 'This one's got her head screwed on.'

Fizzy, however, continued to frown. 'Kip...' She trailed off, eyes sliding sideways to fix her gaze on him. In a matter of seconds, it was obvious that an entire silent conversation passed between them.

'I get a sense of people.' Kip strode to the door. In passing, he dug an elbow into my ribs. 'Look at her,' he said to Fizzy, 'she's raring to go. Firecracker.'

'Sir,' I said, 'I'd still like to talk to you about—'

'About what?' He checked his watch. 'Time and tide wait for no man.'

'I've always looked up to you,' I improvised. 'From afar, I mean. Like a mentor.' *And I'd like to find out*, I added silently, *exactly what you know about Moxham's death.*

Kip's blue eyes lit up. 'Come sailing with me!'

'Kip,' Fizzy said sharply, 'she's working.'

'Tomorrow, then.' He gave a salute and was gone.

I had to laugh at the absurdity of it all. Kip seemed like a doddery old man; easily confused, easily swayed by compliments. Yet, of all the rich people on this island, he was the richest. Brick by brick, acquisition by acquisition, Kip Clement had made himself a king. You didn't do that by being stupid.

Fizzy bustled around to the desk Kip had vacated, the untidy one, which must have been Moxham's. I noticed the laptop bore a sticker featuring a tanned woman, busting out of a neon-pink bikini. She had a T-Rex head, baring a line of deadly teeth. *A smile can change the world*, I wanted to say. It would've made Moxham laugh.

Fizzy yanked a curling edge of the dino-babe sticker and ripped it off. 'Let's get rid of that.' She tapped at the keys with manicured fingers. 'We keep all the passcodes as 1-2-3-4... too many new staff were resetting theirs and forgetting.'

I leaned against the wall and let her work. The sweet-burning smell was giving me a headache.

'My sister swears by sage,' I said, in lieu of the truth, which was, *I think it's a load of old bobbins.*

'Gets rid of negativity,' she said. 'It makes me feel better, anyway. And we're all just trying to feel better.' She squeezed out a tear. 'I miss him already.'

'Me too.' Oh, God – my chest tightened – I was going to cry as well; real, ugly tears. I took in a big gulp of air and concentrated hard on the laptop's loading screen.

Fizzy summoned a courage-under-fire smile and handed me a phone. 'Here's your work phone, and – yes, here we are – all fresh and clean and ready to go.' She nudged the computer in my direction.

'Thanks.' I sank into Moxham's chair and brushed a hand across my face. My bruise was fading, but wasn't completely gone; I had to be careful that my make-up stayed put. Fizzy was hovering over me, her bracelets making music as she tidied away the debris from the desk.

I loaded the email program on automatic. It was empty. I clicked on Documents. Also empty.

'Where are all Moxham's emails? His files?' I asked.

Fizzy's face was impassive. 'I think Kip had the tech people deep clean it all.'

'What? Why?'

'It's a tech issue or a... legal issue. Kip will have had his reasons, I'm sure.'

'But I need—'

'Everyone here is so happy to help.' She slid back into her own desk chair. 'Just ask if you have any questions.'

I turned on the phone, but that was back to factory settings as well.

How was I supposed to take over Moxham's job with no record of his past work and none of his contact lists to help me? It was impossible. To erase everything he'd done was an over-reach of the most insane proportions. And why was Kip getting involved in the minutia of tech stuff?

'I need to buy a fucking unicorn.' I wanted to cry again, but this time out of frustration.

'Excuse me?'

'Never mind.' I batted the laptop lid closed.

Neither Kip nor Fizzy had been outright rude to me today. But they were putting barriers up in front of me. Anything I did to disrupt the status quo of the island would be shut down by Kip and His Girl Friday.

It was a cover-up.

When Diara had dropped her hint, I hadn't wanted to believe it. Now, for the first time, it hit me that Moxham's death wasn't an accident at all.

Across the desk island, Fizzy pressed a finger to her radio earpiece. 'Ah, I think this one's for you.'

'Sorry?'

My hand went to my own radio, twirling the volume knob.

It was Diara's voice. The connection crackled, before re-solving.

'Carolina going crazy in the spa, over.'

8

After Carolina had complained about the windiness of Windy Beach, I'd arranged for her to have a relaxing afternoon of spa treatments. What could go wrong? A lot, apparently.

Diara's was the first face I saw when I arrived at the spa. She burst out of the glass doors. 'I am going to murder that girl. She threw my oils across the room.' Now she mentioned it, I smelled an overwhelming lavender scent on the air. 'Then she clawed at me.'

'I'll deal with it,' I said, but Diara was already stalking away.

The spa was located on the east of the island. From the main complex, it was a twelve-minute golf cart ride, but guests were rewarded with a sanctuary hidden amid thick bush land. Nestled among the trees, the building's green roof merged with the surroundings like a hobbit house.

'Hello?' I pushed through the doors.

I hadn't been inside the spa before. Everything was decorated in corals and oranges. One wall shimmered gold, as if it had been laced through the brick. The lighting was low and moody, creating an effect like a permanent sunset. I circled the water feature in the spa's foyer. The Buddha at its centre, golden and serene, had been knocked off its plinth.

I thought the foyer was empty, until I heard a cry.

It was Carolina, crumpled in a corner, wearing a fluffy white robe. I crouched down beside her. She smelled like the essential oils she'd flung, but when I got closer, I caught the stench of booze.

She was trembling. Make-up was smeared around her green eyes.

'Hi, honey,' I said in my baby-bird voice, 'how are you feeling?'

'… The other girl was mean to me.'

I brushed her matted white-blonde hair off her face. 'Aw, I'm so sorry.' The only way I could keep my tone sweet was to pretend I was comforting my six-year-old niece.

'She should be fired.'

'You won't need to see her again.' I suspected Diara would refuse to be within a hundred metres of Carolina, so it was an easy promise to make.

'I wanted a massage, but she kept touching me,' Carolina mumbled.

'I'm sorry. Why don't we get you back to the villa?'

'No!' Carolina's hand turned to a fist, which glanced off my shoulder. 'Don't want to see him.'

'You two have a fight?'

'He's going to ask me to marry him. I heard him talking to you earlier.'

'Don't you want to marry him?'

'… He wears socks with sandals.'

My mouth twitched, but I kept a straight face. 'Unforgiveable.'

'And he goes through my phone.'

Ahh, so the self-aggrandising arsehole was also a possessive creep. What a surprise.

'We'll take you to a different villa.'

'I want' – Carolina's voice rose as she tried to stand up – 'I want a plane! I want to go home!'

'OK…' I put my hands on her shoulders to steady her, but she shrugged me off, her legs kicking out. In the process, she knocked me on my arse. I yelped as I hit the floor.

'Everything OK?' It was a man's voice. I half-turned to see a guy in a towel had appeared in the foyer.

'Everything's fine,' I said, as Carolina lurched forward and vomited down my front.

*

It could have been worse. She could have vomited in my hair. Really, my shorts and T-shirt had borne the brunt of it. The worst part of the whole incident was the man in the towel had rushed to my aid. The gorgeous, gorgeous man, with tousled blond hair and the body of an Adonis, was handing me paper towels and frowning at me in a sweet, concerned way. Forevermore, his first impression of me would be: Vomit Girl.

The silver lining was that vomiting had taken the fight out of Carolina. I radioed for assistance and Reggie arrived. Five minutes later, the two of them had gone (Reggie propping up Carolina, trying not to look grossed-out by the smell of sick). I slumped onto the floor where Carolina had sat.

To my surprise, the blond man was still here. Still gorgeous. Still in a towel.

'You look like you could use a massage. I'll get Helena to come out. She's a diamond.' His grin was so earnest that I didn't know what to say.

No, Helena would not be giving me a massage. I levered myself up. The man shot out a hand to help me. His grip was warm and strong. My hand, I was humiliated to realise, was sticky with vomit.

'I've interrupted you,' I said robotically. 'I'm terribly sorry, sir. Please, return to your treatment room.'

I suspected Helena – whoever she was – hoped she could knock off early, due to the carnage, but I had no intention of letting her. It was bad enough that we'd had a death on the island this week. I didn't want the guests bothered by a rampaging trophy-girlfriend. I wanted them relaxed and oblivious.

'My pops taught me to never leave a damsel in distress,' he said. 'Gimme a minute to make myself decent, then I'll help you out.'

I was too exhausted to argue, which was how I ended up on cleaning duty assisted by an investment banker named Brady Calloway.

'We've met before.' Brady pushed a mop across the floor. He was dressed in a linen shirt and trousers now, and (I didn't like to judge, but) he handled the mop like someone who thought houses cleaned themselves.

'Don't think so.' I crouched down, scrubbing at the tiled floor.

'You look awful familiar.'

I squinted up at him. 'You say that to all the girls.'

His laughter was a low rumble. 'You're onto me.'

There was admittedly something vaguely familiar about him, although that might have been because he was an actual Ken doll.

'Hey, sorry to hear about that guy,' he said.

'What?'

Brady snapped his fingers. 'Meekham.'

The way Brady was looking at me was too intent. Or was I imagining it?

'Moxham,' I said.

'So it was some freak accident?'

'Mm.'

'Crazy. You don't expect it.'

I murmured 'Yeah, crazy,' and busied myself propping up the Buddha on its plinth. Brady was the first and only guest to comment on Moxham's death. I'd told the hosts we shouldn't mention it, because nothing ruined a holiday quicker than death. So far, it hadn't come up in my conversations. Not even Ford, chummy enough to be jet-skiing with Moxham on the day I'd arrived, had acknowledged his absence.

Most guests must have assumed Moxham was sick or had been called away, if they'd noticed he was missing at all. Brady was sharp enough to have discovered the truth. It probably didn't mean anything, but this fact lodged in the recesses of my mind.

With the clean-up concluded, it wasn't hard to guide the conversation away from death and into lighter realms. Brady gave the impression of a foodie who spunked his cash on daily fine dining. I persuaded him to go to the restaurant for dinner, where Guillaume was cooking roasted pork belly with sweet potato purée.

'Sure you won't join me?' he asked.

''Fraid I can't.'

As he sauntered away, I almost regretted my refusal. It had been drilled into me, from my first hotel job, that fraternisation with the guests was cause for immediate dismissal. Yet on Keeper Island, more than any other place I'd worked, the line between guest and staff was blurred.

There was a line though. While Brady could enjoy his evening in peace, I still had to source a plushie unicorn.

*

The next twenty-four hours, Monday blurring into Tuesday, were frantic with work-work-work. On Tuesday morning, I magicked up a perfect engagement tableau for Carolina and her Prince Charming, in between dealing with one of the swimming pools turning a lurid green colour, due to a broken filter. If I weren't so curious about Our Benevolent Dictator, I might have found a way to put off my sailing engagement with Kip. In case I'd forgotten, a handwritten note on heavy Clement Hotels stationery was delivered to me. *Hidden Cove, 5 p.m.*

As the bush trail opened up onto sands, I kicked off my trainers. True to its name, Hidden Cove was a bit of a secret, on the eastern edge of the island, far from the restaurant and the well-trodden Main Beach. It was also inaccessible by golf cart.

The crescent of pale sand, edged by rocks, was deserted. My footprints joined Kip's solitary trail. It had the echo of a place that might never have been discovered by a human soul until now.

When I spotted Kip in the shallows with his boat, two words nagged at me. Big. Fish.

Moxham had bragged about having a 'big fish on the line'. He was targeting someone on the island, in whatever scheme he was running. And who was the biggest fish of all? Kip Clement. If Moxham had crossed Kip, Kip might have retaliated. This was my suspicion, yet it was hard to hold on to it as I waded into the bathwater-warm sea.

Kip seemed ecstatic to see me. 'Ever sailed before?' he asked.

'On a yacht with a toilet brush in my hand.'

'Then you're an old hand.' He laughed and slapped the water. 'Choppy today, but that never stopped me.'

A swell broke against my legs and I had to dig my toes into the sand to keep upright. Kip began explaining to me the particulars of dinghy sailing; the size of the boat (10 ft), how to steer and what to do if it capsized. I asked if I should change my clothes; I was dressed in cotton shorts and T-shirt, in contrast to Kip's gloves, board shorts and black water-repellent turtleneck.

'Pah, she'll be fine.' He threw me a rope. I fumbled but caught it.

When I'd heard the word 'sailing', I'd imagined Kip and me punting along in still waters, sharing a sun-warmed bottle of wine. It would be the perfect opportunity to ask a few casual questions about his working relationship with Moxham and what he was doing the night of the Alice party.

'Seriously, sir, I don't really know what—'

'Call me Kip, dear girl.'

He pulled at the highlighter-yellow sail of his boat. I could see in his eyes, in the jut of his jaw, that he was leaving. And, if I wanted his respect, I was going with him.

I plunged forward, my toes skating across sand as I skipped-swam to the sailboat. Kip hauled me on deck, and without another word, we were off.

We arced out of the cove, into open water. My legs were cramped up beneath me. The boat was scarcely big enough for the two of us.

'Duck!'

I had to dive under the boom as Kip sent the sail slamming towards me.

We were racing now. Waves slapped against the hull, soaking me, the wind deafening as it thwacked against the main sheet. The sun, scorching earlier, didn't feel so hot anymore. A shiver ran through me; my wet clothes clinging to cold flesh.

Should I be wearing a life vest? I recalled Moxham, shirtless, fearless, as he'd roared across the waves on a jet ski.

'The party!' I half-shouted, dispatching any thoughts of creating a neat conversational segue.

Kip's face was stony with concentration. 'What?'

'Did you go to the party on Saturday?'

The rumour that Kip had gone to bed early with a headache struck me as too convenient.

'Don't lean back,' he said.

I wasn't aware I'd been leaning back. I tried to hold Keeper Island in my sights – it was worryingly far away now – but Kip changed direction again and I had to duck to avoid the boom.

'It was a great party,' I tried again.

'Didn't get to see much of it.'

'None at all?'

'Busy.' The wind wrenched away the word, so I had to lip-read.

Busy with what, Kip?

The boat reared in the water as sickness lurched in my stomach.

To make matters worse, Kip grabbed my hand and put it on the tiller. He stood up and began toying with the main sheet.

Jesus. I clutched the tiller in a vice-like grip. What if I died? It would be so easy. A jab of the elbow was all it would take to tip me into the water. Another accident.

Would anyone bother to investigate my death?

Kip, still standing, tugged at the sail. His arse wiggled close to my face. I looked away, but something snagged at the edge of my vision. My head snapped back. There was a dark stain on Kip's board shorts. It was on the back of his thigh, the size of a handprint, smeared at the edges. He could have put on his shorts this morning without ever realising there was a stain.

I could see the motion now. A hand, wet with blood. Reach back, wipe it on the seat of your shorts. Maybe it was unconscious. He'd forgotten he did it.

Kip sat down with a thump. I leaned back automatically, my eyes scanning his face for—

What? Some trace of guilt only I could intuit?

His hand shot out. My heart plummeted to my stomach.

He was going to push me in. Leave me for dead.

I curled away from his reach. 'Don't—'

The world dropped away. The sea engulfed me, water filling my airways.

With a clunk, the hull flipped on top of me, blocking out the sun.

9

Kip thought the whole thing was hilarious.

'Like a kitten in the bathtub, she was.' He mimed scrabbling.

I gritted out a smile. As it turned out, I wasn't a murder victim. Just an idiot who'd capsized the boat. Kip had straddled the upside-down hull and scooped me up out of the water.

'She was burbling, *no, no, no,*' he said, courting laughter from the length of the table.

A waiter arrived at my elbow, refilling my glass with wine. Before I could thank him, he slipped away into the dark. Across from me, Ford let out a guffaw of laughter. Beside him, Carolina's head was bowed as she cut up her eel into tiny pieces.

'Never sailed before?' Ford asked.

I shook my head. We were seated on the veranda of Kip's villa, the clamour of the waves a backdrop to the conversation. I craned my neck and caught a glimpse of the marble woman out at sea, drowning yet again.

Following my near-death experience, Kip had invited me to dine at the big table. That wasn't what he called it (although the long stretch of mahogany was certainly vast), but I'd picked up the staff slang during my first couple of days on Keeper Island.

In the evenings, the staff typically ate simple fare, delivered to the staff village by Guillaume's team. Dining at the big table, where Kip gathered together a dozen of the island's guests for an impromptu salon, was ostensibly a treat. If I weren't so wrung-out, I might have enjoyed the opportunity to visit Kip's villa, which I'd previously only passed by. Perched on the rocks, at the northwest tip of the island, it was apparently built on the lighthouse ruins that gave the island its name. The white circular tower, imposing against the dark sky, marked it as distinct from the other cube-like villas. Sprawling in size, it seemed built for a family, although as far as I could tell, only Kip lived here.

'This chef's not bad for a fairy,' Kip said, smacking his lips. 'Hell, this eel is so good, it should be illegal!'

At the other end of the table, a paunchy man in a salmon-pink shirt pantomimed a belly laugh. 'I'm off duty.'

The man in pink, I recalled, was the BVI Commissioner of Police, who was apparently a good friend of Kip's. The footballer and his wife were also here, along with the chic Italian woman, not eating because she was on a detox. Creepy Eddie Yiu raised a glass in my direction. Brady, my knight-in-a-towel from the spa, was at the opposite end of the table. He'd shot me a flirty look as I'd arrived, but he was seated too far away for conversation.

I didn't love sitting beside Ford and Carolina, especially when we were only on the third course of ten. Smiling and nodding at first world problems ('you wouldn't believe the tax those bastards want to charge me') was giving me a headache.

I was still in my salt-stained shorts and T-shirt, and Kip was still in his water sports gear. (There was no dress code on Keeper Island, apparently.) I'd had no time to reapply my make-up, so I was sure the shadow of my bruise stood out on my cheek. I was not the only one with bruises though.

Kip pushed up his sleeves and raised a finger. A blotchy-purple bruise covered his forearm. The waiter reappeared, wordlessly refilling glasses. Kip's arm came to rest on the table as he chatted with Carolina about her horses. The bruise looked a few days old. I leaned in, pretending to reach for the salt. There was a bruise on his other arm as well, and the one on his neck I'd noticed a couple of days ago.

He looked like he'd been in a fight.

If I hadn't seen the bloodstain on his shorts, I might have dismissed this thought. It was blood, wasn't it? Not oil, or paint, or shit? Kip caught me looking at him and grinned. I gave a queasy smile in return.

'I have an announcement to make.' Ford stood up, tapping his wine glass with a fork. 'Carolina's going to marry me.'

There were whoops and cheers. Kip wrung Ford's hand like they were on a game show and Ford had won a million dollars.

I turned to Carolina. 'That's exciting.'

She ignored me, reaching out a hand to present her diamond ring to the guests at the other end of the table. She also hadn't acknowledged me when I'd sat down. Maybe the events at the spa had been a particularly erratic version of cold feet. Maybe she and Ford would live happily ever after. Maybe.

The next course arrived. Wagyu beef with oyster mushrooms and wild garlic.

'Get married, stay married.' Kip thumped a hand against the table, making my plate shudder. 'Best advice I ever got.'

'Oh, yeah?' Ford cocked an eyebrow. (I suspected he was planning to trial Carolina for a four–six-year period and then trade her in for a younger model.)

'Love, love, love, all you need.'

Easy for a billionaire to say. I took a bite of my steak.

'Secret to a happy marriage?' Carolina asked Kip, her eyes glassy.

'Never let yourself get angry with each other. People who say couples fight… pah! Relationships are easy with the right person. My lovely wife… we enjoy each other's company. We'd be happy in a shack.'

'Where is she?' Carolina asked.

Kip's face crumpled. 'She passed.' When a tear rolled down his face, he didn't wipe it away, just let it fall into the *jus* on his plate.

There was an excruciating silence. I ate just for something to do.

Now I thought of it, I'd heard something on the news a few years ago about the death of Kip's wife. Cancer or something.

Eventually, the conversation revived, returning to the subject of business (Kip was semi-retired, but still on the board of Clement Hotels). As the steak dishes were being cleared away, Fizzy appeared.

'Join us, my darling!' Kip said.

She demurred, but when he offered her his wine glass, she took a sip. Her hand came to rest in the crook of Kip's arm, as she leaned her slight frame against his back.

'Everything OK?' I asked. I was half-hoping for an emergency to get me out of the remaining six courses.

'No, no, I fixed that problem with the hinge,' she said to Kip. Now I noticed she was holding an electric screwdriver.

I frowned. 'I would have got maintenance to—'

'Isn't it funny how we ever managed before Ms George showed up?'

There was acid in Fizzy's voice, but Kip laughed like it was a joke. 'Fizzy looks after me well.' He patted her arm. 'She's my right hand.'

Scalded, I took a swallow of wine. The waiters arrived with the next course. Fizzy leaned in to whisper something in Kip's ear and then she wafted away.

Across the table, Ford was back to talking about the proposal.

'I wanted to fill the house with red roses and all I got were a few sad, drooping things.'

I tensed, expecting him to confront me. Prick.

Ford turned instead to Kip, clapping him on the shoulder. 'You got quite a place here, my man, but still room for improvement. Trust me, I've been to the best resorts. We'll sit down, man to man, give you some pointers.'

A muscle in Kip's cheek jumped. Kip Clement owned a hotel in every major city in the world. A tech-upstart weasel was going to give him pointers?

'Mmm.' Kip shrugged off Ford's hand.

The dinner ground onward. Course number six arrived. Miso-glazed aubergine with pickled radish.

'What the hell is this shit?' Ford picked up a radish from his plate and pitched it over Kip's shoulder. 'The sloths can have it.'

Kip glanced behind him at the radish lying on the wooden boards. He opened his mouth, but instead of a reprimand to Ford, he seized upon the subject of the sloths. They were his pet project, no pun intended. A rare breed at risk of extinction. He'd introduced them onto Keeper Island some fifteen years ago.

'Isn't that, like, fucking with nature's plan?' Ford asked.

'Ah, no, that's the thing.' Kip gestured with his fork. 'They could have been here originally. The science indicates that, at one point, there was a land bridge from here to South America. A thousand years ago, this place would have been teeming with sloths.'

'They're cute, but they're vicious,' Ford said. 'Tried to feed one a Dorito and it slashed at my hand.'

Kip made a sound in the back of his throat. He lifted his white cloth napkin and wiped at his mouth. I was feeling faint with tiredness at this point, wondering if I could make an excuse and skip the final four courses, when Kip stood up.

'My dear, could you arrange for a boat to be at the pier in ten minutes? I'm afraid it's a little late in the evening for a helicopter.'

It took me a second to realise he was talking to me.

'A boat. Yes, sir.' My hand went to my hip, but I must have left my radio on the beach at Hidden Cove.

'Well' – Kip extended his hand to Ford – 'I'd say it's been a pleasure, but we both know that's a lie.'

Ford shook Kip's hand. There was a confused smile on his lips.

'Let's leave it at... safe travels,' Kip said. 'Lola will escort you to your villa to pack your belongings.' He gave a slight bow in my direction. 'Thank you, dear.'

I stumbled to my feet, still processing what was happening. Kip was kicking them off the island.

Ford faltered for a moment, before he found his voice. 'Not fucking leaving.'

'We paid for three weeks,' Carolina said. She had certainly paid for nothing.

'I'm sure we can rustle up a refund.'

'I don't want a refund,' Ford said. 'I want you to honour the contract. I'll sue your ass.'

'Oh, I do love a good lawsuit.' Kip's blue eyes actually lit up. 'But I'm afraid you'll lose. You see, this island is my home. I am a hotelier at heart, so I couldn't resist the idea of turning it into a little resort. But it is still my home. And an Englishman's home is his castle.'

'What?' Ford's nostrils flared.

'Get out of my castle before I tar and feather you.' Despite his words, Kip's voice remained genial. He cleared his throat. 'So to speak.'

I was still in shock. Beside me, Carolina had begun to cry, her hands crushing the unicorn.

A waiter was standing behind Kip and another appeared at his elbow. Brady rose from his seat and approached Ford, holding up a placating hand.

'Hey now, bud, time to go,' Brady said.

'Fuck off, you meathead cunt.' He elbowed Brady out the way.

Brady's face darkened. 'Lola, would you like some help escorting our friends to their villa?'

'That would be very kind,' I said.

'I'm not going anywhere.' Ford's face was bright pink.

Carolina plucked at his shirtsleeve. 'Baby, don't—'

'Listen to your lady.' Brady squared up to Ford.

'I'm not listening to that bitch.' He was several inches shorter than Brady, but he bumped him with his chest. 'Not listening to any of you!'

Ford took a swing at Brady. It glanced off his cheek. A moment later, Brady wrestled him into a headlock.

'Sue you too.' Ford was gasping, clawing at Brady's forearm. 'Assault.'

'Funny' – Brady winked at me – 'I don't see any witnesses.'

In the end, Ford and Carolina were as meek as drowning kittens. Half an hour later, they were gone.

It was contrary to everything I had ever experienced in the hotel trade. If a guest was an arsehole, they got more bowing-and-scraping from the staff. As long as you had money to grease the right palms, you were untouchable. Nothing, short of murder, could get you booted from an upscale hotel.

Murder. My thoughts returned to Moxham, blood in the water.

'I just didn't really care for him,' Kip told me mildly, when I returned to the villa to tell him Ford and Carolina had departed. In my absence, they had finally reached course number ten. Wild strawberry sorbet with sorrel granita.

Was there enough evidence to point to Moxham being murdered? As Kip resumed his conversation about sloths with the Italian heiress, I realised for the first time that I didn't want to believe it. I grabbed a bite of sorbet and licked my spoon clean. I wanted Kip to be benevolent. I wanted Moxham to have died accidentally. I wanted to have found my dream job, out here in paradise.

10

Time seemed to accelerate on Keeper Island. The days slipped away from me and suddenly, it was Friday. I'd been here almost a week. Even after Ford and Carolina departed, my workload didn't diminish. There was always a disaster to avert.

'I got a craving for McDonald's,' Eddie Yiu said.

'I'll have Guillaume make you a burger,' I said.

'I want McDonald's.'

Every time I'd seen Eddie in the last few days, he'd been on his laptop or his phone. Apparently, he was working on a new business venture. Yawn. He'd been frosty with me since he realised I wasn't going to have sex with him, but now I produced a dazzling smile.

'I promise you, our chef will make something even better. It'll be fifteen minutes.'

OK, it would be forty minutes, because it was just before dinner service and Guillaume would probably pitch a fit, but I wasn't lying about the burger being great.

'It's gotta be McDonald's.'

I gritted out a smile. '… Absolutely.'

I might have understood it if he wanted authentic Chinese food, but American junk food? Really?

When I asked Tyson where the nearest McDonald's was, he told me it was two hours away by boat and I'd need a passport. Jesus. I dispatched Reggie on this errand (he was bleary with weed, so didn't complain too much) and, four hours later, Eddie got his Big Mac. I microwaved it, which only made it look worse, but the guy acted like it was nectar of the gods.

By the time I clocked off, it was past midnight. I traipsed into the staff village. I'd developed muscle memory that meant, like most of the staff, I could make it along the half-mile bush trail from the main complex without needing a torch in the dark.

My sore muscles were compounded by a streak of sunburn across my shoulders. I was ready for a beer and a game of cards. Late at night, when normal people were asleep, you could always find a crew in the team bar. Tyson was a notorious bad loser; Tessa was a hustler; Reggie had once cried over a bad bet and no one would let him forget it. They usually only played childish card games, but I'd seen a table flipped upside down two nights ago.

To my surprise, it wasn't only the card sharks who were awake tonight. A bonfire blazed in the middle of the clearing, flanked by a crowd of twenty or more people. I recognised bartenders and groundskeepers, a couple of the housekeeping team.

'Lola!' Guillaume beckoned me.

Over the last couple of days, I'd figured out the best times to scavenge cordon-bleu leftovers from the kitchen. (Pumpkin and crab bisque, grilled mahi mahi, rabbit tortellini – and that was just Thursday.) In the process, I'd become something of a confidante to Guillaume. He worried his long-distance boyfriend in Lyon was growing too close to a man he'd met at the gym. He worried his temper was getting out of hand. He worried about worrying.

On a fold-out table in front of Guillaume, a paper banner was stretched out. It read: *We'll miss you, Mox*. He scrawled a message in French, then offered me the marker pen. 'You want to write something?'

I rubbed my neck, aggravating my sunburn. It wasn't only a week since my arrival; it was a week since Moxham's death. I scribbled, *Cheers to the man who could fix anything*.

My comment felt inadequate, but how could I describe Moxham? In Hong Kong, he'd taken me out to the karaoke bars. We screamed 90s pop songs at the top of our lungs for catharsis. The city was a culture shock to me. The outdoor markets that smelled of death, the cramped pavements with workshops spilling out, the pollution, the loudness of everything. It was a whole world crammed onto a tiny island. Moxham showed me around, shared with me the best places to eat, taught me bits and pieces of Cantonese (mostly the swear words).

I turned away from the banner. He would have hated all those maudlin comments. The bonfire, on the other hand. Yes, Moxham would have approved of being memorialised with a big fuck-off blaze.

Grey smoke wafted into the dark sky, the column of fire creating a wall of heat. I edged around it, towards the team bar. Inside, Tessa was slumped in one of the squashy orange chairs looking morose, while a bartender (I vaguely recalled he was named Ethan) was shooting darts at a board that bore a pockmarked picture of Kip's grinning face. Diara and Fizzy were at the end of the pinewood bar that ran the length of one wall. Fizzy was murmuring intently, Diara was angled away from her.

'Why are you always so—' Diara spat the words.

Fizzy shot back, 'I'm just trying to—'

They stopped talking the moment I drew near. There was an awkward pause, then Fizzy said loudly in my direction, 'You'll need some aloe for that sunburn.'

'Thanks, I'll get on it.'

She shot me a fake smile and pushed away from the bar. I rescued a couple of beers from the fridge and handed one to Diara. Considering she was my roommate, I'd seen little of her in the past week. She was absent from our room on as many nights as she was there. I wanted to be her friend, but she'd been noticeably standoffish with me.

I told her about Eddie Yiu's McDonald's as the two of us ambled back to the bonfire. I was courting her laughter, but she only raised her eyebrows and said, 'Seen it before.'

'Supposed to be a celebration!' Kip strode into the staff village, his plummy accent ringing out. 'Let's get some real wood on this pyre.'

The chatter around me died down. It was a bit like a schoolteacher showing up at our clubhouse. (What did Kip think of the dart board?) He hauled some more lumber onto the fire, tutting and exclaiming, as if he were more than just a business mogul, he was also a true survivalist. As the bonfire grew, a tickle of smoke lodged in the back of my throat. I took a swig of beer.

Kip clapped his hands. 'We're here to honour our dear friend, Michael Moxham. Who'd like to say a few words?'

There was a hush. Some people bowed their heads; nobody spoke. Fizzy was staring into the flames with a faraway expression. Diara was on her phone. Guillaume was whispering something to Reggie.

I stepped forward. 'I will.'

Kip beamed at me. 'Please, please.'

I moved to stand beside Kip. The firelight flickering across the faces of my new co-workers made them look distorted.

'You don't know me that well.' I cleared my throat. 'But Moxham is the reason I'm here. He wasn't always the easiest person to get along with.' When I raised my eyebrows, there was scattered laughter. 'But he made me laugh.

'He was the first person on the dance floor – we'll forgive him for that, because Mox should never, ever have been dancing.' More laughter from the crowd. 'A couple of times, he pulled me out of a hole.'

My voice dipped. I'd begun speaking without processing what I was going to say. It was almost eighteen months now since I'd got the call from one of my sister's friends. Allie was back on the pills, not eating, not looking after herself. Not looking after Flora. That day, I'd broken down in Moxham's office, heaving out sobs. He pulled me close, smelling of cigarettes. I got snot all over his tailored Italian jacket, but he didn't complain.

I'd been prepared to quit my job on the spot and fly home to London. Moxham told me I could take paid leave for as long as I needed. He lent me money to get Allie into a private clinic. There, I spent weeks seated in a sunny day room, knotting friendship bracelets with my niece, as I hoped and prayed Allie wouldn't succeed in starving herself to death.

Moxham was a big part of the reason Allie pulled through.

Tears made my voice thick. I mumbled my final words, raising my beer bottle. 'He was my friend.'

Reggie let out a whoop. 'Whatta man!' It came back in an echo from the rest of the crowd. *Whatta man!*

My eulogy unstopped the dam, as people rushed in to tell their stories about Moxham. Reggie imitated his dance moves. Tyson told a convoluted story about a series of dares he and Moxham had set each other, culminating in him running naked through the restaurant during dinner service.

When the laughter died down, Fizzy tottered up to the front. 'When I first met Mikey, he said to me, "You'll either love me or you'll hate me, there is no in between." Of course I loved him. We all did.'

There was a snort behind me. I half-turned to catch a look of disgust on Diara's face.

'We'll miss him so deeply,' Fizzy said. (Was she drunk?) 'A chasm in our hearts has opened up.' She dropped her head, her shoulders shaking. Kip swooped in, squeezing Fizzy close as she collapsed into theatrical sobbing, and escorted her away from the gathering.

I shuffled backwards and shot Diara a look.

'Should I start polishing the Oscar?' I slapped a hand over my heart, eyes fluttering shut. 'The chasm – in my heart—'

Diara's face remained blank for a second, then a small smile spilled onto her lips. 'She means well.'

I shrugged. It was probably true. But there was something about it I didn't like. A grab for attention, perhaps. If you knew it would get you the limelight, why not exaggerate your relationship with Moxham? Play the role of the most devastated?

'Were they close?' I asked.

'They worked together a lot.' Diara squinted at me. 'Kip puts Fizzy in charge most of the time. When Moxham came in last year... he thought he should be in charge.'

'Turf war?'

'Yeah, a turf war.' Diara shot me a weird smile. 'But Fizzy won. Fizzy always wins.'

I mulled this over. 'The power behind the power.'

Diara didn't reply and our conversation cooled. Following Fizzy's exit, Tyson was telling a dirty joke to uproarious laughter. Guillaume was hacking at what looked like young coconuts, lining up a dozen of them on the ground.

Kip returned, prowling the edge of the bonfire. 'Moxham is with his people in Australia now, but his spirit remains here.' He flourished a bow at the bonfire. 'He deserves a send-off. A true funeral pyre.'

He grasped the paper banner and let it flutter down into the fire.

Someone bumped into me. 'Coming through!' There was a squeak as Reggie manoeuvred a wheelbarrow through the crowd.

Kip retrieved a brown fedora from the wheelbarrow and held it up.

'Ride on, fierce warrior, ride on.' He tossed the hat onto the fire. It landed with a *pop*, hovering for a split-second before it dipped, puckering into the flames.

I peered over Tyson's shoulder at the contents of the wheelbarrow. Clothes were clumped together: a white button-down, a leather jacket, a logo tee in green. There were comic books. An action figure in moulded plastic.

'A true Viking ritual for a chieftain would involve a sacrifice,' Kip was saying (although I was barely listening, my eyes fixed on the wheelbarrow). 'A slave girl would climb aboard a mighty ship and mount the dead chieftain. Ride off into the afterlife as the ship is set alight.'

A couple of men in the audience chortled, but Kip only bellowed out a command.

'Let's send our dear friend to Valhalla! Let's burn his grave goods. Send our warrior on his journey!'

Kip sent a cascade of pages onto the flames. A few people applauded, but I was speechless. Moxham had been fanatical about his comic books. He was a collector.

Tyson scrambled forward and pitched a balled T-shirt into the fire, as more people got in on the action, flinging clothes and shoes. Someone lobbed what looked like a rugby ball into the air and it landed in the blaze.

What the fuck? I couldn't believe what I was seeing. Up until that moment, I hadn't thought about Moxham's belongings. I'd subconsciously imagined them crated up and shipped back to his parents.

Instead, we were burning them. We were destroying them.

11

The smoke from the bonfire turned acrid, as plastic melted amid the flames.

I coughed. I wanted to scream, 'Stop!'

There was a frenzy as hands groped in the wheelbarrow, flinging items into the fire. I fought my way to the front of the crowd and grabbed at random from the near-empty wheelbarrow. I didn't know Moxham's family. Never met them. Yet I had a primal need to save something of his belongings and give it to them.

I came up with a tie, but, within seconds, someone had ripped it from my grasp. Beside me, Reggie grunted. He lifted a comic book, encased in a plastic sleeve, and sent it arcing into the flames.

The wheelbarrow was empty.

I skip-stepped around the edge of the bonfire, wanting to rescue as much as I could from danger, but it was too late. My shoe kicked something. It was the comic book Reggie had thrown. He must have tossed it too far, clear of the fire. I picked it up. There were burn marks at the edges of the plastic sleeve, but it had escaped the worst of the flames. I shoved it down the back of my shorts and retreated from the blaze.

Ethan the bartender jostled past me, holding two pitchers of swirling, dark liquid. Guillaume was arranging the coconuts at the base of the fire. Now I looked closer, I saw they were not coconuts but creamy-yellow in colour.

'Breadfruit!' he said, catching my gaze.

I was shocked at how quickly we'd gone from Viking funeral pyre to good ol' fashioned barbecue. The incongruous smell of freshly baked bread filled the air, chasing away the tang of burned plastic.

'You ever taste it?' Guillaume was still talking to me. He smacked his lips. 'Delicious.'

I shook my head. I didn't care about breadfruit. The old adage of how to keep a hotel guest happy was to refill their cocktail and offer them a snack; it made me sick how easily the staff of Keeper Island were similarly distracted.

Moxham was dead. And everything that remained of him had burned.

I scanned the crowd for Kip. He was leaning against a wooden railing, his face eerily blank. Crate up Moxham's belongings and you might unwittingly leave behind evidence. Blitz them in an insane ritual and you eliminate all possibility of getting caught. Wasn't this bonfire just a more extravagant version of what Kip had done when he'd wiped Moxham's devices?

As I stumbled away from the bonfire, Diara put a hand on my arm. I shrugged her off and strode on. I'd been stupid to let myself get caught up in island life. I couldn't trust these people. Just as Moxham had warned me.

I hastened clear of the crowd and shut myself in my room. I could still hear the clamour outside, but it was muffled. As I sat down on my bed, a sharp plastic corner of the comic book dug into the flesh of my back. I tugged it free of my waistband. It was all that remained of Mike Moxham. Despite the scorch mark across the sleeve, when I slid out the comic book, it was pristine. Superman flexed, looking beyond me to a crisis he was about to avert.

What had Moxham got out of these comic books? He'd told me once that they were a great investment, worth thousands, but I liked to think he hoarded them like memories of better days. I imagined him as a child with a torch under his covers, paging through stories of damsels in distress, crackpot scientists, heroes and villains.

When I flipped open the comic book, something fell from its pages. It was a slim notebook with an olive-green cover. I thumbed through it. Was it a free gift that came with purchase?

No. Unlike the carefully preserved comic book, the notebook was battered. Greasy fingerprints stained the cover. The pages were crammed with handwritten notes. Moxham's writing, with its odd left-hand lean, spidery as a doctor's prescription.

I read from it at random:

Devil cardinal red pizza bed 1
Devil snake beef canoe bed 11
Devil teardrop blue party bed 3

Well, that cleared up everything.

I snuffled a laugh. It wasn't like I expected a diary, one with a tantalising final entry:

Kip is on my trail. Please, Lord, should whomsoever finds this journal know that Clement hath killed me. Avenge my death!

My fingers trailed down page after page of word-salad notes.

Devil peacock rice and peas vg 2 hours bed 12
Devil spike sick bed 12
Devil stars yellow vg 3 hours bed 12

Was it a code? I tried to separate out the parts that were identifiable. Every entry ended with a bedtime. Was it something as mundane as a sleep tracker? 'Canoe', 'beef', 'pizza' had to describe his activities and food for the day. So far, so boring. 'vg'? Very good? Was Moxham charting his moods? That didn't explain the persistent references to the devil. For each word I could explain, there was another that seemed like nonsense. Creepy nonsense.

I drew a line under 'spike' using my thumbnail. What kind of devils had Moxham been fighting?

Frustrated, I flicked through the notebook at speed. I'd thought most of the pages were blank, the devil notes only filling up 20 or 30. For the first time, I noticed faint pencil scrawl, written sideways, on the central page of the notebook.

$25k Alexandre Jensen
$30k Gordon Howell
$50k Nadine Rowley

There must be 10 names listed, along with generic descriptors like 'CEO' and 'Lawyer'. Each one was matched with a dollar amount. I totted up the total. It was somewhere in the region of $250,000.

The final three names made the hairs on the back of my neck prickle.

Eddie Yiu?
Brady Calloway?
Christopher Clement?

Moxham's voice returned to me. *Big fish on the line.*

'What were you up to?' I asked, my voice loud in the empty room. 'What did you do?'

There was a flicker of movement on the other side of the room. I jumped.

A lizard darted across the floor.

I squeezed the notebook shut, my hands curling it into a cylinder. 'Fuck,' I muttered.

(*What did you do? What did you do?* Blood running down black tile. The splatter of water from a shower head. The distant sound of piano music.)

Moxham had left behind a mess in Hong Kong. It looked like he'd created an even bigger mess here.

He'd been playing with big money, he'd been playing with billionaires' lives. It had got him killed. I felt sure of it now.

12

The next morning, I could still smell smoke. It was in my hair. When I closed my eyes, I saw the sparks as Moxham's fedora hit the flames. In the shower, I scrubbed my scalp hard.

I shuffled down the hall to my room in a towel, my wet hair hanging in ropes around my ears. Diara, who'd been absent when I'd woken up, was back. She was humming as she spread out pancakes on chipped plates. 'I got us breakfast from the kitchen,' she said.

I hadn't realised how hungry I was. I grabbed a plate and took a bite, oozing syrupy sweetness alongside a sharp tang of apple.

'You need to get off this island,' she said.

I made a *huh?* face, my mouth full.

'You're getting that look about you,' she said.

'What?'

'Stressed, squirrelly.'

'I'm fine.'

'It's my day off. You should take a day too.'

I swallowed the last of my pancake and grabbed a bottle of lotion, rubbing aloe over my sunburn.

'There's stuff I need to do,' I said.

A clean uniform had been delivered to my room and I shimmied into it without dropping my towel. You couldn't discover a camera in your room and not become a little paranoid about being observed.

'It'll still be there,' Diara said.

I opened my mouth to argue, but she held up a hand.

'Trust me, you spend too much time in the Keeper bubble, you lose your marbles.'

I laughed. 'Lost those years ago.'

It was still early – barely seven – but the temperature was already building in our cupboard-room. My hair was curling as it dried. Now that Diara had dangled it in front of me, a day off sounded tantalising. I wanted to walk down a stretch of beach without pausing to pick up someone else's sodden towel.

'Where are we going then?' I asked.

'Home.' Diara brushed the crumbs from her fingertips. 'But first' – she dragged the wooden chair to the middle of the room – 'you need a haircut.'

'Really?' I fluffed my hair. 'I think I have a talent.'

Diara shook her head. 'Crazy gyul.'

I sat down and Diara moved to stand behind me. She tugged at a strand of my hair and began to cut.

'You know, my father always say to me...' She sucked on her teeth. 'A woman who cuts her hair is about to change her life. Steer clear or she may cut you.'

'Hell yeah.'

Diara was still a mystery to me. Where did she go when she didn't come back to our room? On one of the nights when she was absent, I'd scrutinised the drawings tacked to her wall. They were only pencil sketches, but they were good enough that I recognised some of the people in them. There was Reggie, smoke curling up around his head. Guillaume's eyes were downcast, his lashes long. There were children I took to be family members, their mouths blurred with laughter. She'd drawn a pair of hands, again and again. Who did they belong to? She was either obsessed with the person or obsessed with getting them right.

'Does your dad live nearby?' I asked.

'Next island over. Born and raised, and my mum both.'

'They like it?'

I shifted my weight, which evidently displeased Diara. She held my skull firm, scissors snipping rapidly.

'Well, it's not this. Not a resort. But it's their home.'

'Yours too?'

I knew Diara wasn't the only BVIslander on staff, but most people were expatriates. Either from far away, like me, or from closer: Jamaica, Dominican Republic, Guyana.

Diara made a clucking sound. 'S'pose so.'

In halting tones, she told me her dad worked in construction, while her mum ran the office. Three sisters, all of whom worked in financial services. A million cousins. Her family were 'old-school Christian', obsessed with doing the right thing.

I got the sense Diara didn't love talking about herself, but I was curious, so I persisted. 'How long have you been working here?'

'Three years. I got my associate's degree, thought about transferring to university in England, but...' She shrugged. 'People always need their hair done, always want a massage.'

I was surprised to learn that, for all Diara's world-weary attitude, she was only twenty-six. Part of me was jealous. When I was twenty-six, I'd never met Moxham, never met Nathan. That year, I had a job offer in Seoul. I turned it down because Hong Kong offered more money. Just think: I could have become a completely different person.

'You prefer living here, rather than over there?' I asked. If Diara's family lived on a neighbouring island, why not live there and commute by boat each day? There was a staff ferry.

'I like it here,' Diara said. 'We a bunch of misfits. Don't fit in nowhere? You fit in here.'

'Did Moxham fit in?' The question was out of my mouth before I could stop myself.

The overhead fan whirred.

'Moxham was too brisk.' She circled the chair and bent down, her face in front of mine, eyes blank. Her earrings were simple silver pendants today. Teardrops.

'That boy was always pushin' his luck.' She drew out my hair, snipping a side fringe. 'But luck runs out.'

Ping.

My head snapped up, but it was Diara's phone. As she flicked open a message, a sweet smile crossed her face.

'Do you need to go?' I asked.

The smile disappeared. 'I still have the back to fix.'

For a minute, there was only the click of steel, the whir of the fan.

'What did you think of last night?' I asked.

'The bonfire?'

'Mmm.'

'So much emotion. I'm allergic to it.'

I smiled. Diara reminded me of my younger self, when I'd acted so tough. I was alone and I didn't need anyone. Then Allie needed me and I learned that the toughest thing in the world is to care about someone else.

'You and Moxham, you were close, right?'

'No.'

'Oh.'

I was surprised. When I couldn't sleep last night, I'd opened my social media. There'd been a few follow notifications from my new colleagues on Keeper. Guillaume's profile was an extremely effective combo of gourmet dishes and thirst-trap selfies. Tessa had a Birkin bag and felt the need to show it off in every photo.

Lying in bed in the dark, I'd navigated to Moxham's profile. It was eerie to see the posts halt and know there would never be any more. He mostly posted pictures of ocean sunsets, but in the few selfies he shared, he was smirking, his brown hair sticking straight up, a cigarette dangling from his fingertips.

Standing next to Moxham in one of the shots was a girl. It took me a second to recognise her profile. I flicked the screen, zooming in to see her face more clearly. Diara. She was looking at Moxham, wearing a big smile. The picture was dated three months ago. The caption was: *loml lmao*

Love of my life.

'Who did he hang around with?' I asked.

'He liked being with the guests, I tell you that.'

'Guests like Eddie? Brady?'

'The richer the better.' She exhaled. 'Keeper Island can mess with your mind because it feels like everyone's the same. Everyone rich, everyone here to party. Some people forget they're playing at living the high life. Moxham had that look about him. Like he forgotten he was the staff.'

'I guess he was the same in Hong Kong,' I said.

I'd always thought Moxham was good at his job precisely because he treated the guests like equals. He was never awed by them and could always crack a joke at the right moment.

'He told me about his childhood once, where he grew up,' Diara said.

'Sydney, right?' I said.

'No, he grew up in some beach town. Rich people with second homes. They used to swamp the place in summer, leave it a ghost town in winter. His parents owned a café or a shop or something. I think it messed him up, being around rich kids and having nothing.'

I frowned. Moxham had told me about growing up in the shadow of the Sydney Opera House, skipping school to be at his father's law office. He used to help him write briefs. I was sure Diara must have it wrong. Or Moxham had lied to one of us. Lied to both of us.

'All done.' Diara dusted the back of my neck. 'You're respectable.'

I ran a hand through my hair. The texture of my cut felt better, less choppy. 'Thanks.'

'What, you want a mirror like at the salon?' she asked.

I laughed. 'I mean, I wouldn't say no.'

Ping. Another new message. She returned to her phone and tapped out a response.

'There's a mirror in the drawer,' she said, without looking up.

I got up and went to Diara's dresser. I don't know why I opened the bottom drawer, except that it was half a centimetre open already and I could slide my fingers into the gap. I scanned the contents for a mirror. A grey sweatshirt lay on top and I moved it aside.

'Not that one!'

Diara leaped to my side. She pushed me out the way and slammed shut the drawer. It was too late. I'd already seen it.

A gun.

13

My fingers recoiled. 'Why do you…' The question died on my lips.

Diara was glaring at me. She yanked open the top drawer and shoved a hand mirror at me. To break the tension, I held the mirror up and looked at myself. My new look was pixie-ish and cute: layered, dark hair falling to my jaw. But my face in the mirror was ashen.

'A toy, that's all,' Diara said.

I didn't respond. The gun didn't look like a toy. Nathan would've known the make and model. I only knew it was a revolver. Black and shiny and deadly.

'Fake. My cousin give me it for protection.'

'Protection?' It wasn't like we were in a big city. Who did Diara need protection from?

'Not everyone in this world is a good person.'

I had a flash of blood running down black tile in my bathroom in Hong Kong. No, not everyone was a good person.

'It's nothing,' Diara said. 'Forget about it.' When she squeezed out a smile, it didn't reach her eyes. 'We should clean up, get going.'

She bent down to pull a dustpan and brush from under her bed. In a few strokes, she swept up the hair from the floor. I watched her, unable to stop picturing the gun in the drawer. Nearby, a wild rooster crowed. I flinched, still unused to the sound.

When she rose to her feet, I reached out a hand. 'Diara…' I tried to grab her arm, but she twisted away. 'You feel the same thing I do. You said it, you said they'd hush it up. There's a bonfire, all his stuff burned, all his files wiped…'

Diara shook her head, teardrop earrings shuddering. 'I'm trying to do my work, keep my head down.'

'Come on… tell me I'm not crazy. There's something wrong.'

Diara released a heavy breath. 'You don't understand how things are around here.'

'So, tell me.'

'Two years ago,' she said, 'one of the guests stabbed a waitress.'

'What?'

A glimmer of humour appeared in her expression. 'He a Hollywood producer or something. He was drunk, of course, bet someone a thousand dollars he could throw a knife at the wall next to her, hit a target. Hit her shoulder instead. She was pinned there, screaming. He was laughing.'

'Oh, my God.'

'She should have had him locked up. Instead, everything hushed up. Accident, accident.'

I rocked back on my heels. I was still holding the hand mirror and a shaft of light bounced off it. I should have been horrified by Diara's story, but I wasn't. When you managed a high-end resort like this, you internalised the fact that reputation mattered above all else. Guests paid for luxury, yes, but they also paid for discretion.

I was no stranger to being paid for my discretion.

'Everything with Moxham, it doesn't make sense,' I said. 'Why was he out at night on a jet ski? Even if he crashed, he was a good swimmer.' I was speaking faster now, tapping my fingers against my thigh. 'Moxham had a dark side and I worry… I worry…'

I didn't want to say it, I wanted her to say it, but Diara's lips were pressed together. A month ago, murder was a remote concept to me. After Hong Kong, after Nathan, death loitered at the edge of my mind permanently.

'I worry he was murdered,' I said. 'And I think some people here are hushing it up.'

I expected Diara to snort, to shake her head, to say, *you* are *crazy, gyul*. Instead, all she did was twirl an earring between thumb and forefinger.

'D'you ever get a bad vibe from Kip?' I asked.

This, at last, elicited a response. She barked out a laugh. 'You think Kip Clement killed Moxham?'

I told her about sailing with Kip, about the fresh bruises on his neck and arms, about the blood on his shorts.

'He coulda sat in wet paint,' Diara said. 'None of this is proof of anything.'

'That's why we need to find proof.'

'We?' she asked flatly.

'You know everything that goes on here, better than me.'

Diara rolled her eyes. 'What's the best-case scenario? Mr Clement, your boss. You want him in jail?'

'If he deserves it.'

'Next thing, you're gonna start talking about Meredith.'

'Meredith?' The name rang a bell.

Diara turned away. She didn't respond.

'Who's Meredith?'

'I don't wanna have this conversation here. Come on, London, I need to get off this island for a few hours.'

*

We hitched a ride to Virgin Gorda on a powerboat with Reggie, who was heading on to the next island of Tortola. Over the roar of the engine, I tried to ask Diara about Meredith, but she shook her head, the word 'later' wrenched away by the wind.

Reggie dropped us at the marina, among sleek sailing boats. 'Bring me back some johnny cakes,' he said, by way of farewell, 'Guillaume can't make 'em right.'

94

Five minutes later, we were bombing along hilly roads in the back of a taxi. The interior was held together with duct tape and my whole body juddered as we hit a pothole. Diara leaned forward, resting her elbows against the top of the passenger seat. She was chatting with the driver in rapid Creole; her relaxed manner was noticeably different from the stiff way she often spoke to me.

I sagged back in my seat, which was comfortably worn down from ten thousand previous passengers, and let my gaze roam out the window. My brain was lighting up with The New. Ever since I was eighteen and stumbling around Spain in a drunken daze, I'd been addicted to this. New places could wash away your worries. For a time, at least.

At the marina, everything had looked freshly painted. The gardens were lush with eruptions of red blooms. As soon as we headed inland, the resorts were replaced by cheerfully ramshackle villages. The houses stood out in sun-baked colours – oranges, pinks, yellows – but their exteriors were shabby. Scrub grass grew long, waving in the breeze.

The taxi driver, compact and jovial, one eyebrow cocked, sounded his horn as we passed another vehicle in a rush of exhaust fumes. There was a break in his conversation with Diara, so I asked, 'What happened there?' Many of the houses we passed had a cobbled-together look, rebar sticking up from their flat roofs like porcupines. A couple were demolished.

'Irma,' the taxi driver said. 'She got us good.'

Under today's blue skies, it was hard to imagine a hurricane so brutal it ripped the roof off your home.

'Did you evacuate? During Irma?'

'No, I stayed.' His voice was upbeat. 'This my home, where else I gonna go?'

I wanted to ask Diara about her experiences with hurricanes, but she was on her phone. The taxi driver slammed on the brakes. He gave me a grin and said, 'Enjoy.'

At the airport, on my way to the BVI, I'd scrolled distractedly through pictures of the Baths, the area's top tourist attraction. Located on the southwestern tip of Virgin Gorda, they were a collection of huge granite boulders on a white sand beach. A geological wonder, millions of years in the making.

'So, Meredith…' I said to Diara, as we traipsed down a trail to Devil's Bay.

The boulders were impressive, scattered like pebbles at the shoreline, as if dropped by a careless giant. But I was more interested in what Diara had to tell me.

'Would you just enjoy this?' She headed for a crevice created by two boulders shouldered against each other, and ducked inside, disappearing from view.

I squeezed through the gap, blinking against the half-dark. Stacked on top of each other, the boulders created a cave effect, but there were glimmers of sunlight slanting through crevices above.

I lost Diara for a second, went the wrong way and doubled back again. That was when I spied it: a very unnatural set of wooden steps. It was like being a child again, in a playground, grasping at ropes to climb over particularly tricky boulders.

'Wow,' I said.

I splashed down into a sun-dappled cavern. We were beyond the shoreline now, swells of seawater swirling around my ankles. Everything glowed green. Preternatural. I breathed deep the scent of salt and rock and algae.

The Baths lived up to the hype. Within this place, there was a hush. It was the type of place that made you believe in God.

Diara cast a look over her shoulder. 'Not too bad?'

The wonderland belonged to us for ten minutes. Then I heard them, the brash exclamations. 'It's like the Grand Canyon in here!' An orange backpack was discarded against a rock wall. A pair of girls were shooting a video. Magic gone.

I gave a rueful shake of my head. We exited the cavern on the other side, climbing into the fresh air. When we reached a particular rock, at the edge of the shore, Diara took a seat and I dropped down beside her.

'You're lucky, growing up here,' I said.

'I know it. Spent a few months in London and it was all noise, dirt, people pissing in alleyways.'

'Sounds familiar.' I took off my sodden trainers and dangled my feet in the seawater. It swirled and frothed around my toes.

I hesitated. 'Are you going to tell me about Meredith? You're the one who brought her up…'

'The statue,' she said.

'What?'

'The one on the west side of the island. You know, Kip sends Shirley out to scrub the algae off her every month. He obsessed.'

'Obsessed with a statue. Is this like men who marry their cars?'

I leaned my palms against the surface of the boulder. It was porous, pleasantly rough to the touch, but warm, too, retaining the day's heat.

'It's a memorial. Meredith Clement was his wife. She died… I don't know, ten years ago?'

The wife. The one Kip never fought with. The name was familiar. All I could recall about her was raising money for children's hospitals.

'Cancer, wasn't it?'

'I think they put that rumour about. But what happened is she went for a swim, got caught in a rip tide. Drowned.'

'Shit. It was an accident?' I asked.

'Before my time. Only thing I know is the body ended up in Caracas.'

'What?'

'First time I heard of that happening, body floating into open water…' She shuddered.

I stared at the horizon, as if Meredith's body might drift into view. My mind was whirring. Moxham's words returned to me. *Drowned, my arse.* Could he have been talking about Meredith?

There were all sorts of reasons for husbands to decide they'd be better off if their wives were dead. Was there anywhere more perfect to get rid of your wife than on your own private island? Had Kip killed Meredith and covered it up?

'Kip thinks he can get away with anything,' I said.

'I knew if I told you this, you'd jump to conclusions.' Diara snapped her tongue. 'You know, after Irma, Kip helped a lot of people on Virgin Gorda, helped my family. There's not much money around here. Kip is important for us.'

A wave crashed against our boulder, splashing my knees, making me jump. I cast a sidelong look at Diara, who was twisting her mass of braids into a knot. Could I trust her? Should I tell her my suspicions? The wind and the waves collided in a cymbal-clash.

'If he didn't like Moxham, he could fire him. For that matter, if he didn't like his wife, he could divorce her.'

Diara was being rational; perhaps she was even correct. Yet a darker possibility nagged at me. What if Kip had killed Meredith and Moxham had found out? Knowing Moxham, he would have used the information for blackmail. That gave Kip one hell of a motive for murder.

14

Underwater, sunlight created marble patterns on the seabed. My arms churned as I swam further from Virgin Gorda's shore. Electric blue fish darted away from me, hiding among the coral. The sensation of breathing through the snorkel wasn't weird anymore, now I was used to it. The trickle and glug, the click and snap, of life underwater blotted out the rest of the world.

Then came the shark.

It grabbed my ankle.

Diara and I surfaced at the same time. I spat out my mouthpiece, spluttering. 'You scared the shit out of me.'

'You're like the monster from the black lagoon.' She thrashed in the water. 'Don't swim with your arms, use your legs.'

I ducked beneath the water, kicking the fins on my feet. Diara had borrowed snorkelling gear from a dive shop where she knew the owner. We'd only been out on the water for a couple of hours, but I could feel myself becoming obsessed. I wanted to hold my breath and go deeper, down to where the light dwindled. I wanted to discover the mysteries at the bottom of the sea.

Diara finally dragged me back to the shore. I protested, but my legs had turned to jelly and my breathing had become raspy. I lay on the beach, exhausted, letting the sun bake me dry. I was wearing a fussy green bikini with too many straps, which I'd liberated from Lost Property on Keeper Island. There was sand stuck to me, but I was growing immune to this scratchy, irritating feeling.

We were at a locals' beach on Virgin Gorda. Families chattered and laughed nearby, and the smell of barbecuing meat wafted on the breeze. Beside me, Diara sat cross-legged. She'd thrown a sheer white kaftan over her orange swimsuit. Her notebook open on her lap, she was sketching a small boy who kept running in and out of the water, playing chase with the foaming shallows.

I wanted nothing more than a nap. I closed my eyes, red searing against my eyelids. I drifted into sleep, but an insect whined nearby.

Moxham's white face floated through my dreams. It never got easier, seeing him dead. *Gwáilóu*, that was the Cantonese word they used in Hong Kong when they talked about Westerners. *White devil.*

Bzzzzzzzz.

The insect was back.

I didn't know if I was dreaming or not. An enormous wasp-like creature zoomed towards me.

There was a scream.

I opened my eyes, propping myself up on my elbows.

Another scream.

My eyes struggled to adjust to the sunshine. It was the boy; a wave had got him.

I blinked rapidly. There was something I needed to hang on to from my dream. Something I'd seen.

Moxham's white face, a sting across his cheek.

I remembered it now: when I'd seen him floating in the water, there'd been two red marks on his face.

I sat up straight. A sting? No, it hadn't been a sting from an insect.

I'd seen those type of marks before. A thick-necked man, ranting and raving, had entered the Clement Hong Kong last year. He'd lumbered behind the bar, torn his shirt from his back with a howl and begun smashing bottles. Nathan had taken him down with a shot of electricity from his Taser. Two red welts were tattooed on the man's chest afterwards.

The marks on Moxham's cheek had looked the same. Someone had Tased him.

'Diara!' Next to me, there was only an empty patch of sand.

'What?'

I whipped around. She was ambling towards me, her hands cradling a yellow paper napkin.

'I got us ribs.' She sat down beside me, spreading the napkin between us. 'They're good, Toots makes them special.' She ripped off a strip of meat with her teeth. 'Spicy.'

'I remembered something.' I glanced around, but there was no one nearby to overhear. The beach was clearing out, our shadows stretching.

In a low voice, I told her about my dream. 'Someone Tased him, before he died.'

Diara was gnawing on a bone. 'Just a dream,' she said at last.

'No, I remember now... I can see it, I can.'

I picked up one of the ribs but didn't eat it. The glaze turned my fingers brown and sticky.

'Someone fucking Tased him,' I said.

Diara wasn't looking at me. She stared out at the sea, which glinted gold. I thought she was going to mollify me. *You can't know for sure. You probably imagined it.*

'There's still six keys,' she said instead.

'What?'

She plucked another rib from the napkin. 'Try them, they're good.'

Reluctantly, I took a bite. It was good. The meat was juicy; the glaze was sweet and spicy, with a kick of rum.

'Six keys,' I said. 'To the villas?'

'No. Jet skis.' Diara dabbed at the corner of her mouth with her thumb. 'I was in the boathouse a few days ago. Six keys hanging up.' Her voice was placid, like she was discussing the weather. 'Each key only fit one jet ski. There are six because there used to be six jet skis.'

I wasn't sure I was following. 'OK...' I finished my rib and discarded the bone, licking my fingers.

'Except one got crashed,' she said.

'Right.'

'Moxham's jet ski. It got crashed, but the key still hanging in the boathouse.'

Midges were gathering around my head, unfazed when I batted them away.

'So, how did it get crashed?' I asked.

'I don't know, London.' She turned her head to look at me. 'But no one could have ridden it out that night. Not without a key.'

'The crash was staged.' I grabbed her arm, my nails digging into her skin. 'It can't have been an accident.'

I didn't know enough about boats to know exactly how it was staged, but I could take a guess. Tow it out to sea on a powerboat and dump it? It didn't sound difficult. Something nagged at me. Hadn't I seen a light on the water, the night of the Alice party? Could it have been a boat?

Was Moxham alive or dead when he was dumped in the water? Was he Tased to knock him out before—

I shuddered. All the weirdness of the last week, every time I'd told myself I was imagining things – I was right to be suspicious.

'This is proof,' I said. 'Foul play.'

My body was vibrating with a morbid triumph. By contrast, Diara looked tired. She gave a tiny shrug and my grip on her loosened.

'They can say there was a spare key or something.'

'It's a start. If there's one thing, there could be more.' I pounded a fist against the sand. 'An autopsy report.'

'Is there one?'

'There must be. It'd confirm he'd been Tased. Other injuries. That would be proof. Do you know any police here?'

'My auntie... but she not gonna tell me anything.' Diara shook her head. 'Confidential.'

'Could you ask?'

'London, you just got here, but this... this is my life. If we go looking, we find things we don't want.'

Light was seeping from the sky, darkness descending.

'I don't care.' I flexed my toes against the warm sand, digging down to where it was cooler. 'I want to know. I need to know, for Moxham.'

Diara rubbed her neck, her kaftan drooping off her shoulder. There was a gremlin tattooed there; it gave me the stink eye. She didn't reply.

'There's something I need to tell you,' I said. 'Kip had a motive to kill Moxham.'

I needed to trust someone. I needed an ally.

Diara, despite her prickliness, had an affection for Moxham. I knew it, from that photo on social media. She deserved to know what was really going on.

I took a deep breath and told her about the notebook, about Moxham's plans to pull me into his schemes. I also told her an abbreviated version of his operations back in Hong Kong. She didn't need to know the full story, but I wanted her to know that Moxham had been playing with fire.

'Moxham crossed Kip,' I said, 'I'm sure of it. Kip must have been desperate to shut him up.'

Shit. Diara mouthed the word, rather than spoke it. She was rubbing at her neck rhythmically. (Was there a bruise there?)

'You'll help me, right?' I said. 'Find out the truth?'

'Cheeeeese an' bread,' she muttered under her breath. 'I'm gonna regret this.'

15

Hong Kong, one year ago

We were still in the lift when Nathan started kissing me. I swatted him away but only half-heartedly. He drew me close again and kissed my neck and I stopped resisting.

The lift could grind to a halt at any moment; a guest could waltz through the doors and catch us.

A thrill chased up my spine. I was getting in too deep with Nathan.

It was supposed to be stress relief. That was how it started. A couple of times a month, we'd sneak into a suite. Now it was happening almost every day. He would come to my office and give me that look. Two minutes later, we were in the lift, kissing like it was our last day on Earth.

It wasn't professional.

Ding! The lift doors slid open.

The hallway was blessedly empty. We stumbled-and-kissed our way along the swirling carpet. I fumbled the master key from my pocket and – *buh-leep* – the door swung open.

The butterscotch-coloured carpet of the presidential suite was soft and thick underfoot. The smell of white jasmine blooms overflowing from the vase on the glass table filled the air.

I put both my hands on Nathan's face and leaned in to kiss him again, slow and deep. 'Baby, I missed you,' I said inanely, because I'd seen him yesterday and the day before and the day before. I missed him on a visceral level, every second we weren't together.

Nathan didn't reply. He'd gone rigid, gaze locked over my shoulder.

I twisted my neck. The suite was not empty.

'Ahh, lovebirds. Makes your heart swell. Makes something swell, anyway.'

The surprise wasn't in seeing Moxham there. He had access to the rooms the same way I did. The surprise was that Moxham was crouched beneath the mahogany desk. He clambered free of the wooden legs and brushed down the knees of his black trousers.

'Shit, Mox,' I said, 'I'm sorry, we were—'

'I should have you fired for this.' There was a snap as he pulled off his blue disposable gloves. Why the hell was he wearing those?

Beside me, Nathan flinched. Moments before, I'd been pleasantly giddy, but the feeling had turned to seasickness in my stomach.

Moxham broke into his hyena laugh. 'I mean, I won't. But I could.'

I heaved out a sigh, caught between relief and irritation. Moxham tapped his lips using something I mistook for a pen. When I looked closer, I saw it was a screwdriver. Was he doing room maintenance?

There was a scuffing noise behind me. 'Sorry, sir,' Nathan mumbled, groping for the door handle. 'I will return to my post.'

'No, no.' Moxham crossed the room and nudged Nathan out of the way. 'Stay, stay, have a good time.'

He turned back to look at me, gave a lazy salute, and then he was gone. The door's soft-close mechanism made a *shhh* sound.

'He is firing us?' Nathan's face was ashen.

'That was a joke.'

'I like this job. It pays well. My parents depend on—'

'I know,' I said, although I didn't, not really. I'd made it a point not to know too much about Nathan, beyond the sweet nothings he whispered to me in bed.

Out the window, Victoria Harbour was spread out, container ships inching towards the dock. The view was framed by a chandelier worth more than Nathan earned in a year. His parents lived where the skyscrapers and bright lights gave way to shabby small-town life. They ran a neighbourhood shop, I remembered that much. I burned with shame to realise I'd never asked what the shop sold.

'Everything's fine,' I said. 'You can go downstairs.'

Nathan's broad shoulders were flexed inward. He hadn't been fired, but I could see he'd lived the experience in his head. My chest felt tight. He should find a nice girl, a local girl; one who was capable of loving him with all her heart.

'Kiss me before you go,' I said, because I couldn't resist it.

Usually, he was passionate, overeager, but there was some hesitancy as he leaned in to peck me on the mouth. I drew him into a deeper kiss and his tentativeness fell away. I was tempted to rekindle the moment, but there was something niggling at the back of my mind.

What had Moxham been doing under the desk?

*

I wasn't stupid. I knew what went on at the Clement Hong Kong. I knew how to spot drug residue in the bathrooms. I knew how to identify sex workers, the expensive ones, who would flow in through the lobby, wearing chic pencil skirts and nude lipstick, and head straight for the lifts. When I threw them out, they were back an hour later. 'This is a friend of mine,' Moxham told me, grinning at one of the frozen-faced girls.

I noticed certain guests were over-friendly with Moxham, leaning in close to *whisper-whisper-whisper* in his ear. Moxham's pockets would bulge with money, often in foreign currency; too much to constitute a common tip. Those guests always needed to speak to Moxham specifically, even when I offered to help. The police visited one day and I was alarmed, but Moxham laughed it off and said the police were friends of his too.

Once, I gathered up my courage and asked him flat out. 'What are you up to?'

He gave his best innocent face.

'I need to know,' I said.

'Trust me, Showgirl, better if you don't.'

I searched his office when he wasn't there, but of course there was nothing incriminating. I wasn't stupid, but neither was Moxham. More than once, I walked in on him in a hotel room, rearranging the curtains.

He proffered a smile. 'Just enjoying the view.'

*

After Nathan left the presidential suite, I crawled under the desk. There was nothing except a line of dust next to the skirting boards and a lead plugged into the telephone port. The white plastic wall plate was sitting ever so slightly askew.

I got a screwdriver from the maintenance locker and removed the wall plate, revealing a rough-cut hole in the wall. There were wires inside the hole but also plenty of room to spare. I ferreted around inside and came up with a roll of bank notes and a big lump of white powder in a bag.

*

I wrenched open the door to Moxham's office. 'What are you up to?'

'I'm about to absolutely murder these fish balls. What are you up to?' His eyes darted to one side. A woman, round-shouldered, her black hair in a bun, was sitting beside his desk. I recognised her as one of the cleaning staff.

'I'd like a word,' I said.

After the woman had left, Moxham reared back in his chair. 'Shut the door,' he said with a yawn.

Moxham's office was tucked away in a rabbit warren of rooms far from the view of the guests. Here, the walls were yellow and the carpet was thinning grey.

'You're dealing drugs now?' I put bag of white powder on the desk.

'I dabble, sue me.' He stabbed his chopsticks into the take-away container.

'Mox, this must be a hundred grams. You're dealing.'

'I assume you also found the money.' He shovelled a pair of fish balls into his mouth but didn't stop talking. 'Or are you planning to keep that for yourself?'

I tossed the rolled notes onto his desk. 'Yes... and no.'

Moxham swallowed, laid down his chopsticks and began counting the cash. 'It's no big deal. Just useful to have a little coke around the place. Anytime some British banker shows up, I run low.'

I wanted to storm out, scream at him that this was wrong. Black-and-white was never my style though.

'Sit down and take that scandalised look off your face,' Moxham said. 'It doesn't suit you.'

I slumped into the plastic chair the cleaner had vacated.

'Get mixed up with the big dealers and you could end up dead,' I said.

'I'm not El Chapo.' He chuckled. 'I like to make people happy, that's all. And you know that what makes the punters happy isn't always legal.'

If a guest wanted something, it was our job to make it happen. *I'm a fixer*, Moxham had said to me once. *Whatever the problem, I fix it.*

Wasn't it what everyone in hospitality was paid to do?

I heard the whine in my voice as I said, 'It's not worth it. Breaking the law. If you get caught...'

'Won't get caught.'

We sat in silence. Moxham's eyes flicked up to meet mine. A long look. We'd been working together long enough that sometimes we had these moments of telepathy.

'You're going to dob on me?' He cocked his head to one side.

I swallowed past the lump in my throat. 'It's wrong.'

He laughed at that, a screeching yelp, and a flush rose in my cheeks.

'Mate... let's not fall out over this.' He re-rolled the notes, snapped an elastic band around them and chucked them into my lap. 'That's ten grand US. You keep it. Tip for all the help.'

I'd never stood in his way. Did that count as helping? My fingers tightened around the roll of cash.

'Don't you have dreams?' he asked. 'Don't you and that bloke of yours wanna leave this stinking island one day? You need money for that. You need money for other things too.' His eyes narrowed. 'How's your sister?'

The question was like a physical blow. Allie had been out of the hospital for almost five months. She was still thin, but no longer skeletal. She was coping – as long as she had weekly therapy and a nanny to help her look after five-year-old Flora. None of it came cheap.

'Allie's fine,' I said.

Across the desk, Moxham went back to eating his fish balls. He'd always been erratic; prone to yelling at employees, apt to fire someone on the spot (and not always as a joke). Yet his vicious streak had worsened in the two months since the abrupt departure of Violet, his girlfriend, who'd been a calming influence on him. I'd seen on social media that she'd got a new job in Paris. I'd written to congratulate her, but she'd never responded.

I stood up. I didn't want to be in this stuffy little office that smelled like curried fish anymore. I hesitated and pushed the roll of cash into my pocket.

'I think you should be careful,' I said.

Moxham gave a gurning grin. 'Always am.'

*

For the next month, I was paralysed with fear. In taking the money, was I complicit? I should have given it back. Instead, I hid the money inside a sock at the bottom of my drawer and tried to forget about it.

Allie called me. There was a school she was looking at for Flora. One of those hippy-dippy private ones which was all about soul-nourishment and charged through the nose for it. She needed money. She didn't say it out loud. She didn't need to.

I fished the roll of notes out of my drawer and wired the money to Allie.

A few weeks later, I was staring into space in my office, a yellow box identical to Moxham's except half the size, when Moxham came charging in.

'Listen, Showgirl, I'm shipping out.'

He told me about his job offer. Private island in the Caribbean, picture-postcard stuff. I felt the usual professional envy. It seemed a big step up for Moxham; unattainable for me.

'You know, you could carry on my business,' he said.

For a split-second, I pictured it. I could probably do it better than Moxham. I was more organised than he was and I could be more charming. But it would be a Faustian bargain. To live like Moxham, you traded a piece of your soul.

'No,' I blurted out.

There was steel in his eyes as he met my gaze. 'And if anyone comes around asking for me?'

I shrugged.

Moxham's voice dropped. 'You'll keep my secrets?'

Allie had called again this morning, Flora singing Disney songs in the background.

'What's in it for me?' I said at last.

'Good girl,' Moxham said. 'Asking the right questions. What do you want?'

I sat up straight. The words came out my mouth before I had a chance to second-guess myself. 'I want your job.'

16

Knock, knock. Silence. I unlocked the door to Villa Copper using my master key and gave another rap. 'Hello?'

No answer.

Inside, it was cool and shadowy, with curtains drawn and the air-conditioning running on a low hum. I spent a few minutes flicking on and off light switches, shifting furniture to look for mould spots. I even tapped my chin with the screwdriver, in a pantomime of a busy worker deep in thought. I had a paranoid sense that someone might be watching me. My gaze slid along the tops of the picture frames, remembering the spy-cam I'd found in my own room. Not such a paranoid thought, then.

Aware of time slipping by, I abandoned my pretence, prying open floor vents and dismantling air-conditioning panels. I eased the pictures off the wall, one by one, peering behind them. I squirrelled under the desk, unscrewing the wall plate for the phone jack. A mess of wires sprang out, but there was nothing hidden inside there except dust. I wiped my hands on my shorts and jumped to my feet.

Every empty hiding place made me feel more agitated. Blood hummed in my veins. I wasn't even listening for the click of a door opening, or the shuffle of footsteps. I was deep in it.

The curtains! The glass doors that opened onto the veranda were draped with heavy vanilla-hued curtains. I dropped to my knees, wincing as I reawakened old bruises, and fumbled along the hemline, coaxing the fabric.

Still nothing.

I scampered upstairs to the master bedroom. More curtains. More crawling on the floor.

By now, I was drenched in sweat. (I'd turned off the A/C so I could check the vents.) My hands were coated with dust. My knees were throbbing.

I didn't care. Moxham had left something behind and I would find it.

In the hem of the bedroom curtains, my fingers caught on a lump.

Outside, a bird called. My head snapped up.

The lump in the curtains wasn't large enough that it upset the line, but that was the beauty of it. You'd only find it if you knew to look.

The bird hooted again. Shit. I needed to get out of here.

Instead, I groped for the flathead screwdriver. One more minute. I tore open the stitching of the hem.

Downstairs, there was the unmistakable sound of a door swinging open. *Shit, shit, shit.* My fingers pawed at the fabric. *Come on.*

Footsteps. Someone was climbing the stairs.

I wrenched the object – a USB stick with a red shell – free from its nest. Standing up, I shoved it into my bra and kicked the curtains back into place. I withdrew my phone from my pocket and snapped a random photo of the ceiling, composing my features into a look of bored contemplation.

'Good morning.' I took another photo, narrowing my eyes at an imaginary crack in the plaster.

'Excuse me.'

His drawl was so pronounced, I mistook it for sarcasm. I wheeled around, ready to grovel, to magic up a bottle of champagne.

Brady Calloway was grinning, hands in the pockets of his shorts. He was also shirtless.

'Routine maintenance,' I said. 'Sorry to intrude.'

I wiped my brow with the back of my hand and sidestepped towards the exit. The USB stick was digging into the skin of my chest. Any second, it would drop through my T-shirt, clattering as it hit the tile floor.

'Wait, wait.' Brady made a hand motion like he was swinging a tennis racket. 'You've been holding out on me.'

I stilled, the smile freezing on my face.

Brady was looking down. Had I been a moment too slow? Had he watched me pull the USB stick from the curtains?

'Hong Kong.' His green eyes flicked up to meet mine.

'What?'

'I finally figured it out. Where I know you from.'

I stared at him blankly. What did he know about Hong Kong?

His dimples deepened. 'Am I that forgettable?'

'Sorry, I don't think…'

'The Clement Hong Kong. I used to stay there a lot on business. Couple years ago, maybe? My wife, Jessica, would come sometimes – ex-wife, she liked it there.'

'Oh… yeah.'

When I slotted him into context, I remembered too. He wouldn't be flattered to learn that he existed in my mind as just another American arsehole in a suit. His wife had been skittish; brown hair, doe eyes, milk-white skin. I'd once organised rose petals to be strewn across the bed and a violinist for their anniversary. They hadn't tipped well.

I knew I should say something complimentary, but I was too distracted. The beginnings of a headache were pulsing at my temples.

'The other guy too.' Brady snapped his fingers. 'Moxham.'

'Yeah.'

'I didn't recognise him at first either. You two musta been close, working together all that time.'

'Sure.' What was Brady insinuating? Was I being paranoid?

I cleared my throat. 'I should be getting back to work. Need anything before I go? Tempt you with a drink?'

'Nah…' Brady licked his lips. 'I'm headed out sailing with Mr Clement.'

'OK. Wear sunscreen!' I skipped backwards towards the door, unable to stand the conversation any longer.

'Hey…' Brady tapped his foot and I noticed it was bandaged. 'They never found out anything more? About what happened to Moxham?'

'It was an accident.'

'Damn.' Brady shook his head. 'He was a heckuva guy.'

The sorrow in his expression looked sincere.

'I was wanting to make a donation,' he said, 'to a charity, or… maybe help out his family. Could you make that happen?'

'No problem.'

I checked his face for ulterior motives and found none. Maybe he was just a nice guy. He remembered Moxham from his visits to the Clement Hong Kong and he wanted to honour his memory.

Except Brady's name was written in Moxham's notebook. That wasn't a good sign.

Before he could say more, I slipped out of the room and down the stairs.

*

Outside the villa, a bird appeared from within the foliage. It was a rather large bird.

'Cheeeese an' bread, my heart is going. Why didn't you leave?'

Diara flexed her hand, eyes darting side to side.

'It's fine,' I said.

'He catch you?' she asked.

'It's fine.' I cast a look behind me and hustled Diara down the path. There was a scuffling sound on the ground. A lizard flashed past.

'I found something,' I said, once we were clear of the villa and heading along the paved path that skirted the shoreline. I extracted the red USB stick from my bra and held it up. She reached for it. I had an urge to close my fist and stop her, but my hand slackened and I let her take it.

She held it between thumb and forefinger, like she was examining a diamond. 'What's on it?'

'I don't know. But you don't hide something that well unless it's important. And if there's one, there's more.' I was sweating, despite the breeze that flowed off the sea. 'I need to check the curtains. I need to check all the villas.'

'I can't help you.' Diara's hand closed around the USB. 'I have to be back at the spa.'

As we walked, a golf cart rolled past, carrying a guest in a floppy hat. We both waved automatically, identical fake smiles on our faces.

'I'll do it without you,' I said, when the buggy had passed. 'Reggie took most of the guests out to the shipwreck, their villas'll be empty.'

'You gotta be careful.' Diara lowered her voice, emphasising the last word.

Before I could argue with her – it was worth the risk – there came a shout. 'Lola!'

Tessa was jogging towards us, her face bright pink. 'It blew up! It just blew up.'

'What?'

Once Tessa caught up to us, she bent over double, panting. In typical Tessa style, it took far too many words to establish the facts: Mrs Park, the other half of a property tycoon from Korea, had switched on the coffee maker in Villa Queen Conch this morning and it had blown up in her face. She was uninjured but shaken.

'It's the humidity,' Diara said to me. 'Happens all the time.'

'I don't get paid enough, I don't get paid enough...' Tessa was muttering.

One of the housekeeping staff, Shirley, was passing in a golf cart piled high with linens. Diara flagged her down and climbed onto the back seat. She waved goodbye. 'That other stuff can wait,' she called to me.

I shook my head and turned back to Tessa. 'She still got her eyebrows?'

'Yeah.'

'Then it's fine.'

When Tessa snuffled a laugh, I suggested she take Mrs Park to the restaurant and fix her a coffee with a shot of liqueur. I wasn't really paying attention though. The exploding coffee maker had given me an idea.

I was halfway down the path to the nearest villa, Mangrove, when I realised. Diara had taken the red USB drive with her.

*

Moxham's covert filing system was extensive. As in Hong Kong, he knew it would be too easy to link him to items in his office or his apartment in the staff village. Something secreted away in guest quarters, on the other hand, couldn't be tied to him.

I'd expected to find drugs and money. What I found instead, hidden away like treasure, were more USB drives. With each one I unearthed, the disquiet in me grew.

They might contain nothing. That was what I kept telling myself. The USB sticks might be backups of bank statements, dental receipts, childhood snapshots. Moxham could have hidden them for safekeeping, not for nefarious reasons.

I couldn't make myself believe it.

I searched all five of the guest villas. The malfunctioning coffee maker was a neat excuse for the few guests I encountered. I even tried to get into Kip's villa, but the master key didn't work. As I was fruitlessly pushing at the door, there was a clatter of footsteps on the other side and it opened an inch. Fizzy's face appeared in the gap.

'Kip around?' I hid the keys behind my back.

Considering she shared seniority with me, I saw Fizzy rarely. Beyond shop talk, we'd never had a real conversation. She didn't spend time in the team bar after-hours. I was used to seeing her alone, sitting at the end of the pier with a book or doing yoga on the beach. Friendship groups on the island tended to run along work lines. Fizzy was an island all of her own, both in work and in leisure.

'He's upstairs,' she murmured. 'Sleeping.'

Wasn't Kip supposed to be sailing with Brady? I narrowed my eyes. Who was lying and why?

'There's been a problem with the coffee makers.'

Fizzy gave me a long, slow blink like a cat. 'Kip's coffee maker is fine.'

'I can check it, I don't mind. Two secs.'

'I handle anything to do with Kip's villa. That's the way he likes it.'

She shut the door with a snap.

I backed away from the villa, with its stylised tower, the windows of the observation room smoked black. It had the look of a fortress about it; the lighthouse keeper of Keeper Island in his own little world.

*

It was dark by the time I returned to the staff village. Diara was seated on her bed, stooped over her sketchpad, making harsh black lines against the page. I bent to look at what she was drawing, but she flipped the pad shut. The red USB stick lay on top of the chest of drawers.

'Did you look at it?'

'Yes.' She drew out the word into multiple syllables, clicking her tongue at the end.

I pulled three more USB drives from my bra and dropped them onto the chest of drawers. Their shells were plastic, cheap. Blue, green, yellow, like a child's crayons.

'What's on it?' I asked.

Diara exhaled long and hard. 'See for yourself.'

17

Hong Kong, three weeks ago

Someone was playing the piano.

I trotted through the hotel's entrance hall, my heels clicking against the marble. It struck me as strange to hear piano music in the middle of the day, but the thought was crowded out by other worries. The meat shipment was late, the sommelier had quit and my phone was buzzing.

Allie: You should have a party. Come and visit.

It was another two hours before I had time to sit down and respond to Allie's text message. In my office, I kicked off my heels, flexing my toes against the grey carpet.

A party? The fact that I was turning thirty soon made me want to crawl under the desk. I was inclined to let the day pass without a fuss. Allie was half-right though. I was overdue for a visit.

There was a knock.

'Come in!'

Nathan's face was solemn, peering around the door, until he saw I was alone. A smile cracked him apart and he bounded inside like a naughty schoolboy.

'You ever been to London?' I asked, a second before he kissed me.

*

The next day, it rained. It wasn't like London rain – the air remained dense and humid – but it still made me think of home.

What would Allie and Flora make of Nathan? They'd like him, of course. Everyone liked him.

The hotel's glass doors flowed open to admit me and I shook the water off my raincoat. Again, I was greeted by piano notes floating towards me.

It was nice, actually. We used to have a pianist who played for two hours in the mornings and two hours at night, but Clement management had tightened our budgets, so we had to fire him. We only paid a pianist for special occasions now.

The piano music sped up, a flourish of notes. My dad would have known the name of the piece. Not because he had a passion for classical music, but because he thought it made him look cultured.

'Who's on the piano?' I asked the doorman.

He shrugged and turned away, rushing towards a woman who was struggling with shopping bags and an umbrella.

It was probably a guest playing for fun. Across the lobby, the receptionist was signalling to me. I held up a finger – one minute – and diverted left. There were shallow steps that led to a raised area of the lobby, dotted with upholstered antique armchairs. In the afternoons, guests liked to sit here and pick at tiny sandwiches, sip from teacups and pretend they were back in the glory days of Empire.

I expected the person sitting at the piano to be one of these paunchy, glassy-eyed Englishmen, who had a story of visiting Hong Kong during the 1960s.

Instead, the man was Chinese, terribly thin and hunched over the piano. I waited for him to finish and applauded.

'We should be paying you,' I said. 'You're better than the last guy we hired.'

He didn't turn to face me, his hands still hovering over the keys, but swivelled his sunken eyes to graze mine.

'Pay me,' he said in an undertone.

I waited for him to continue, but he didn't, so I went on. 'What's that piece you're playing? I almost recognise it.'

The man slammed shut the piano lid. I jumped.

When he twisted around to look at me, the cords in his neck stood out. 'Mr Moss-ham?' He stressed *Moss-ham* like it was two words.

'He's left the business. I'm happy to help though.'

I said it on automatic. My brain was ahead of my mouth and it was blaring a warning signal. When people asked for Moxham, it was never a good sign. In the year since his departure, many guests had requested special treatment and I'd pretended not to know what they were talking about. I'd had to fire a bellboy who was dealing drugs. I might have taken Moxham's hush money, but I wouldn't condone these activities moving forward.

'We make money together.' With bony fingers, the man reached for my hand.

I jerked away. 'No.'

'Big money.'

'You need to go. This isn't happening.' I fumbled for my radio, speaking into the mic. 'Security to the lobby.'

He held up his hands, rising from the piano bench. 'You think about it.'

'No.'

The man's voice got more urgent. 'I make money, you look the other way. Moss-ham make big money, you make big money. Coke, heroin, whatever you like.'

'That's over. I'm not interested.'

Footsteps echoed in the entrance hall as Nathan hurried towards me. 'OK? OK?'

He raised his eyebrows and said something in Cantonese to the man. The pianist gave a mournful shake of his head and made a reply, longer than I would have expected.

I backed away and one of my heels slipped on the marble floor, my ankle rolling sideways. 'Shit.'

It wasn't until I was in bed that night that it struck me. There was something off about their interaction. Nathan usually took security threats seriously, bearing down on anyone who was being the least bit aggressive. Yet, when he'd spoken to the pianist, his demeanour had been almost relaxed. There was a familiarity between the two men.

I rolled over, seeking out a cool spot on my pillow. Beside me, Nathan let out a light snore.

*

'Who was he?' I asked the next morning.

I was leaning against the counter in my tiny kitchen, sipping from a mug of coffee. Nathan, fresh out of the shower, was rummaging through his gym bag, humming a pop song under his breath.

'Who?' Nathan asked, without looking at me.

'You knew him. The man at the piano.'

'Ahhh.' There was a tiny hesitation before Nathan looked at me and said, 'He was a dishwasher. At the hotel. Then he went to prison.'

I didn't say anything and Nathan punctuated his comment with a *doo-doo-doo*, conducting the end of the song with his forefinger. 'Shin,' he said at last. 'Name is Shin.'

I took a swig of coffee. 'What did he say to you?'

'Wants his job back. I mean... you could give him a chance.' Nathan looked so sweet and full of optimism that I smiled.

'He didn't want that job back,' I said.

I'd never told Nathan what Moxham got up to, or the fact that I'd looked the other way.

'Moxham... he did certain favours for people. Got them what they wanted, got them out of trouble. Shin must have been one of Moxham's drug contacts. Wanted to start it all back up again: dealing to the guests.'

I waited for shock to register on Nathan's face. He was a clean-living type. He worked out every day. On New Year's Eve, I'd offered him a joint and he'd looked so affronted, a giggle had lived in my throat for hours. But Nathan's expression remained impassive. He fidgeted with the zip of his gym bag. I put down my coffee cup on the kitchen counter with more force than I intended.

'You knew about this?'

'Not really.' He shrugged his big shoulders. 'I heard rumours. That's all.'

I opened my mouth to say something more, to ask another question, but Nathan crossed the room and put his arms around me. He smelled clean, of the pine body wash he always used. I pressed myself against him automatically, my eyes drifting closed.

'If Shin comes back,' he said, 'I'll take care of him.'

It was a line from a movie. Nathan loved those mindless action films.

I smiled. My protector.

*

There was no piano music the next day, or the day after.

Thank God. Shin was a chancer, nothing more. Now he knew Moxham was gone, he wouldn't come back. I gave the doormen his name and description and told them not to let him in the hotel.

Still, I couldn't shake the coiled anxiety in my chest.

(*Moss-ham?*)

A large wedding party descended on the Clement Hong Kong and I ended up working late three days in a row. On the third night, I snuck into my office for a break. The wedding reception was being held in the ballroom at the other end of the hotel, but I could hear the music's bass line. It was bedlam out there. A hundred guests, getting progressively drunker. I should go out and check on things. Instead, I reached for the bag of coconut candy in my desk drawer. Munching automatically, my eyelids drooped. I was so tired, I might fall asleep here and now.

My phone buzzed.

Allie: Booked your flights yet?

Yes, I'd do that, before I changed my mind. Nathan and I would go to London; we'd be a real couple, in the real world.

There was a knock on the door. I broke into a smile, convinced it would be Nathan, summoned by my thoughts. 'Come in.'

The door opened a few centimetres and then stopped.

My smile faded. 'Hello?'

It was probably the father of the bride with yet another request. So why had my whole body gone rigid?

'Hello?'

Shin squeezed inside the room, leaning against the door as it closed behind him. His eyes were roving, looking everywhere except at me.

'You need to go.' The words came out as a command, even though I couldn't get my body to move.

Shin shambled closer to my desk. He was stringy, smelling of sweat and something meaty, reminiscent of the outdoor markets here in Hong Kong. Tattoos snaked up his arms. I reminded myself it didn't mean anything; plenty of people here had tattoos and weren't Triad. My heart raced as I tried to push down the feeling of panic.

'I been thinking.' He made a closed-mouth smile, then licked his lips. 'You do nothing and I make my business.'

'No.'

'Nothing trouble for you.'

He didn't raise his voice. He was soft-spoken, a rarity in this city, where everything was loud-loud-loud.

'No.'

I reached for my phone, but once it was in my hand, it was slippery with sweat. I couldn't seem to unlock it.

'Leave,' I said. 'I'm calling the police.'

'No police. I not go back to prison.'

He took out the gun from his trouser pocket almost shyly, like he was Flora, showing me a pine cone she'd found at the park. He didn't point it at me, just held it limply at his side, but still fear throttled me.

'No police,' he said again.

I dropped my phone onto the desk. 'OK...'

'Money. I need money.'

'I don't have anything.' I fumbled my wallet from my desk drawer and flung it at him. It landed at his feet with a thump.

He picked it up left-handed and ran a thumb over my credit cards.

'Take them!' The panic was ringing in my voice now.

'Moss-ham owe me. Now I owe other people.'

I stood up. 'That's not my problem!'

He was shaking his head, not in a furious way, but like a mourner at a funeral. He shuffled closer, sliding around the desk, tapping the gun against the wood.

Tap.

'Please...'

Tap.

I was trapped here, with the wall at my back.

Tap.

'You need. Get me. Money.'

Before I could reply, he cold-cocked me, slamming the barrel of the gun against my cheek.

I hit the floor before I even registered the pain.

Hours seemed to have slipped away. Shin had kicked me hard in the head and my vision was like static. I'd probably passed out for a while.

I cowered beneath my desk, knees bunched up to my chest, waiting for Shin to return. This time, he'd use the gun to shoot me.

I hadn't even tried to fight him. I was a fucking coward. I didn't have the type of money that would satisfy him. If he came back, I would die. I felt certain of that.

I wanted to give in to the pain, to pass out again. Tears coursed down my cheeks — half fear, half humiliation — but I forced myself to find my phone.

*

'Lola... Lola... Lola...'

When I opened my eyes again, time had sped forward. Nathan was crouched beside me, saying my name over and over, until it lost all meaning. Maybe it never had any meaning to begin with.

He cradled the joints of my shoulders with his hands. 'Are you OK?'

'Yes.' My voice came out hoarse. I cleared my throat. 'I'm fine.'

Nathan helped me to my feet. 'What happened?'

I shook my head and winced.

'Shin?' Nathan asked.

'Yes...'

The name triggered something in my body. I ground my fists into my eye sockets to keep from crying. Nathan tried to hug me, but I shrugged him off.

'This was a warning,' I said. 'Next time...'

With Nathan at my side, my fear was receding, replaced by anger. It was a burn-you-up-inside type of rage I'd never experienced before.

'Next time.' My teeth clicked as I enunciated each word. 'He'll kill me.'

'What...' Nathan gulped, gasping like he couldn't breathe. 'What?'

'Is that what you want? You want them to find me on a rubbish heap?'

What if Shin *was* Triad? What if he and his friends raped, tortured and dismembered me?

Nathan formed his mouth around a word – perhaps *what* again – but didn't speak.

'Don't just stand there.' I pushed him. 'Do something!'

As Nathan staggered backwards, a sob rose in my throat. 'You were supposed to protect me.'

It was nonsense. When had I ever wanted or needed anyone to protect me? I'd been on my own since I was eighteen. Yet I felt a soul-deep grief, that there really was no one I could count on. Not even Nathan, who claimed to love me.

'I throw him... away.' Blood flooded Nathan's cheeks.

I don't know if his English failed him. I don't know if it was a mistranslation, a stock phrase that came out wrong, but it made my brain pulse.

'Yes. Throw him the fuck away.'

When I imagined Nathan ramming Shin's skull into a wall, it felt good.

Crack. Nathan pounded his fist against his open palm.

A second later, he was gone and the door slammed shut behind him.

18

A drum 'n' bass beat shuddered through the open window, syncing with my quickened heartbeat. I took a deep breath and shoved the red USB stick into my laptop.

A wall of photos loaded in the browser window. There were hundreds of them. These weren't family photos from good old Oz. The first image I clicked on might have been porn. A woman, voluptuous, with a heavy curtain of hair, nuzzled close to another woman in bed. She was spiky-haired and bird-like. Both of them were naked.

Heat crept up my face. I was perched on the edge of my bed, laptop balanced on my knees. I tapped at the arrow key. Like a stop-motion animation, the women stretched, laughed, kissed.

These women weren't playing to the camera. Even if the director was going for an appearance of faux-voyeurism, the angle wasn't good enough to pass muster, limbs cut off by the frame. This was candid photography, taken without the knowledge of its stars.

I also recognised the wall-hanging behind the bed. It was Villa Queen Conch where I'd stayed my first night on the island.

Diara crossed the room and sat down next to me.

'That's Meghan Shaw.' She pointed at the full-figured woman. 'Christian. Family values. Husband's a Congressman, Alabama or something. That's not him.'

I pressed so hard on the arrow key that the photos flashed past in split-second intervals. I slowed down when the players in the scenes changed.

A man tottered across the tiles of Villa Flamingo, wearing a nappy, with a dummy in his mouth.

'You probably recognise him,' Diara said.

'Do I?'

She said the name of a film star. In spite of myself, I laughed. Peering at the screen, I sought out his familiar features.

'Been here a few times. Friends with Kip.'

'And this is what he gets up to?'

'Everyone has secrets.'

A woman bent down for a snort of coke from the coffee table in Villa Copper. In the next shot, she reared up, flushed and grinning at a person just out of sight.

There were videos too. They captured the curl of smoke from a heroin foil. A man sucking a big toe into his mouth filled my laptop screen.

'I don't understand how he got all this.' Diara, who must have already seen everything on this drive, only glanced at the screen.

My initial surprise was congealing into a sick feeling. I reached for my water bottle and gulped down its contents, which were unpleasantly warm.

'Cameras.' I wiped my mouth with the back of my hand. 'They're easy to hide.'

It was lucky I'd found the camera recording me and stopped it. God knows what Moxham would have done with the footage if he'd lived long enough to use it. I wanted to close the laptop and push it away, but morbid fascination won. I returned to the files.

How many of the acts were truly spontaneous? If the person in question didn't have any juicy secrets, Moxham could have enticed them with drugs, made dares, acted like it was a joke, all while capturing the moment for posterity.

The videos were soundless, but there were audio files too. I opened one at random. A rustle of white noise filtered through my speakers. There were voices, but they were far away.

Moxham: '*Ever cheat on your wife?*' (I could hear the grin in his voice.)

There came a laugh, low and deep. The other voice was South African: 'I'm a red-blooded male, bru.'

Moxham: 'Tell me about it, bru, I'm stuck here with a bunch of frigid bitches.'

'Scunt,' Diara muttered.

There were too many recordings to pore over – it would take hours to listen to them all – but some of the files had been clipped. These must be the nuggets of gold.

I hit play on an audio file that had been edited to forty seconds:

Moxham: 'He died?'

Unidentified man: 'We were kids, man, just kids.'

Moxham: 'That's heavy.'

Unidentified man: 'I think about it every day. The look on his face. Right before we' – sobbing – 'killed him.'

I closed the file, not wanting to hear any more. Beside me, Diara kneaded the muscles of her neck.

'We found a motive,' she said.

All those dollar amounts in his notebook. Pay-offs. He'd collected smears on people and blackmailed them.

'This is… so fucked up.' I sucked in a breath, but it didn't seem to reach my lungs.

'Profitable, though.'

A woman with a no-infidelity clause in her pre-nup caught cheating on her husband would be left without a penny in the ensuing divorce.

A film star caught dressed as a baby would never live down the humiliation and would never be a leading man again.

A business leader caught doing heroin would be considered an unstable element; he'd be removed from the board of the corporation he'd built.

In the hotel business, it was our job to protect guests from extortion. Even when he'd crossed the line in Hong Kong, I'd thought Moxham had built his career on discretion, finding inconspicuous sex workers, providing drugs that could never be traced to the dabbler in question. Whatever they wanted, no matter how illegal, he delivered it with a smile. What had prompted his about-face?

Maybe it was something small. A tip that was $100 and not $1,000. A female guest who laughed when he tried to kiss her. A sneering remark from a guy like Ford. 'Be a good little donkey and fuck off now.'

Perhaps Moxham simply considered it a savvy business move. You can earn X dollars by catering to a guest's every whim; you can earn Y dollars by threatening to destroy their life. Y is greater than X, ergo, investment in Y is recommended.

When confronted by an embarrassing photo or recording, Moxham must have calculated that most people would consider $10–50k an easy pay-off. They'd be angry, but they'd cough up.

The stakes were high though. Millions of dollars, lifelong reputations, hanging in the balance. When Moxham made his ultimatum ('pay up or I put it online'), all it would've taken was for one of them to let their anger boil over.

I had wondered if Moxham had found out Kip's darkest secret, but now I knew he was blackmailing dozens of people – all of them with a reason to want Moxham dead. The scale of it was overwhelming. So many suspects.

I nudged the laptop accidentally and a video opened and began to play. The toe-sucker.

'You know who that is, right?' Diara asked.

I squinted at the screen, shook my head.

'Howell,' she said. 'Big cheese in the BVI police.'

'Shit. Well, that explains why no one was too bothered when Moxham wound up dead.'

Outside, a rooster squawked. I shoved the laptop aside and let my head sink to my chest. 'Moxham wanted me to help him.'

'What?'

I told her everything Moxham had said during our conversation in the beach hut, during the Alice party.

Diara snapped her tongue. 'Count yourself lucky.'

'What?'

'You coulda ended up in an accident too.' She stressed the word *accident*.

The room was getting smaller, closing in on me.

'What if they think I'm in on it?' I said.

All these new suspects, everyone with a reason to kill Moxham. If they thought I was helping him, they had a reason to kill me too.

My fingernails scraped at my neck. I couldn't fucking breathe.

19

Hong Kong, ten days ago

Alone in my apartment, I crawled into bed with an ice pack and cried, my fingers turning stiff where they clutched the ice against my cheek.

I must have fallen asleep, because the noise wrenched me awake. There was a scrabbling sound at my front door.

My heart lurched. Fuck.

It was Shin. He'd found out where I lived. He'd brought his friends.

He'd fire the gun this time.

I crept from my bed into the hallway, dressed in a threadbare oversized T-shirt and nothing else. On tiptoes, I approached the front door.

'Lo?' His voice was hoarse, muffled by the door. 'Let me in.'

I released my breath. Nathan.

He had a key. Why not let himself inside? Why scare me half to death?

When I swung the door open, I saw why.

He must have been leaning against the door, because when I opened it, he slid forward and stumbled to his knees. I reared backwards. When he turned his face up to look at me, I gasped.

One eye was swollen shut. He had a fat lip. A red welt was spreading across his throat.

'Nathan...' My hand went to the crown of his head, my fingers burrowing into his black hair, which was damp with sweat.

With a groan, he hoisted himself upright, faltering, like he'd forgotten how to work his legs. He shuffled inside and the door shut behind him. He leaned heavily against the black IKEA table, the one which was perpetually in the way, too big for the space.

'I'm fine.'

It was such a perfect reversal of our earlier conversation that I almost laughed, but the sound that came out of my mouth was a cry.

'You need a… hospital,' I said.

From Nathan's ragged breathing, I guessed he had a broken rib or two. Concussion?

He stumbled past me into the bathroom. 'Aspirin.'

Each surface he touched, he left a smear of blood. His T-shirt and trousers were black, so I hadn't noticed at first, but now I saw they were soaked in a rusty-brown liquid. Was there a stab wound under his shirt? Was he dying?

'What happened?' My voice rose an octave. 'What did you do?'

I followed him into the bathroom, grasping at the hem of his T-shirt. It was stuck to him with blood.

Nathan batted my hand away. 'Nothing.'

He flipped open the medicine cabinet and grabbed an aspirin bottle. His hands were shaking so badly, he couldn't overcome the child lock. I eased it out of his hands, unscrewed the top and handed it back to him.

'I'm calling an ambulance.'

'No.'

He poured a handful of pills into his palm without counting and dry-swallowed them. His eyelids were fluttering. 'Sleep.'

If you had a concussion and you went to sleep, you could fall into a coma. Was that real science or a TV thing?

'Shower,' I said.

Nathan was the same height as me, with twice the heft, but it required barely a shove to get him into the shower cubicle. He teetered like a zombie, then braced himself against the wall. I'd hated the black tiles when I'd moved in, but now I was grateful for them.

I yanked the dial on the shower and water drenched us both. The spray always took a minute to heat up, so it was icy cold. Crammed in next to me, Nathan let out an almighty shudder.

'Try and take off your clothes.'

His fighting spirit was gone. He did as I said, stiff arms working robotically. When he was naked, he stared at me, a dog waiting for his owner's next instruction. He was so out of it, I could have called for an ambulance and he wouldn't have argued.

For a second, I rewound the evening in my mind. The moment Shin left my office, I should have called the police. That would have unravelled everything Moxham had done and perhaps even incriminated me. If I'd been thinking clearly, maybe I would have done it anyway. But it was too late for that. I wasn't calling the police now. I wasn't calling an ambulance, either.

As the water rippled over Nathan's body, his skin washed away to an unblemished golden brown. The blood belonged to someone else. We were washing away evidence. Everything he'd done, I was in it too.

After the shower, I helped Nathan into bed.

'Thank you for taking care of me.' He gave me what would have been a lovely smile, if it weren't for the Picasso state of his face.

'Tell me what happened. Exactly.'

His smile faded. 'He is gone. He will not hurt you.'

The bedroom was dim, the only light coming from a bedside lamp.

'Oh, fuck, Nathan…' I'd been hoping, insanely, that it wasn't as bad as I'd feared.

'Now he cannot hurt you.' The sheets crackled as he pulled them up over his body.

'I thought you'd...' I let out a keening sob. 'I don't know, scare him off. Not kill him. I didn't want this.'

Nathan's eyebrows knitted together, his mouth going slack. Outside, a siren filled the silence. I tensed, until it faded away.

He reached for me, but I shrank back, half-falling off the bed. 'Don't touch me.'

His expression went blank. When I shuffled out of the room, he didn't call after me. I slumped onto the sofa and turned on the TV, watching without seeing.

Minutes later (or was it an hour?) I heard him snoring. I hated him for that. What kind of psychopath could kill someone and have a peaceful night's sleep? I wasn't sure I'd ever sleep again. I couldn't stop replaying our earlier conversation. I wanted to pretend Nathan had misunderstood me. It happened all the time. Little blips of mistranslation. I'd ask for a green tea and he'd bring me a black tea.

Except it hadn't been a misunderstanding. I'd wanted Nathan to kill Shin. I'd wanted revenge and I'd sent Nathan to do my bidding. What kind of person was I to do that? If I wanted my boyfriend to kill for me, wasn't I culpable too?

*

The next day, Nathan made a dogged decision that he was going to cook breakfast. The kitchen was a disaster zone, with every cupboard thrown open and dishes cluttering every surface. Apart from a stiffness in his movements, he whisked eggs with surprising dexterity. Either he was pushing through the pain or he'd inflicted a lot more damage the night before than he'd received.

I sat at the table, the IKEA one that he'd helped me build one lazy Sunday. When he produced a plate with a flourish, I didn't even try to eat. While he had slept, I'd scrubbed clean the blood. Now all I could smell was bleach.

'What are we going to do?' I said.

Nathan's mouth was full. His eyebrows stretched upwards, optimistic, as if I might be asking how we were going to spend a day off together. A trip to the zoo gardens?

'What could your alibi be?' I went on. 'Do I need to lie and say you were with me?'

His face dropped. 'I'm sorry.' He swallowed, reached for my hand. 'It was the only way.'

'It wasn't.' My fingers remained limp.

'It's what Moxham would have done.'

The words hit me like a punch.

'How do you know what Moxham would have done?'

*

'I did it for us,' Nathan kept saying.

The conversation was going round and round in circles. Nathan was squeezing my fingers so hard, pins and needles shot through my arms. He lifted my numb fingers and kissed them, one by one. Another thing he'd seen in a movie, perhaps.

Nathan didn't tell me the details of exactly what he did for Moxham – 'protection,' he said – but I could guess. If a drug dealer was ripping off Moxham, Nathan could intimidate them. Maybe all it took was a tough look. Maybe it was an easy job. At first.

Stroking the palm of my hand, he began telling me about our future. We'd buy a house somewhere hot and beautiful. It would be us, an island of us.

'I didn't spend the money,' Nathan said. 'I saved it. For us.'

I'd thought everything stopped when Moxham left. I was an idiot.

Of course Nathan didn't stop. He would have been better at it than Moxham. He was friendlier, able to speak to his contacts in Cantonese. He kept the drugs flowing into the hotel. He kept the favours coming from the local police.

'Shin. Is he…' I said, 'is he. The first person you've killed?'

'He was scum, he hurt you.'

'So he deserved to die?'

'Yes.'

I was crying again, but Nathan's hands were clasping mine, so I couldn't wipe the tears away. I let them fall, blurring my vision. I didn't want to look at him anymore.

'You've done it before,' I said.

Nathan didn't reply.

*

That night, we made love ever so gently. I don't think either of us were in the mood, but we were determined to prove we still loved each other. With the heat of his body smothering mine, it was almost possible to block out everything else.

When he fell asleep, I eased out of bed and crept to the bathroom. I sat on the floor, knees under my chin. My phone was slippery in my grip. I tried to calculate the time difference in my head. It would be afternoon in the Caribbean.

Calling Moxham was like calling the devil for help, but with the situation I was in, it felt like only the devil could save me.

'Something's happened,' I said, when he answered.

'Showgirl!' He rolled the R, sounding like the ringmaster at the circus.

'This guy named Shin showed up.'

'Oh, yeah?' His voice flattened.

'Things went bad.' I didn't want to say too much on the phone.

I pushed at my cheekbone with my knuckles. Pain jolted through me. On the mirror opposite, dead eyes reflected back at me. There was a tiny fleck of blood that I'd missed during my clean-up.

'Well, shit.'

'Mox…' I worked my jaw, trying to get my words out. 'I'm fucking terrified.'

'You're fine. That big dumb lunk will protect you.'

I wanted to scream at him. *I don't want that kind of protection. I don't want a man who'll kill for me. Because that kind of man could end up killing me.*

'I need to get out,' I said. 'Away from here.'

'Showgirl…'

'You need to fix this, Mox. You're the fucking fixer, so fix it.'

'How about a new job? A fresh start.'

'Where?'

'Paradise.'

20

'**B**reathe,' Diara said. 'Concentrate on breathing.'

She made me count to five as I breathed in, then count to five as I breathed out. The two of us sat like that for a long time, Diara counting, me remembering how to breathe.

'You're safe.' Her fingers dug into my forearm.

I wasn't sure she was right. But at least the room was no longer closing in on me.

Once I'd stopped hyperventilating, she went down the hall to the kitchenette and brewed a bush tea for me. It tasted of lemongrass and made me feel better, although my chest remained sore, like my heart had swollen and didn't fit in my ribcage anymore.

'You should get some sleep,' she said.

I let out a bristly little half-laugh, half-wheeze. 'Don't think I'm ever gonna sleep again.'

Heaving myself up, I crossed the room to the chest of drawers. The three other USB drives (blue, green, yellow) remained there. I glanced at my watch. It was past ten, but there was still work for me to do; I should check in with the hosts, make sure all the guests were happy. Right now, I didn't care. These USB drives held the answer to Moxham's murder. I needed to know what was on them. I fumbled the blue drive into my laptop and its files appeared on my screen.

'Who was on Keeper that night?' I asked Diara. 'Howell?'

Could it have been the police chief himself who shut up Moxham for good?

'No. He wasn't there… that night, he wasn't.'

'You sure?'

'I'da remembered. He always drops by the spa, likes to flirt with Helena.'

Distractedly, I clicked through a gallery of naked women. 'So who was here?'

Diara ticked them off on her fingers. 'Guests on the island... Ford, Carolina, Brady...'

Together, we filled in the list. There was the footballer and his wife, the German condiments guy, the Italian heiress...

'... and Eddie Yiu,' she said.

'Plus Kip,' I said. I was scrolling at speed through the contents of the drive. When I caught sight of a bald head, my heart leapt. On closer inspection, I didn't recognise the guy who was in bed with two women.

'Did you see any of them on the red drive?' I asked.

Diara shook her head. 'No.'

I flung aside the blue USB and grabbed the green one, jamming it into my computer. 'You do yellow.' I tossed the remaining USB stick to Diara.

It clattered onto the floor, but she stooped to retrieve it.

'In that case' – she released a long sigh – 'I need some coffee.'

She went back to the kitchenette and returned with two mugs of coffee and a packet of plantain chips. Studying the footage was a long and tedious task. The weird camera angles and unfortunate cropping made it difficult to identify the stars of the show. I had to go frame-by-frame, scrutinising every expression. It was voyeurism in the extreme. What was disturbing was how quickly I became desensitised to seeing people's most vulnerable moments.

'Can you check green?' I punted the USB across the room. I wanted a second opinion on a blond-haired man in lacy underwear. 'Is that Brady?'

'Nope, not him.'

An hour had passed. I rubbed my eyes. The effect of the coffee was wearing off. While I'd been checking the videos, I'd let one of the recordings play, muffled voices fading in and out. I hit pause.

Across the room, Diara stretched, rearranging herself on her bed. 'Tell me what you think of this.'

I perched beside her and peered at her screen. A video was playing, showing a man dancing around Villa Flamingo. He was naked, clothes scattered on the floor around him.

'Who is that?' I asked.

The man's physique was puffy and his teeth flashed, whiter-than-white. His dick jiggled.

'Eddie Yiu.'

'Is it?'

His face was partly concealed by a blue baseball cap, bearing a logo that looked vaguely familiar.

'That's his investment company.'

'Well, he's having a good time,' I said, managing a tired smile.

'Wait for it.'

As the video continued to play, the dancing turned to martial arts, with Eddie squatting and lunging at an invisible assailant. His cap fell off and his face was captured by the camera. Even though the footage was shot at a distance, I could tell there was something wrong with his expression.

He grabbed a belt from the floor. *Whack*.

I flinched. He whipped the belt against his thighs, then up over his shoulder, hitting his back. His mouth stretched in a soundless howl.

'He looks... fucking unhinged,' I said, not wanting to voice the rest of my thought: he looked like the type of person who could kill.

'Embarrassing, if that got out.' Diara shot a distasteful look at the screen. Naked Eddie was bloody and writhing on the floor.

'It would tank his career,' I said. 'That new business he's starting…'

I leaned over to Diara's laptop and paused the video.

'What d'you know about him?' I asked.

'Not much. First-timer. He's been to the spa, but he's not… chatty.'

I pulled up Google, tapped in *Eddie Yiu + Hong Kong*. I scrolled until—

'Oh, fuck, I just found his mugshot.'

In the photo, there was a dazed appearance to him, skin sallow, black hair falling across his eyes. The accompanying article was in either Cantonese or Mandarin and running it through a translation program produced garbled results. With a pang, I wished, stupidly, that I could ask Nathan to translate.

As far as I could work out, Eddie was fresh off a two-year stint in prison.

'Assault. That's what it says, right?' I shoved the laptop in Diara's direction. I felt sick.

If Eddie had murdered Moxham and he suspected I was in on the blackmail, he'd come after me too.

I clenched and unclenched my hand, trying to get rid of the pins-and-needles feeling.

'He left, right?' I said. 'Left the island.'

Diara shook her head, feather earrings brushing her shoulders.

In the nine days since the Alice party, obviously Ford and Carolina had gone. The Italian, the German and the footballer and his wife had also departed. I knew Eddie had been due to leave this morning. Yesterday, I'd asked Tessa, his host, to prepare an elaborate goodbye hamper: designer-scented candles, freshly baked cookies, a cuddly sloth with the Keeper Island key logo embroidered on its belly.

'Extended his stay,' Diara said.

'No…' Why the hell hadn't Tessa told me?

'I gave him a massage at four.'

I cringed, pulling at the neck of my T-shirt.

'He tipped well,' she said.

'Great,' I muttered sarcastically, 'as long as he tipped well…'

Diara kissed her teeth and we turned back to the screen as I played the video again. Eddie Yiu was obviously not a man with a lot of self-control. For his new business venture, he'd want to project to the world that he was a changed man. Moxham's footage would directly contradict that. Was it worth killing him over?

Hong Kong. It all came back to Hong Kong. My thoughts were spiralling. What if Moxham, when he was at the Clement Hong Kong, had known Eddie? What if Moxham had black-mailed him before? Was it possible he'd had something to do with his incarceration?

If Eddie recognised me from Hong Kong, if Moxham had insinuated I was helping him…

'If he knows I have all this, he'll come after me.'

'He doesn't know you have it,' Diara said. 'Don't worry.'

She was fidgeting with her earrings, pulling at her lobes. Should I tell her the full extent of what I was running from in Hong Kong? If she knew, she might not sound so confident.

The air felt thick. Oxygen was hard to come by or I'd forgotten how to breathe again.

'I need to get some air,' I said.

'How 'bout a midnight snack?'

*

Under white lights, the restaurant kitchen gleamed. Everywhere I looked, I saw weapons. Knives regimented in size-order on their magnetic rack, enormous hooks used to hang meat, pans that you could swing like a bat.

Oil hissed in the skillet. I flinched.

'Don't tell Chef I was in here.' Diara adjusted the burner.

'Trust me, I can keep a secret.' I pulled myself up onto the stainless-steel counter next to her.

At least our surroundings were bright and clean. Eddie Yiu couldn't sneak up on me in here.

Diara was making johnny cakes, a type of dumpling. Methodically, she flattened blobs of dough into circles and dropped them into the bubbling oil.

'My granny make 'em better, but...' She shrugged and handed me a plate. 'Here you go.'

I broke open the first johnny cake, hot from the pan. It was crispy on the outside, soft and fluffy on the inside. 'These are yummy,' I said, with my mouth full.

Diara gave a tiny eye roll, but she was smiling. I finished my second johnny cake and let my gaze roam the kitchen. The windows were a wall of black rectangles.

'How long do you think Moxham was blackmailing people?' I wondered aloud.

'All that footage...' Diara said. 'Months. Musta been.'

'He had cameras in every villa. Every room, almost.'

I'd been enjoying my food a moment ago, but now I could only nibble on my second johnny cake.

'Cameras still there?' Diara asked. 'Did you find them?'

'No...' I frowned, set down my plate. 'There was nothing.'

'He must have taken them down, before he—'

'Why would he?' I cut in. 'He was trying to get dirt, he needed them recording. But now they're gone.'

Diara raised an eyebrow. 'They self-destruct or something?'

She was thinking the same thing as me. Someone had destroyed the cameras, after Moxham's death. They couldn't have known locations of the hidden USBs, but they'd known about the blackmail and they'd known it needed to be covered up.

'He had an accomplice,' I said.

It made sense. During our shifts at the Clement Hong Kong, I'd learned Moxham hated grunt-work. That was why he and I always worked so well together; I picked up the slack. But who had been picking up Moxham's slack before I'd arrived on Keeper?

Diara retrieved another golden-brown dumpling from the oil. 'Has to be someone on staff, someone he trusted...'

'Who did he trust?'

'... Didn't know him well.'

The photo of Moxham and Diara laughing together flashed in my mind. *Love of my life.* I blinked it away.

'What if... his accomplice killed him?' I said.

Diara screwed up her face. 'How's that?'

'Mox was making hundreds of thousands of dollars. What if the accomplice wanted that money for themselves?'

'That's a motive,' Diara said.

I pressed clammy palms against the cool countertop. It was not only the blackmailed guests who might want Moxham dead. I glanced at the knives on the magnetic rack.

Anyone on this island could be the killer.

21

The following morning, I awoke at dawn to Keeper Island being the most glorious version of itself. Now that I'd discovered the blackmail and violence hidden in the heart of the place, it felt as though evil should permeate every grain of sand.

Instead, it was heaven.

Monday meant the whole week lay ahead, full of possibilities. The sky was impossibly blue, with towering clouds. The sun, where it broke through the tree canopy, was a balm on my bare skin. As I hiked from the staff village to the main complex, I encountered one of the island's sloths, half-concealed by the foliage. Big eyes, long arms, furry face. I let out a shout of laughter. The sloth gave me a look – not frightened, more like a disapproving librarian – and began a slow munch on a leaf.

Above me, there was a rush of wind. Someone was on the zip-line; they sped by too fast for me to identify them. I had yet to try out the zip-line that stretched from Keeper Peak to Hidden Cove, but I wanted to. A bucket list item.

Better get cracking, might not have much time left.

Last night, Diara and I had agreed a plan. We had suspects, but what we needed was concrete evidence. The when and where.

We'd discussed, briefly, whether we should hand over the blackmail material to the police and let them handle it. 'Not a good idea,' Diara had said. 'Not till we sure of things, not till we have evidence they can't ignore.' Howell had a big, embarrassing reason to bury it. For my part, I didn't want to draw any attention to the Clement Hong Kong.

Instead, Diara would get in contact with her auntie, who was a local police sergeant, and who would keep things discreet. On Keeper, we would do some digging. There were witnesses to interview about what they'd seen on the night of the Alice party; we could build up a timeline of the events leading to Moxham's death.

I was also determined to sift through the blackmail material again for anything we'd missed. I was cognizant of the audio recordings; hours and hours of conversations that might feature Eddie or Kip or anyone else with a mind to kill again. With a mind to kill me if they knew what I was doing.

In the tree, the sloth slowly climbed out of sight. I sighed and continued my trek. A big wedding party from San Francisco was arriving today and I was expected to be a wedding planner. When I ran into Tessa (sullen, slurping a green smoothie), she told me the island's remote IT server was glitching, which apparently made it impossible for her to do anything.

I sent her to pack a cooler for a guest excursion to the island of Anegada, due to leave in – I checked my watch – one hour.

There was a murderer on the loose, but that didn't mean life – or work – stopped in the meantime.

*

A sleek red and white bowrider was tied up to the pier, ready to take the guests to Anegada. When I arrived, I noticed a smaller, shabbier boat out on the water, motoring close to shore. A hand popped up, waving at me.

'Good morning!' A baritone voice rose above the roar of the engine.

The boat rocked closer. Doc's lined face broke into a broad smile.

'I'm terrible with names,' he said breathlessly, once he was on dry land.

Earlier, I'd seen news of a tropical storm heading towards St Kitts, some 130 miles away. I wasn't clear on how badly this might affect us. The sea appeared choppy but not catastrophically so. I didn't have the bandwidth to worry about the weather, as well as everything else.

I reintroduced myself to Doc and he doffed his hat. 'Bad with names, but I never forget an ailment,' he said. 'How are you feeling after your tumble?'

'Fine, no worries. What brings you to Keeper?' If the doctor was here, someone might be injured.

'The big man himself.'

'God?'

He chuckled. 'Is that what Kip's calling himself these days?'

I radioed Fizzy to find out Kip's location but got no response, so I escorted Doc to his villa myself.

'Nothing's wrong, I hope?' I steered the golf cart past the swimming pools at the main complex, which were sparkling blue again, since I'd got the filter fixed.

'Kip's a fighter.' Doc tapped his cane against his leg. 'Recovery's been good.'

'Recovery?'

'Stroke took it out of him.'

Kip had a stroke? When? During the time I'd been on Keeper Island, I'd never considered Kip's health. He always seemed to be going sailing or kayaking or hiking the island's trails. He might be over sixty, but he didn't strike me as unfit. Yet if he was still recovering from a stroke, he must be fragile. I wondered why I'd never seen his health problems reported in the press. For that matter, should Doc be telling me this? I made an *mmm* sound, hoping he'd continue.

'Made everything worse,' he said, rolling his neck. 'The Von Willebrand, in particular. Very rare, you know.'

'Right.' Was Doc under the impression I already knew about Kip's health problems? Or, more likely, was he indulging in a spot of gossip? 'Von Wille…'

'Von Willebrand's disease.' Doc puffed out his chest, showing off his expertise. He explained that it was an inherited disorder where your blood doesn't clot properly, causing bruising and nosebleeds, among other things.

Bruises? Bleeding? My mind was whirring by the time I deposited Doc at Kip's villa. He walked to the entrance and knocked.

'Oh, no.' When Kip opened the door and clocked Doc, he tried to shut it again.

Doc jammed the door with his cane. 'Not getting rid of me that easily.'

Kip sounded plaintive. 'I thought you were coming on the thirtieth.'

'Yes and the rumours are true,' Doc said, 'it's the thirtieth today.'

Kip smacked his forehead. 'Dammit.'

I hid a smile as I manoeuvred the golf cart away. I'd never seen anyone call Kip on his bullshit before.

*

Back at the pier, I rifled through the mounds of supplies that were to accompany the guest excursion. Tessa was supposed to have packed a hamper of towels. (She hadn't.)

I was still thinking about Kip. The bloody handprint on his shorts, the bruises that suggested a brawl. Surely, it could all be explained away by Von Whatsit disease? For that matter, did Kip, with his many ailments, even have the strength to kill a man? I still didn't trust him – he'd lied about the circumstances of his wife's death, for one thing – but I couldn't hold on to my suspicion of him as the prime suspect. There were so many other people out there with a reason to kill Moxham.

I was so lost in thought that I barely noticed Brady's approach. 'Hey there!'

I squinted into the sun. He was huge in silhouette, ambling down the pier towards me.

'We've gotta stop meeting like this!' he said.

I laughed. 'An island this size... it's a crazy coincidence.'

He was dressed in Superman colours, red shorts and a blue T-shirt, tight enough to show off his muscles. Not that I was looking, of course.

A cluster of guests arrived, along with the bartender, Ethan. He was a handsome American lad; lanky and dark-haired with a Roman nose and tattoos crawling up his arms. When Tessa finally materialised with the towels, she dumped them on the ground and began a long conversation with Ethan, ignoring my pointed looks.

'You coming to Anegada with us?' Brady asked me.

'No... no rest for the wicked.'

My radio flared up with chatter about the tech glitch. Not so much a glitch anymore as a heart-monitor flatline.

'Aw, c'mon... it'll be fun.'

'Seriously, have a great time.' I sidestepped away from him. 'I have to get back to...' I gestured in lieu of saying, *this avalanche of shit I'm dealing with.*

'How about this?' Brady said. 'I need you to come.'

He popped out a hand to steady me, as if I'd been about to fall into the water. (I hadn't.) His green eyes were sparkling. God, he was cute.

'Guest request,' he said. 'Can't say no to that.'

I hesitated. No, I didn't want to spend this beautiful day rushing around, fixing other people's problems. I also didn't want to sift through clues for a murder that was frighteningly close to home.

I wanted to escape it all; sail away, visit new places and flirt with a hot guy. A hot guy who was one of the suspects in Moxham's murder. My taste in men was flawless.

Reggie arrived, urging guests onto the bowrider. Ethan piled supplies into the back of the boat.

'Come on…' Brady said.

Once he'd climbed aboard, he turned back and held out a hand to me.

22

Anegada, the 'drowned island', was completely flat and invisible from a distance. As we motored closer, Reggie at the helm, the island's foliage resembled parsley on a slab of fish. It was significantly less populated than Virgin Gorda, but a few businesses were thronged around the mooring point.

Reggie chatted with the owner of a moped rental company and, minutes later, our party was bumping along the cracked concrete of Anegada's one and only paved road, in a cloud of exhaust fumes. I pulled out in front on a red moped, savouring the speed and the growl of the engine.

At the salt ponds, the famed flamingos were so far away, they appeared as pink smudges even through binoculars. According to Tessa, who was giving the guests tourist-guide spiel in a tone of profound boredom, Anegada's flamingos had been hunted to extinction, but conservationists had re-established them and the flock was thriving again. Thriving but shy.

Nearby, Cow Wreck Beach offered us white sands, palm trees waving lazily in the breeze and rum cocktails that came in plastic cups from a turquoise beach bar. It was easy to forget I was working. At lunchtime, a cluster of local men waded into the water, hauling in a trap teeming with lobsters. The lobster tails, served half-an-hour later drowning in butter, were the freshest seafood I'd ever eaten.

Finally, it was time for horse riding. It was a surprise for the guests, but even though I knew to expect it, the sight of a pack of horses trotting towards us along the beach was strange and delightful. Anegada might be home to fewer than two hundred people, but it had a horse sanctuary.

'Ah, they're precious!' Tessa clapped her hands together. For the first time ever, I saw her eyes light up.

The horse, blotched white-and-chestnut, which was assigned to me, was not precious. In fact, I had the distinct impression she was a bit of an arsehole. When I tried to stroke her nose, she jerked away with a whinny. It was worse when I attempted to mount her. I got one foot in the stirrup before she jolted to the side, leaving me dangling in the air, unable to get on top and unable to get down.

'Steady on, girl. Steady on.'

I thought Brady was talking to me, but he laid a hand on the horse's neck. He gave a gentle tug on the reins and released a long breath, like he was instructing the horse to do the same.

'Since when do they ride horses in New York?' I asked, after Brady had given me a boost onto my saddle.

'I was born in South Carolina. Country boy.'

I didn't trust my horse, but when I squeezed my legs against its flank, as Brady suggested, she strutted forward. The way she shook her dusty-brown mane made me feel she was only tolerating me. The rest of the guests trotted ahead of me, along the beach. It was nothing like the starched horse riding I'd seen on TV. Two of the women were in bikinis; most of the men were shirtless; everyone was barefoot.

I expected Brady to canter off with the rest of the party, but he remained beside me, apparently content to make slow progress. He spoke often to his horse – 'there we go' and 'you're a wonder, my girl' – and smoothed his big hands over her mane. I gave my horse a single wary pat.

In the silence that settled between us, my mind inevitably drifted back to suspects. Brady's name was written in Moxham's notebook. And, though he'd always been friendly to me, I couldn't shake the feeling there was something off about him. He'd known Moxham, as a regular visitor to the Clement Hong Kong. Was that mere coincidence?

'Tell me about South Carolina,' I said.

Wouldn't now be a good opportunity to get to know him? Purely for investigative purposes, of course.

Brady rubbed his chin, where golden stubble was growing in.

'In the summers, we'd go to my daddy's ranch… been in his family a hundred years. That land stretches way off into the distance, right down to the train tracks. When I was five, I thought that was where the world ended.'

'Oh, yeah?'

I squeezed my legs and the horse increased its pace, kicking up sand. Brady pulled up beside me. 'I was a little rascal.' His dimples deepened when he smiled. 'Got obsessed with them end-of-the-world trains. Got to knowing exactly when to cross the tracks. Freighters roaring past and little old ninety-pound me staring 'em down, playin' chicken.'

His Southern accent had grown thicker. I imagined him as a boy with gangly legs and a blond mop of hair. In my mind, he ran full tilt across the train tracks. I couldn't help but feel a twang of understanding. I'd played chicken as a child too. Maybe I was still playing chicken.

'My daddy got out his belt when he found out what I'd been doing.'

'That's rough.'

'Naw, he wanted me to know right from wrong.'

I let that settle into my bones. My father had certainly never taught me right from wrong. We trotted on. The tide was coming in, waves foaming on the beach.

'What brings you to the Caribbean?' I asked.

He was quiet for a long moment, rocking back in his saddle. 'Can you have a mid-life crisis at thirty-five?'

'I'm the wrong person to ask.'

Our horses splashed into the shallows, hooves digging into the wet sand.

'I'd been doing the whole suit-and-tie thing in New York and I was… burned out. My marriage was over. Felt like my life was over.'

'Shit.'

'Yep, sums it up.'

'Anyway, I ran into my buddy, Andy. He suggested I come out to Keeper for a month, clear my head.' He laughed. 'Already been here more than a month. Maybe I'll never leave. Take that guy's job.'

He indicated to Ethan, who was crouched twenty metres away beside a cooler, organising drinks and snacks for the guests when they looped back around. Ethan inclined his head, like he'd heard. I'm sure he was used to this joke from men who'd never worked a day in the service industry.

Brady launched into a long story about getting lost in the bush, trying to find his way up Keeper Peak. As I wobbled along on horseback, I could feel a soreness building in my legs. Beside me, Brady looked as relaxed as if he were on a golf cart.

'And then I saw one of them sloths and, I swear to God, he pointed me in the right direction,' Brady was saying. He turned and gave me a lazy wink that made my stomach flip. Did I really fancy someone who would wink at you?

I accidentally squeezed my legs too hard and my horse let out a whinny and kicked the air.

'Jesus!' The horse tossed her mane, threatening to throw me off. She calmed, but I read it as a warning.

'How about a drink?' I said. *How about getting off these godforsaken beasts?*

Ethan laid out a beach blanket for us, deep red and soft to the touch. I felt guilty that he was waiting on me, but not guilty enough to stop it. He mooched away, sneaking his phone from his pocket. The other guests, who had to be half a mile away, were lost to the curve of the shore.

'So, you've been on Keeper a whole month?' I asked Brady, as we settled on the blanket. 'Shows you're enjoying it.'

I poured him a generous measure of El Tesoro, chilly from the cooler. I knew from his guest file that it was his favourite tequila. I poured myself a smaller dose.

'You were at the party the day I arrived, right?' I asked.

'When was that?'

He nosed his tequila like it was a glass of whiskey, then took a sip.

'The Alice in Wonderland party.'

'Sure, sure. You guys know how to put on a shindig. Had to have someone carry me home, of course.' He waggled his eyebrows and made a weird flip with his feet, a bandage unravelling from one of them.

There was a buzz and he fished out his phone. 'Sorry, I hate to be this guy.' He swiped across the screen. 'Should throw it in the ocean.'

'No worries.' I took a sip of tequila. It was fruitier than I expected, good enough that I went back for more.

Brady dropped his phone onto the blanket between us. 'What were we talking about?'

I stretched out my bare legs, nudged my toes against Brady's ankle, halfway on purpose, halfway not.

'Alice in Wonderland.' I kept my voice casual. 'You didn't see anything out of the ordinary?'

'Oh, yeah!'

I held my breath, waited for him to continue.

'Man in a bunny suit tried to wrestle me.' He slapped a hand against the sand.

'Huh.' I forced a chuckle. 'That's funny. Nothing else you remember about that night?'

His voice darkened. 'Just a shit hand at cards and' – he swigged his tequila – 'too much to drink.'

I glanced at him, studying his profile. The laughter was gone from his face, replaced by a strange rigidity in his jaw. I hadn't heard him swear before; he seemed to have a Boy Scout aversion to it.

'That's… too bad.'

'I'll get over it.' He smiled, his voice relaxed again.

My toes were still tickling his ankle. Brady reached out and swept my legs across his lap. I should have resisted, but I didn't want to. The weight of his palm was heavy on my thigh.

'Y'know' – he gestured to the expanse of white-sand beach – 'I'd like to buy an island of my own. Looking into it. For serious.'

'You'll have to invite me to stay.'

'Top of my list.'

We sat and listened to the waves crash, Brady's thumb making distracted strokes against my thigh. Without noticing, I'd finished my drink and my body felt loose.

Brady was trying to catch my eye. I knew if he did, he'd kiss me.

It was part relief, part disappointment when a horse nickered nearby. The rest of the party had returned, trotting along the beach towards us. I cleared my throat and disentangled myself from Brady.

'Get you another drink.' I hastened towards the cooler. A cloud of biting midges had descended and I swatted them away.

He stood up, stretched, and I made a point not to notice the way his shorts were slipping off his hips, revealing a hard belt of muscle.

'I gotta find a bathroom,' he said, 'or a… bush. You'll excuse me.'

As he wandered away, I busied myself by spreading out more beach blankets, ready for guests to relax after their horse ride.

I was still processing everything from my conversation with Brady. What had he said? *Had to have someone carry me home.*

So, Brady had been drunk at the party, drunk enough that he couldn't make his own way home. It wasn't a crime. It wasn't even unusual. Except he may not have gone to bed after he got home. He might have gone back out, tracked down Moxham, confronted him about the blackmail. Drunkenness and rage were a scary combination.

Bzzz. I glanced around automatically. Brady's phone was still on the sand. The screen was lit up with a new message. Then there was the buzz of another message, then another.

Curiosity overtook me. I picked up Brady's phone. Three messages stacked on top of each other:

I'm sorry
Play it cool
They can't prove anything

All the texts were from someone named Andrew Reisslenger. Can't prove anything? Prove what?

'Hey.'

Brady was standing over me, back from his bathroom break. There was a crease between his eyes.

I almost dropped his phone, but I recovered and fumbled it in his direction.

'This is yours,' I said stupidly.

'Thanks.' He took it.

'Wouldn't want to lose it!' I coughed, covering my mouth. 'Well, this has been fun, but… can't stay out much longer. Better get going before the insects eat us up.'

'Sure.' Brady met my eyes, but I couldn't read his expression.

Play it cool, I thought, and forced myself to return his gaze with a blank stare and a bland smile.

23

The following day, the island's remote server was still down. A cyber attack to the data centre in the US was having a knock-on effect on our IT infrastructure. The tablets in the villas didn't work, which meant guests couldn't order food or book excursions. At the spa, there was chaos, because guests started turning up unannounced, taking previously filled slots. It was my job to sort it all out. In addition, there was tomorrow's wedding to organise and Saturday's gold-themed beach party to plan.

I'd been on the phone to Zack, our tech-support person in Florida, on and off all day. He was less effective than a chocolate teapot in tropical heat. I would have screamed at him if I thought it would do any good. Instead, I poured honey on my voice and asked him to please, please try to rectify the situation by the end of the day.

'Try my best, Ms George,' Zack said, sounding petulant.

I ended the call and flopped onto one of the sun loungers beside the pool. I was drowning in sweat. The temperature was up at least five degrees today.

All I wanted was to stay here and nurse a Painkiller in a frosty glass. It was one of the BVI's signature cocktails: orange, pineapple and coconut with an aftershock of rum. My eyes fluttered shut, imagining the taste. Stupid job. Stupid work.

'Hello, hello.'

At the sound of his voice, I flinched so violently that Eddie Yiu continued, 'Hey, you OK?'

He was in a baseball cap, the same one he'd worn in the video. I hadn't seen him since I'd watched him whip himself.

'Fine, fine.' I levered myself up. 'What can I do for you?'

'I want to go scuba diving.'

'Great!'

I spied a welt on his arm. God knows what else was beneath his pressed polo shirt.

'Tried to book it, but the tech wasn't working for me…'

'Yes, sorry about that. We're fixing it. But I'll set up scuba diving for you, no problem.'

As I watched him walk away, I had a stray thought that one of my former colleagues at the Clement Hong Kong might have intel on Eddie. He'd been a guest when I was working there. Was the assault charge his first crime or were there more? Wenjing, the gossip-hound of the housekeeping department, would probably know. Except, to call her would send up a flare to Nathan about my location. I didn't want that.

I'd been so busy, I'd made no progress on investigating Moxham's murder. Though I'd loaded a bunch of his covert audio recordings onto my phone, there were hours of them and I hadn't had time to listen to much of it. Could there be more from Eddie on those recordings? For that matter, could the recordings reveal something about Brady? The mysterious text messages from Andrew Whatshisname were still bugging me. But when I'd told Diara about them last night, she'd been unimpressed.

'Evidence,' she'd said. 'We need cold, hard facts.'

Our plan had been to spend the day working on our time-line of events, asking a few delicate questions of staff members who'd been working the Alice party. Instead, Diara was fighting chaos at the spa, and I was contemplating flying to Florida and beating Tech-Support Zack over the head with a giant foam mallet.

I radioed Reggie about organising a scuba diving trip for Eddie and sought refuge in the storeroom. It was overcrowded with dusty boxes, but it had two distinct advantages. One, the air-conditioning made it feel like a snow day in London. Two, the guests couldn't find me in here.

I slumped onto a crate labelled 'Manuka honey' and drew my phone from my pocket. In the time since my last call to Zack, I'd received another four missed calls from guests with problems I was supposed to fix.

Diara might think Brady's text messages were a distraction, but I was convinced they were a clue. I pulled up Google on my phone. What was the name of the guy who'd been texting Brady? Andrew Reiss-something. I googled a few variations, until I hit upon: *New York City, Andrew Reisslenger*. In pictures, he had a brown Caesar haircut and a straight-line smile. He was a lawyer, working for a firm with a name like Boring Borington and Boringdale Associates.

The text messages could be business-related. *Play it cool, don't show your hand, they can't prove you're bluffing*. If Brady was in negotiations to buy an island of his own, he might be strategising with his lawyer, Andrew. Or the messages could be proof of his guilt. Brady was a murderer who knew he was about to be arrested. His lawyer was counselling him not to incriminate himself.

I continued scrolling through the search results. Apparently, Andrew was also an author. *Order in Court, Faith in My Heart: A Lawyer's Journey Back to Christ*. Jesus. I'd have to buy that one for the next time I needed help getting to sleep.

A glance at his book showed that Andrew had, in the past, drunk too much, dabbled in drugs, had premarital sex. It sounded like a good time. However, he'd found God now and God had forgiven him.

I returned to his law firm's website. On impulse, I hovered over the phone number. I checked my watch. Mid-afternoon.

We were in the same time zone as New York. Fuck it. I'd ask the man himself.

As I listened to my phone dial out, my heart rate quickened. What the hell was I going to say? *Hello, are you Brady's lawyer? Do you think he's dangerous?*

A receptionist answered in two rings.

'Andrew Reisslenger, please,' I said.

'What is it regarding?'

'I'm… looking for representation. Andrew came personally recommended to me.'

I tensed, anticipating more questions from the receptionist. Instead, there was a click and the phone was ringing again.

'Andrew Reisslenger.' He had a nasal voice. I imagined him reclining in a chair in his cubicle. Cubicle? I mentally relocated him to an office with a window, the Empire State Building perched next to his ear.

'Hello, my name is' – I cast around for ideas – 'Sophie Sea… more, Seymore.' I cringed. It wasn't quite Jane Palm-Tree, but it was close. 'I'm looking for representation.'

'You've come to the right place. What's the trouble, Ms Seymore?'

'Got myself into a sticky situation.'

'Sorry to hear that. Can you go into any detail?'

'Probably not over the phone. You know. To be on the safe side.' I had to choke down a laugh. God, I should be better at subterfuge.

'OK…' Andrew said. I could hear the frown in his voice. Maybe he thought this was a prank call.

'Could you tell me a bit about your services?' I asked.

That set Andrew off on what was clearly a well-practised spiel. It turned out he specialised in contract law. Yawn.

'You sound like a good Christian man,' I said, when he paused for breath.

'Thank you. Are you a follower of Jesus Christ?'

'Absolutely. You know, I think we might have a friend in common?' A giggle slipped out. 'Apart from Jesus, I mean.'

'New York's a small town... although you sound like you're from a ways away. You from England?'

'Mmm, good guess.' I made my tone kittenish. 'It was actually Brady who recommended you. Brady Calloway.'

'Brady.' Andrew's voice went flat. 'How do you know Brady?'

'Socially. But you two are tight, right?'

Andrew released a noisy breath. 'Haven't heard from him in years.'

'Oh...' *Why are you lying to me, Andrew?* 'I thought...'

There was a rustle and I heard the laughter and conversation of an office setting, as if Andrew had pulled the phone away from his ear. 'Sorry, I gotta go.'

Click.

I lowered my own phone. That was weird. Andrew was chummy enough with Brady to be texting with him, but he acted like the two barely knew each other. What motive did he have to lie?

I redialled the number of the law firm, but the receptionist told me Andrew was in a meeting all day.

My phone lit up in my hand.

'Well,' I said, taking the call, 'if it isn't my best friend, Zack.'

*

That evening, the sun was low in the sky as I slipped onto a stool at the tiki bar. Close by, one of the hosts, Maria – petite, baby-faced, with blue streaks in her black hair – was filling the pools with floating tea lights. Guillaume was preparing an actual suckling pig for dinner and the smell of it wafted over to me. I put my head down on the wooden bar. God, I could sleep right here.

'Something to drink?'

I looked up to see Ethan passing with a wine bottle in his hands. Dinner service was getting started at the nearby restaurant, talk and laughter creating a background hum.

'Painkiller,' I said. He darted away to make it, but I called after him. 'Joking! Just a pineapple juice. Thanks.'

When my juice appeared, it was all dolled up like a cocktail, with a tiny umbrella and a maraschino cherry, which I plucked out and ate straight away. I slipped the damp cocktail napkin from beneath the glass and scrounged up a biro from my pocket.

Evidence. Cold, hard facts. Diara was right. I was getting distracted by going down rabbit holes. I needed things I could prove.

On the napkin, I wrote:

Timeline of events:
10 p.m.: Moxham visits Villa Queen Conch to see Lola.
12 a.m.?: Moxham on Main Beach, hurries off because he's late for something. Fireworks.
7 a.m.: Body discovered.

It wasn't much. Moxham had said he was late for a very important date. I'd assumed he was making a joke about *Alice in Wonderland*, but what if he was actually meeting someone?

I racked my brains for memories of that night. There'd been a person running down the beach, hadn't there? That was strange.

Later that night, I'd woken up to a light on the water. I was convinced it was a boat. Disposing of Moxham's body perhaps? What time had that been? Three o'clock, maybe? I added both incidents to the timeline.

Diara arrived, leaning on my shoulder to look at what I was writing. 'Ready to go?'

'Almost.' I took a final slug of my drink. 'How's the spa?'

'Nightmare.' She hid a yawn behind her fist.

An hour ago, Tech-Support Zack had assured me he'd fixed the problem, except only 50 per cent of the system worked. I couldn't bring myself to care anymore. Diara and I were going to spend the evening interviewing as many people as we could.

'Hey, what do you remember about that night?' I slid off my stool and shoved the napkin in my pocket.

She shrugged. 'I was working. Went home.'

'But you were at the party? The staff one by the pool.' It occurred to me that I hadn't seen Diara after her collapse into the fern.

'Only for an hour or so.'

'Didn't see anything?'

'Nope.'

I was delicate enough not to mention that she'd been drunk as a skunk. No wonder she didn't remember much.

Diara cracked a smile. 'Sorry to disappoint you.'

'Hope the other witnesses are better than you,' I said, raising an eyebrow.

24

'What's this about?' Tessa folded her arms across her skinny body.

Villa Copper was blissfully cool and smelled like fresh flowers (and a little air-freshener, shh). I sneaked the thermostat down a couple more notches, to feel the air-conditioning turn Arctic.

'The Alice party,' I said. 'Where were you that night?'

Diara and I had tracked down Tessa in the middle of sunset turndown. This was one of the more tedious host duties, involving spot-cleaning, tidying away the guests' belongings and preparing their beds for sleep. When we'd arrived, Tessa had been doing none of those things. She'd been snapping selfies.

'I was working,' she said. 'Everyone thinks I don't work—'

'Who said that? I know you're a soldier.' I managed to keep a straight face with effort. 'That's why I came to you, I knew you'd remember everything that happened that night.'

Behind her, out the floor-length windows, the sun was setting over the waves.

'Told you, I was working.' Tessa pushed out her bottom lip. 'Am I in trouble?'

'No, no, I just need to know about that night because…'

'Fizzy,' Diara said. 'Doing an investigation into Moxham's death. For the insurance company or something.'

We'd come up with this cover story, hoping insurance stuff was boring enough that no one would question it. Tessa, however, didn't look satisfied.

'What did she say?' Her voice rose. 'Talking absolute shite, like always. I told her, I was getting my sweatshirt. Left it in there. Needed it back.'

'What?'

Trying to follow a conversation with Tessa was like trying to reason with my niece.

Her cheeks had gone pink. 'She's never liked me, probably 'cause Kip thinks I'm cute. She's jealous.'

Ah, yes, few knew the pain of being a pretty young woman. Diara flicked a miniature eye roll in my direction and I smothered a laugh. It had been at least twenty-four hours since Tessa had last threatened to quit; we were overdue another meltdown.

'Did you notice anything weird that night?' I prompted Tessa.

Since she wasn't making a start on turndown, I shook out the bed sheets and began pleating the top sheet in the Keeper-mandated pattern. Villa Copper was Brady's villa; it was tempting to imagine him slipping, naked, between these sheets. I had a wild urge to rifle through his possessions, partly for clues, but partly because I was curious. I wanted to know what type of underwear he wore, to spray his cologne, to uncover any embarrassing quirks, like a collection of tacky gold bracelets.

'Well.' Tessa watched me work but didn't move to help. 'I heard shouting in the village. That was kinda weird.'

'What time?'

'I don't know, eleven, maybe earlier. I went back to my room, wanted to call my boyfriend back in Dublin. He's dealing with a family thing. And it's not like I was gone for ages. I was back at the beach by half-past, totally on top of my work—'

'Who was shouting?' I tucked in the end of the bed and smoothed a hand over the sheet.

'Dunno, it was over quick. Sounded like a woman.'

'There's always someone shouting in the village,' Diara said. 'You see anything else?'

Tessa guffawed. 'I saw Reggie running along the beach, round about midnight, he was proper sprinting. His shorts kept falling down, so he was basically mooning us.'

'Reggie? He was running?' I asked. 'Are you sure?'

The running man was one of the few clues I had. I'd hoped, inanely, that I might have seen the murderer in pursuit of Moxham.

'I'm not blind, he went straight past me.'

*

'We need to find Reggie, find out why he was running,' I said to Diara, as we were leaving Villa Copper.

'Probably a prank.'

All the golf carts were in use, so we returned to the main complex on foot. Diara was using a long-stemmed torch to light the way. Somehow the torch made it creepier than if we'd been walking in pure darkness. The light bouncing off trees and ferns made everything look alive, ready to pounce on us.

'What about the shouting Tessa heard?' I asked.

Diara shrugged. 'Can't look for boogeymen everywhere.'

Actually, I was inclined to do exactly that. Then something else occurred to me.

'Dublin's in the same time zone as London.'

'If you say so...' Diara squinted out a smile.

'Tessa said she was on the phone to her boyfriend at eleven. It would have been, like, three in the morning in Dublin.'

'Maybe he was up late. Maybe she was slacking off and wanted an excuse. You're jumping to conclusions again.'

I sighed. 'Yeah.'

Reggie, as it turned out, had gone off-island and was due to return from Tortola in the next hour. While we waited, Diara and I looked elsewhere for interviewees.

Guillaume was in the kitchen. It was peak dinner rush. His face was sweaty and his chef's whites had dark, smiley-face stains under his armpits.

'Everyone thinks parties are a great time, but I did not have a great time,' Guillaume said, when I brought it up. 'I have to make fucking jam tarts into haute cuisine. This bunny party, it is gauche.'

I made an *mmm* noise and tried to look sympathetic.

'As soon as I finish the food for the party,' Guillaume was saying, 'people are going back to their villas and ordering room service. It is a nightmare. Kip, he order crispy veal and then leave it on his doorstep.'

'His doorstep?'

'The waiter tells me he doesn't even open the door. The veal is still there the next morning. *Merde, merde, merde.*'

The exasperation was reverberating off Guillaume. I glanced at Diara, who raised her eyebrows. Guillaume had already thrown a hissy fit today over an inadequate seafood order, lobbing handfuls of mussels at the wall.

Is this crazy-French-chef thing an act, or are you really this ridiculous? I wanted to ask, but it was no use upsetting Guillaume further. We said our goodbyes and hastened out of the kitchen, onto the restaurant floor.

'Why would Kip order room service and not even bother to eat it?' I asked Diara, under my breath.

Diara clicked her tongue. 'You met these people, right?'

'Alright, alright. But maybe he was busy doing something else.'

'We got too many suspects, that's the problem.'

'What a problem to have.'

*

In the dining room, I was flagged down by Mrs Park and spent an hour hearing about her 'wellness' philosophy, which sounded suspiciously like a cult to me. It was past eleven by the time I persuaded her to go to bed.

Diara had been mixing with the bartenders and waiters; her eyelids were drooping. 'Let's do this another time.'

'We'll just talk to a couple more people,' I said, feeling left out.

'Make it quick.'

Now that the restaurant floor had cleared out, Ethan was bent over a table, dark hair falling in his face, as he set out cutlery for tomorrow's breakfast service. Tyson from the kitchen, with his red bandana tied around sweaty hair, was refilling salt shakers.

'I was fucking slammed,' Ethan said, when I asked about the night in question. 'Right through till one, even though most of the staff had fucked off to their own party.'

Tyson gave a guilty guffaw. I grabbed a handful of napkins and began folding them into lilies.

'What else do you remember?' I asked.

Ethan huffed out a sigh. It must have been a gruelling dinner shift. 'That Brady guy wanted tequila, and not the regular stuff, so I had to go to the storeroom. I was busy, dude.' With a clatter, he grabbed another handful of forks. 'Why does it matter?'

'Dickhead, she's your boss,' Diara said. 'Answer her questions.'

Ethan blanched but didn't apologise. 'I already talked to Tessa, I know you're sniffing out deets, how Moxham ended up kaput.'

'It's for an insurance—'

'Yeah, yeah, I don't give a shit.' Ethan flicked his nose ring distractedly. 'If you want the truth, I saw someone skulking around that night.'

My ears pricked up. Diara's back straightened.

'Who?' I asked.

'Didn't see his face, but he was tall.'

'Was it Moxham?' I asked.

'No, he was *tall*. Like, well over six feet. I was on my way to Hidden Cove.' Ethan folded a napkin, evading my gaze. 'Two o'clock in the morning, maybe. There was someone lurking near the pier. He clocked me, stepped behind a tree. That struck me as pretty fucking weird. Why didn't he want me to see him?'

'Why were you going to Hidden Cove, mate?' Tyson asked.

'Don't need a reason,' Ethan said.

'Out for a little night-time stroll, eh?'

Ethan whipped him with a napkin. 'Fuck off.'

'What were you really doing?' I asked.

Ethan's lip curled. Diara pulled at my arm. 'Leave it,' she said to me.

*

Later, as we were walking back to the staff village, Diara explained. 'Only one reason you go to Hidden Cove after dark, and that's to hook up.'

'Who's he hooking up with?' I asked.

'Tessa.'

'Tessa with the boyfriend in Dublin?'

'Everyone who comes here has a boyfriend and they always break up. Get swept up in something new. Tessa right on schedule. That's probably why she was lying about calling her boyfriend.'

The bush was creepy at night and I was glad to reach the village, with its lit windows and reggae beats floating from the team bar. Before I could ask Diara more about Tessa and Ethan, she called out, 'Reggie!'

His springy head of hair popped upwards. Reggie was seated on the tree-stump bench, nursing a beer. When Diara beckoned him, he came ambling over. Not for the first time, I noticed how tall he was. As head of the water sports team, wouldn't Reggie be the most likely to be lurking near the pier?

'Why you mooning everyone?' Diara asked him.

Reggie twisted around to look at the seat of his shorts, as if he might have forgotten to get dressed. 'Whatcha talking about, woman?'

I recounted what Tessa had said, about him running along the beach the night of Moxham's death.

'Me ain't mooning!' Reggie made a puppy dog face, as if hurt by the implication. 'Running for the fireworks.'

'What time you set them off?' Diara asked.

'Not late, not really. Ten past midnight, absolute latest.'

Apropos nothing, he began complaining about Fizzy, who, according to him, didn't do anything she was supposed to do and spent all her time fussing with crystals. I steered the conversation back to the night in question.

'Someone saw you at the pier,' I said, improvising. 'About 2 a.m.?'

'Nooo, no. I was there earlier. Hadda drop the steel drum band back on VG, but that was early… ten-thirty or so.'

'You weren't there at two?'

'Nah, we were limin' hard. Over by the pool. Drinks, music, good times.' He nudged me, his Jamaican accent thickening. 'You was there! Dee so drunk, she pick up a coaster instead of her phone.'

A muscle in Diara's cheek twitched. I grinned at her discomfort and then made an effort to stop.

'A coaster!' Reggie roared with laughter.

Diara swiped at him. 'Not that funny.'

Reggie swaggered away in the direction of the team bar, still laughing to himself. His shorts were baggy, drooping low on his hips, as if they might fall off at any moment.

'Reggie no criminal mastermind, London.' Diara gave me a thin smile. 'Now we cleared that up, I'm going to bed.'

I should have felt exhausted, but I was wide awake. I wasn't completely ready to let Reggie go.

'Night.' I took a couple of backwards steps away from her. 'I'm gonna grab a new shampoo from the commissary.'

The commissary was a tiny store cupboard in the staff village; you were supposed to leave money in an honesty box, but Diara had told me no one ever did. I skipped right past it, into the shabby team bar. Reggie was popping open another bottle of beer.

'Couple more questions,' I said breathlessly. 'About Moxham.'

'This is an insurance thing, right?' Reggie squinted at me. 'Hope his family gets some money or something. Doesn't make up for it, but… shit, I don't know.'

He was the first person today who'd expressed sorrow that Moxham was gone.

'D'you know if Moxham was seeing anyone?' I asked, imagining Hidden Cove in the moonlight.

'Ah.' Reggie took a long pull on his beer. 'You know he was sweet on Diara.'

I nodded, like, *sure, sure, common knowledge*, but my heart was pounding. Recalling the photo of the two of them on social media, I was eager to hear more about this.

'He was so hot for her. Like a puppet on a string. Roses in her room on her birthday, that kind of shit.' He laughed. 'Dat ain't impress her. You know Dee.'

A room full of roses. I had a vague memory of Moxham doing the same thing for his girlfriend, Violet, back in Hong Kong. It had already occurred to me that this could this be the real reason Diara had agreed to help me investigate. Now I wondered if she missed him, if she wanted justice for him.

I pressed Reggie further about the staff party by the pool. Could he remember exactly who else was in attendance? Not really. There was a wrestling match going on. People were popping in and out, their movements lost to a cloud of smoke.

I said goodnight to Reggie and wandered back to my room. It was dim inside: no lights on. Diara's covers were pulled up over her face, only the edge of her bonnet visible. Her breathing was slow and even.

On her nightstand, her phone lit up. I couldn't resist glancing at the message that appeared on the lock screen.

Elizabeth: Goodnight sleep well x

Diara's phone dulled to black. I crossed the room. My bed gave a squeak as I sank onto it.

Who was Elizabeth? I ran through a mental list of people on the island, but I couldn't place an Elizabeth. Maybe it was a relative over on Virgin Gorda.

There was a scuttle nearby, which I tried to ignore. We'd had an ant infestation yesterday. Diara maintained that it was best to let the lizards eat them, but their tiny dinosaur bodies still freaked me out worse than the bugs.

Sweat was beading on my forehead. It was too damn hot; I wouldn't be able to sleep. From my pocket, I pulled out the white cocktail napkin, creased and curling at the edges. I filled in some of the gaps:

Timeline of events:

9 p.m.: Dinner over; Kip goes back to his villa, orders room service.

10 p.m.: Moxham visits Villa Queen Conch to see Lola.

11 p.m.: Tessa hears shouting in the staff village.

11:45 p.m.: Moxham on Main Beach, hurries off because he's late for something.

12:05 a.m.: Reggie running down the beach.

12:10 a.m.: Fireworks.

2 a.m.: Ethan sees a figure lurking near the pier.

3 a.m.: Boat on water.

7 a.m.: Body discovered.

I sat hunched in the darkness, going over and over the timeline by the light of my phone.

Who was shouting in the village? Who was the tall man near the pier?

At the memorial bonfire, Tyson had said he and Moxham used to play dares. I'd got the impression from their stories that it had been something of a boys' club between him and Ethan and Reggie. Could any of them have been Moxham's accomplice?

For that matter, could I discount Diara? She and Moxham had obviously been closer than I'd imagined. What else was she hiding?

From across the room, she let out a snore. *They're all back-stabbers. You'll see.* Those had been Moxham's final words to me.

Diara and I weren't really friends; I barely knew her. The thought stirred a feeling of loneliness in me. I turned off my phone-torch and burrowed under the covers, into the blackness. I could feel the hard edges of the USB drives where I'd hidden them inside my pillowcase.

If only I could know exactly where Moxham had gone after our last conversation. Who had he been meeting?

I cursed Kip for deleting all the files from his devices. Maybe it had only been an overzealous digital deep-clean, but I couldn't shake the feeling that, if I could look at Moxham's emails, his text messages, I'd have the key to his murder.

25

The couple from San Francisco was getting married. It was my job to make sure we didn't get swept away to sea. Literally.

My bare feet sank into the sand as I measured out the size of the islet. It was seventy-six of my feet in length, and forty-eight in width. By the time I hit forty-nine, the tide was lapping over my toes. Seagulls laughed overhead. I strained to see the nearest landmass, which was nothing more than a green hump at this distance. Now that the speedboat had disappeared, the howl of the wind sounded louder, more ominous.

'Is this safe?' I asked Ethan, who was kneeling on one of the beach carpets, trying to pin it down.

'What?' He sat back on his haunches, raking a sweaty lock of dark hair off his forehead. The corner of the carpet whipped up in the wind.

There were a dozen chairs for the guests. They were arranged on either side of an aisle, created by thirty giant conch shells, which had been motored over from the Keeper storeroom.

'I feel like the tide's gonna wash us away.' I forced a smile, like I was teasing, but I was deadly serious.

When I'd heard the Keeper resort offered intimate weddings on nearby Seashell Island, I'd imagined something similar to Anegada, with its beach bars selling lobster tail. Instead, we were encircled by water, on a strip of sand the size of my Hong Kong apartment. It didn't even have a palm tree in the centre, like it would if it were a child's drawing. I stooped to pick up a tiny seashell. The islet might be better named Desolation Island.

'Not till eight,' Ethan said. 'Hand me that lantern?'

I did as requested, then set about decorating the wedding arch with fresh flowers. This morning, I'd seen another alert online about the brewing storm, which would theoretically (although not definitely) miss the BVI. Oh well, if we were going to die stranded out here, I should make sure the happy couple had a hell of a wedding first.

The bride was due to sail in during golden hour, which meant the rest of the guests would need to be seated within thirty minutes.

The roar of a boat engine swelled closer. Reggie and Fizzy arrived with the last of the supplies, plus a steel drum trio to accompany the bride down the aisle.

'Gorgeous… gorgeous…' Fizzy would be performing the ceremony, because she was an internet-ordained minister (of course she was).

I waded into the water, leaning into the boat to grab two bottles of champagne from their case. 'Fizzy, grab the rest for me?'

Fizzy's lip curled. She was looking at the champagne like it was poison. 'I need to practise my speech.' She turned and swept away, bracelets jangling.

'Well, OK then,' I said under my breath.

I unloaded the last of the supplies and Reggie sped away to collect the guests. As I ran around, stopping carpets and flowers and even the wedding arch itself from blowing away, I was aware I was the only one who seemed concerned. Ethan was on his phone, while Fizzy was staring out to sea, lips churning silently through a monologue.

There was a buzz against my thigh. My work phone. It reminded me it had rung earlier while I'd been chasing decorative palm leaves across the sand. I pulled it out.

The call was from Allie: the only person from the real world who had my work number.

I was about to answer it when there came the rumble of the approaching bowrider. It was Reggie with the guests. I declined the call and turned my phone to silent.

As soon as Reggie jumped off the boat with a splash, I knew something was wrong. His grin was too large, too rigid. I rushed to his side, producing a fake-grin of my own. 'What?' I whispered.

'The bride, she not coming.'

'Like… cold feet or…' I mopped at the sweat trickling from my brow.

Perhaps the bride had realised that being trapped on a deserted islet with one other person was a terrifying metaphor for wedlock and decided to flee.

Reggie's eyes were bulging. 'I don't know.'

My phone vibrated again.

'Oh, shit…' I aimed another grin at the guests, who were climbing down off the boat, assisted by Ethan. 'Don't worry, I'll come back with you, sort it out.'

Reggie and I left Ethan and Fizzy with the guests and returned to Keeper Island. As we rocketed across the waves, the wind thundering against my eardrums, I pulled out my phone.

There was a message from Allie: *I'm freaking out, call me back.*

Was this a real emergency or an Allie emergency? An Allie emergency was 'someone looked at me weird on the Tube,' or, 'I saw a dead pigeon in the park.' I loved my beautiful, sensitive sister, but she could be a lot to handle.

I dashed off a message – *call later, love you* – and returned to thinking about my runaway bride.

*

During the ceremony – which took place at sunset, rather than golden hour – we all pretended not to notice that the bride had been crying. She was beaming now, but her make-up showed signs of wear and tear. We pretended not to worry that the arch, swaying in the breeze, was about to bolt upwards and fly away. We pretended not to watch the tide lap in, soaking the beach carpets and shrinking the islet.

By the time Reggie whisked away the newly-weds and their guests in the bowrider, I had a pounding headache. In the dimming light, I dragged myself down the aisle on hands and knees, rolling up sodden carpets. A bouquet of pink-and-white flowers unhooked itself from the arch and hurtled away, skimming the waves before it disappeared.

Fizzy was circling the islet with hands clasped. 'Wonderful, wonderful, absolutely magical.' She kept saying it on repeat, like a talking doll that had got stuck.

I pulled out my phone to check that no one from Keeper had called me. Six missed calls. All of them from Allie. Wrinkling my brow, I collapsed onto the sand and hit redial.

'Allie, what's wrong?'

'Nathan?' Allie's voice was an octave higher than usual. 'Nathan's your boyfriend?'

'What?'

'This guy named Nathan, he called me. Says he's your boyfriend, he needs to find you.' Allie's voice was strained, the words tumbling out. 'He was – he said – he kept asking – oh, my God, I was trying to call you and you didn't answer and I'm freaking out—'

'Slow down, OK?' When Allie didn't react, I said, louder, 'Tell me what happened.'

Out of the corner of my eye, I saw Fizzy's head jerk. I clambered to my feet and turned away, traipsing to the other side of the islet. The last thing I wanted was Fizzy overhearing my conversation.

'Is this the same guy from Hong Kong?' Allie asked. 'He got really aggro on the phone. He was screaming. Flora could hear him, she started crying.'

'Stop, stop…' It sounded like Allie was crying too.

I'd fled so far from Fizzy that I'd run out of dry land. Water slapped at my calves.

'Start at the beginning,' I said. 'What did he say exactly?'

'He wanted to know where you were.'

My whole body stiffened, but I tried not to let it show in my voice. 'What did you say?'

Twilight was almost gone. The sea was turning black.

'He thought you were here. He kept asking. Finally I had to say you were in the Caribbean. I thought that would be the end of it.'

Shit, shit, shit. 'Did you tell him the name of the island?'

'No, I couldn't remember it…'

'Good, that's good.' Thank Christ. Finally, my sister's forgetful nature came through for me.

'That's when he started shouting. I hung up on him—'

'Good.'

'—but he called back. He wouldn't stop calling. I blocked him, but he called from a different number.'

There was a ringing in my ears. It was louder than the wind. I took another two steps into the sea and a wave rocked against me.

'You'll have to change your number.'

'He scared me, he really scared me…'

'I'm sorry, Allie, I'm sorry.'

'He was talking about a man who died. Someone died… I don't understand…'

I tried to take a deep breath, but my heart had swelled to fill my entire chest.

'Allie, Allie, listen to me. Get a new phone, I'll pay. Forget about him.'

'He said he was coming to London. He said he'd come to my flat. I don't want to see him!'

'He doesn't know where you live. He can't.'

How had Nathan got Allie's number? It was possible I'd left it lying around for him to find. It was also possible he'd paid an investigator. Shit. If he'd found Allie's number, he could also find her address.

'Oh God, Flora's crying again. I have to go.'

'OK, OK, tell Flora I love her. Allie, listen to me…'

There was only silence on the other end of the line. She was gone.

I wanted to call her back, make her tell me exactly what Nathan had said, but it would only upset her more. I took a few panting breaths. Nathan could be on his way to London right now. Would he do that? Would he go that far?

As I'd learned two weeks ago, I had no idea how far Nathan would go.

There was a tap on my shoulder. I jerked away, splashing sideways.

'Are you OK?' Fizzy asked.

'Fine, fine.'

In the dregs of twilight, her face was shadowy.

'Who was that on the phone?'

'My sister. It's fine.'

'Come out of the water, you're getting wet.'

I let her lead me onto dry sand. She'd got wet as well, the hem of her floral maxi-dress drenched.

'Sit down a minute, catch your breath.' Her voice was so sweet, I tried to detect sarcasm in it.

'I need to…' I gestured, wavering on my feet. 'The arch, the chairs—'

'We'll do all that. You take a minute.'

I wanted to argue, but I worried I might fall over if I didn't sit down. I sank onto the sand, pulling my knees up to my chest.

There was sand stuck to my soles. The sandpaper feeling helped, in a weird way; a reminder that I was here, in the Caribbean, and not back in Hong Kong. I concentrated hard on pulling in breath after breath. One, two, three, four, five. I imagined Diara counting.

Occasionally, Fizzy's voice filtered through my stupor. She was directing Ethan in the clean-up, clicking her tongue when he wasn't quick enough. There was the sound of an engine and I raised my head. It was Reggie. I tried to get up and help with loading everything into the boat, but my legs were wobbly.

'Lola's a little sick, shouldn't be on a boat right now.' Fizzy's voice floated over to me. 'Come back and get us on the next trip.'

I wanted to protest, but Fizzy was right. If I rode on the speedboat right now, I'd puke my guts out.

A tangle of chairs and half a dozen carpets, rolled tight, remained in the centre of the islet, like the centrepiece on a cake. Ethan climbed aboard with the rest of the wedding decorations. The boat disappeared almost instantly into the near-dark, although the ghostly drone of the engine remained for several seconds more.

Fizzy wafted over, smelling fragrantly herbal. She sat down beside me and rearranged her dress over her knees. 'Do you get a lot of panic attacks?'

On the darkening horizon, there were a few twinkling lights from a faraway island, but otherwise nothing.

'World closing in?' Fizzy said. 'Feel like you're dying?'

'Sounds familiar,' I mumbled.

'Wanna talk about it?'

'Not at all.'

The water was nibbling at my toes, so I shifted back a metre. Fizzy moved with me. A glance over my shoulder confirmed that the islet had shrunk to less than half the size it had been when we'd arrived.

'How long till this island disappears?' I asked.

'Another hour, don't worry.'

'I love it when people tell you not to worry, it's always so effective.' I sounded like a petulant teenager, but I didn't care.

Fizzy pulled something from her pocket. Her bracelets jingled as she shook a pill into her palm. 'Make you feel better.' She extended her hand.

I hesitated. The wind breathed a huge gust and my T-shirt rippled.

'It'll calm you down,' she said.

I took the pill and dry-swallowed it.

'Is your sister OK?' Fizzy asked.

'No.' I barked out a laugh. 'And it's my fault. Always my fault.'

'I'm sure that's not true.'

I couldn't be bothered to respond and sifted a handful of sand instead. The wind whipped the grains away from me. What the hell was I going to do about Nathan? Should I go back to London? Find a new flat for Allie, a new school for Flora?

'My ex...' I'd been quiet for long enough that Fizzy's head bobbed up when I spoke. 'He's looking for me.' I dragged in a breath. 'Calling my sister in London, I don't know how he got her number.'

'Who is he? The ex?'

My breathing turned ragged again, but thanks to the pill the panic felt more distant this time, as if someone had draped a veil over me, like a bird in a cage.

'Can't talk about it,' I muttered.

'Here.' Fizzy swept her black hair over one shoulder and pulled a necklace up over her head. I hadn't even known she was wearing it, the pendant nestled against her chest. Now she reached over, uncurled my fingers and pressed it into my palm. The crystal was warm and jagged. It appeared colourless in the dim light, but looking closer, there was a hint of pink.

Before I could say anything, she began to murmur under her breath. 'This fear, I accept it, I release it and I let it go.'

She turned my hand over and tapped the edge of my forefinger with the crystal. 'Say it. This fear, I accept it, I release it and I let it go.'

I squeezed my eyes shut. I'd been denying it, but I was petrified.

'I accept it,' I whispered. 'I release it and I let it go.'

The only light came from the moon. The sand glowed white, but Fizzy was swathed in shadow. I hoped she wouldn't be able to see my tears.

'You know,' she said softly, 'I have a contact at the airport on Beef Island.'

I made a *huh?* sound.

'I used to get him to send me passenger lists. I knew everyone who was arriving.'

My fist was still clenched around the crystal, its hard edges digging into my palm.

'It was my night-time reading,' Fizzy said. 'When I couldn't sleep, I'd read those passenger lists. Check his name wasn't on there.'

I swivelled around to face Fizzy, but it was too dark to see her expression. Her voice was calm, eerily so.

'I did it for years,' she said. 'Years and years of thinking about him. Even when he was in prison in New York, I'd imagine him doing a jailbreak, getting on a plane. Showing up in the BVI, looking for me.'

'Who?'

'My ex.' Fizzy waved a hand, like she was brushing him away. Her bracelets shot down her arm with a clatter. 'A bad ex.'

'Ah.'

'After a while, you're not scared of the person, you're locked up inside your own head.'

'... I'm sorry' was all I could manage.

'Don't be sorry. It was just a moment in time. Kip would always tell me, Keeper Island's the safest place in the world. It took me a long time to believe him. Now I think he's right. There's something about it that's magical, a little cocoon against an unforgiving world.'

'What did he do? The ex?'

'Oh... he loved me, I suppose. Loved me too much.' Fizzy lifted up her hair, angling her long neck. 'I have a scar here. It's too dark, you probably can't see.' She let her hair fall. 'He broke a wine bottle, said he was going to slit my throat because I flirted with one of his friends. He said sorry afterwards though. He was world-class at apologies. So sweet, so tender.'

'Shit. You said he's in prison?'

'Oh, no.' She gave a tinkling laugh. 'Not anymore. He's a reformed character. They made him swear, Scout's honour, he wouldn't torture any other girls.'

I thought about putting an arm around her, but her posture was stiff.

'I'm sorry.'

'Me too. Meredith used to tell me, you never know how strong you are until someone tries to break you.'

It was one of those stock phrases that would have made me roll my eyes usually, but right now it made me want to scream and weep. All these vibrant women in the world, beaten to a pulp by their men, saying affirmations to try and renew themselves.

'What was Meredith like?' I asked.

'Meredith?'

'I wondered... if she was... if someone broke her.'

Had Kip terrorised Meredith the same way Fizzy's ex had terrorised her?

There was a long silence. The tide had caught us again, swilling over my feet, soaking the edge of Fizzy's dress. I didn't move and neither did she.

'I always thought it was brave,' Fizzy said at last. 'I don't think I could do it.'

'What?'

'She was decisive. I admired that about her. It got too much, so she ended it.'

'She... she what?'

Fizzy's voice was matter of fact. 'She killed herself.'

'Oh, my God.'

'Sorry, I shouldn't talk about it. Kip likes to think of it as an accident. He finds it easier that way.'

'What happened?' I managed.

'She had her reasons, I'm sure. Kip's not a perfect man. There were... women. Whatever the reason, she made the decision. There's something beautiful about it, don't you think? Her way of reclaiming herself. Slipping into the water.' She sighed. 'For a while, she was lost. It was a relief to get the ID from Caracas.'

I kicked my feet into the wet sand, submerging them in the tide. After my first conversation with Diara about Meredith, I'd done some research online. Apparently, if bodies in these waters weren't recovered quickly, they could be attacked by sharks. Was that a beautiful ending?

'Fizzy, are you OK?'

'I'm wonderful.' I caught the flash of white teeth. She was smiling.

'Do you still check the flight lists?'

The distant whine of an engine drifted towards us. I unclenched my fist and dropped the crystal into her lap.

'Sometimes.' There was a hint of mischief in her voice, like we were schoolgirls playing hooky. 'I'll send them to you if you like.'

Was that even legal? To access passenger lists?

Fizzy swung the necklace over her head. I rubbed my arms. I had an itchy feeling. She and I had too much in common. I didn't want to be like her, terrified in the middle of the night, poring over the lists, looking for Nathan's name. It was a kind of suicide, to live like that.

I needed to stop hiding from him.

A light was bobbing through the blackness. The sound of the engine intensified. The boat was here to collect us.

26

In my room, I lay flat on my back, arms crossed like a corpse. A piece of obsidian was between my eyes. It was mid-morning and the heat was building, thickening the air. I was trying to breathe long and smooth, but I felt like I was on the verge of another panic attack.

Fizzy had left the crystal as a gift for me. It gleamed like gunmetal. *Obsidian protects against negative energy*, the pink Post-it in her handwriting had read.

Earlier this morning, Allie had called me from her new phone. She'd sounded calmer. She was getting extra locks fitted on her doors and windows.

I sat up. The crystal bounced into my lap. I reached for my phone. It was my personal phone, rather than my work phone, and I usually kept it switched off in my bottom drawer. Now I turned it on and accessed the list of blocked contacts.

Blood roared in my ears. The ringing at the other end of the line went on for such a long time, I thought he wasn't going to answer.

'Lola.' He sounded hoarse.

'Hi.' I couldn't help it, I was crying. 'I missed you.'

*

The trouble started with an IKEA table.

I regretted ordering it immediately. I wasn't staying long-term in Hong Kong. My job was a stepping stone, a way into the Asian market. Like most Hong Kong apartments, my flat was minuscule: a glorified crash pad. Yet I was sick of eating meals while sprawled out on the sofa or propped against the kitchen counter. I ordered the table because I wanted a table.

In quiet moments, I pictured Nathan and me sitting there, eating breakfast, our feet kicking each other lazily.

Another job had come up last month, in Tokyo. It was a bigger hotel, more prestigious. I'd almost taken it. At the last minute, I'd said no.

Without meaning to, I'd built a life in Hong Kong. On days off, Nathan and I went to the movies or wandered the city parks. We sat in brightly lit Cha Chaan Tengs, raising our voices to be heard over the hubbub, as we slurped macaroni soup and talked about the future. We took mini-breaks to Thailand and Vietnam. Nathan's constant smiles were not an act. He was a happy person and he made me happy too.

Putting together the table was supposed to be a mindless job for my day off. It was supposed to ease my stress, not add to it. I'd forgotten that IKEA furniture was designed by sadists.

Nathan returned from a morning at the boxing gym to find me spread-eagled on the floor. I was trying to find a screw that had either gone astray or was never in the packet to begin with.

'Need help?' he asked.

I rolled over onto my back. 'I want to die.'

'OK.' Nathan crouched down. 'But instead, I will help you and you will not die.'

'God, this is humiliating.' I put my hands over my face. 'It's just a table.'

Nathan glanced at the instructions and then flicked them aside. He whistled as he arranged pieces of wood on the floor. I slumped against the end of the sofa and watched him work. The thing that bothered me most about Nathan was that he was actually smart. I'd denied that fact to myself for months. He'd left school without qualifications and become a security guard due to his muscles rather than his brain. If he was dumb, it was fine for me to have an affair with him. Whenever I got the next job offer, I could kiss him goodbye and barely think of him again.

If he was smart…

Shit, I might be in love with him.

*

On the other end of the call, there was a rasping inhalation.

'I need to see you,' Nathan said.

I squeezed the obsidian crystal, flexing and unflexing my hand.

'I can't,' I said.

'Where are you? I'll come. I'll catch a plane, I'll—'

'Stop. Please stop.'

'Lola, I did it for you, I did it for us.' He was crying; I could hear the hitch in his voice.

'I know.'

I closed my eyes and pictured the two of us sitting at the black IKEA table. It was the morning and we were eating breakfast: scrambled eggs with Hong-Kong-style French toast, oozing syrup and butter.

'I love you,' he said, 'I love you so much.'

'I love you too.'

'So come back.'

'No.'

I didn't hesitate. Nathan heard it too, the certainty in my voice. He sniffed. I imagined him dragging a hand across his face, scrubbing away the tears.

'They're not investigating it,' he said. 'I heard from someone in police. A drug deal went wrong. That's what they said.'

'Don't… we can't talk about it like this,' I said reflexively.

'Come home. We talk about it. When you come home.'

'I need a fresh start,' I said. 'You should get one too.'

'A fresh start with you?'

'No. Nathan, you need to stop. Stop calling my sister, stop looking for me. This is the end.'

'It's not the end. I love you. Love is… love makes the world go around.'

It was such a weird cliché that I laughed. Nathan laughed too, and in that moment, the last year was erased. We were back in the lobby of the Clement Hong Kong and Nathan was fanning a deck of cards in my face. *Don't you want to be amazed?*

The laughter died in my throat. 'Love isn't the problem with us.'

Nathan's voice was low. 'I'm the problem.'

Tears were building behind my eyes. I sucked in a breath and tried to swallow them down. *No, I'm the problem. I asked you to kill for me. Now I can't forgive you for that.*

'Nathan…' I took a deep breath. 'Could you help me with something?'

He grunted.

'I… I need to know if you ever heard the name Eddie Yiu?'

'Eddie Yiu.'

'You know him?'

'I heard the name.'

'Was he friends with Moxham?'

'… No.'

'Are you sure? Did Moxham screw him over in any way?'

'Why you ask?'

'It's important. Was Eddie Yiu someone with a grudge?'

'He' – Nathan released a noisy breath – 'he committed a big fraud. Before you came to Hong Kong. It was in the newspapers. Big story. But they only got him for hitting a police officer. I never met him. Moxham neither. As far as I know. It was a finance story. Famous.'

I'd been so convinced there was a link between Eddie Yiu and Moxham. Now it seemed like there wasn't one. If Eddie was already infamous in Hong Kong as a white-collar criminal, did one more leaked video of him acting crazy really matter?

Eddie as the killer would have been a neat solution. Too neat.

I lay down, head against the pillow, listening to Nathan breathe, wishing I could inhale the pine-musk scent of him. This was supposed to be my goodbye call, but I didn't want to hang up.

'What time is it there?' I asked.

'Eleven.'

'You should go to bed, huh?'

'No, I need to—'

'Go to bed. When you wake up, it'll be two years ago.'

'Lola—'

'The two years you knew me, they're gone, OK? Never happened.' Despite all my efforts, I was crying now. 'Everything with Shin, never happened. You never loved me and you never...' I mouthed the final words instead of saying them. *You never killed for me.*

'Lola—'

'Please. This is what I want. So go to bed. Turn back the clock.'

27

Keeper Island's only ATV wouldn't start.

'Motherfucking bloody hell!' I kicked the off-road vehicle, which was a piece of shit but still solid enough that I stubbed my toe.

Tessa took a step backwards, her eyes wide. 'We'll have to cancel the picnic.'

'We're not cancelling.' I danced on one foot. My toe was smarting.

It had rained in the night and the bush trail was muddy. There was no relief from the heat though. It was 11 a.m. and a thick mugginess had descended. Hosts on Keeper uttered the word *picnic* the way other people used the word *tsunami*. Over the next two hours, I learned why.

Brady, Eddie and the other guests were to enjoy a scenic picnic this lunchtime. The set-up for the picnic involved hefting not only blankets and cushions but tables and chairs. (Rich people apparently misunderstood a key part of the picnic concept.) The food was not sandwiches in wax paper but a gourmet spread of French cheeses, thyme crackers, pâté, tarts and tiny cakes.

Keeper Peak, once volcanic, now wild with forest, didn't have a steep incline, but the bush was so overgrown, it was impassable in a golf buggy. With the ATV broken, the only way to get there was a mile-and-a-half trudge up a winding trail, loaded up like a packhorse. (Tessa, unsurprisingly, made a particularly slow mule.)

At the top, the view was spectacular: to the south, the undulating foothills of Virgin Gorda with sailboats bobbing in the marina; to the north, an endless expanse of water. The zip-line tethered to the peak meant that guests could glide down the hill instead of walking. I wanted to zip away and never return, but I had a job to do. By the time I'd made the trek up the hill three times, I barely even glanced at the view. My eyes were stinging with sweat.

The only good thing about this march up and down Keeper Peak was that it gave me a chance to put in my earphones. I cued up Moxham's covert recordings. I was determined to find new evidence. Previously, I'd only managed to listen to a few minutes here and there. Now I had a chance to immerse myself in what Moxham had recorded. Most of it was numbingly boring, muffled voices and circuitous conversations, but some parts were more interesting. Disturbing, even.

'*You see the real person when you strip them down. Put a man's feet in the fire and all the artifice falls away.*'

The nasal voice who spoke was American-accented. I almost recognised it, but it wasn't Brady or anyone else I could identify. As I trudged through the bush, I was sweltering, but on the recording, the man was describing a dark winter night. On a nameless college campus, a group of students were hazing their peers.

'*It was cold, man, really cold. We'd been pouring buckets of water over the pledges, making them do burpees, stress-testing them, y'know.*

'*I remember… I remember everyone screaming with laughter. Jackals. Giving me a headache. I wanted to go home, but… we were on duty, making sure the pledges did a shot every minute. Gets you closer to heaven, that's what we'd say.*'

Moxham replied, his voice indistinct, and then the man spoke again:

'*Yeah... yeah... The night always ended in the backyard. We made them dig a pit. A grave. It was a trust exercise.*' (A pause. Laughter or tears, I couldn't tell which.) '*It was a fucking joke.*'

As I stopped to rest on a fallen branch, I heard the conclusion. The pledge who was buried alive – '*a joke, a fucking joke*' – didn't get out alive.

'*I think about it every day. The look on his face. Right before we – killed him.*'

The recording dissolved into sobbing and static. I clicked it off. Around me, the sounds of the bush renewed, insects rasping, birds whistling.

Who was this man? How much had Moxham blackmailed him for? How much was a life worth? I couldn't connect any of it to Moxham's murder – the man on the recording was a stranger – but it bothered me. There was something familiar about that voice.

If only I could get inside Moxham's head, know everything that he knew.

Wait a minute. The nasal voice...

I did recognise it.

Andrew Reisslenger, Brady's God-fearing lawyer.

*

It took another hour, but the picnic set-up was complete. In twenty minutes or so, the guests could enjoy a stroll up the hill and be rewarded with a lavish feast. I radioed Tessa, who was carrying up an extra cooler of drinks, and she claimed to be on her way. Not with any sense of urgency, apparently.

Exhausted, I leaned against the heavy wooden pole that braced one end of the zip-line. While I'd worked, I'd listened to Andrew's confession three more times. Andrew hadn't been on the island the night of Moxham's murder, but he certainly had a motive to want him dead. The hazing ritual gone wrong was manslaughter, at the very least. He could be convicted.

Did Andrew tell his good buddy, Brady, about the blackmail? Had the two of them concocted a plan to take out Moxham? It seemed farfetched that Brady would be willing to kill for Andrew, but after what Nathan had done for me, maybe I shouldn't rule it out.

I recalled the text messages on Brady's phone. They looked even more suspicious now. Had Moxham confronted Brady with blackmail about his own dirty deeds – whatever they were?

It was another frustrating what-if. Maybe it meant everything. Maybe it meant nothing.

I fluffed a few cushions and checked my watch. No rest for the wicked. I considered tracking down Diara to share what I'd found out, then decided against it. I still wasn't sure what to think about her and Moxham's secret relationship (if that's what it was), or the fact that she'd concealed it from me. I wished I had a true friend to talk to.

As I swallowed down the lump in my throat, my gaze came to rest on the zip-line. I'd been meaning to try it out. Up close, it looked home-made, with a handhold and a seat like you'd get at a playground. No harness. There was some rust on the cable, and the sign instructing riders to wear a helmet was sun-faded. For that matter, there were no helmets anywhere nearby. I peered at the wire's trajectory. Once the flattened area on top of the peak fell away, it was a long way down into tangled forest.

Probably safer to stick to walking down the hill. My work phone rang as I was contemplating this. When I saw the caller ID, I rolled my eyes.

'Hiii!' I answered in my fakest voice. 'How are youuu? How are the kids? See the big game?'

'Uh, Ms George, this is Zack from ICO Tech Support—'

'Zack, I've been thinking about you non-stop. I live, breathe, die for you, Zack. If I get murdered – and, boy, oh boy, that might happen – I'll leave you everything in my will. I burn for you, Zack.'

He cleared his throat. 'Your computer system is completely back online now, Ms George.'

'It is?!'

'Yes, you'll have access to all your booking functionality and—'

'Well, fan-tas-tic, and it only took you four fucking days to fix it. Great work.'

'Apologies, ma'am.' Zack sounded as sarcastic as me now. 'Is there anything else I can do for you?'

Yes, Zack, my sweet, there is something you can do. The thought occurred to me in a flash of inspiration.

I needed to get inside Moxham's head. And, short of bringing him back to life, I needed his data footprint.

'I need you to recover some files for me, Zack.'

*

Zack let me down yet again. He couldn't recover Moxham's emails and messages from the cloud for me without author-isation from 'Mr Clement or Ms Manolo'. Even my threats of murder (joking, joking) didn't sway him. The only way to get ICO Tech Support to send over the files was to connect to Zack using Kip's or Fizzy's computer. I knew neither of them would agree to it.

I ended the call with Zack and strode over to the zip-line. My skin was prickly with heat. No way in hell I was taking the bush trail down from the peak yet again.

Tessa had arrived while I'd been on the phone. 'You can handle the guests, right?' I said.

She gave a sullen shrug, which I took as a yes.

I grasped the zip-line's handhold. Above, on the metal cable, the pulley stirred, desperate to pull me along.

Within seconds, I was in flight. The ground dropped away and I skimmed the tops of the trees, leaves brushing my bare legs. The beach below, the shimmer of water, was rushing to meet me.

It was fucking amazing. I leaned back on the little seat and crossed my ankles to increase my speed. For the minute I was airborne, all my fears and irritations fell away.

I knew what to do. If I was going to recover Moxham's text messages, I needed to think like Moxham himself.

28

Friday was manic with preparations for the weekend's beach party, which was to be gold-themed; a twisted Midas fantasy. There'd been some suggestion that we should cancel the party, due to the incoming storm, but I was keeping my fingers crossed it would miss us. I couldn't let my hard work go to waste.

It was 4 p.m. by the time I made it back to the office. Empty. Good.

Fizzy's desk was as tidy as ever. A row of pink Post-its were lined up beside the laptop; one of them read, *Be kind to yourself.* My heart gave a little skip as I reached for the yellowing spider plant. The leaves made a dry rasping noise as I pushed them aside, my fingers closing around the spy camera.

It was warm from recording. Finally, I was getting somewhere.

'Great stuff, great stuff.' Outside the window, there was a baritone laugh. The crunch of footsteps against the shell path.

Shit. I shoved the spy-cam back into the plant pot and bolted across the office. The door opened.

'Hi, what's up?' I said it too loud.

Kip's eyebrows flicked upwards. 'Gorgeous girl... you should be outside on a gorgeous day like today.'

He was dressed for the water in a royal-blue windbreaker. There was the blue shadow of a bruise visible on his neck.

'Just finishing up some paperwork.' I wilted into my own desk chair.

He strode over to Fizzy's desk. 'Tut, tut. All work and no play.'

'Can I help with something?'

'Ah, no, no.' He scratched the dome of his bald head.

His gaze was roving across Fizzy's workspace. He shuffled aside a pair of cloudy crystals and sent a pen rolling across the desk. I tried not to stare at the spider plant. A slice of the spy-cam's lens was visible if you looked for it.

The pen dropped to the floor. I reached to pick it up. 'Kip?'

'Hm.' He moved the plant pot an inch to the left.

I froze. Had he seen the camera?

Keep calm. On my computer, I made a point of tapping open an email, trying to look busy.

Across the desk island, there was a rattling sound. My eyes darted to Kip again, but he'd turned away. He appeared to be tucking something inside his jacket pocket.

'Right!' He patted his thighs. 'I was looking for my... you know, whachamacallit?'

'Sorry?'

'I thought Fizzy was going to leave it here for me... Ah, well, chalk another one up for the scatty old man.'

I stared at him. I didn't know what to say.

'Don't work too hard.' He grinned. 'I pay you to have a grand old time.'

A moment later, he was gone, windbreaker rustling as he strolled out the door. My foot bounced against a wheel of my chair. Outside, there was the squawk of a rooster. I let a few more seconds drag by – he was really gone, right? – before I crept over to Fizzy's side of the office.

The spy-cam was still there. I scanned for anything that looked out of place. There was the pill bottle discreetly placed behind the plant pot. I assumed they were more of the tranquilisers Fizzy had offered me on Desolation Island. When I picked up the bottle, it gave a rattle.

What had he tucked inside his jacket? For that matter, why was he even wearing a jacket on a sweltering afternoon? I sagged into Fizzy's chair. I was being paranoid. Kip had just stepped off a boat, he'd come to see Fizzy and he'd wandered off again. Nothing more.

I made an effort to stop my leg from jiggling. This morning, when I'd retrieved the camera from inside a sock at the back of my drawer, I'd thought only of the positives. I'd been thinking this was the best way to find out Fizzy's password and use it to recover Moxham's files. I hadn't anticipated the slimy sense of shame that came with spying on someone. I didn't have Moxham's heart of stone.

Oh, well. I was in too deep now. No going back.

I reached into the spider plant and grabbed the spy camera.

*

Of Kip, the footage showed only the blur of his sleeve. If he'd done something to Fizzy's pills, it wasn't captured on the recording. When I skipped back to earlier in the day, however, it did record Fizzy's fingers as they skated over her keyboard.

The Nutcracker. I wondered if Fizzy had some particular memory of it, either watching or starring in a production as a child, whirling around onstage. I didn't have time to contemplate it further. I tapped in her password, *Drosselmeyer*, the name of the toymaker from the ballet, and logged into her computer.

Twenty minutes later, Zack had restored all of Moxham's files and I'd downloaded them onto a USB drive. It was almost too easy. I shut down Fizzy's laptop and squared it on the desk, praying she wouldn't notice any disturbance.

I hoped Diara would be in our room, but it was empty. I was too impatient to wait until she arrived home, so I settled cross-legged on my bed and pulled my laptop onto my knees. When I inserted the USB stick, months' worth of messages appeared on my screen. Everything that had been deleted from his phone and laptop was here.

I scrolled. Every cheeky reply from Moxham (*'you naughty lil muthaducka'*), every reference to a future that never was (*'we'll meet up in Road Town next month'*), made my stomach squeeze inward.

The light was fading, but I didn't bother to turn on the lamp. From outside, someone called my name. It sounded like Reggie, probably summoning me for a card game. He gave up when I didn't reply.

I skimmed the phone messages until I got to the twenty-first. This was it. The date of Moxham's death.

There were dozens of messages relating to logistics-planning. The steel band was delayed. The Beluga caviar didn't arrive.

I kept scrolling, my eyes flickering in and out of focus. The last few texts he'd received, which had been sent in the early hours, held an echo of my own sudden departure from Hong Kong.

Hey, man, where are you?
Everything OK?
What's going on?

11:45 onwards. That was when Moxham had rushed away from me on the beach. I scrutinised the messages sent and received in the minutes before midnight.

One caught my attention:

I'm sorry. I want to talk. Meet me at the boathouse at midnight.

My mouth had gone dry.

I read the name attached to the message three times because I couldn't believe it.

Diara.

This would make her one of the last people to see Moxham alive. Why hadn't she told me she'd met him at the boathouse?

I was pacing my room, eyes flicking over the ugly boat painting, when it occurred to me. There could be proof of Diara's whereabouts at midnight on the twenty-first. Moxham had placed a camera above my bed to track me, but what if Diara was also caught in the frame? If she'd been at home in bed at midnight, as she claimed, that proved her innocence.

Retrieving the spy-cam's SD card from my sock drawer, I inserted it into my laptop and opened the file labelled with the date of Moxham's murder. Hurriedly, I clicked through to 23:45.

Diara's bed was visible. It was empty.

On fast-forward, I let the footage play, willing Diara to return. The timestamp clicked past midnight and still there was no sign of her. I allowed the video to play past 1 a.m., past 2 a.m., and still Diara didn't come home.

She'd lied. She'd said she'd gone home to bed. I remembered how drunk she'd been that night. Was it possible she'd blacked out and didn't remember meeting Moxham? I'd suspected a secret relationship between Diara and Moxham. It could have turned toxic. She'd killed him in a lovers' quarrel. In the last week, she'd helped me to investigate, but only because she was covering her own tracks. She was keeping tabs on me. If I got too close to the truth, she'd kill me.

A shiver shot up my spine.

No, that was crazy. Right?

*

There had to be a reasonable explanation.

One problem: I couldn't find Diara.

I called her, but there was no response. She wasn't in the team bar, where Reggie, Tyson and a few others were grousing over their card game. She wasn't at the spa. She wasn't in the restaurant or the kitchen or sitting by the pool. When I sent out a message on the radio ('anyone have eyes on Diara?'), I got nothing back.

No one had seen her.

After I called her again with no luck, I texted her.

Where are you?

No response.

I messaged again, three times more, not caring how insane I seemed.

Nothing.

Was it possible Diara had left the island and wasn't coming back?

29

The evening unspooled as I sat in my bedroom, hunched over my laptop, the glow from the screen providing the only light. I was supposed to be prepping for tomorrow night's party, turning the island into a golden wonderland.

Instead, I returned to Moxham's messages, looking for confirmation of his relationship with Diara. Looking for evidence of her guilt.

A lizard scuttled across the floor, but I didn't react.

Grab em by the balls till the money comes out of they filthy mouths. Hahahahahahahaha.

I scrolled past the text exchange and then up again. Diara? No. I read on:

Moxham: Keep digging. Find out what he wants. You're a good listener.
Tessa: Is that code for I got a nice arse?
Moxham: Haha. You be the carrot ill be the stick.
Tessa: Yes boss;)

Tessa. As I continued to scroll through the days preceding Moxham's murder, I found countless messages from her.

Dim-witted, petulant Tessa had a side hustle. She was Moxham's accomplice.

A memory popped. Tessa's social media, all those selfies of her with a Birkin bag, togged out in designer clothes. Before, I'd assumed she had been wheedling good tips out of soft guests. Now I knew it was more than that.

Moxham must have been paying her for months.

The door opened.

I jumped, my laptop leaping sideways.

'Fucking hell!'

In the darkness, I almost imagined it was Tessa, wearing a smirk and aiming a gun – *you caught me, did you?* – but the figure in the doorway was my roommate.

Actually, based on what I'd just found out, and the gun I knew to be in her possession, perhaps the sight of Diara wasn't any less disturbing.

She stumbled into the room and switched on the light. 'Cheeeese and bread, what's up, London?'

At the same time, I said, 'Where have you been?'

'Visiting my family on VG.'

'Why didn't you text me back?'

'I was busy.' She exhaled a laugh. In the enclosed space, the rum on her breath smelled sickly.

'Need to show you something.' I unfolded my tensed limbs and stood up. I grabbed my laptop and crossed the room to where Diara was teetering on one leg, unfastening her sandal.

She yawned. 'Tomorrow.'

'No, right now.'

I showed her the Tessa text messages first. When she asked, 'how did you get this?', I waved her question away. She grabbed the laptop from me and began skipping through the messages.

'This is big,' she said, without taking her eyes from the screen. 'Never woulda guessed it…'

I tried to make my voice casual as I asked, 'Hey, did you speak to your auntie?'

'What?'

'The autopsy report.'

'No, didn't get a chance.'

She perched on the edge of her bed, still reading Moxham's messages. I crossed my arms, checking her face for clues.

'But that's evidence we need,' I said.

'You want me to break into the police station on wires like *Mission: Impossible*?' She shot me a brief smile and returned to the screen.

'I want you to tell me why you keep lying.'

She screwed up her face. *Huh?*

'I know you met Moxham at the boathouse, right before he died.' Blood pounded in my ears. I grabbed the laptop back from her.

'You lost your damn mind.' She didn't sound tipsy anymore.

I found the text message and shoved it in her face, the laptop balanced on her knees. 'You texted him, right before he died.'

'No, I didn't.'

The laptop slipped an inch. I reached out to grasp it. 'You did.'

'No.'

I'd hoped she would explain it all away. *Oh yeah, I totally forgot, I met Moxham in the boathouse to talk about our favourite puppies; it was all fine.*

'How, then? How did that message get sent by you?'

'Not sent by me, sent by my phone.' Diara closed the laptop. She pulled her knees up to her chest.

'I lost it that night,' she said, 'Reggie found it in the morning. Anyone coulda picked it up. You know all the work phones have the same passcode. Unlock it, send the message as me, put it back down. Easy.'

'You lost your phone?' Reggie had said something about that, hadn't he? Diara trying to pick up a coaster instead of her phone?

'Yeah, embarrassing… I was drunk that night. Everything's a little fuzzy.'

'Blackout drunk.'

'No.' Her voice was sharp. 'Not blackout drunk.'

We were both silent for a while. Diara was fidgeting with her earring. For the first time, I noticed the S-shape that dangled from her ear was a snake.

'Listen, London,' she said at last, 'me and Moxham, we was… whatever… we was friends. For a time. If someone wanted to guarantee he'd show up to meet them, it makes sense… they use my phone.'

I let her words sink in, trying to picture the scene. It would be a calculated act, to see Diara growing drunker and drunker, to swipe her phone when she wasn't looking, to make Moxham think he was headed to a romantic tête-à-tête. It was a killer lure.

'I'm sure I saw Tessa buzzing around the night of the party,' she said.

'Tessa?'

'She was there, coulda been her.' Diara was deflecting. Her gaze was evasive. 'Should speak to her.'

It was true that only staff members would know the code to unlock Diara's phone. Tessa had given a nonsensical story about calling her boyfriend in Dublin at the staff village. Perhaps she'd been inventing an alibi for herself.

'OK…' My hands had turned to fists unconsciously, but I made an effort to unclench them. 'Let's see what she has to say for herself.'

Diara finally met my gaze. 'Hey… you trust me, don't you, London?'

It was the bottom-line question. If I trusted Diara, I had to believe her story. If not… well, there was no one I could really trust on this island.

'Yeah, I trust you,' I said.

*

It was past midnight. As I stepped out into the square, the only sound was the coo of a bird. Even the card sharks had gone to bed.

Knock, knock. At Tessa's door, there was no reply. I hammered harder with my fist. Diara was hovering at my shoulder.

The more I thought about it, the more evidence stacked up against Tessa. No wonder she wanted to quit so badly. She could see the ship was sinking and she wanted off.

One of the other hosts came to the door. It was Maria, who was from the Philippines originally and had a round baby face. Her black hair, streaked with blue, was loose around her shoulders. She rubbed her eyes, voice hoarse. 'I haven't seen her.'

'Do you know where she is?' I asked.

'She'll be with Ethan.'

Diara knew which room belonged to Ethan. He'd been on the island long enough that he'd snagged a single. There was no answer when I knocked. Were Tessa and Ethan off somewhere together? Hidden Cove, perhaps? Or had Tessa finally made good on her bluff and left the island for good?

The staff village was eerie in the darkness. We were surrounded by the heavy-breathing rattle of insects.

'Do you think she left? Or...?' I let the question hang.

'She around here somewhere.' Diara shook her head. 'Gyul like that, she wouldn't leave without getting something out of it.'

I dropped my voice to a whisper. 'Tessa... maybe she wanted to take over Moxham's business. Get all that money for herself. So, she took him out. She could be the murderer.'

'Don't jump to—'

'I know, I know.'

I'd always thought of Tessa like an annoying cousin. She was lazy – manipulating me and the other hosts into doing her work for her – but I'd wanted to believe I could train her up. Now I felt stupid.

I had a flash of her laying down a winning hand of cards during one of our late-night games in the team bar. She wasn't dumb. She'd been playing me since the first moment I arrived.

30

In the dawn light, the boathouse was gloomy. It smelled of motor oil undercut with a hint of something herbal burning. Diara and I let ourselves in through a side door. In the shadows, I rammed my knee against a metal rod and swore under my breath. Behind me, Diara made a tutting noise and turned on the lights, flooding the space with harsh blue-white illumination.

Half an hour ago, I'd shaken Diara awake. 'The boathouse! We need to check the boathouse.'

I'd only slept for an hour or two, but the idea had been pulsing in my head the second I opened my eyes. No matter who had lured Moxham here, we now knew for sure that he had visited the boathouse just before his death.

This could be the crime scene.

It was a shed of a place. Concrete floor, wooden beams overhead, with a metal up-and-over door that faced the sea. I squeezed past the racks of kayaks and canoes, and almost got kneecapped again by a metal winch that was attached to one of the boats. It wasn't just water sports equipment that jostled for space. The boathouse had the appearance of a dumping ground. In the corner, there were teetering stacks of metal chairs, which I guessed were used for events. I was surprised at the griminess, considering the pristine perfection of the rest of the island. A shovel was leaning against the wall. I picked it up.

'Could you use this as a weapon?'

Diara's eyes were slits. She didn't reply.

I weighed the shovel in my hand, inspecting it for signs of blood. There was only a white crust. This must be used to keep the pier clean of bird shit. With a grimace, I replaced it and continued my survey of the boathouse.

'OK.' I clapped my hands. 'Let's recap what we know.'

Tossing and turning last night, I'd decided the best way to keep an eye on Diara was to pretend things were fine. We were still Holmes and Watson. I couldn't imagine her as a murderer, but if I observed how she acted at the crime scene, I'd have a better sense of what she was thinking.

'No one saw Moxham after midnight.' I ticked off facts on my fingers. 'He wasn't there during the fireworks. The killer drew him away. Nice and isolated here, a mile away from the party. No one would hear a fight.' I paced the length of the boathouse. 'It would also fit with what Ethan said about seeing a tall man skulking near the pier. Maybe the killer was on his way home after the murder.'

Diara was leaning against the hull of a boat. She said nothing.

'We should do a re-enactment,' I said brightly. 'Do you want to be Moxham or the murderer?'

I'd been half-joking, courting her laughter, but Diara remained silent. She gave a one-shouldered shrug.

'I'll be the killer.' I ducked down behind a nearby boat. 'I could be hiding when you arrive, to make sure you're alone. We know Moxham was Tased, so I would be holding the Taser.' I crouched against the crusty hull of the boat and grasped an imaginary Taser.

'If you wanna kill someone, why bring a Taser?' Diara asked.

I popped up from my hiding place. Her arms were crossed.

'Why not a knife or a gun?' she asked.

At her words, I couldn't help but think of her gun, hidden in her bottom drawer.

'I guess the killer would have a Taser because...' I trailed off.

I'd been imagining the Taser as a supplemental weapon, a way to immobilise Moxham, so he was at the killer's mercy. But Diara was right. That was a long-winded way of murdering someone. It would be easier by far to grab a knife from the kitchen and stick it between Moxham's ribs.

'You use a Taser because you're scared,' Diara said.

'Scared…' I said. I supposed any blackmail victim would be scared of what Moxham would do. Yet my mind flashed to sitting on Desolation Island with Fizzy, talking about being locked up inside your own fear.

'Whoever it was, there musta been a fight,' Diara said.

I roamed the space, examining a tool kit in the corner. There was the remains of a bundle of something burned inside a teacup. A joint, perhaps?

'Look at this.' Diara beckoned me to an open section between two boats.

'What?'

'The floor.'

She toed at it emphatically, but I was lost. 'What am I looking at?'

'Exactly. The floor here is clean. Reggie and those boys never clean more than they can help. Housekeeping doesn't come to the boathouse. So why the floor clean?'

The concrete on the other side of the boat was blackened, covered in sand, pieces of fluff, stray screws and nuts that were dusty from how many times they'd been stamped on and kicked around. By contrast, this patch of floor was a pale grey, only lightly strewn with debris.

'Clean-up job,' I murmured. A memory surfaced. I reached out to clutch Diara's arm. 'Shirley! Someone stole her cleaning supplies the day after I arrived. You went and dealt with it, remember?'

Diara nodded. 'Question is, did they clean up everything?'

Around this patch of floor, I began pushing aside life vests, racking, paddleboards. Diara did the same.

'They must have left something behind…' she said.

'They?'

'The killer.'

'The way you said "they", I thought maybe… it was more than one person.'

'How should I know?' Diara gave a thin smile. There was something unsettling in that smile. The hairs on my arms rose.

'I just mean…' I paused, breathing heavily from the effort of shifting a boat's hull. 'If we follow it through: the killer murders Moxham, then cleans up. It's a mile to the storeroom to get cleaning supplies. He also has to dump Moxham's body at sea, tow out the jet ski to make it seem like an accident. That's a lot for one person.'

'Not impossible, if they're strong.'

'Not impossible…' I repeated, thinking out loud. 'But if I killed someone and didn't mean to do it, the first thing I'd do is tell someone. Someone I trusted. I wouldn't be thinking straight, I'd need help.'

Diara didn't say anything. She was still checking the floor. 'They didn't do a good job of cleaning.'

She'd shifted aside an old-fashioned wooden rowing boat. Beneath it, there was a sprinkling of green shards, and a dark splatter of –

I crossed the space in two strides and bent down to make sure.

– blood.

The sight of it hit me in the chest. For the past twenty minutes, I'd been in detective mode. Working through the case had been like something from a story. Something abstract. Now the horror of it crashed over me. Moxham had walked into this boathouse a living, breathing, complicated human being, and he'd been dragged out a corpse.

Gingerly, I picked up the largest fragment of glass. 'What d'you think?'

'Could be a bottle. That would make a good weapon.'

Diara mimed slicing the air with an imaginary bottle. There was an ashy tint to her dark skin.

I had a flash of Moxham weaving towards me in the dark. 'A champagne bottle.'

The tube lighting hummed overhead. I held up the piece of glass to the light. There was a smudge on it and—

'Is that a fingerprint?'

Diara eased the fragment from my grasp, holding it by its edges. 'Might be good enough to get a match. I can give it to my auntie.'

'We should go to the police.' I reached out to reclaim the piece of glass, but Diara withdrew her hand.

'My auntie is police.'

The same auntie who was supposed to get us Moxham's autopsy report? The same auntie who Diara had not spoken to yet?

My jaw clenched. No, Diara wasn't going to spirit away what looked to be our best piece of evidence. 'We need to find a bag or a box or something to put it in, so it doesn't get damaged.'

Behind me, there was a grinding noise.

I jumped, looking around. Glass crunched against my shoes. Shit, I was destroying evidence.

Light blazed into the boathouse. The grinding noise was the up-and-over door rising.

I put my hand out to Diara. 'Just give me the—'

She took a step backwards. There was an almighty crash, as she upset a stack of chairs.

The light from outside was shining directly in my eyes now.

'Who's there?' I said.

No response.

Could we have been followed here? If the killer realised we'd found the crime scene, if they realised we had fingerprints—

'Hello!' I yelled.

No response.

I shielded my eyes. I still couldn't see anything.

'Good morning!'

The person was silhouetted in bright light. It took me a second to identify his fedora and cane.

'Care to help me with my vessel?' Doc asked.

*

In the space of five minutes, the boathouse went from a murder site, hushed and horrible, to a hive of activity. Reggie arrived to help Doc with his boat. Doc was here for the gold party, either because Kip had invited him as a guest, or because someone had died last time Keeper had a blowout party, and having medical assistance on hand could prove useful.

The rest of the water sports team were dragging out kayaks and paddleboards for an early-morning guest excursion. Tyson swung by with coffee and bacon baps from the kitchen. I took a bite of one, but it was difficult to swallow.

Diara had disappeared, carrying with her the piece of glass. I had to believe she was only concerned with keeping it safe.

As people swarmed around me, grabbing life vests and paddles, I pulled listlessly at the tangle of chairs Diara had toppled. My cover story was that I was unpacking them for tonight's party.

'Zip-line's down.'

'Hm?'

Reggie was talking, but I wasn't listening. I couldn't keep my gaze from straying to the floor where we'd shifted the wooden rowing boat. The brown spots remained on the concrete, but now that the light had shifted, they could have been oil or petrol.

The glass was reduced to a green glitter, barely there unless you knew to look for it.

I wanted to take pictures, but people were walking all over the crime scene. They'd been walking all over it for two weeks. The clean-up job might have been poor, but time eroded all evidence.

'Zip-line,' Reggie said again. 'Noticed on the way here. Cable detached – *whump* – on the ground.'

'You're not supposed to bring me problems,' I said. 'You're just supposed to tell me I'm pretty.'

Reggie was open-mouthed for a second, like I was serious, before a smile spread across his face. 'Sorry.'

The zip-line, though old, had seemed fine when I'd used it the day before yesterday. When I'd landed at Hidden Cove, the seat had whirred away on an electric system, travelling back up to the peak, ready for the next rider. I'd have to find a local repair company, if one existed. Add another dollop to my shit sandwich. Well, that was Future-Lola's problem. I had the gold party to get through first.

I gave up on untangling the chairs and left the boathouse, hitching a ride in a golf cart with Doc. He kept up his usual patter of stories about his patients, which meant I didn't need to talk. I was brooding on Diara's reactions to the murder site.

On the way to the main complex, we met Brady, sauntering home from Hidden Cove. Doc slowed and Brady climbed into the back of our buggy.

'How 'bout a drink?' He flashed a flirty smile.

'Rustle one up for you.'

'No, a drink with you.'

'Maybe tonight.' I twisted around to face him. Despite the coil of apprehension in my chest, a smile slipped out.

'Maybe?'

'Definitely. Pinkie swear.'

We locked our littlest fingers together and I felt a tingle.

'And how's the foot, young man?' Doc asked, as we resumed our buggy ride.

Brady dropped his hand from mine and turned to the doctor. 'Getting there. Not much pain anymore.'

'You hurt yourself?' I asked.

'Stepped on a piece of coral, sliced up my foot. Doc here was very obliging, bandaged me up, told me to quit whining.'

'I hope my bedside manner was a little gentler than that.' Doc braked to let a family of chickens cross the path.

'When was this?' I asked.

'Day of that crazy party, Alice in Wonderland. I'm all trussed up like a turkey. I'll tell you, my ego was bruised worst of all. I had to have this German dude, twice my age, practically carry me to my villa.'

Brady shook his head, laughing. I felt like I was seeing him anew.

He'd told me before that he was incapacitated the night of the Alice party, but I'd assumed he meant he was drunk, not injured. I'd seen plenty of fall-down-drunk people lash out in violence. A foot injury, on the other hand, rendered him helpless – especially when combined with too much alcohol. There was no way he could have killed Moxham.

Brady had an alibi.

31

At first, I didn't recognise the woman dancing on Main Beach. Her brown skin contrasted with the bright orange wig, which fell in soft waves to her shoulders.

Beneath an electrical rig I'd rented for the evening, a local fungi band was setting up. Each member of the foursome was dressed in gold. The soothing rhythm of drums drifted on the breeze. In the orange glow of the sunset, the tables draped in gold cloth shimmered. The absurdly expensive decorations included a hundred roses dipped in wax and sprayed gold.

I scuffed closer to the dancing woman, my bare feet sinking in the sand. As I passed an enormous bowl filled with foil-covered chocolates, I stole one and razored it open with my thumbnail.

'You look nice,' I said.

Diara was dressed in a sunshine-yellow romper with a fringe. She looked up at the sound of my voice. Her lipstick was purple and her eyes were winged with liner.

'I hear the surprise in your voice, you know.' She laughed and cut me off before I could protest. 'I know how to have a good time.'

For my part, I was wearing a bright gold halter-necked dress with a circle skirt, from the rack of clothes I'd had rushed in from Florida especially for the occasion. I'd slathered gold body glitter across my chest and arms, although I suspected the effect was less 'golden fantasy' and more 'thirteen-year-old let loose at Claire's'.

I munched on the chocolate, which was sweet with a hint of bitter sharpness. It had arrived from Switzerland two days before. Nothing but the finest for Keeper Island.

Diara shimmied over to the drinks table and grabbed a champagne bottle. *Pop!* She took a long pull and then handed it to me.

I held the bottle loosely by its neck. I couldn't help but think of the shards of green in the boathouse. 'The piece of glass—'

'Stop.'

The band had grown louder and I had to raise my voice. 'I was just—'

'I gave it to my auntie, she getting it tested.' Diara swiped the champagne from me and took another swallow.

'OK… but…'

'Nothing else we can do now.'

'I talked to Brady. He has an alibi.' I explained about my conversation with Doc.

She nodded, but I got the sense she wasn't listening. 'Nothing else to do today. So, we limin', right?'

I wanted to argue. For a start, Tessa's absence was gnawing at me. It turned out Maria had been covering her work for her. When I'd checked with Ethan, he hadn't seen her in a couple of days. According to Reggie, she hadn't left on the staff ferry that made the rounds of the islands each morning and evening. But that didn't mean she hadn't departed on another vessel. I was increasingly sure she'd fled, taking her knowledge of Moxham's schemes with her. Was it possible to track her down? Talk to Fizzy's contact at the airport?

I exhaled a long breath. I was sick of the whatifs. It would be good to take a night off from everything. Diara held out the bottle again. This time, I gulped from it long enough that bubbles frothed in my nose. The beat of the music was irresistible. I rolled my head back and let myself dance. My dress flared out when I turned. Diara shook her hips and the fringe of her romper rippled.

It was getting dark and I was enjoying the music, so it took me a few minutes to notice what was different about Diara. There was a looseness to her dancing, a bleariness in her eyes.

The champagne wasn't her first drink of the day.

'Hey, are you OK?' I put a hand on hers, but she ignored the question and took it as a cue to spin me around. Sand sprayed my ankles. I laughed in spite of myself.

Behind me, there was the clink-rattle of bracelets. I knew without looking that it was Fizzy.

'Didn't know the bash had already begun.' She swished her long black hair off her shoulder and fixed me with a tight smile.

'Come join us,' I said, breathless. Diara's hand was still clasped in mine. I nodded to the rows of champagne flutes. 'I'll even get you a glass.'

'No, thank you.'

'Don't be like that.' Diara gave a broad grin and rolled her shoulders. 'We limin'. It's a party.'

Fizzy spread her arms wide. She was holding a long-stemmed torch, although it wasn't yet dark enough to require it. She aimed the torch beam in a semi-circle.

'Doesn't look like a party to me,' she said. 'The candles aren't lit. The beach carpets aren't down. And you're goofing off.'

'It's fine.' I dropped Diara's hand and took a step towards Fizzy. 'I'll get a couple of the guys to—'

'No offence, but you're brand new.' Fizzy wrinkled her nose. 'I know how things are done.'

'God, could you stop being an officious bitch for five minutes?'

I didn't mean to say it out loud. The champagne and the music had done a number on me. My words hung in the air. There was a horrible silence. Of course the band had chosen that moment to stop their warm-up.

Fizzy tapped her torch against her thigh. Her ears had gone pink.

'I'm an officious bitch, am I?' Her eyes flicked to Diara. 'That's what you think too?'

'Sorry, I didn't mean it,' I said.

Diara stepped between us. 'Elizabeth.' She released the name in a sigh. 'Let's have a drink, have a dance…'

The band had started up again, a slow, sultry song. She palmed a hand against Fizzy's shoulder.

Fizzy pushed her away, hard. Her bracelets whipped with the force of the motion. Diara stuttered backwards, into the table. A row of champagne flutes rattled. The bottle fell to the sand with a crash, gushing foam. Diara landed on her arse with a thump.

I looked to Fizzy, wide-eyed. What the fuck?

'I could have you fired.' Fizzy's voice was shaky. 'Don't forget that.'

She stalked away, shoulders hunched, sandals slapping against the sand.

I huffed out a breath, half a laugh. 'Shit, what's going on with her?'

Diara remained silent. I stuck out a hand to help her up, but she waved me off and levered herself up.

'Are you alright?' I asked.

'Fine.' Her orange wig was askew.

I waited for her to spew out a rant about the absolute nerve of Fizzy, as I would have done. I wanted to hit Fizzy in the tit with the crystal she'd given me. *Negative energy, be gone!*

'Talk to Kip about her. You should—'

'Forget it.' Diara dusted down her romper.

'I'll talk to him, then,' I said. 'Seriously.'

'Don't.'

'She could have hurt you.'

'She didn't.' Diara's expression was blank. 'I need to check in at the spa.'

She didn't wait for me to respond before she left. Diara and I hadn't been friends for long, but when you shared a room with someone, you became attuned to their moods.

I knew she didn't want me to see her cry.

*

Hours later, fire streaked across the black night. One of the fire dancers rotated a fireball on a leash. She leaned back, face to the sky, and the flame circled above her like a shooting star.

I weaved through the crowd, retrieving dropped napkins and offering more drinks. Each time I sneaked a look at the night's entertainment, I felt sure the fire dancer was about to burn herself to ash. I was relieved when her performance ended.

I needn't have worried about the party; everything was perfect. Kip approached me, grinning and slurring. 'You get the gold medal for this one.' He gave an awkward fist bump. His sequinned jacket made a *shh* sound as he shuffled away.

I'd sent racks of designer rental clothes to each villa earlier in the day. Most of the women in attendance had embraced the opportunity to wear a Gatsby-ish embroidered gold dress or a sweeping lamé gown. Of the men, only Kip had gone all-out, in a gold suit with a gold fedora. All the wait staff who didn't refuse had been slathered in gold body glitter, which looked better under twinkling fairy lights.

Diara reappeared around 11 p.m., as the fungi band was finishing and an overpriced DJ was taking centre stage. She was apparently recovered and definitely drunk. When I asked again if she was OK, she drew me into a sloppy hug and said, 'You're annoying, but I like you.' She let out a cackle of laughter.

I saw Fizzy again only once. She was still brandishing her torch, like a night patrolman. I opened my mouth to say something to her, but she looked right through me.

I'd been cornered by one of the guests, a stout man with a patchy beard. I was trying to evade his wandering hands, when someone bumped my elbow. I turned, wearing a fake smile, ready to rebuff another admirer old enough to be my grandfather.

It was Brady, holding a champagne flute. 'Lemme steal this pretty lady for a dance.'

If he was good looking in board shorts, he was dazzling in a suit. His top button was undone, gold bow tie unravelled. He touched me again, a tap to my hip this time.

'I'm working...' The other guest had shambled away, but out of the corner of my eye, I could see ten things that needed fixing.

'You deserve a break.' Brady handed the glass to me.

It was champagne, mixed with elderflower liqueur and vodka, swirling with edible glitter. I'd asked Ethan to invent a specialty cocktail for the evening. He'd wanted to name it the Golden Shower, to his own endless amusement, but I'd taken the executive decision to rename it the Midas Touch. I sipped at it, warmth spreading through me. God, these were lethal.

I wondered if Fizzy was still nearby. I hoped she was, so she could see me swigging the cocktail.

'C'mon,' Brady said. 'I want to dance with the most beautiful woman here.'

I mimed looking around. 'Where is she? I'll set you up.'

Brady appeared not to hear me. He grabbed me hard enough that part of my drink spilled. He spun me around and my dress flared.

When I came to a halt, he nuzzled in close. 'Please? When I drink, I dance. Them's the rules.'

I laughed in spite of myself. Brady was a goofy drunk, all droopy eyes and big teeth. I downed the last of my cocktail and set it on a table. I'd spent the evening catering to other people's enjoyment. Didn't I deserve a few minutes' break?

It wasn't like other guests weren't dancing with staff. I'd seen Reggie with a yummy mummy fresh off her divorce from a pharma CEO, and Kip had worked his way through every one of the female wait staff. The lines were getting blurrier as everyone got drunker.

Brady drew me close and I let myself relax into him. His size was undeniable up close, that wide expanse of muscular chest. 'I like you, Lola. You're different.'

He seemed like he was about to say more, but at that moment, Ethan raced towards us. 'The fireworks are late.'

I checked my watch. 'I have to get back to work,' I said to Brady.

*

I found Reggie by the pool at five past midnight. He was smoking a blunt and he looked at me groggily when I said, 'Fireworks?' His eyes widened and he jumped to his feet, dropping the joint in his agitation.

'Shit, I'm doing it, I'm doing it. Fizzy normally remind me.' Reggie took off running, his shorts dipping low on his hips. It was such a perfect recreation of what must have happened the night of Moxham's death, I felt a dull ache.

A few minutes later, the first firework exploded and there was a collective gasp from the crowd. I returned to the beach, going through a mental checklist. The number of guests had thinned out. There were also fewer people serving drinks. I suspected another parallel party among the staff must have cropped up elsewhere.

I could only see one of the hosts, a couple of the waiters. I'd give them a bollocking if the rest of them were—

From behind, a pair of hands grabbed me around the waist. There was a burst of light, the scream of a firework.

I jumped.

'Guilty conscience?' Brady whispered in my ear. As he laughed, his stubble scratched my cheek.

I leaned back against his hard mass of muscle, my heart pounding.

'I'm trying to kiss you and you're running away,' he said.

My stomach flipped over. It wasn't just the Midas Touch that had hit me full force.

'I told you, I'm working.' Scanning the crowd, I tried to extricate myself from him.

'The party's over.' He let me loose and then, playfully, pulled me close again, my chest against his. I couldn't summon up any resistance.

When I breathed in, he smelled like soap and sunblock and a spicy-sweetness that reminded me of gingerbread.

I was so tired of being good. I wanted distraction. Oblivion. I was due a rebound.

I licked my lips, anticipating his kiss. Then I remembered where we were.

'Not here.' I gave him a gentle push. 'Wait two minutes and head in that direction.'

I inclined my head to the right. At the edge of the party, there was a cluster of tamarind trees swaying in the breeze. While the beach glittered with candles and string lights, the copse hid pools of darkness within it.

I trotted to the shelter of the trees, stumbling on a root as I went. I heard something stir nearby, but my mind was filled with static. There was an ache in my thighs.

Brady didn't wait two minutes. I glimpsed him through the trees. He looked like a naughty schoolboy, trailing after me. He stopped at the tree-line, blinking and uncertain. I realised I must be invisible to him. I darted forward and grabbed his shirt front.

God, the size of him. He could crush me.

I closed the gap between us, easing my lips over his. Brady urged me back against a tree trunk and I almost lost my balance. Twigs snapped beneath my bare feet. I sensed a disturbance nearby, as if I'd unsettled a nest of birds.

He buried his hand in my hair, securing me to him. He was a guy who liked to be in charge.

Birds again. Flapping wings. Scurrying feet.

Enormous birds. Human-sized birds.

The delayed realisation came to me and my eyes flew open. We were not alone.

32

The copse of trees was dark, but it wasn't hard to deduce what we'd stumbled across.

Another couple.

I disentangled from Brady. I was coming back to myself. What was I, a hormonal teenager? This could only end badly. Fizzy would relish having me fired because I'd been fraternising with a guest.

Fizzy. As if I'd conjured her, she appeared.

There was a jingle-jangle sound from her bracelets as she wrenched up the neckline of her floral-print dress. Her voice rang out, sounding like a pissed-off headmistress. 'What are you doing here?'

'Sorry,' I said reflexively, taking a step back. Brady's hand came to rest on my waist.

'Nice night,' he said, with a nod.

Fizzy ran a hand through her mussed hair and shot him a look like she didn't recognise him.

She brushed past me, away from the trees and back towards the party. I didn't watch her go because another figure materialised out of the darkness. This woman was wearing an orange wig, set awry on her head. Her purple lipstick was smeared. She didn't say anything before she bolted.

I scrambled after her. 'Diara…'

A dot of something wet landed on my cheek. Brady reached for my hand. I ignored him, ducking under a branch to get clear of the trees.

Fizzy and Diara. Diara and Fizzy.

I couldn't get my head around it all. Why hadn't Diara told me? Did she think I'd judge her?

Back at the party, the DJ was packing up. He hailed me, probably wanting to ask about payment, but I held out a hand. 'Five minutes.' A second droplet landed on my shoulder, another on my forearm.

Rain? Was it raining?

I edged past a knot of remaining guests, who were laughing as they drank their Midas Touches. On one of the trees, the fairy lights now dangled like a noose. I still couldn't see Diara.

Brady appeared at my elbow, droopy with puppy dog eyes. 'You're running away again.' He put a hand on my hip, rolling me towards him. The night air was cooling, but he was a wall of heat.

I felt a flutter of my earlier lust. Diara and Fizzy were probably cosied up together somewhere. Why shouldn't I do the same with Brady? I turned in his arms, hands moulding against the muscles of his chest. We stood in a pool of golden light created by a spotlight. (The spotlights were a rental. They'd been a pain to source and they needed to be packed away before they were destroyed by the rain.) This was too public a place for us to be embracing. Someone would see and report back to Fizzy.

Fizzy. I had a stray thought that I could use my new knowledge about Fizzy's love life against her. It was what Moxham would have done.

Above us, there was a crack of thunder. Rain came down like a bucket being emptied.

*

I fell asleep to the sound of the rain drumming on the roof, exhausted from battling the weather to clean up after the gold party. When light from a lamp filled the room, I thought it was morning and tried to rouse myself.

230

'Sorry.' It was Diara's voice. With a click, she turned off the lamp again. The room blackened.

I twisted myself free from my sheets, trying to make out Diara's form. 'You OK?'

'Yep, yep, yep.'

There was a squeak as her mattress dropped. I struggled into a sitting position. It was too dark to see more than the curve of her back, hunched over.

'What's the time?' I asked.

'Late… too late.' She stood up, unsteady on her feet, and then collapsed onto the bed again.

'You sure you're OK?' I reached for my phone (it was 3:26 a.m.) and aimed a beam of light in her direction.

'None of us is OK.' She gave a dark little giggle. 'Everything gone to shit.'

'You and Fizzy?'

'No, that wa' always shit.' Another laugh, harsh and low.

I turned off my phone and lay down. Darkness enveloped the room.

'Diara…' I said at last. 'How come you lied to me about you and Fizzy?'

There was a long pause and I thought Diara wasn't going to reply. She was wrapping her hair in jerky movements.

'I didn't lie,' she said.

'OK…'

The silence this time was so long that I added in, 'You can talk to me. If you want.'

'Listen…' Diara heaved out a sigh. 'I'm private, but I'm not in the closet.'

She lay on her back. Her voice was low and I had to strain to hear.

'My family like to pretend I'm not gay,' she said, 'so I don't shout about it. But I'm not ashamed.'

'I didn't mean to…'

Diara raised her voice. 'I'm my own person.'

Outside, the wind was whistling. I rolled over in bed and a streak of gold glitter appeared on my pillow.

'That's brave,' I said. 'It's a hard thing, being true to yourself.'

'Not that hard.' Diara snorted. 'Fizzy… she has this fantasy of who she is and when real life gets in the way of that, she pretends it's not happening.' Her voice sped up. 'We been doing this dance for months. We hook up, she gets scared, says it won't happen again, and then, oh wait, it happens again.'

I wondered if Diara would be so candid if we were sitting across from each other in the middle of the day. The darkness gave the room the quality of a confessional booth.

'You know, it was her who kissed me first.' She paused and I got the sense that she was reliving the moment in her head. 'I wasn't trying to get involved with no self-hating straight girl, but…' She released a deep sigh.

'When she pushed you—'

'That was nothing, she was upset.'

I frowned. It had seemed fucked-up at the time, and it seemed more so in light of their true relationship.

'What about her and Kip?' I'd assumed, almost automatically, that Fizzy and Kip must be sleeping together.

'What, a woman can't get ahead in business without sleeping with her boss?'

Diara made a *pfft* noise. I felt ashamed. She was right.

'If you'd been here longer, you'd get it,' she said. 'Elizabeth loves this place, really loves it. And she loves Kip because he lets her live in this perfect bubble.

''Course, she don't want Kip to know about the two of us because' – (I heard her kiss her teeth) – 'I don't know. He's a homophobic bastard and she's his perfect surrogate daughter? He likes Elizabeth because he thinks he can control her.'

I let this information sink in. I waited for Diara to say more, but all that followed was the rustle of sheets, the squeak of the bed. When I glanced over, I saw that she'd turned to face the wall.

'Do you love her?' I asked.

Silence.

I curled up and let the rain lull me to sleep. Was this the only secret Diara was hiding from me? Or were there more?

*

It continued to rain the next day. In this weather, all the guests wanted room service or a spa treatment or both. Diara was working around the clock; she'd been gone when I'd woken up and I hadn't seen her since. The hosts were so busy they'd stopped answering their phones, so the guests rang me instead. Every golf cart was in use, so I trudged from villa to villa on foot, making apologies and buying favour with alcohol.

Guest after guest asked the same question: 'When's it going to stop raining?'

Let me snap my fingers and control the weather for you.

To make matters worse, the boat with supplies hadn't come in. I found Guillaume pacing the kitchen, muttering under his breath. 'No lobster, no beef. They want me to serve chicken? Five-star chicken?' When he began making *pock-pock-pock* noises and flapping imaginary wings, I made a swift exit. Once outside, I heard an explosion of shouting. '*Merde! Connard!*'

The sea was fierce, churning against the shore. As expected, the storm had struck St Kitts and we were receiving only its reverberations. However, the bad weather brought home the fact that our position here, perched on a rock, was precarious.

I asked Reggie how long we could be stuck without provisions. 'Probably only a few days,' he said.

233

'Days?' Even that sounded awful. For the past two-and-a-half weeks, I'd been blissfully ignorant to the fact that we grew nothing on this island, we manufactured nothing. If money could buy it, we had it. Except money couldn't buy you some things.

Mid-afternoon, I remembered I hadn't checked out the downed zip-line yet. This chore suddenly felt like an escape. By climbing Keeper Peak, I could avoid another guest interaction ('my room service arrived cold, what kind of place is this?').

On top of the hill, I pushed my weight against the zip-line's wooden mast. It seemed solid. In fact, everything about it looked fine, apart from the fact that the cable hung slack. It must be the Hidden Cove end that had snapped.

Wind rippled through the jacket I'd borrowed from the storeroom. I wiped the rain from my face and peered over the rocky edge, scanning the place where the cable disappeared downwards, into thick forest. Obviously I didn't have the expertise to fix this.

A piece of white fabric far below caught my attention. I thought, stupidly, that it was a white flag. Surrender.

I looked again, my eyes focusing.

Fifty metres below, a mannequin in a white T-shirt was twisted in the branches of a tree.

33

Tessa.

For God knows how long, she'd been left out in the rain, thrown away like a piece of rubbish. I'd been totally absorbed in planning some pointless party. It hadn't occurred to me to really look for her.

'How do we get her up?' I waded through the undergrowth to the edge of the plateau, but Kip caught me by the arm.

After I'd radioed for help, a motley crew had assembled on Keeper Peak. Fizzy and Maria were crying, useless. Ethan stood with his head bowed, his face obscured by a black rain hat. Kip, with Doc at his side, droned on about fall trajectories.

The rain continued, slithering inside my windbreaker, but my body flushed hot with anger. No one was doing anything.

'We need a rescue helicopter,' I said.

'Not in weather like this,' Doc said.

'We have to get her out of there!' What if there was a chance she was still alive?

Kip drew me away from the edge. 'We will.'

I ground my teeth, knowing if I let go of my anger, I'd have to face the emotions that lay underneath.

I had no idea how to rescue Tessa; rescue being the wrong word, anyway. According to Kip, the terrain was too rough to bushwhack through to Tessa at ground level. Instead, he was formulating a plan to lift her out, using the ropes and equipment Ethan had brought from the storeroom.

Brady arrived, underdressed for the wet weather in a T-shirt. 'I just heard.' He pulled me into a hug.

I didn't react at first, but when I inhaled the smell of him, ginger and musk, my body slackened.

'Are you OK?' He raked a hand through my wet hair.

'No.' I closed my eyes and pressed myself into him.

Brady volunteered to climb down and strap Tessa to a solid rescue board. He'd done a lot of mountaineering, apparently. As I watched him descend, it occurred to me: how had he heard about Tessa? Had someone told him or had he already known?

I'd been hanging on to the faint possibility that Tessa might merely be unconscious. Ethan hauled her up the cliff using a pulley system, with Brady pushing from below. They set her down on the ground gently, but there was no disguising the fact that Tessa's skeleton had collapsed. Her legs stuck out at unnatural angles, her torso was twisted, there was a rib bone protruding from her chest. Blood caked one side of her face, wounds mashed up with mud.

Doc checked for a pulse. Crouching down beside him, I touched her arm. She was cold. And there was… a smell.

I recoiled, covering my nose with my sleeve. Ethan took my place. He was heaving in gasps, tears shuddering free.

'I blame myself,' Kip said. 'We should have taken down that zip-line years ago.'

My anger roared back to the surface. 'You're not saying it was an accident?'

'Of course it—'

'Someone did this to her!'

'Hysterical,' Kip muttered.

'We need the police, an investigation.' I stamped out the words. This wasn't happening again; not another murder swept under the carpet.

'Calm. Down.' Kip's voice was severe, like a slap across my face. 'We don't want a panic.'

'Kip…' Fizzy had been hovering at his side, but now she pulled at his arm. 'We need to—'

His voice rose. 'Don't start.'

Fizzy dropped her hand as if scalded. More tears leaked down her face. I blinked, feeling the heat in my own eyes. Dad was shouting.

'All these women' – Kip's lip curled – 'twittering around, making a nuisance. It's not the time.'

He looked to Doc, then to Brady, as if hoping for reassurance. Doc's face was blank. Brady shouldered away from Kip and wrapped an arm around me. It was a relief to let him hold me up. I'd begun to worry I might faint.

Tessa was bundled in a blue tarp. The only visible part of her was a few strands of hair. The idea hit me as Kip and Brady were carrying her away: the physical evidence of her murder had been destroyed, partly by the storm, partly by the rescue.

*

I drummed my hands against the curved bar that cut across one corner of the deserted restaurant.

'Cocktails, cocktails, cocktails!' The rows of bottles were lit from behind. I took a swig of rum, then tequila. 'That'll do it. Let's do a tasting. Can't tell the guests there's been another murder. Oh-ho-ho, nooo, that would ruin a good time. Cocktails…'

I was still in my windbreaker, still muddy and damp, but I didn't care. I offered Diara the bottle. Before she could take it, I slugged from it myself. Whiskey? I was losing track.

'I can only stay a minute.' Diara was perched on a bar stool, her jacket slung over the neighbouring seat, water seeping onto the floor. 'Spa is hectic. Just wanted to check you're OK.'

'I'm spectacular!' I slammed the bottle against the bar and Diara flinched.

From the kitchen, there was the distant clang and clatter of food prep. Normally, the smell of jerk chicken would have made my mouth water, but tonight it only made me think of the meat locker. Tessa's body was in cold storage, right next to the cuts of Iberico ham. Tomorrow morning, when the weather was better, we'd load her onto a boat headed to the morgue. The idea of it made me want to cry and scream and—

'Cocktails! Circus theme. That'll cheer everyone up. Get out the clown wigs.'

'Clowns are creepy.' Diara eased the bottle from my grasp. 'No one needs a cocktail tasting right now.'

No, I needed to organise something. It wasn't five-star service to let the guests sit inside and watch the rain. Everything, absolutely everything, was going to shit, but the guests should be happy.

I grabbed for a different bottle, but Diara grasped my hand this time.

'You're not helping Tessa by getting drunk,' she said.

Hearing her name made something inside me crumple. I squeezed Diara's fingers, hard enough that it must have hurt, but she didn't complain.

'She was a baby,' I whispered.

'Yeah.'

Two hours ago, I'd psyched myself up to call Tessa's parents. It was a drawn-out process. No one answered. I called again twice, left a message, then they rang back on the landline. Fizzy, who was in the office with me, picked up the call. Her face went pale and she handed me the phone. *Gee, thanks.*

I couldn't stop replaying the keening cry Tessa's mother had released when I'd broken the news that her only daughter was dead.

'She was, what? Twenty? Twenty-one?' I said to Diara. 'If I met Moxham when I was that age, who knows what he would've talked me into…'

Diara extricated her hand from my death grip. 'He didn't talk her into anything.' Her words were slow and deliberate. 'She made a choice.'

'She deserved it?'

'Didn't say that.'

We lapsed into silence. There weren't enough lights on in the restaurant and the swaying palm trees outside created eerie, shifting shadows.

'This is really fucking bad,' I said in an undertone. 'The killer's out of control. Tessa knew too much. She had to go.'

Diara grabbed the rum and took a drink. 'Do we know when Tessa was killed?'

'No fucking idea. Believe me, I wish we could get CSI out here. But I bet Kip gets his old pal, Howell, on the phone, drags his heels, tells him, oh no, we don't need any of that…'

As I spoke, it hit me that I was drunk. The alcohol wasn't making me feel tingly-good; it was making me feel jangly-weird.

'Who saw her last?' Diara asked.

'Ethan, probably.' God, Ethan. I couldn't stop picturing him on Keeper Peak. A man torn open.

'I talked to him, he's in pieces. But last he saw her was Thursday morning.'

'Thursday…' That was three days ago. Surely, she hadn't been on the peak for three days? 'Thursday was the picnic. I used the zip-line myself. It was fine.'

'That means… sometime after that, it broke'

'Oh, Jesus, it was my fault. I left Tessa to do the clean-up after the picnic. That's when she used the zip-line. I sent her to her death.'

I gripped the bar, curling my toes to try and stop the seasick feeling.

'Not your fault.' Diara slid off her bar stool and got a bottle of water from the chiller. 'Drink this.'

'I should have gone instead of her. The killer expected me to go back up there. They must have seen me on the zip-line, figured I'd use it again. Fuck. They were trying to kill me.'

'You don't know that.'

I heard the uncertainty in Diara's voice. She nudged the glass bottle towards me. I gulped water but ended up coughing.

'I don't think I can do this anymore,' I said. 'I think I need to leave.'

'Leave?'

'Leave and keep my fucking life.'

'Listen, London…' She reached out and anchored my shoulders, forcing me to look at her. 'We don't know anything yet. So don't go off the deep end.'

I squeezed my eyes shut (too fucking late; I was off the deep end and falling), but Diara kept talking, her voice low and calm.

'The rain will be gone by tomorrow. We'll go to VG, see my auntie. She'll know what to do.'

I sniffed hard in an effort to stop myself from crying. 'OK.' It sounded like the best plan we had.

Diara let me go. She retrieved her jacket and pulled it on. 'Hafta go to the spa, but I'll see you at home in two hours.'

Despite myself, I cracked a tiny smile at the word home. Yes, I'd go home, lock myself in our cupboard-room, where nothing could hurt me.

'Drink some water,' she said. 'Get some sleep.'

'If I'm sleeping… it's with a knife under my pillow.' I wasn't sure if I was joking. I could steal one from the kitchen.

'Ohh-kay.' Diara gave a dark laugh. 'And when you wake up in the middle of the night in a panic? Waving that knife around? Remember I'm your friend.'

*

The following day, I had the hangover from hell.

I stumbled around my room in a towel, looking for clean underwear, before giving up and going without. I strapped on my radio. It was still raining, which meant I had to brace myself for another day of complaints from the guests. Maybe I could organise a poker game? Decorate the restaurant like Vegas and serve lots and lots of drinks? The smell of rum lifted off my skin and I almost retched.

Diara had left before I'd woken up, presumably headed back to the spa. I wasn't a meteorologist, but the weather was looking worse than yesterday, not better. The ferry wasn't running. We were short-staffed, because those who lived off-island couldn't get to work. God help us if there was a problem with the power, because the chief engineer lived on Tortola.

Still, I wasn't giving up hope. It was just rain, right? There had to be a chance we could take the bowrider over to Virgin Gorda to see Diara's auntie. In my windbreaker, I trudged along the muddy bush trail towards the spa. Diara was a BVI native; she'd lived through hurricanes; surely she wouldn't be put off by a mere storm?

'*Help me! Somebody!*'

The voice was faint. It took me a second to realise where it was coming from. I spun the volume on my radio. Reggie's voice grew louder.

'Heeeeeeelp! She dead.'

34

Hidden Cove was shrouded in a pearly mist, the wind and the waves creating a background roar. I pelted across the sand, with the rain whipping into my eyes. There were three figures; one standing, one kneeling, one laid out on their back. Fizzy.

Her patterned sundress was spread out over the sand, the material soaked through. The tide was coming in. A rush of foamy white tickled at her feet. Still, she didn't move.

A sick feeling rose in my throat. Not again. Not another body.

'What happened?' I stooped down next to Fizzy. She was so pale. 'What happened!'

Reggie knelt with his eyes screwed shut, reciting the Lord's Prayer. He didn't reply.

Guillaume, head bowed against the rain, had his phone pressed to his ear. 'The helicopter – the boats – they do not know if they can come in this weather,' he said to me.

'Fizzy?' When I touched her, the cold feel of her skin made me shudder.

Everything about her appearance convinced me she was dead. Then I found a flutter of a pulse at her neck.

'Fizzy!' I shook her shoulder. 'Fizzy, wake up.'

Was she breathing? I was so jumpy, I couldn't tell. I tried to find her pulse again, but either it was gone or I didn't know what I was doing. I glanced at the other two, hoping to abdicate responsibility, but Reggie still had his eyes shut, while Guillaume was staring at me, slack-jawed.

Shit. My first-aid training consisted of a one-day course, too many years ago. Did I even remember how to do CPR? I braced my arms straight and placed my palms on the clammy material that covered Fizzy's chest. I laced my fingers together and pumped hard, counting in my head.

Within a minute, I was exhausted. I kept going. I was so fixated on my task that I almost missed the tiny jolt of Fizzy's chest.

She coughed.

I sat back on my haunches, panting. 'Fizzy?'

She let out a moan and rolled over, knees up to her chest.

'Fizzy, what happened?'

Her eyelids were fluttering, but she didn't reply. At least she was breathing.

'What the hell is going on!'

Kip was running full tilt across the wet sand. He shoved me aside and crouched down beside Fizzy, cupping her face. 'Sweetheart... sweetheart...'

She let out a faint cry. Kip picked her up like she was a rag doll.

'Sir.' My voice rose an octave. 'I don't think we should move her. Wait for the ambulance.'

'Ambulance? No, no, no, we don't need that,' Kip said.

'Paramedic say one or two hours for boat to come,' Guillaume said.

'What are you playing at?' Kip's nostrils flared. 'Paramedics? This is a private matter. Call them back and say you made a mistake.'

Guillaume looked from Kip to me and back again. I was horrified. What if Fizzy lost consciousness again?

Guillaume nodded slowly. 'Yes, sir.'

Apparently chain-of-command trumped common sense. He pulled out his phone.

'Guillaume...' I said, but he didn't meet my gaze. I wheeled around. 'Kip, she needs a doctor.'

Kip blew out a breath, looking down at Fizzy in his arms. 'Clarence Jeston knows what to do, and God knows, he can keep his mouth shut. Someone find him.'

Rain was dripping down my face, obscuring my vision. I was so cold I'd begun to shiver.

'Let's get her home,' Kip said.

Fizzy was alive. I should have felt relief, but I only felt a creeping dread. The killer had tried again but failed. That only meant Fizzy was still in danger.

*

In the circular tower of Kip's villa, Fizzy was draped across one of the white sofas. There was a sour smell of vomit from where she'd thrown up. I'd taken it as a good sign that she was getting something out of her system, but I honestly wasn't sure.

On Kip's orders, Reggie had gone to find Doc, who was staying in the staff village (no way to get home with no boats running), while Guillaume had returned to the restaurant to secure it against the storm. He'd tried to make me go, too, but I'd refused. Now I hovered at the end of the sofa, straining to hear each laboured breath Fizzy inhaled.

She still looked so pale, her lips shading into blue.

I checked my watch. Where was Doc?

Kip must have been thinking the same, because he muttered, 'Tiny bloody island and can't find...'

I curled my fingers into my palms, nails digging into the skin. I wanted Doc here. It wasn't the same as a helicopter whisking Fizzy away to a hospital, but at least Doc might be able to tell what had happened.

Over the last week, Kip had receded in my mind as a murder suspect, especially since I'd found out about his health problems. Today, however, he didn't look like a frail old man; quite the contrary. Had he killed Tessa to shut her up? Had he tried to do the same to Fizzy?

One thing was for sure: I didn't trust him to be alone with her.

The villa's smoked glass, combined with the stormy skies outside, gave the room's curved interior a gloomy feel. I was used to the pristine cleanliness magicked up by the housekeeping team. By contrast, there was a dustiness to Kip's villa, drifts of papers on every surface.

He was doing a tiger walk, back and forth, back and forth. Watching him was adding to my anxiety, so I forced myself to sit down. I had to move a stack of papers from an armchair in order to do so. Distractedly, I flipped through a printout of a web page about CBD oil, a proposal for a golf resort in Madagascar, a flight confirmation to Venezuela, a letter about Pay Per Click advertising. If not hoarder level, this stuff amounted to 'Grandpa doesn't throw anything away.'

Fizzy let out a murmur, her eyelids flickering, and Kip rushed to her side.

'Darling, darling... tell me what you need.'

Her eyes closed and she didn't respond.

Kip sank to his knees on the floor. 'Please, please... I can't do this again.' There came the wet sucking sound of someone trying and failing not to cry. 'Not Meredith all over again...'

God, he was pathetic. Making this all about himself. People were dying here on his private island and he was doing nothing to stop it. What secrets was he keeping? I rose from my chair, advancing on him.

'What did you do to Meredith?' I was tired of varnishing my words; I wanted the truth.

His head whipped around, face crimson. Before he could speak, there was a bang, followed by a howl of wind.

The front door flew open. Doc's fedora was missing, his glasses cloudy.

'Now, now, what's all this?' he asked. 'Bit of a mishap?' I was used to his persistent joviality, but today it struck a disturbing note.

Doc edged past me, his shoes squelching, and dragged a chair to the sofa. A hush fell over the room as he set down his bag and checked over Fizzy.

'I'd say it's benzodiazepines,' Doc said.

Fizzy twitched.

'Benzodiaz-uh…?' I approached Doc. 'What…?'

'Valium, Xanax, prescribed them to her myself. A lot of people don't mean to do it, take too many pills without realising.'

That was much too neat of a solution. 'Are you sure it wasn't—'

Doc cut in, 'You say she stopped breathing?'

I explained how Reggie had found her and Doc said, 'Her respiratory rate's on the slow side, but I'd say she's out of the woods. She'll need monitoring, of course.'

Kip clapped his hands. 'She needs rest. Peace and quiet!'

He was looking at me, obviously expecting me to leave. No fucking way. Before I could respond, the front door opened again.

It was Diara. She tripped on the rattan rug in her haste to get inside. Raindrops glistened in her braids; her T-shirt was soaked.

'What happened?' She was out of breath like she'd been running.

Slipping past Doc, she crouched by the sofa. When she put both hands on Fizzy's face, the other woman mumbled but didn't open her eyes.

'Baby, can you hear me?'

Diara tried to lift her up, get her into a sitting position, but she kept flopping down again. Kip cleared his throat and took a step towards the pair.

'She too cold.' Diara glanced at Doc. 'Why she not talking?'

Doc busied himself with repacking his satchel. 'She's had a lotta excitement…'

Understatement of the century.

Diara's fingers twined through Fizzy's hair. She pressed a kiss to her lips. 'Wake up, love, wake up.'

Kip stood with his arms crossed, watching the scene unfold. Fizzy released a long, laboured breath. She said something under her breath, but I didn't catch it.

'Leave me alone,' she said, louder this time.

There was a stunned silence. Diara's face crumpled. She angled away from me, rubbing at her eyes.

Kip grabbed a caramel-coloured blanket from an armchair and lay it over Fizzy. In the process, he nudged Diara out of the way. 'Too many people, too many people.'

Fizzy moaned, her body convulsing. She threw up again into a decorative glass bowl I'd emptied of shells and placed beside her.

Blood. There was blood in her vomit.

Diara rushed back to her, but Fizzy flinched away. She curled up beneath the blanket. All that was visible was a shroud of black hair.

'We hafta get her to the hospital,' Diara said and I echoed a 'yes'.

'Easier said than done, weather like this,' Doc said.

'She just needs rest,' Kip said. 'Quiet.'

The room was already so quiet it felt like a morgue. Seconds dragged by, all of us standing around like mourners.

Finally, I grabbed the vomit bowl from the floor. 'Help me a minute,' I said to Diara with a pointed look.

Diara's body was limp. She resisted, but then let me drag her down the hall. I led us inside a bathroom and made sure to lock the door behind us. After I'd washed out the bowl in the sink, I left the water running.

'This feels wrong,' I said.

Diara didn't reply. She balanced on the edge of the whirl-pool tub.

'Why would she collapse like that?' I said. 'Except – poison. I keep thinking poison. Blue lips, right? Blood in her vomit.'

'I don't know…' Diara's voice was hoarse. 'Someone poisoned her? You think so?'

'What else? Two bodies in two days. I'm… I'm fucking scared.'

From the tap, water gushed, hypnotic white noise.

'She knew a lot,' Diara said. 'Fizzy. She been here the longest.'

'She knew too much?'

As Kip's Girl Friday, hadn't I always suspected Fizzy knew where the bodies were buried? Now it seemed all too literal. The killer wanted to bury that knowledge forever. I recalled Kip's odd behaviour in the office. Had he been tampering with Fizzy's pills?

'Too much.'

I barely heard Diara, because she'd covered her face with her hands, knuckles digging into her eye sockets.

Fizzy knew too much, but then, so did Diara and I.

'What do we do?' A sob threatened to erupt from my throat.

'Get her away from him.' Diara lifted her head and met my gaze, her expression hardening.

*

It took some of my best coaxing (downcast eyes, *sotto voce*, 'whatever you think is right, sir'), but I persuaded Kip we should move Fizzy to her own apartment. Reluctantly, he stayed behind, while Doc, Diara and I transported the patient to the staff village.

Doc held an umbrella over us, but it didn't stop the rain from splashing our faces as Diara and I lifted Fizzy from the golf cart, in through the door and onto her bed. Unlike most of the rooms in the staff village, which had a student-y air, Fizzy's apartment looked more like a grown-up home, with striped wallpaper and blush-coloured curtains. A mirror to my left was decorated with colourful slips of paper. One of them read, *I am worthy of admiration.*

Fizzy burrowed under the covers, as if hoping to make the world disappear. I'd expected Doc would stay with her, but after he checked her vital signs again, he seemed satisfied she was in a stable condition.

He patted his stomach. 'Know where a hungry man can find a bite of sustenance?'

'You're leaving?' I said.

'I'll check on her in an hour or two.'

Across the room, Diara was leaning over Fizzy, stroking a hand across her cheek. Fizzy recoiled from her. Hurt registered on Diara's face.

'Come, come,' Doc said, 'she'll want to sleep.'

Diara dropped into an armchair. Her expression had turned stony. 'I'm not leaving.'

'I understand,' Doc said, 'she gave us a scare, but—'

'I'm not leaving her side.'

I was relieved. Diara would protect Fizzy.

Doc exhaled a breath through his nose, but he didn't argue. He picked up his leather bag and ducked out of the apartment. I wavered, not sure if I should stay or go.

'Be safe,' I said to Diara quietly. 'Lock the door.'

'Trust me.' She reached for the long-stemmed torch that lay on Fizzy's nightstand and brandished it like a weapon. 'Kip comes in here, I'll kill him.'

35

The next day, I woke with a start. Someone was humming.

'Good morning.'

I sat up and rubbed my eyes, registering grey daylight. Across the room, Diara was dressed not in her uniform but in a khaki tank top that revealed the edge of the tattoo on her shoulder. She was rolling items of clothing into a sports bag.

'Is it still raining?' My voice came out hoarse.

'Listen.' Diara flashed a smile.

I didn't have to strain to hear the horror-movie howl of the wind or the percussion of rain on the window. There would be no rescue helicopters arriving.

'Shit,' I muttered.

'If you say so,' Diara said.

I scrubbed the sleep dust out of my eyes and swung my feet out of bed. I'd asked Diara the wrong question.

'How is she?'

'Much better,' she said.

'Oh.' A big breath flowed out of me. I'd been tensed for bad news. 'That's great.'

'Can't keep that woman down.'

'Who's with her? Doc?'

'No, he's eating breakfast. That man has a clock in his stomach.'

'Is she by herself?' My voice rose an octave.

There was a bang. Something (a tree branch?) hit the window. My head whipped to one side, but Diara didn't react.

'Fizzy?' I said. 'She shouldn't be by herself.'

'She sleeping.'

'We should go and check on her. If she's alone, she could be in danger.'

If Fizzy was recovering, that made her a greater danger to Kip. I had a vision of him slipping into her room right this second, administering another dose of poison.

Diara gave me a sidelong look. 'She fine.'

I shoved my bare feet into shoes and ran a hand through my sleep-rumpled hair.

'I'll check on her.' I crossed the room, but before I could open the door, Diara darted forward and blocked my path.

'She fine. You go and see her, that'll only upset her.'

'What are you talking about?'

'She told me, last night. She took the pills on purpose. By the time she collapsed, she was already regretting it.'

I rocked back on my heels. 'She tried to kill herself?'

Diara raised one shoulder in a shrug.

'No,' I said, 'you must have it wrong. It was Kip. He's trying to kill her.'

Her laugh was derisive. 'That's insane.'

'Diara... he was in the office the other day. He swapped out her pill bottle or something. I saw him. Everything we've uncovered... it all points to Kip. He's the killer.'

Here, now, it was so obvious. Kip had lifted Fizzy yesterday like she weighed nothing; clearly, he had the strength to kill Moxham. The night of the Alice party, he could have swiped Diara's phone and used it to message Moxham. The tall man seen near the boat-house? Kip. He must have murdered Tessa when he found out she was Moxham's accomplice. And, when he realised Fizzy, his keeper of secrets, was getting suspicious, he tried to kill her too.

'It was him.' I stabbed the air using my finger. 'And if we don't stop him, he'll kill again.'

I waited for Diara to react, but she remained impassive. Her serenity was unnerving. She leaned against the door, fingering her earring. Today's fashion choice was a red bird with a sharp beak. Something about it snagged at the edge of my brain.

'Are the boats running?' I said at last. 'Can we get off the island?' My voice sounded plaintive. 'I really think we need to leave.'

Diara smacked her tongue. 'The waves are ten feet tall. Nothing leaving this island today.'

'We need to protect ourselves, then.' (Why had I only joked about stealing a knife from the kitchen? I wanted a knife.) 'Do you still have that gun?'

Diara let out a humourless laugh. 'Stop. You're letting your imagination run away. It's all coincidences.'

She shook her head and her bird earrings jangled. Red birds. What were they called? Cardinals.

'That's not true,' I said. 'There's evidence. The jet-ski key was still in the boathouse.'

She turned away. 'I don't remember.'

'The blood—'

'Kip gets nosebleeds.'

'But the boathouse was cleaned up.'

'Shirley did a deep-clean after Kip complained.'

'That can't be it. The fingerprints on the broken glass—'

'Someone musta dropped a beer bottle.'

'Why are you saying all this?'

Diara didn't respond. She returned to her bed and shook out a T-shirt, before rolling it tight. I focused on the tattoo on her shoulder blade.

It was a devil.

'Your tattoo,' I said. 'What does it mean?'

'Nothing. Family joke.'

'Devil. Did Moxham call you that?'

There was a long silence. Diara turned to look at me, all camaraderie wiped from her expression. Her lips remained in the barest quirk of a smile, but her eyes were dead.

'He wrote about you,' I said, 'in his notebook. Pages and pages. About you.'

The words from the notebook returned to me. Teardrop, peacock, snake. Cardinal. These weren't random words. They were descriptions, of Diara and her earrings. The notes encompassed what she wore each day, where she went, what she did.

'Stop.' She zipped up the bag on her bed. When the zip snagged, she yanked at it. The material split.

'He was... tracking you.'

'Stop.' Diara rounded on me. 'You love to stick your nose where it don't belong. Get you in trouble one of these days.'

She socked me on the arm as she swung the bag onto her shoulder. I let out an *ow* sound, but she didn't even look at me. Two steps and she was at the door.

'Diara, wait,' I said.

She ignored me.

'Please, tell me what's going on.'

The door slammed shut behind her.

*

Despite everything, I'd thought I was safe here at home.

Now, I flipped over my pillow and rummaged inside its case, looking for the olive-green notebook. I'd hidden it here days ago. What other clues from it had I overlooked? I'd wondered for a time if Diara and Moxham had been in a relationship. Finding out Diara was seeing Fizzy had put paid to that theory. Yet Moxham's notes about Diara had the ring of obsession about them. He must have followed her movements closely. Stalkerish.

The worst part was, I wasn't shocked. In Hong Kong, Violet's break-up with Moxham had been bad. I'd got the impression his love for her had tipped over into obsession. Maybe the same thing had happened with his feelings for Diara.

I shook the pillow out of its case. Where was the notebook?

For that matter, where were the USB drives? I kept those in my pillow too. I turned the pillowcase inside out. I balled it up.

Nothing.

Someone had taken them. The suspect list wasn't long. Diara was the only person who knew they were there.

I needed to go after her and continue this conversation. Stripping off the T-shirt I wore to sleep, I scrounged up a fresh pair of shorts and T-shirt from the drawer. While I was looking for socks, my hands closed around a lumpy pair.

It was the spy-cam I'd found, my first night in this room.

I froze. The final puzzle piece slotted into place.

The camera I'd found in my room hadn't been for me. Moxham wasn't obsessed with me. He was obsessed with Diara. Long before I arrived, the camera had been watching her every move.

36

I shoved the spy-cam's SD card into my laptop, which still bore the sticky residue of Moxham's busty dinosaur sticker. It made my skin crawl to imagine him watching Diara in this way.

The files on the SD card were automatically labelled by date. I located the twenty-first, the date of Moxham's murder, and hit play. The camera software created a new file each day at 6 a.m. I'd already watched the part of the footage that captured midnight till 2 a.m., but what about the rest of the day and night?

I should have pored over every second of footage before now, but I'd wanted to believe in Diara's innocence. I'd thought she was my friend. It was my biggest blind spot. I didn't want her to be a murderer.

Once my eyes adjusted to the monochrome of night vision, I saw my room and the spot on the bed where I was seated right now. Diara appeared on the screen. On fast-forward, she dressed and sped around the room, before leaving. The rectangle of footage brightened and dimmed.

Diara re-entered the room at – I checked the timestamp – 22:46. She roamed around, picking up discarded items of clothing, plugging in her phone to charge. I was about to hit fast-forward again when her head turned.

It was the jerking motion of a cornered animal. Someone else was there.

Diara's lips were moving; I didn't need sound to know she was telling someone off.

Moxham stepped into the frame. My heart dropped. If it was 10:46 p.m., this must be about half an hour after he'd left me in the Jacuzzi at Villa Queen Conch. He crossed the room and put his hands on her shoulders. She attempted to shrug him off, but his grip on her tightened. I tried to imagine what they were saying. Diara's face was still scrunched up. Maybe he would be placating.

Get out of here! she'd say.

Listen, he'd say, *I want you to listen...*

He shook her hard. She slapped him.

All at once, the pleading was over. The screen was a flurry of movement. Moxham grabbed Diara by the neck. Her face stretched in a scream, but he clamped his other hand over her mouth. She was struggling, legs kicking, fingers scratching, but he was stronger than her. He pushed her onto the bed.

I didn't want to watch anymore. My hand hovered over the pause button, then slackened. I wanted to know. Good or bad, I always wanted to know.

I let the video play.

Diara's body had gone dead beneath Moxham. He rose above her, one hand holding her down, the other unzipping his trousers.

Please, don't.

I've seen the way you look at me. You want it. Stop pretending.

Please, please, please.

I imagined Diara breaking down in desperate sobs, but the Diara on the screen had other ideas. Moxham was too preoccupied with his dick to notice, but her left hand was snaking under the mattress. She withdrew the gun, gripping it awkwardly. My heart was in my throat. For one terrible second, I thought she was going to drop it. Her grasp tightened around the gun. She slammed the barrel against the side of Moxham's head. He recoiled.

Diara scrambled backwards, away from Moxham, so that her back was against the wall. Both hands were clamped around the gun.

I'll do it. I will shoot you in the face.

A second later, he was on his feet. He was gesturing, saying something to Diara. In response, she waved the gun in the air. Moxham backed away. He was evidently moving too slowly for Diara's liking, because she trained the gun on him again. He was still talking. Then, with a flourish like a bow, he was gone.

What had his parting words been? A threat, undoubtedly, but what kind?

I felt numb as I watched the rest of the video. Diara sat holding the gun for a long time after Moxham left. Both she, and I, kept expecting him to return.

He didn't, though. Fifteen minutes later – the timestamp read 23:01 – she put on a pair of jeans and tucked her oversized T-shirt into them. She left the room. But not before she shoved the gun into the waistband of her jeans.

Little more than an hour later, Moxham would be dead.

*

The air in the room felt thick; memories of what I'd seen on screen layered over the present moment. Diara couldn't have known the extent of Moxham's obsession with her – the hidden cameras, the stalker behaviour – but an instinct must have flared inside her. Moxham's lingering looks, his overfamiliarity, the winking way he'd brush off her rejections; they were all signs that must have kept her on edge.

'Sorry, I'm seeing someone,' I imagined her saying.

He would've shot back, 'I'm not giving up.'

After the attack, Diara must have been distraught. If she went to Kip, would he believe her? If she went to the police, would they take her seriously? Even if they did, she wouldn't be Diara anymore. She'd be the rape victim. What to do next? Live on an island with her attacker? She could take a job elsewhere, but why should she leave when he was in the wrong?

'You absolute fucker!' someone yelled.

My whole body tensed. Someone outside was shouting. A man. The accent sounded Australian. Moxham returned from the dead.

'I was trying to sleep, you maniac.'

No, not Australian. South African. Tyson, the sous-chef. I heard his laughter, brash and low. Nothing like Moxham's hyena laugh.

I sucked up the threat of tears, wiping my nose on my sleeve. It was only banter in the staff village.

A realisation dawned on me. Tessa said she'd heard shouting in the staff village the night of Moxham's death. Diara had brushed it off as nothing; another boisterous night in the staff quarters. The shouting must have been Diara and Moxham. Right from the start of our investigation, Diara had been misdirecting me, working against me.

I thought back to the stumbling, drunken Diara I'd met the night of the Alice party. Now I knew it had been less than an hour after Moxham attacked her. Had she been faking her drunkenness and plotting murder? She certainly hadn't seemed hungover the next day.

It was her text message that had lured him to the boathouse. In the drama of the video, I'd half-forgotten that Moxham hadn't been shot. He'd died of blunt force trauma, but did he have a gun trained on him when he met his end?

Then there was Tessa. When Tessa had revealed she'd overheard her shouting that night, had Diara realised that if she wanted to cover up her first murder, she needed to commit another? Once you'd killed two people, did it become easier?

'Fizzy,' I said aloud and scrambled to my feet.

Fizzy was in danger.

I'd thought Kip wanted to eliminate her because she knew too much. What if Diara wanted to take her out for exactly the same reason?

Pillow talk could be dangerous. Diara might have confided in Fizzy late one night, cocooned in the feeling of intimacy. She'd expected absolution from Fizzy – *I had to do it, baby, I had to kill him* – but instead Fizzy was appalled. I understood that reaction all too well.

How could you? I don't even know who you are anymore.

It would have been as simple as putting Fizzy to sleep. Crush up the pills and put them in her drink. Call it an accidental overdose or spread the word that Fizzy was suicidal.

Fizzy's recovery would be a blow, but it would be easy to take another crack at poisoning her. Diara was Fizzy's guardian angel. She'd been with her all night. At any point, she could have pressed another spiked drink into her hands.

Drink this, baby, you'll feel better.

I threw on a jacket and wrenched open the door. Rain whipped against my face as I rushed across the square.

'Fizzy!' I yelled.

I banged on her door with both fists.

'Fizzy, open up.'

I knocked harder, kicking the door with the heel of my trainer.

'She left already.' It was Tyson, squinting at me through the rain.

'Where?'

'Breakfast?' he said with a shrug.

The bush trail was awash with mud. More than once, I almost slipped. Even in waterproofs, I was drenched, but I didn't slow down.

The roar of the wind merged with the static hum in my brain.

I had to find her. I had to make sure she was safe.

37

At the restaurant, what was alarming was how normal everything seemed. I was greeted by the tinkle of conversation, the clattering of plates, the smell of bacon. As I pushed through the doors, Ethan was escorting a guest inside, shielding her with an enormous umbrella. He looked gaunt, with sunken eyes, yet it was he who asked me, 'You OK?'

'Yeah, yeah.' I swept past him.

The guests must have got tired of staring at the four walls of their villas, because the restaurant was busy. There were more staff members than usual as well, keeping dry and twiddling their thumbs. I stumbled into another waiter, almost upsetting a plate bearing steaming eggs Benedict. Where was Fizzy? Was she here?

'Another dandelion tea, thank you.'

Her voice drifted over to me. There! In the corner, half-obscured by a potted palm.

'Fizzy!' I landed at her table with a great gasp of relief.

She sat alone, in front of a white china teacup and a plate loaded with untouched croissants and fruit. Dressed in a pink patterned sundress, at a glance, she looked her normal self. Up close, her eyes were hollowed and there was a grey tint to her skin.

'Lola, you look appalling.' Fizzy's voice was hoarse. 'Are you OK?'

The windows had steamed up, rain seething against the glass, but inoffensive chill-pop blotted out the sound of the wind.

'I'm fine.' I gave a dizzy laugh. 'And you're fine too.' I wanted to hug her, but she flinched backwards.

'Of course I'm fine.' With a tremor, she reached for her teacup.

'Please, stop drinking that.' I swiped her near-empty cup and tossed the remaining liquid into the potted palm.

'What are you doing?'

'Trust me. Please. I know we haven't seen eye to eye, but you have to believe me.' I was gabbling now, but I didn't care. 'We need to leave. Now. We'll go to the hospital on Tortola. It'll be safe there. Please.'

'You're not making sense.'

I sensed someone behind me and half-turned to see Kip. The noise level had dropped. The more tactful guests were pretending to study their plates, but many of the staff members were staring with undisguised interest at our table.

'Now, now, what's all this?' Kip put his hand on my shoulder.

I shrugged it off. Obviously, I looked like a lunatic, but if I could persuade Fizzy to come with me to the hospital, everything would be OK.

'The hospital,' I said. 'Please. That stuff could still be in your system.'

'The doctor has been taking good care of her,' Kip said.

'She almost died.'

'Let's not be melodramatic.'

'I'm taking her to the hospital.'

Kip started to reply, but Fizzy cut him off with a stern look. He wilted backwards by a step.

'Lola, darling,' she said, 'the boats can't make it out in this weather. Shame, really. I'd prefer it if you were gone today.'

She hugged her arms across her abdomen, as if she were still in pain. But when she lifted her gaze to meet mine, her eyes were hard.

'What?' I said.

'I've been indisposed, so I haven't been able to draw up the paperwork. Usually I would insist on a meeting, but these are unusual circumstances.' She cleared her throat, strengthening her voice. 'I'm afraid you've been terminated. Effective immediately.'

'What?' I couldn't parse what Fizzy was saying.

'If it had been just a few bottles, maybe we could have overlooked it. But we both know that's not the case. Shouldn't come as a shock to you. It amounts to gross misconduct.'

'You're firing me?' My voice came out loud enough that everyone who'd returned to their mimosas and their breakfast conversation now swung their heads back around.

Fizzy's lips puckered. 'Yes.'

I turned to look at Kip, who was still standing nearby, hands clasped at his groin, looking like Fizzy's bodyguard.

'You can't fire me,' I said.

'Let's not do this here, gorgeous girl.' Kip cupped my elbow. I didn't resist as he guided me towards the kitchen.

I was in shock. I'd worried Fizzy wouldn't believe me, that Diara might try to convince her everything was fine. I'd even wondered if Diara might try and shut me up by force. I hadn't expected to be fired.

My face flushed as we passed a gawking Guillaume.

Kip nudged me through the door into the pantry. Fizzy followed, wafting a herbal scent.

'There's been a misunderstanding,' I said, as the pantry door clanged shut.

Inside, it was cool and dark. My shoulder connected with a shelf weighed down by a dozen types of flour. It reverberated and Kip made a tutting sound. He was blocking the door. When I realised this, the muscles in my legs tightened.

'I'm sure you thought you were being ever so clever,' Fizzy was saying. 'Taking the odd bottle of wine while you were doing inventory. Putting it down to breakage. Charging guests for five bottles, only delivering four. Who'd notice? It must have been a nice sideline for you. Of course, it's also fraud.'

I stared at her. Frankly, I was offended. It was a poxy scheme. I'd caught drinks managers doing the same in the past and fired them unceremoniously.

'I didn't do this!' I said it to Fizzy at first, but her face was a brick wall. I swivelled around, my voice turning pleading. 'Kip, I didn't do this.'

His face was regretful, although maybe it was a lifetime of phony corporate empathy.

'I'm afraid this is the situation,' he said.

Fizzy cut in. 'I had someone check your suitcase in the storage room. There were twenty bottles hidden inside, ranging in value from five-hundred to five-thousand dollars.'

'Anyone could have put those there! It wasn't me.'

'I also called your former employer,' Fizzy said. 'Moxham never bothered to take out references on you, but I did.'

Her lips twisted into an insincere smile. It made me want to punch her.

'Very strange,' she said, 'they couldn't understand why you left without notice. They're checking paperwork, making sure nothing's amiss.'

I stayed very still, trying not to react. There was nothing to find at the hotel in Hong Kong. I'd never stolen from them, never laundered money or cooked the books. However, if my former bosses began digging deeper, they might uncover a trail that led from Moxham to Shin to Nathan. Despite everything, I wanted Nathan to be safe.

'This place,' Fizzy was saying, 'it's more than a job to me, it's my home. I couldn't sleep at night thinking something might be wrong.'

The statement made my blood boil. 'Something's wrong, alright. I don't know if you're all in on it together' – I flicked a look of contempt at Kip – 'but it's fucking wrong.'

Kip raised his voice, acting as if I hadn't spoken. 'I'm afraid I'll be contacting the local police. And your position here is terminated with immediate effect.'

'Kip, her radio,' Fizzy said, gesturing.

'If you'll just unclip it for me now…' He reached out but stopped short of touching my waist.

I bundled the radio in his direction. 'Take it! I'm fucking gone. There is nowhere in the world I want to be less than this godforsaken island.'

Fizzy made a *hrm* sound in the back of her throat. For a second, she looked incredibly frail. 'She needs to be contained.'

'We'll set you up in my guest room until the storm calms down,' Kip said.

'What? Under lock and key?' God, there was no way out. I was at their mercy.

'Room service,' he said. 'A lovely soft bed.'

'More than you deserve.' Fizzy was looking at me like I was dirt on her designer shoes.

'Come now.' Kip extended a hand, like he was expecting me to promenade with him.

I shrank backwards. 'Don't fucking touch me.'

He advanced on me again. This time, his smile was gone.

I panicked. I didn't want these people anywhere near me. I grabbed at random from the shelves around me and batted a bag of flour in his direction. It exploded against his shoulder.

Shock caused him to stutter sideways. I took the opportunity to open the door, scarpering out the back of the kitchen, ignoring Guillaume, who called after me.

Outside, the rain was falling harder than it had been before. I could barely see. I ran anyway, without knowing my destination.

If I went back to my room, they'd find me there. Lock me up. Or worse.

I took the paved path westwards, running parallel with Main Beach. At least it was solid ground here and not a muddy mess.

I needed somewhere to hide.

I needed to get away from Kip and Fizzy and Diara.

They're all backstabbers. You'll see.

Was there anyone left I could trust?

38

By the time I reached Brady's villa, I was shivering so hard, my teeth were chattering out of my skull. I braced myself against a gust of wind and hammered on his door.

What if he wasn't home? I didn't remember seeing him at the restaurant, but he might have arrived as I was leaving. I knocked again and the door swung open. Brady was dressed in a towel. His hair was as wet as mine, his bare chest glistening, but he looked flushed and warm.

'Can I come in?'

His eyebrows flicked upwards in surprise. 'You're drenched.' He held open the door. 'Let me get you a towel.'

I took a step inside, dripping on the tile floor. I aimed a look behind me, scanning the gloom for signs I'd been followed. He scampered upstairs, tightening the grip on his own towel and taking the steps two at a time. I shut the door. The snap of the lock made me feel more secure.

When Brady returned, he was dressed in a bathrobe. He offered me one as well. I had a vague sense that I should make a joke – *let's get out of these wet clothes* – but I was too numb for flirting.

'Something to warm you up,' he said. 'Bloody Mary?'

It was barely 9 a.m., but the storm made time feel irrelevant. I left Brady mixing drinks and slipped into the downstairs bathroom. I peeled off my jacket and clothes and draped them over the shower screen to dry. The robe felt heavenly soft against my chilled flesh. It was embroidered with a key logo and the words *Keep Keeper Island a secret*. At least I'd stopped shaking.

In the living room, I curled up on the sofa, the same white as in all the villas. I was sipping distractedly from my Bloody Mary, but after a drop of it spilled on my robe, I put down the drink. Too much like blood.

'Wanna hear something funny?' I asked.

Brady was in the armchair, his eyes on the enormous picture windows that framed the water. Waves galloped across the rocks, white spray flying. The unfettered sea formed a permanent thunder, one that made my jaw clench.

He glanced at me. 'Sure.'

'I got fired today.' I tried a *shit-happens-right?* grin, but it collapsed on my face.

'What? How is that possible?'

'Long story.'

'You're freakin' great at your job, they can't fire you.'

Brady's fist bounced against the arm of his chair. I was touched at how outraged he appeared. 'I'll talk to Kip. He'll have a change of heart.'

I shook my head. 'He won't.' When Brady opened his mouth to say more, I cut him off. 'Can I borrow your phone?'

Without hesitation, he unlocked it and tossed it to me. The irony didn't escape me. A week ago, I'd been obsessed with the messages on his phone from Andrew. Now that seemed much less significant than Diara's deception and the fact that Kip and Fizzy were closing ranks.

I dialled a number, the only one I had memorised, and pressed the phone to my ear. It rang out, then clicked onto voicemail: 'Hi, you've reached Allie and Flora, leave us a message, or send a text like a normal human being.'

A sob rose in my throat at the sound of my sister's voice. I wanted a hug from her. I wanted to tell her everything and receive the warm glow of her sympathy. I also knew that telling her the truth would only terrify her.

'Hi, lovelies, it's me,' I said in my cheeriest tone. 'Hope things are sunny in London. Speak soon.' My voice caught in my throat. 'I love you.'

I ended the call before I started crying. Shielding my eyes, I let the phone fall between the sofa cushions. Brady moved to sit beside me on the sofa.

'Hey, hey, you OK?' He wrapped his arms around me.

I resisted his hug for several seconds, my elbow firm against his ribs. He hugged me tighter and I collapsed against him. My tears and snot soaked into the collar of the bathrobe. I cried and cried, until I was heaving dry sobs.

'That's a lot you've been holding in,' Brady said in a low voice.

'You have no idea.'

We stayed like that for a long time, listening to the clamour of the storm. Despite my current emotional state, my lizard brain was enjoying the closeness of Brady. I wiped away the last of my tears and leaned against his chest. The steady rise and fall of his breathing calmed me.

My robe had got twisted on my body, falling open to reveal my bare leg. As we hugged, Brady had been stroking my knee, the barest of caresses. Now his hand moved up my thigh. His lips grazed my temple. I hesitated. I caught the green of his eyes, blurred at close proximity, and I angled my face towards him.

Tap, tap, tap.

I started at the sound.

Tap, tap.

Someone was at the front door.

'Don't answer it,' I said.

Brady gave me a quizzical look. I pressed myself closer and kissed him hard.

'Stay here,' I murmured.

The tapping on the door turned to knocking. 'Brady, let me in.' Kip's voice.

Brady was visibly conflicted. 'Don't worry, I'll get rid of him.' He pecked me on the lips and unfolded himself from the sofa.

I grabbed a fistful of his robe. 'You answer the door, I'm screwed.'

'I can talk to him about—'

'Listen to me. They think I did something wrong, but I didn't. Do you believe me?'

'Of course.' He tugged himself free from my grip with half a shrug.

As he strode towards the door, I crumpled to the floor and scooted out of sight.

'Hello, sir!'

'Apologies for the interruption,' Kip said. (I couldn't see him, but I pictured him swathed in wet-weather gear, looking like a fisherman.) 'You haven't seen Lola, have you? Our dazzling manageress.'

I held my breath, my cheek pressed against the fabric of the sofa-back.

'What's going on?' Brady asked.

'Small matter to clear up.' (I imagined Kip angling his neck, trying to see inside the villa.) 'Thought she might have paid you a visit.'

Balanced against the cold tile floor, my hands were in fists. This was it, the moment when Brady would sell me out. What did I matter to him? Rich people always stuck together. I glanced sideways at the glass doors that led out to the beach. Should I make a run for it now? Back out into the storm?

'Haven't seen her,' Brady said.

'You sure?'

'Just me on my lonesome.'

'Ah, well, there's plenty of people at the restaurant if you fancy some company.'

'Maybe later.'

I released a breath, sagging against the back of the sofa. Brady had come through for me.

'If you see that girl, let me know, though,' Kip was saying. 'Between you and me, she's having psychiatric problems, needs support.'

Heat rose up my face in a scratchy flush. Psychiatric problems?

Brady and Kip said their goodbyes and the door shut. When Brady came into view, he extended a hand to help me up.

'Want to fill me in?'

'I'm not crazy,' I said. 'It's them! They're out to get me.'

Brady's eyebrows crept up his forehead. I cringed.

'I know,' I said, 'that's exactly what a crazy person would say. But you have to trust me.'

Brady's hand was still entwined with mine. He swept it up to lay a kiss on my palm. Despite myself, I felt a tremor in my legs.

'I do trust you,' he said. 'Now you need to trust me. Tell me what's going on.'

*

Brady made another round of Bloody Marys. I gulped mine down automatically, before I considered it would be better for me to stay sober.

There was a bang outside. I whipped around.

'Just the storm,' he said.

Shit. I was still jittery from my close shave with Kip.

'D'you think he'll be back?'

'No, you're good.'

'Yeah... yeah, I guess.'

The rain outside the window, whipped along by fast winds, had taken on the appearance of smoke. I shivered. I wanted to get off this island, but there was no way I was leaving today. It was a case of waiting till the storm died down.

Brady handed me a fresh cocktail. I sipped from it, savouring the warmth pooling in my belly, and forced myself to take a few deep breaths. No one would be looking for me here. I was safe. We settled on the sofa, close enough that his thigh was pressing against mine.

Brady was looking at me with penetrating eyes. 'This is to do with that Moxham guy, ain't it?'

I released a breath. 'I think Moxham and Tessa were both murdered.'

My story came out in a jumbled mess. Brady listened intently.

'He was blackmailing people...' he said. 'So my buddy, Andy, was right.'

'Andy?' I feigned innocence.

'He comes to Keeper on the regular, he's how I met Kip. Anyway, I see him in Manhattan a couple months ago and he's got this crazy story about how someone recorded him while he was drunk at Keeper.'

I took a swig of my cocktail and wiped my mouth.

'It's some so-called confession,' he said, 'but it's all bullshit, right? Like the guy fed him the lines and then accused him of... I don't even know what.'

When I told Brady the extent of Andrew's confession, his eyes widened.

'Wow, I know Andy paid out some money, but... jeez, he really did that?' He jerked his head. 'Don't know what to think anymore.'

'Moxham had a pretty sophisticated operation going on,' I said.

'Well, he sure as heck didn't try and blackmail me.' Brady rubbed his face. 'Too boring, I guess.'

'I think the murderer... I think it was someone close to Moxham.' Still, after everything, I didn't want to say Diara's name.

'Not someone he blackmailed?'

'… Not sure of anything anymore.' The alcohol had made my mind fuzzy. Did Kip care enough about Diara to cover for her? Had I fitted the puzzle pieces together correctly?

Brady draped his arm across the back of the sofa. 'Where's the footage?'

'Long story.'

'Are the police involved? I could make some calls. Don't know if the NYPD has any influence down here, but at least we could get advice.'

Part of me wanted someone to swoop in and take the burden of the situation away from me, but what jurisdiction would the NYPD have? Brady was either naïve or arrogant. Still, at least he was on my side. We fell into silence. He drew me close and it was comforting to burrow into his embrace. I finally felt warm, my hair dry and my muscles relaxed.

'Once the storm dies down, we need to get you out of here,' Brady said.

'Trust me, I know.'

'Pick a place,' he said. 'I'll pay for the ticket.'

It sounded tempting. Get on the next flight to… Singapore. Cape Town. Medellín.

'Heck, come to New York,' he said, taking my hand and squeezing it.

'What would I do in New York?'

'Whatever you like.'

A queasy, euphoric feeling washed over me. I stole my hand back from him and took another gulp from what turned out to be an empty glass. The room was spinning. Everything felt unreal. Maybe it was the cocktails, or maybe it wasn't. My real life had been Hong Kong. This, here and now, was something else. I was treading water in the middle of an ocean. I couldn't find land anywhere.

Outside, there was a flash of lightning.

Brady shifted closer to me, big and solid. Maybe he could be the land I needed. For now.

His first kiss was feather-light. He smelled like gingerbread and he was warm. So warm.

'I'm serious,' he murmured. 'I want to be with you.'

I kissed him this time, a deeper kiss, and then let my lips stray to his neck. His skin was salty.

I could be that girl, I supposed. Follow a guy to a new place; be the window dressing of his life. That was how my mother had lived her happiest years, creating a home for a man who was hardly ever there. Home. I had a crazy desire to be at home. I just didn't know where that home might be.

'You'll love it there.' His voice was husky. His hands tangled in my hair. 'City of light.'

'That's Paris.'

'Fine. The big apple.'

I pressed myself against his chest. Any separation between us felt unbearable. I could feel his muscles beneath the softness of the bathrobe.

I put my lips beneath his clavicle, opened my mouth and mimed taking a bite, feeling the give of his skin. 'Big. Apple.'

Brady drew in a shaky breath. 'Do it again for real.'

This time I bit down.

39

blinked awake. Sunlight seared against my eyes, so I shut them
again. I rolled over in bed, escaping the light, and collided
with the hard mass of his body.

Eyes closed, I breathed in the smell of Nathan.

No. Wrong.

I blinked again and remembered where I was. It was Brady's
fair hair and sleep-slack face that greeted me. I pulled away,
stretching my neck. I had a woozy sense that the bed was
moving, rocking with the tide.

Outside, the weather was still raging, wind howling, waves
crashing. Through the open curtains, there was the glare of the
sun, like it was fighting the storm for supremacy.

'Hungry?' Brady's eyes were slits. He tugged me towards him.

Earlier, I'd sunk into him, but now our limbs didn't fit together
right. I twisted myself loose, sitting up in bed. Sweat prickled at
my hairline.

'What time is it?' I asked. How long had I slept?

Brady groped for his phone. 'Almost four.'

'In the afternoon?' I said stupidly. It felt like days had passed,
but it was only a few hours since I'd been fired. God, was I still
drunk? I let myself collapse against the pillows.

Brady began kissing my neck. 'I. Am. Starving.'

'So go eat something.'

'I want ribs.' He dug his thumbs into the flesh beneath my
breasts, a breathy laugh hot against my collarbone.

I angled away from him. It was no good. Whatever fantasy
we'd created was evaporating. I liked Brady, but surely we both

knew this thing wasn't real? Reality was a murderer with me in their sights.

He yawned without covering his mouth. 'Guess I'll go shower. Then we can get breakfast. Dinner, I don't know.'

I didn't reply. The flirting was getting on my nerves. Beneath me, the bed shifted as Brady got up and went into the en-suite bathroom. I struggled out of bed, naked, leaving a tangle of white bed sheets. It was stuffy in here. Was the air-conditioning off?

I went to the glass doors, planning to go out on the veranda and gulp in fresh air. When I tried to open the door, a gust of wind slammed it shut again. The curtains flared. They were soft, thick cream-coloured fabric, but my toe grazed something solid. Looking down, I expected to see a watch or a piece of jewellery, but there was nothing on the floor.

I was yanking at the bottom of the curtain before I'd finished processing what I was doing. The hard object wasn't on the floor. It was inside the hem of the curtain. In my hunt for Moxham's hiding places, I'd missed one. When I'd been in Villa Copper a little over a week ago, Brady had interrupted me; I'd never finished my search, had I?

I'd found one data stick, but there'd been two squirrelled away. Now, as I tore at the hem, a USB drive fell into my hands.

Part of me wanted to wrench the door open and throw it into the storm. What was the use in knowing more of Moxham's blackmail secrets? Where had following this trail got me?

The other part of me had no choice but to look. I recalled speaking to Tessa's mum, her cry of anguish. How could I let that murder go unpunished? One more piece of evidence and surely I'd know who killed Tessa and Moxham.

Flash drive clenched in my fist, I cast around for a way to view its contents. The tablet! Every villa had one.

I took the stairs two at a time and made a pit stop in the down-stairs bathroom. My shorts and T-shirt, laid over the shower screen, were dry, so I got dressed. My jacket and trainers were still sodden. I left them behind.

In the living room, the villa tablet was on the table. I took a seat and jammed Moxham's data drive into the USB slot. A window appeared on the screen, filled with photos. The first picture showed a dozen men, all of them young and strapping, posed against a stately white building with pillars either side of the entrance. I swiped through the photos at speed. Some featured the rolling green lawns of a campus. Stencilled on one of the sweatshirts, I caught the name Attley College.

I flicked through the photos faster and took a sharp inhale as a dimpled young man filled the screen. Brady. He was clean-shaven, his blond hair buzzed short. There was something stiff about his shoulders, the way he was posed against a blue background. Brady was smiling, but his eyes were flat.

I glanced at the staircase, aware that Brady – my Brady, not this younger version – could be finished with his shower any minute. It wasn't a surprise to know that Moxham had been investigating him, but these photos were so innocuous. No violence. No nudity. No sex. Why had Moxham even bothered to hide them? I scanned for swastikas or white power tattoos, but found none. I had to be missing something.

The third time I went over the photos, I spotted someone else in the back row of the group shot. Straight-line smile, brown Caesar haircut. He looked the same as he did on his law firm's website, only half a stone lighter and a few years younger. Andrew Reisslenger.

Underneath the photo of Andy, there was a caption. *Confirmed! Members of the Rites. Secret Society at Attley.* Moxham must have screenshotted the image from the internet. I connected the tablet to data and it only took me a minute to pull up the original webpage.

Killer secret society! All true! Not a hoax!

I skimmed the text. I'd never heard of the Rites, but according to the internet hive mind, they were a clandestine club, all male, who'd formed at Attley College. Their tendrils of influence stretched from Wall Street to the White House, with former members of the Rites apparently wielding an incredible amount of power among the world's elites. The page was edging into conspiracy theory territory, although in my mind, the situation seemed much more banal than that. Of course intelligent, ambitious, white men got ahead by banding together. It was a story as old as time.

Except, there was more: the mysterious death of someone named Rory Palmer.

A zoomed-in version of the group photo Moxham had saved showed this guy, Rory, hunched in the back. A flame of red hair was his only distinguishing mark. He must have been university-age, but could have passed for sixteen.

According to the website, Rory's death had been reported in the press as 'party culture gone wrong'. The cause of death was ruled 'undetermined', although his blood alcohol level was high and there were signs he may have choked on his own vomit. Someone online had got hold of the autopsy report, which showed minor defensive wounds and soil particles in his airways. No one was ever charged. *They killed one of their own and got away with it*, the blogger wrote.

Rain lashed against the windows; the sun had dimmed again. From upstairs, there was the sound of footsteps. I tensed, but Brady didn't appear on the stairs. A klaxon was blaring in my head. *Go. Leave now.*

I knew from Andrew's recorded confession that a pledge at his college had been force-fed alcohol and buried alive. Afterwards, perhaps Rory's secret society 'friends' had dug him up, cleaned him up and acted like it was a tragic accident. No wonder Andy was racked with guilt: '*I think about it every day. The look on his face. Right before we – killed him.*'

We. The Rites. The whole group of them killed Rory. Did that include Brady?

I stood up with such force that my chair tipped over backwards with a crash. Cringing, I crept through to the bathroom to retrieve my shoes, taking the tablet with me. I closed the door behind me, but the sensor light failed to turn on. (Was the electricity off?) The only light came from the tablet's screen. I clicked through to an obituary of Rory Palmer. If I could figure out the year of his death, I could find out if it coincided with Brady's time at Attley.

My trainers squelched as I pushed my feet into them. I was torn between wanting to continue my research and wanting to get the fuck out of here. Where could I go? People would be looking for me at the staff village. My circle of friends on this island had shrunk to one. Zero, if Brady had been lying to me.

Perched on the closed lid of the toilet, surrounded by darkness, I returned to reading the tablet. Rory's obit – *an engineering whiz, a keen golfer* – included a picture of him with his girlfriend, Jessica. (Quote: 'He is in my heart. Always.') There was something vaguely familiar about her. Dark hair. Pale skin. Big eyes.

Rory had died 15 years ago; Brady would have been 20. What was the name of Brady's ex-wife? I googled to be sure. Their wedding announcement came up. A photo showed the same Jessica in a froth of a dress, Brady in a tuxedo.

He'd married Rory's girlfriend. That threw everything into harsh relief. Had Brady killed Rory deliberately to get to Jessica?

'Shit.' My hands were trembling as I pulled on my jacket. It was still wet, but I didn't care. *Get the hell out of here.*

I pushed open the bathroom door, ready to sneak down the corridor and out of the villa.

'Heyyy!' Brady swept me into his arms. 'Thought you ran away from me.'

He was naked, preening like a peacock, as he leaned in to kiss me. Instinctively, I turned my head away. 'I have to...' My voice came out faint. I nudged Brady with my elbow, but there was no give to his wall of muscle.

'Going somewhere?' Brady's smile deepened, showing dimples. 'Don't know if you noticed, but it's a bear of a day. Think it's fritzed the shower.'

I was still clutching the tablet. When I glanced at it, Brady followed my gaze.

'You're not working? Best thing about getting fired, you don't need to work anymore.'

Playfully, he swiped the tablet. I tried to pull it back, but it was too late. The wedding photo of him and Jessica was plainly visible.

'What are you doing?'

'Nothing.'

'Turning into a stalker on me?' Brady still sounded amused, but there was a furrow between his brows. He took a step backwards, breaking contact with me.

'I was... curious.' I grabbed for the tablet, but he twisted away from me, flicking through the open tabs. 'It's stupid. Let's go back to bed... come on...' I made my voice coquettish, my fingers trailing his flank.

'What the fuck?'

With a single movement, he sent the tablet crashing to the tile floor. *Hulk smash.* I wanted it to be funny – ha-ha Hulk – but Brady's hands had curled into fists. A deep flush was rising in his cheeks.

'You're picking up where that weasel left off?'

'No—'

'Knew you were in on it with him.'

When he grabbed my upper arms and shook me, it was hard enough that my skull jolted. He released me only to retrieve the tablet from the floor.

'You got proof? Come for me, you better have proof.'

I skidded backwards. Brady's eyes flicked from the cracked screen to me. Something had morphed in his appearance. The handsome face had turned ugly. I didn't quite recognise him anymore.

I threw myself at the door. With a twist of the lock, it was open. A gust of wind hit me full force, rain splattering my face.

I made two stumbling steps and then I was running.

40

I made it onto the wide, paved path that curved around the villas. It was as close as Keeper Island came to a main street. Today it was deserted. I had an eerie feeling everyone else had left and Brady and I were the only two people who remained on the island.

Glancing over my shoulder, I scanned for him. The shrubbery, blurred by rain, which discreetly shielded the villas, could also conceal Brady. I gulped in a breath and renewed my run, feet pounding. The only thing I had in my favour was that Brady would need to get dressed before pursuing me. That gave me a couple of minutes' head start. I still wasn't sure I could outrun him.

Moxham's excited voice returned to me: '*got a nice big fish on the line*'. When he'd tried to blackmail Brady, he must have expected him to break down in tears like his friend, Andy, beg him not to say anything. Instead, Brady had... what had Brady done?

Today, the switch in him had been terrifying. From flirtatious to vicious in a split-second.

My lungs were burning. I had to stop and wheeze for a second, bent double. Rain thumped against my head.

I'd thought his foot injury alibied him for Moxham's murder, but now that seemed foolish. He could have been faking. He must have murdered Moxham and rigged it up as an accident. (The tall man Ethan saw near the boathouse? Brady.) When he realised Tessa had dirt on him too, he took her out. That explained his appearance on Keeper Peak. ('I just heard.' How? Because he'd known for days she was dead.)

No wonder he was so interested to hear my story this morning. He wanted to find out how much I knew; if I was another accomplice he needed to kill.

My muscles were screaming. Wet hair was matted in my face. I forced myself to resume running. A place to hide. Somewhere far away from Brady. That's what I needed. A plan could come later.

I'd reached the main complex. The sloping roof of the restaurant loomed up ahead, but its shutters were closed. I rattled the door, hoping someone might appear and usher me inside. No luck. I cut around the back of the restaurant to the office. Its pink door, which normally stood open, was shut. Worse, it was locked. I pushed against it. I hadn't even known it was a door that locked.

Jesus Christ, why couldn't I catch a break?

Wind rippled through the trees, driving a deckchair up over the canopy. I whipped around, expecting Brady to come lumbering around the corner. The deckchair crashed to the ground. It was close enough that my whole body flinched.

I stooped to pick up a rock, a heavy one, from the makeshift zen garden outside the door. I slammed it against the door handle. Once, twice. It was cathartic.

The door sprang open and I ducked into the office.

It was galvanising to be inside, in the dry, even if the door would no longer close properly. I nudged the light switch with my elbow. No light. I went to the HVAC unit, flipped the switch. Nothing.

The electricity was definitely down.

A shiver went up my spine. Had Brady cut the power lines? No, that was crazy. It had been hot in the room when I'd woken up an hour ago, back when Brady was just a harmless body sleeping next to me. It must have been the storm that had knocked out the power.

I spluttered out a laugh. It sounded loud in the airless room. I doubled over and laughed again, a long, bitter cackle.

I was fucked. I was so completely fucked. No power. No way off the island. And a killer was hunting me.

The adrenaline high of my run was subsiding. Using the last of my energy, I heaved one of the desks across the floor, so that it barred the door.

Hopefully that would keep Brady out, if he even knew this office existed.

Water sluiced off my jacket as I collapsed into Fizzy's chair. My eyes lit upon the landline phone.

God, why hadn't I called the police before? I'd counted on Diara to contact her auntie at the police department, if that auntie even existed. I'd thought only about myself. In the moral grey area I'd inhabited in Hong Kong, the police were only useful if they could be bought. I had feared the influence of powerful men, like Kip and his police chief buddy, Gordon Howell. I hadn't known who to trust.

All of it seemed like a poor excuse. I should have talked to the police the morning Moxham's body was discovered, Kip's need for discretion be damned.

When I lifted the receiver to my ear, there was no dial tone.

'Shit!' I lobbed it across the room. It strained against its cord before smashing against the desk.

A second later, I noticed Fizzy's work mobile, squared up neatly on her desk, next to a mottled pink crystal. Thank fuck. The passcode of 1-2-3-4 unlocked the phone. I almost fainted with relief. It was 8 per cent charged (*low battery warning*) and there was one bar of signal. That was all I needed.

I jabbed the numbers 9-9-9, although I wasn't sure it was the right number for the BVI. Imagine being so stupid you didn't know what to dial when you were being hunted by a killer.

'What is your emergency?' a voice with a soothing BVIslander accent asked.

I pressed a fist to my shuddering chest. This woman, with her honeyed voice, was going to save me.

'Someone's chasing me. I need to get off this island.'

'What is your location?' The woman's voice had gone faint, overtaken by a crackle.

'Keeper Island. I need a boat. Can you send a boat?'

'No boats are running.'

'But – for emergencies. Must be something. This man's a killer.'

'You say there is a man,' she said, and I could hear her typing. 'Do you know the name of this man?'

'Brady Calloway. But I don't think it's just him. Kip Clement is involved. I know it.'

'Kip Clement?'

I cringed at the way her voice changed. *After Irma, Kip helped a lot of people… Kip is important for us.* That's what Diara had said.

There was a whine on the line, followed by silence.

'Hello?' I jumped out of my chair. 'Hello!'

'Yes, madam, I hear you.'

The phone signal appeared to be stronger now I was on my feet. It also placed me next to a window. I scanned for signs of Brady.

'There was a murder. Two murders.'

'Someone has been killed?'

'Mike Moxham. They said it was an accident, but it was a murder.'

'Mike Moxham?' Her voice was neutral, but again, there was the sound of typing. 'Are you with the deceased now?'

'No, this was two weeks ago. But someone else died, a couple of days ago. Tessa…' God, I couldn't even remember her surname. 'I'm telling you, there's a killer on the loose.'

'Madam, I am not understanding you.'

There was a noise outside. A thud, followed by a snap. Jesus, it was him. He was coming.

'I need a boat!'

'We are getting weather updates every hour.' For the first time, there was a hint of irritation in the woman's voice. 'As soon as it is possible for the boats to run, the boats will run.'

'When? I need one now!'

'Madam, I know you are agitated, but there are a lot of other emergencies right now.'

'That doesn't fucking help me!' My voice came out shrill. If Brady was outside, he'd be able to hear me.

'Please do not swear at me.'

I ducked down, crawling under the desk. 'He could be coming any second.'

'How are you hurting? What has he done?'

'Nothing – yet. But this guy's like the fucking Hulk.'

'Madam, please do not swear at me.'

The crackle was back. I could barely hear her.

'I wasn't swearing at you.' I dug my nails into the palm of my hand. 'I was swearing in general. Fuck, fuck, *fuuuck*.'

I waited for her to reprimand me again. It was comforting, like getting attention in school for being naughty.

'Hello?' I said into the phone.

There was no crackle anymore. Only silence.

'Hello!'

Nothing.

Under the desk, it was dusty, the remnants of a spider's web clinging to the wooden underside. I stayed with the phone pressed to my ear, hoping the honey-voiced woman would return. The only sound was the howl of the wind outside.

There was no emergency boat coming to rescue me. Even if the police believed my fractured story, there was nothing they could do. When I lowered the phone, it flashed a message – *shutdown warning* – and went black.

I couldn't breathe. The room grew smaller and smaller and smaller. And I grew smaller with it.

41

Weirdly, it was the smell of sage that brought me back to myself. Wasn't that why Fizzy used it? To cleanse the room of bad energy?

I sucked in a deep breath. Allie was the type to light a bundle of sage, waft it around and hope it would magically ward off anything bad. Allie. Her face bloomed in my mind. Despite my desperation, I had to remember there was life beyond this island.

Every time I breathed, there was still a slight rattle, but my heart rate had slowed. The room was no longer shrinking.

I hauled myself up and rummaged through Fizzy's desk drawers, looking for anything useful. There was a long-stemmed torch, although no weapons of any kind. Still, it would be getting dark soon and I'd need it.

I was going to get the hell off this island.

*

I heaved the dinghy sailboat out of the boathouse. It was heavier than I'd expected. I was still panting from my mile run from the office. The rain had got inside my jacket, so I was drenched and shivering. The rain felt lighter though. I was trying to convince myself of this. I hadn't heard any thunder in the last half hour.

It was only two miles to neighbouring Virgin Gorda. All I needed to do was sail two miles to safety.

I glanced over my shoulder. I was jumpy enough that, when a palm tree swayed across my vision, I mistook it for a man sprinting towards me. I blinked away the mistake.

I needed to hurry.

There was a metal ramp, which allowed me to shunt the dinghy to the waterline. The sea was a churning grey; the sky darkening. A gust of wind made the boat's highlighter-yellow sail buffet wildly. I clung to the rope, fearing the dinghy might gallop away without me. I'd been sailing exactly one time before and I'd capsized.

What the hell was I thinking? I was just as likely to drown myself as to reach safety.

The rope jerked in my grip, burning my palm. Through the stormy sky, a toxic yellow was smudging the horizon; it was almost sundown. I sagged against the red hull of the boat, trying to figure out my Plan B. (Find somewhere to hide? Go back to the office?) With my free hand, I turned on the torch.

'Lola!'

As I wheeled around, the torchlight illuminated him.

'Baby, I've been looking everywhere for you.'

His teeth flashed white, his smile taunting.

Brady.

He was inside the boathouse, fifteen metres away and advancing.

I stuttered backwards down the ramp, plunging into the sea. All other paths of escape were blocked.

I scrambled into the boat. A swell propelled it forward. My grip on the torch slipped. *Zzzzt*. Electricity crackled. I'd hit a different switch by mistake. It wasn't just a torch. It was a Taser as well.

I waved it in the air – I could hit Brady with a bolt of electricity – but the boat rocked beneath me. To stop myself from falling, I clutched the mast of the dinghy, letting the sea take me away.

Brady reached the ramp. The tide soaked his shoes, driving him backwards. My chest filled with relief.

Two miles. I just had to make it two miles.

The sail billowed and the boat surged forward.

A second later, a wave broke over the hull. My face caught a pelt of freezing water.

At least I was moving. Only two miles.

The sail obscured my vision. I yanked on the rudder, but it didn't seem to do anything.

Another wave sideswiped me. The Taser-torch was gone, wrenched from my hand.

The boat tilted.

Fuck.

My body dropped like dead weight. The cold was overwhelming. Needles pricking every part of my skin.

The current was dragging me under, even as I churned my arms and legs. My surroundings were a blur of blues and greys.

Could I swim two miles? I wasn't sure I could swim ten metres. I wrenched my body upwards and broke the surface with a great gasp.

Kick, kick, kick.

Miraculously, I felt sand beneath my feet. I staggered upright. The tide must have pushed me back towards shore.

My eyes still burned with seawater. I couldn't see anything, but I concentrated on breathing. Oxygen! I loved oxygen. I couldn't wish for anything more than not being underwater.

He grabbed me by the scruff of the neck, like I was a dog.

I squirmed, trying to get away, but he held me firm.

'Thought I might need to catch you with a net, you slippery little bitch.'

Brady punched me in the face.

*

When I regained consciousness, it was with a feeling like surfacing. I gasped. There was a pounding in my head that merged with the *tap-tap-tap* of rain on the tin roof. I squeezed my eyes shut and opened them again.

Blue-white tube lighting flickered overhead. Was I in the boathouse?

'Easy, easy.'

I bucked automatically at the sound of his voice. That was when I realised I was tied to a chair.

'Nice to get out of the rain, ain't it?' Brady said.

He strutted the width of the boathouse. With his billowing raincoat removed, his white T-shirt was dry. My clothes were plastered to my body. Every few seconds, another shudder racked my body.

'Heck of a show you put on out there.' Brady sounded genial. I wondered how deep his Southern gentleman bullshit ran.

'I was contemplating whether to dive in and save you,' he said. 'Be the chivalrous thing to do. But you're a modern sort of gal.' He chuckled. 'Save yourself, all that.'

'Fuck you.' I writhed against the ropes that bound me to the chair, trying to manoeuvre myself loose. It was no use. He'd tied me tight.

Why hadn't he let me drown? A swift kick back into the sea and I'd have succumbed to the waves. The fact that he'd kept me alive...

The gooseflesh that rose on my skin had nothing to do with my bedraggled state. I was well and truly in the shit.

I screamed. 'Fucking let me go!'

He took a step backward, making an *oh-shit* face. It took me a second to realise it was pantomime. As I screamed for a second time, my voice hoarse, he also let out a scream. It was high-pitched, mocking.

'Everyone's at Kip's. Must be two miles away, don't ya think?' He cupped his hands into a megaphone. 'Anyone hear me?'

The only response was the *drip-drip-drip* from a leak in the roof. I spluttered out a cough and made another rat-in-a-trap attempt to free myself.

'Easy.' He was using his midnight voice, like this was foreplay. He tucked a strand of wet hair behind my ear. 'Lola, I don't want to hurt you. So, take it easy.'

My stomach turned. The smell of gingerbread from his cologne mingled with the motor-oil-and-mould of the boathouse and something else. Sweet smoke. I wanted to vomit in his face.

'I liked you, I really did.' He made a pouting face. 'I thought you were different. But you're the same.' His voice grew cold. 'A petty liar. My ex, Jessica, she lied and lied and lied.'

Brady must have registered the scorn in my eyes. His face flushed pink. He straightened up and crossed the floor.

The boathouse was cluttered, as always. My gaze darted across the shelves closest to me. If I could loosen my hands, was there something I could use as a weapon? There were three stones, balanced precariously, like something from a stock photo. Too small to do much damage, even if I bowled them like a cricketer. When I squinted, I realised they were crystals, one mottled pink, one cloudy-white, one black. Beside them, there was a pink ceramic bowl, incongruous amongst the grime of the boathouse. It looked familiar.

Something stirred in my memory. It was a tip-of-the-tongue feeling. Sage, that was what I could smell. Fizzy had burned sage in that pink bowl.

Clang. My eyes snapped back to Brady. He'd unearthed the shovel used for cleaning up the bird shit that accumulated on the pier.

'This'll be useful.' He clanked the metal tip against the concrete floor again.

My back flattened against the chair. *Don't panic.* I twisted my wrists into an unnatural position. They ached, but my fingers were now able to scrabble at the knotted rope.

'What do you want?' I asked, hoping to keep his attention on my face and not my hands.

'I want… you to tell me a few things.' Brady hoisted the shovel onto his shoulder as he came towards me. 'This can go good for you or it can go bad.'

He hesitated. Just long enough that I had to see it coming. He swung at me.

The bird-shit metal slammed against my chest.

42

'That's what happens if you lie to me.'

All the breath was knocked out of me. I pitched forward, the ropes cutting into my flesh.

'What do you know about me and Rory Palmer?' Brady asked.

Pain pulsed through me. *You fucking animal.* I tried to say it out loud, but the hit had knocked out my voice.

He scraped the metal part of the shovel across the floor. I wflinched, but the blow didn't come.

'Tell me,' he said.

I coughed. It was painful to suck in oxygen. 'I don't know anything.'

'Whatever photos, whatever video… whatever you have on me, I'm gonna need it.'

'I don't have. Anything.' I raised my head to stare him down.

'Liar.' He spat the word. 'That little pussy, Andy. He gets born again and can't keep his mouth shut. What else did he say?'

My hands were shaking so badly that I'd abandoned trying to unpick the rope knot. 'I don't know.'

'You do know,' Brady said.

'It was Moxham, it wasn't me.'

Moxham's flaw had always been that he assumed logic would prevail in every situation. He was transactional in his soul. *I'll trade you incriminating information in exchange for money.* Simple. He didn't factor emotion into the equation.

'Stroke of luck when he died, but you… always poking around, aren't you, Miss Lola?'

Brady hadn't been orbiting me because he liked me; he'd wanted to know what evidence I had on him. He and Andrew must have discussed the phone call from 'Sophie Seymore'. When Brady had found me researching him this morning, all his worst suspicions were confirmed.

'You killed Moxham.' A sob rose in my throat. 'You did it. Tessa…'

'People get what's coming to them. I truly believe that.' Brady tapped the shovel against the floor twice. 'But, for the record, I didn't kill them.'

'Don't believe you.'

My mind was muddled. I was feeling woozy. This boathouse was where Moxham had died. Was it fate that I would die here too? Fizzy must have tried so hard to cleanse it of bad energy, but it was no use.

Brady barked out a laugh. 'Lola, I don't think you understand. I am the good guy in this scenario. You know how much money I give to Christchurch Hospital in Charleston? To charities in New York? You, on the other hand, are a dirty little blackmailer.'

If I were to get out of this situation, it wouldn't be through untying my ropes – Houdini-style – and scurrying out while Brady's back was turned. I needed to negotiate.

Moxham was collecting material on Brady, but according to the flash drive I'd found today, he hadn't got very far. It only contained photos anyone could find online. Of course, there was Andrew's recorded confession, but I didn't have that anymore, did I? When someone had stolen the USB drives from my pillow, they'd also stolen my leverage in this scenario.

Despite this fact, I needed to bargain for my life. No one was coming to save me. That meant, as Brady had taunted, I needed to save myself.

'Andrew named you,' I blurted out.

Brady had been pacing, but now he stopped in his tracks.

'He claimed you were the ringleader,' I said. 'Killed Rory so you could take his girlfriend.'

Brady swung the shovel. I cringed away from him, my head snapping back as I anticipated a new wave of pain.

It didn't come.

He was beating on a jet ski two metres to my left, stabbing and swiping at its shell till it ruptured, parts rolling on the floor.

'That fucking rat.' He brought the shovel down on the jet ski's engine like he was performing a decapitation. 'Fucking. Piece. Of. Shit.'

Brady's rage made the hairs on my arms stand on end.

The jet ski lay in pieces. I waited till Brady's hands slackened around the handle of the shovel. He exhaled a shaky succession of breaths, not unlike the way he sounded when he came.

'You want the recording?' I made my voice kittenish-sweet, as if we were in bed. 'I can give it to you.'

He glanced at me, a glassy look in his green eyes. 'Where is it?'

'I hid it.'

'Tell me where.'

My lower lip was fat from where he'd punched me earlier, but I dragged my tongue across it. 'Untie me and I'll take you.'

'Nice try.' He let the shovel fall to the floor with a clatter. I jumped, ropes straining.

'I buried it. But I – I told someone, a – a friend, where to find it. I disappear, they'll go looking for it. Whole world gets to know about you and Rory. So, trust me. You need it. I'll show you the hiding place.'

'Tell me where it is,' he said.

'You'll never find it, it's well-hidden.' I hoped I didn't sound too desperate.

Brady hesitated, visibly weighing his options.

I held my breath. I prayed. *Please be just a little bit stupid.*

He scuffed through the wreckage of the jet ski towards me. I shrank back, anticipating pain. Instead, he dropped to his knees and yanked the ropes loose.

I heaved out a breath, glorying in the sensation of being able to move and the possibilities that gave me. Brady must have sensed my relief, because his fingers went to my throat.

'Remember, I can kill you with one hand.'

43

The trail was slick beneath my feet. Brady, a few steps in front of me, jerked the rope that was looped around my neck. It was dark and he was using his phone as a torch, the beam bouncing off trees. My hands were tied in front of me, so I couldn't push the foliage out of my way. The rain had abated, but moisture still dripped from every surface.

My injuries were settling in. My torso ached and my face was swelling up. As I walked, I stumbled more than I would normally, catching my feet on tree roots and rocks.

Brady quickened his pace, seemingly for no reason other than to fuck with me.

'Easy…' I tried to make my tone flirtatious, as if this were a thrilling adventure and not a march into danger.

I scanned the trees, hoping for a saviour. Surely there was someone enjoying a casual stroll through thick bush, at night, during a storm? Around me, there was only a wall of darkness.

At least I was out of the boathouse. I had more options now. Though my hands were tied at the wrist, I lifted them and stroked my fingers along the small of his back.

He jerked away. 'Which way?'

We'd reached a fork in the trail. We were on the east side of the island, which was barely developed.

'Left.' I picked at random.

I kept close to Brady's broad back as we traipsed left. The fabric of his white T-shirt had grown clingy.

'I bet Jessica never let you tie her up,' I said.

He exhaled hard and the muscles of his solar plexus flexed. 'Don't say her name.'

'Jessica, Jessica, Jessica.' My voice was sing-song.

He whipped around and grabbed me by the shoulders. 'Don't say her name.'

Instead of flinching away from him, I leaned in close. Licked my lips.

My face must've looked puffy, but my breasts were heaving against the soaked fabric of my T-shirt and his eyes took on a glazed quality. He dragged his teeth across his bottom lip, apparently without realising.

'What we had was good, wasn't it?' I asked. 'I wasn't faking. Neither were you.'

'You're a liar.' There was something feeble about the insult. I could see his heart wasn't in it.

'We're both liars.' I made my voice honey smooth. 'We understand each other. The problem with Jessica—'

'Don't—'

'She never understood you. But I do.'

I leaned up and kissed him. My fat lip caught the side of his mouth. The act came with pain. I tasted blood.

'You think I care if you killed someone?' I asked. 'My last boyfriend was a murderer.'

He shook his head. 'You're some piece of work.'

'That's why I get you like she never did.'

This time it was he who kissed me. Hard. He slammed his lips against mine, one hand still holding the rope, the other mashed against my breast.

It was a dizzying moment. To realise that a sliver of desire for him remained in me. That I could enjoy kissing him even as I wished for his death.

He pushed me against the tree, grabbing my buttocks. The rope slipped from his hands, falling to the ground, and the noose around my neck slackened. My bound hands lay awkwardly against his chest. I could feel the beat of his heart.

'Let me touch you,' I breathed.

He hesitated, then his fingers picked at the knot.

My hands freed, I rewarded him by tearing at his chinos, grasping his cock. His body shuddered against me, causing the tree to shake, moisture raining down around us.

I took aim.

I kneed him in the balls. Hard.

He howled. Doubling over, hands tearing at the air.

His meaty fists swiped at me, but I was too quick for him. The tail of the rope attached to my noose gave a flick as I turned, but before Brady could catch it, I darted into the bush. My lungs burned, but I knew I still had energy left. I would run until I'd put a good distance between me and Brady, then I'd climb a tree and hide out. Quiet and placid as a sloth.

Pink fabric fluttered in the wind. A figure in the bush.

I recognised that raincoat.

'Fizzy,' I gasped.

Her presence was incongruous, but my heart leapt. She was not on the trail but off to the side, her back to me, half-concealed by a thicket of trees, fifty metres away.

I veered towards her. 'Fizzy, help me. Please…'

Fizzy and I had had our differences, but she wouldn't leave me to die. I felt like a child again, lost in a supermarket. My mum had always said that if I got separated from her, I should find a woman and ask her for help.

Women weren't dangerous the way men were. Women would help you.

Except women did kill. Push them and they were capable of it.

'Fizzy!'

There was something ghost-like about her, golden skin turned deathly. She was doing something to a tree, trying to measure it. Was this real or a mirage?

I increased my pace, grabbing at tree branches to try and pull myself along. My legs were jelly and it was becoming harder to suck in oxygen. 'Fizzy...' I meant it as a scream, but it came out as a whisper.

To my horror, when she was still twenty metres from me, she turned away and set out in the opposite direction.

Within seconds, I'd lost sight of the pink of her raincoat.

I scrambled after her, not looking at my feet.

Thump. I landed on the ground.

The shot of pain was nothing new. The fact that I was swimming in mud bothered me more than the dull ache in my ankle. I dragged myself to my feet and resumed running.

My left ankle collapsed under me.

'Ah!'

I hauled myself up again and tried to bear weight on it. No good. It was twisted at a weird angle.

That's when I heard it. The snapping of twigs beneath a heavy footfall.

44

I was in a hole, digging myself deeper.

The rope was knotted around my neck, with Brady grasping the other end, like I was a dog on a lead.

'We're doing things differently this time,' he'd said.

I'd been digging for a long time. Stoop down, shovel in, kick the dirt out. Over and over and over.

All I could smell was dense black mud, mingling with the metal of blood.

My ankle still throbbed. I had to lean against the side of the hole for relief. But if I ever stopped digging, Brady would grasp the rope, pulling the noose tight around my neck, till I gasped and spluttered and, yes, begged.

'Please... please don't do this.'

When you were digging your own grave, it was pointless to cling to your dignity. I was begging for my life.

'I won't tell anyone.' I bent over to shovel out more earth. 'I promise.'

'Shut up.' He gave the rope a lazy flick that burned against my neck. The beam of his phone-torch arced over me.

'Please...'

I thought of Allie and Flora. I thought of Nathan.

Brady pulled the rope tight. 'Get on your knees and dig.'

When I didn't move, he yanked on the rope again, gathering up slack. 'Give me the shovel.'

He advanced on me, scrambling down into the hole. I had a sudden idea that I could hit him with the shovel.

As soon as my hand twitched, he shouldered against me and manhandled the shovel from my grasp. For good measure, he thumped my chest with the wide metal edge.

I went down, stumbling onto hands and knees. The pain in my ankle screamed. The rope stretched taut, strangling me. My fingers scrabbled at my neck, until Brady let out enough slack that I could breathe.

Breathe, breathe, breathe, just breathe.

While he climbed out, I sat down in the middle of the hole, gasping. Surrounded by soft, wet earth, I felt like I was sinking.

'Dig using your hands, you weasel.'

Robotically, I stuck my arms elbow-deep into the soft earth and dug. The only person who knew I was in the bush was Fizzy. Had that been real or a hallucination?

'You need me.' I shuddered out a breath. 'If I'm gone, the recording of you goes public and the whole world finds out about Rory.'

From up above, Brady laughed. The beam of his torch dazzled me as he peered down to look in the hole.

'You're a dealmaker, Lola.' His voice was jovial, like he was delivering a hilarious joke. 'How's this for a deal? You tell me where the files are. I bury you alive. Once I find them, I come back and dig you up. Incentive for you to tell the truth, don't you think?'

I bit my tongue, so he wouldn't hear my sob. I was going to die in this grave.

*

Death had always felt like something that happened to other people.

I did my first bungee jump, aged twenty-eight, with a company named BungeeHey! In Macau, I jostled along the ledge at the top of a building, waiting for my turn to throw myself into the abyss.

The bungee jump was Moxham's idea. As the guide, who only spoke English in stock phrases, clipped me in, Moxham leaned over, grinning. He told me BungeeHey! was notorious for flubbing its safety protocols. Just two weeks earlier, the rope had snapped and a Swedish woman had fallen to her death. It was all hushed up to preserve the tourism trade.

I made an *oh-wow-that's-crazy* face at Moxham. Maybe he was razzing me. Maybe not. Either way, I didn't care about the Swedish woman. I was certain I wasn't going to die. Not because of any sense of faith in a higher power or trust in BungeeHey! If anything, it was sheer cockiness. I take after my dad. I'm sure he was absolutely convinced his wife would never find out he had another family, fifteen miles down the road.

I plunged downwards, my eyes peeled open, blood rushing to my head. I didn't die.

Over the years, I'd rattled through the air in tiny planes in developing countries, beside people who gripped the arm rest and said, 'OhGodohGodohGod.' I'd been on wilderness treks and signed waivers to say that if I got eaten by a bear, my family couldn't sue. I was reckless with my life and, each time, I didn't die.

Death was something that happened to other people.

Now, as I huddled in the hole, sinking in the earth, I knew I'd been wrong. Every bout of recklessness had amounted to a mark against my name. I'd been courting death and now it had come to claim me.

From above, there was the scrape of metal against earth. The first shovelful of dirt hit me square in the face. I swallowed earth, choking on it. More dirt rained down on me. It was in my eyes, my nose. Great lumps of earth landed on my shoulders, on my head.

I spat the mud from my mouth and wiped at my eyes with the heel of my hand. I strained for something, a tree root, to grab hold of. Brady's light passed over my head. I cringed away as the shovel arced towards me. If I'd stayed where I was, it would have struck me in the face. Instead, I fell backwards into the hole, gasping and crying.

The rope was still around my neck and it choked me.

Bang.

When I heard the sound, my first thought was that it was my brain exploding. I was dead.

Above me, there was a bellow. I flinched, still half-convinced I was dying.

The rope went slack. Brady's light retreated away from the edge of the grave. Drawing deep breaths, I tilted my head up. All I could see was blackness overhead.

Bang.

This time, the noise was louder. I recognised the sound. It was a gunshot.

'Help...' My voice started out a whisper but rose to a shout. 'Help me!'

'You shut up!' Brady roared, but his voice was distant, as if he'd taken several paces from the pit. He was spooked.

I clawed at the sides of the grave, heaving myself into a standing position.

'I'm down here, help me!'

The gunfire was loud enough that I flinched, but what really made my heart jump was the thud that followed. The ground shuddered. There was a scrabbling, a wretched moan. Stamping footsteps. Finally—

Silence.

I strained for more sounds, for a sense that this was the rescue I'd hoped for.

Nothing.

'Hello?' I craned my neck upward. 'Is anyone there?'

Silence.

A sob rose in my throat. 'Please…'

Footsteps. I shrank back, expecting to see Brady.

A torch beam shone into the hole. I glimpsed brown skin, the flash of a yellow raincoat. Dangly earrings. Diara. There was a gun in her hand.

It was a testament to her unflappable calm that when she saw me, caked in mud and hyperventilating, her only response was:

'Hold on, I'll get you out.'

45

Propped up by Diara, I advanced through the bush, half-hop-
ping, my bad ankle useless. The trees pressed in on us. The
torch beam didn't seem to penetrate the blackness. There was a
scurrying sound, the chuckle of a bird.

'Not far now,' Diara said. 'Almost home.'

My body was still tensed, racked with shivers. I'd lost track
of where we were – it could be as far as two miles to the staff
village – but the certainty in her voice made me want to cry with
relief. Despite not trusting her, I had to depend on her right now.

'How did you find me?' I asked.

Her voice was flat. 'God works in mysterious ways.'

There was a noise behind us. I yelped, craning to look over
my shoulder. My eyelashes were heavy with soil.

It was him. Brady was back.

Diara slowed, scanning the darkness with her torch. The
wind shuddered through the trees, branches clashing. Though
the rain had stopped, a dump of water fell on us from a tree.

I knuckled my eyes clear. No Brady in sight.

'Don't worry. I think I hit him,' Diara said.

'You think?'

'I know. He not coming after us.'

Diara raised the barrel of her gun. I shrank back, but she took
my hand and forced the gun into my limp grasp. 'Here.'

My fingers were slippery with mud. Without thinking, I tightened my grip.

'If he shows up,' she said, 'you kill him.'

The two of us continued through the bush, Diara lighting the way, me clutching the gun.

'What did he do to you?' she asked.

I took a few deep breaths. I was still covered in mud and the smell of it roiled my stomach. It was too raw for me to process much of what had happened, but I managed a fractured account of it. The more I spoke, the more cogent I felt.

'What a lunatic,' Diara said.

'He thought I was in on it with Moxham. Blackmailing him for Rory's murder.'

'Makes sense.'

'Does it?'

Diara didn't reply. Talking at length had taken it out of me. She was practically dragging me along at this point. When we came to a fallen tree, she helped me to sit down. Wooziness overtook me for a second, the pain redoubling when I stopped to think about it.

'We should keep going,' I said.

'Just rest a minute.' Diara skimmed the darkness with her torch. It reminded me of the Taser I'd found in Fizzy's desk drawer.

My brain was tired, but the pieces were coming together. I glanced down at the gun in my hands. My finger was on the trigger. It rested there lightly, but still, I liked the feel of it.

Fizzy and Diara. Secret lovers who'd do anything for each other. The video of Moxham's rape attack flashed through my mind.

'Brady has an alibi for Moxham,' I said. 'Doc.'

'Musta paid him off, got him to give a fake alibi,' Diara said. 'Happens all the time. Hush money.'

'Money... money again.' I flexed my ankle, wincing. 'Moxham never understood people, did he? Thought they were cash machines. Thought they were rational.'

I recalled the marks on Moxham's face. From Fizzy's Taser. Vengeance.

Diara inhaled, like she was about to say something, but she remained quiet. Her gaze dropped to the gun.

I stroked the trigger. I wasn't holding the gun anymore but pointing it. At her.

'He didn't get it,' I said. 'Blackmail makes people lose their minds, makes them lose... everything. The person who killed him... it was someone who had so much to lose. So much more than just money.'

'Brady,' Diara said.

'You know it wasn't Brady.'

Diara stood up. She made the movement so suddenly that I jerked the gun on automatic.

'If you wanna shoot me, you'll need to cock the hammer,' she said, turning her back on me.

I lowered the gun, noticing for the first time the curl of metal at the back of the barrel.

'The fireworks were late,' I said.

Diara acted like she hadn't heard me.

'The fireworks were late because Fizzy wasn't there at midnight to remind Reggie to set them off,' I said. 'She was at the boathouse. With Moxham. She used your phone to lure him there.'

Fizzy had never wanted me here. I was a stranger with a beaky nose who might figure out what she'd done.

Diara gave an irritated shake of her head. From somewhere nearby, there was the long groan of an animal.

'Did you know about it?' I tried and failed to stand up from the log. 'Did you help her? Did you tell her to do it? Please, I want the truth.'

'If you'd been here longer, you'd get it,' she said. 'The truth is whatever's convenient.'

Again, I tried to stand up, pain shooting up my leg. I swayed on my feet. The gun was still clamped in my hand. I was exhausted.

'I thought we were friends…' I was crying. I couldn't help it. Everything hurt.

The sounds around us seemed to amplify. Insects clicking, birds hooting. There was an animal on the prowl: squelch-thud, squelch-thud.

'We are friends.' She held out a hand.

I hesitated. Did I trust her? Did I trust anyone?

She stared at me, imploring me to believe her.

I fell into her arms.

'I never meant to hurt you.' She was crying too. I could hear it in her voice. 'But you need to understand. The truth… can get you in trouble.'

Thump.

I jumped, reeling away from Diara.

There was a bellow, like an animal attacking. It took me a second to parse out the words.

'Lo. La.'

Brady's voice.

'Lawdjesus,' Diara muttered.

I scanned the bush. Diara's torch beam shuddered. Where was he? The gun was still in my hand. I aimed wildly, fumbling with the hammer.

'Fuckfuckfuck,' I chanted as Diara murmured a prayer.

Brady appeared in the light of the torch, drenched and ruddy-faced.

I snapped the gun upwards, so it was pointed at him.

'Don't – fucking move.'

'Whatyougonnado?'

His voice was a growl. His eyes were out of focus. He took another stumbling step.

'Shoot him, shoot him, shoot him,' Diara was murmuring now. I wondered how her god felt about that.

When I didn't pull the trigger, she grabbed for the gun. It went off, a ringing explosion.

It was so loud, the recoil so intense, that I almost dropped the gun.

Brady shrank back like he'd been shot but recovered a second later. The bullet hadn't hit him. He advanced another half-metre.

'I'll kill you,' he muttered.

I cocked the hammer. Aimed the gun at him again.

'No,' I said.

I would kill him. He deserved it.

His eyes met mine. For a second, the grimace on his face was replaced with a smirk. He knew I was wavering.

Was this how Nathan had felt? He'd slid the knife into Shin's chest and made the decision.

Allie's face sprang into my mind; curly hair mussed, cheeks flushed with laughter. How could I do that to her? Allie wouldn't want me to become a killer.

I lowered the gun – and shot him in the leg.

46

Water bubbled over my shoulders like champagne. I slipped down another inch, sliding against porcelain. Beneath the fizz of the Jacuzzi, I could isolate the slap of waves against the villa's wooden struts. The storm may have passed, but the sea remained ferocious.

The heat and jets felt good against my naked body, unknotting my sore muscles. In the two days since Brady's attack, the swelling of my face had gone down, though one eye remained flooded with blood and there was a memento of mottled bruises on my torso. Yesterday, I'd been checked over at the hospital on Tortola. It turned out my ankle wasn't broken; it was a bad sprain, but a couple of weeks of hopping around on crutches and it would heal.

I opened my eyes a slit and reached for the drink on the rim of the Jacuzzi. I'd been prescribed pain pills, but I preferred my Painkiller cocktail. I grazed on dark chocolate Florentines from the wooden platter that rested beside my drink, less because I was hungry and more because they were delicious.

As I ate, I found I missed the familiar crackle of my radio. At Villa Queen Conch, it was peaceful, the breeze stirring the palm leaves that overhung one end of the veranda. Once the storm had blown itself out, I'd heard from Guillaume that we'd had a mass exodus of guests. That included Eddie Yiu, who was never more than a pest, after all. Whether it was because rain lashing against your windows for four days made paradise less palatable, or because rumours of Brady's arrest were already leaking out, I wasn't sure. Either way, I'd been installed in an empty guest villa to recuperate.

The luxury villa felt too clean, too beautiful, when the inside of my head was still clogged with mud and terror.

'Lolo, stop pretending.'

This morning, I'd called my sister. There was no point in scaring her with the truth, but I'd wanted to hear her voice. Though I'd tried my best to sound upbeat, Allie had guessed something was wrong.

'I'm fine.' Tears threatened to overwhelm me, my phone slipping in my hand. 'Fine.'

'Tell me what's wrong.'

The whole story tumbled out of me and we were both sobbing by the end. Afterwards, Allie said, 'You don't always have to be the strong one, Lo.'

The words stayed with me. I should stop treating Allie like my baby sister; I should trust her more.

I squinted at the sun, which was dipping low towards the horizon. I needed to get dressed soon. I had a dinner date.

Brady was in jail, but there was still a killer on the loose.

*

'You're looking better,' Kip said.

When I hobbled towards him on crutches, he leaned in to kiss my cheek. He was dressed in a suit with a starched white collar, wafting citrus-cedar cologne.

Queen Conch's veranda was set up for what we, behind the scenes, called a 'violinist fuckfest'. There was a table for two, laid with a white cloth. Tea lights, arranged in circular patterns on the deck, glowed as the sunlight faded. The setup was popular with unimaginative men who wanted to propose (or, at least, remind their bored wife-of-twenty-years that they used to be in love). Thankfully, the violinist, who charged $900 to hover nearby playing Tchaikovsky, was absent tonight.

'Since my accident, you mean?' I gritted out a smile.

It was Guillaume who'd first called it an accident. I'd had a few visitors over the last two days. I'd been too out of it to keep up much in the way of conversation, so those visits had amounted to people talking and me watching, as if from a distance. The hosts, Maria and Alex, had come together, chattering about an apocalypse-themed party they were planning for the staff. Guillaume, on his visit, was unusually upbeat. Apparently, the storm had worried his boyfriend in Lyon so much that he was being particularly attentive and planning his next visit to Keeper.

According to the island rumour mill, I'd been terribly upset about my wrongful dismissal (I was now all but certain Fizzy had planted the wine bottles in my suitcase to get rid of me). In my agitation, I'd been caught in the storm, clobbered by falling debris. It was Reggie, alone, who accompanied the word 'accident' with a quirk of his eyebrow. He'd mooched in smoking a joint, said little and left not long after. Diara had not visited me. Nor had Fizzy, who was apparently 'under the weather'.

'Yes, your accident.' Kip's voice took on a distracted air.

He pulled out my chair and I made an awkward swinging motion into my seat. I was wearing a tailored maroon dress (not my style at all) that Maria had provided for me from the guest racks. Kip took my crutches and tidied them away behind a potted palm that had lost half its leaves in the storm. Maybe he meant it as a benign gesture, but I noted that they were now out of my reach.

Ethan bustled onto the veranda, holding a bottle of red wine swaddled in a napkin. After he poured, Kip took a sip and smacked his lips.

'Ah, yes, I think you'll enjoy this one.'

I caught Ethan's eye. He still looked gaunt, his face blotchy. He'd arrived a few minutes before Kip and drawn me into a one-armed hug. 'Make sure you bleed him for all he's worth,' he'd muttered.

At the table, I tore apart a hunk of bread, still warm from the oven.

'Why haven't the police spoken to me?' I asked Kip.

Out of the corner of my eye, I saw Ethan incline his head.

'My dear,' Kip said, 'you have been very poorly indeed.'

The light was dimming, sunset casting orange hues over the veranda. Kip's face was sinking into shadow, but when he met my eye, I saw a flash of emotion there.

Fear.

Kip was afraid of me.

'You wanted to wait,' I said. 'Speak to me first.'

Ethan served two plates of crispy rabbit with piccalilli. There was no hint we were in the Caribbean tonight. The bespoke menu on the table reported we'd be having steak, followed by apple tart. Kip was wining-and-dining me like we were at his private members' club in London.

He made a performance of waiting for Ethan to leave the table and go inside.

'Now you're better, of course, we can—' Kip cleared his throat. 'We can arrange it. My old friend, Howell, he'll take your statement. Best in the biz.'

'And what – exactly – should I say?' I heard the anger reverberate through my voice. Judging by his expression, so did Kip.

'Why... the truth. About your ordeal with that Calloway chap.'

'Not the truth about you and Fizzy?'

Kip acted like he hadn't heard me.

'I know she killed Moxham. I know you covered it up.' I let out a bark of laughter. 'Badly. Pretty fucking badly.' No wonder there was broken glass and blood left in the boathouse; Kip had never cleaned a day in his life.

'And Tessa?' I said. 'I assume it was Fizzy who killed her. Could've been you.'

At my words, Kip did not break down or freak out. In fact, he gave the appearance that he hadn't heard. He sawed off a section of rabbit and chewed methodically.

There was a rattle of crockery from behind the glass door. I wanted Ethan to come out, to learn what had happened to Tessa, but the door remained closed.

At last, Kip swallowed. 'And you have proof?'

The piece of glass with the fingerprints, Diara had taken. For all I knew, she'd destroyed it, along with the notebook and the USBs. Covering up Fizzy's crime.

My voice rose. 'It was you hiding behind the tree at the boat-house the night Moxham was killed. Ethan saw you.'

'Ethan's a good lad,' Kip said.

'His girlfriend died. Because of you.'

'Ethan's getting a promotion. A new start at my Tuscany resort.'

I gripped the table. Did Ethan believe Kip's lies? Or was that all that Tessa had ever meant to him? Their relationship, her life, was worth less than a promotion?

'You're a clever one, Lola,' Kip continued. 'I think a promotion is in order for you as well. Executive Manager. With a commensurate pay rise.'

'You think I'm staying here?' I said. 'On this fucking island?'

'Is it so bad? Really?'

He had me there and he knew it. I loved this island. Waves lapped over the rocks beneath us. The smell of salt was sharp.

I'd thought it through: I could sue Kip. I could go to the papers. ('My private island hell', complete with a picture of me in a bikini.) I could also blackmail him, as Moxham would have done.

I wasn't Moxham though. There were more important things in life than money.

Over Kip's shoulder, a white mound out at sea glowed in the remnants of the sunset light. It was Meredith, drowning again, as the tide came in.

Had her death been suicide? I knew Moxham well enough to guess he'd looked into it. What had he found out?

I now knew for sure Kip was capable of covering up a murder. This might not be the first time he'd done so.

'Why did you kill your wife?' I asked.

Kip's face flushed. 'I loved my wife.'

'And if the police looked into her death, that's all they'd find? Love.'

Across the veranda, the door opened, glass singing with the impact.

The figure was haloed in light for a moment, before she stepped towards us. Her black hair was uncharacteristically tangled. Draped in a shapeless white dress, she looked like a wraith.

Fizzy.

Kip rose, advancing on her. 'Darling, you should be resting...'

'No.' Her voice was hoarse; I had to strain to hear it. 'I want to speak to Lola.'

'Now is not the time.' He put an arm around her, but she shrugged it off.

'You can go, Kip.' She sat down in the chair Kip had vacated.

'I'm staying.' He puffed his chest. 'I haven't had my filet.'

I laughed involuntarily, but Fizzy's face remained blank.

'Ethan will serve you in your villa,' she said. 'Now go.'

'You're being silly...' Kip tugged at Fizzy's arm, but she didn't react.

'Go, or I'll throw myself into the sea here and now.' She sounded dead calm. 'Perhaps you'd prefer that. No loose ends.'

It was breezy tonight, but that wasn't why I shivered. The rocky outcrop beyond the veranda had disappeared into darkness. Meredith had sunk beneath the waves.

Kip sloped away, blustering that he'd be back shortly, making it clear that Fizzy hadn't dismissed him, he'd chosen to leave. His eyes darted in my direction a couple of times. Perhaps he was relieved to escape my questions about Meredith.

When Fizzy and I were alone, I noticed how waxy and strange her appearance was.

'I'm sorry…' she murmured. 'I didn't know… I didn't know Brady would do that to you.'

'Well, he did.'

'I'm glad you're OK.' She tried for a smile, but it flickered and died immediately.

'Are you?'

'It would… it would be easier if you'd died. But. It wouldn't be right.'

I laughed again; I couldn't control myself. 'That's honest, I s'pose.' God, what a night. I couldn't handle any more bullshit. 'You wanna tell me why you murdered Moxham and Tessa?'

My tone was flippant. I wasn't actually expecting the truth, not from a serial liar like Fizzy, but her face crumpled. Her nose was running. She dragged the back of her hand through the snot. It was so unladylike that I wondered where the Fizzy I'd known had disappeared to.

'I guess it starts here.'

She retrieved her phone from her pocket. For the first time, I noticed she wasn't wearing any of her usual bracelets. The lines on her wrists were unmistakable.

'What?'

On her phone, she showed me a photo of herself.

Bruises mottled her cheek, one eye turned red with blood; not so different to how I looked now. The state of her face wasn't the worst part though. It was the defeated expression in her eyes.

47

Maybe for you, the worst thing in the world would be people finding out you cheated on your wife or that you liked to pretend to be a giant baby in a nappy.

Forget that. Imagine something worse. What if you'd spent fifteen years running from your abuser and someone threatened to tell him exactly where you live?

Blackmail.

I could see it from Moxham's perspective. It made me sick, but there was something alike about the two of us. Our worldview. When he had a problem, he made it go away.

Moxham's problem was Fizzy. They must have riled each other. Fizzy, the lifer on Keeper Island, would have hated how smoothly Moxham ingratiated himself into Kip's good graces. She might be Kip's surrogate daughter, but wouldn't a son always trump a daughter? For his part, Moxham must have got a nasty shock when he realised why he didn't have a shot with Diara.

I tend to imagine Moxham interrupting Diara and Fizzy kissing in a copse of trees during a party, although I know it's me transposing my own experiences onto this story. However it happened, Moxham twigged that his path to true love with Diara was compromised.

True love? More like obsession. I'm not a psychologist, but I'd guess Moxham's feelings for Diara had gone beyond hearts-and-flowers and descended into the pathological. He set about getting Fizzy out of the way. He did it using his tried and tested method.

Blackmail.

Fizzy went by her childhood nickname on Keeper Island, but Moxham, as general manager, could have easily discovered her legal name: Elizabeth Rose Manolo. Armed with that information, everything that happened to her was only a Google search away.

Fizzy's abusive boyfriend, Grant, had only served five years for her kidnap, rape and torture. Maybe he was a reformed citizen. Maybe not. It would have been effortless for Moxham to drop him a message through social media. I imagined Moxham taunting Fizzy: 'Top bloke. He'd love to see you again. Wouldn't you like that?'

If it had been me, I would have left Keeper Island in the dust. *Run, run, run.* Moxham must have assumed the same would be true for Fizzy. She'd pack up and leave so he could have Diara – and the island – all to himself.

Fizzy hadn't run. When the blackmail didn't work, Moxham went for Diara anyway. If I'm generous to him – and the part of me that once considered him a friend wants to be generous – I think he was so obsessed with Diara, he'd convinced himself she was in love with him too. When he went to her room and tried to rape her, he deluded himself into thinking it was an act of love.

Or else he was just a fucking bastard.

*

It was fully dark now, the LED tea lights on the veranda providing only specks of light. Fizzy had both elbows on the table, chin resting in her hands. It was a girlish pose, like we were teenagers sharing secrets.

'This is my haven, you know.' Her expression was shrouded in darkness, but I heard the smile in her voice. 'Keeper Island saved my life. Friend got me the job. Kip wanted a pretty girl to type up his emails for him. I was overqualified, but I needed to be as far away from Grant as possible.

'I remember my first day, getting the tour of the island, and I thought, *it doesn't matter, I'm going to kill myself.* I decided I'd wait till my thirtieth birthday and then I'd do it. My birthday came and went. I looked out at the sea and realised I didn't want to die anymore. This place, it's special… in my whole life, it's been my only real home.

'Then he came along. Ruined everything.' Her head drooped. 'I wish, I wish, I wish…'

Sucking in a breath, I could smell sage smoke. It must be clinging to Fizzy's clothes. I suspected that, over the last two weeks, she'd returned to the crime scene again and again, burning sage, using crystals, desperate to cleanse the space.

Despite everything, I felt sorry for her.

'What really happened… the night of Alice in Wonderland?' I asked.

Above us, clouds shifted, the moon draping us in silver.

'I've never seen Diara like that.' The corner of Fizzy's mouth quirked. 'Never even seen her cry. But that night… she was out of her mind. Couldn't stop shaking. She must have drunk half a bottle of rum before she could even speak. I don't think she meant to tell me Moxham tried to rape her. That girl is a steel trap, she'd rather die than show weakness. But she needed to tell someone.'

I had a flash of Diara at the party, drunk and unsteady, before she collapsed in the shrubbery. Fizzy's plan must have already been formulating.

'You used Diara's phone,' I said.

'Yes, that was my stroke of genius.'

Fizzy broke into a smile. Not the tremulous one she'd used earlier. This one filled her whole face. It was terrifying.

'Moxham shows up at the boathouse,' she said, 'like the cat that got the cream. Thought it was a hook-up with Diara. Instead, it's me with a Taser. The look on his face.

'I thought it was quite fitting actually. He tried to blackmail me into leaving the island. It was nice to give him a taste of his own medicine. He could get in a boat and go, leave before daybreak. Or I tell everyone about the rape. Put his ass in prison.'

My stomach contracted as I pictured the scene. *Leave*, I wanted to scream at Moxham. *She's giving you a way out.*

A ghost of a smile remained on Fizzy's lips and a shiver shot down my spine. 'You never really intended to let him go, did you?'

'I gave him a choice. He was cocky, swigging champagne. Didn't take me seriously. Even gave me the bottle, offered me a drink.

'He was a prize psychopath, that man. Said something about how sorry Kip would be to hear about this. How I threatened him. My mental illness, my tragic, tragic past. If I didn't leave, he'd persuade Kip I was touched in the head, have me shipped off somewhere.

'He was always twisting the truth, twisting everything to his advantage. I could see it all playing out the way he described: I'd be bundled away and he'd be left here. With Diara.'

Fizzy had been gazing out at the darkness beyond the veranda, but now she looked me in the eye.

'I couldn't let that happen,' she said. 'I fired the Taser at him and it caught him on the cheek. He let out this howl, barely human. He didn't stop coming at me though. It only made him angry. So, I swung the champagne bottle at him. It cracked against the side of his head. He fell – he – he must have hit his head again when he fell to the floor.'

My stomach was churning. I didn't have to ask what happened next; I'd pieced it together. Someone had towed the jet ski out to sea – I'd seen the boat's light out on the water. They'd unloaded Moxham's body into the water; set it up as an accident.

'What about Tessa?' I asked.

Fizzy's voice was sharp. 'She was no better than him.'

'You found out they were working together?'

'Caught the little snake breaking into Moxham's apartment. Said she left a sweatshirt in there. Didn't take long to get the truth out of her. She turns it round on me, acting all high and mighty. She'll go to the police if I don't pay her off.'

Tessa must have been panicked in the days following Moxham's death, worried their scheme would get discovered. She'd taken down all the cameras. It wasn't a surprise to learn she'd also tried to get her hands on any evidence hidden in Moxham's quarters. No wonder Fizzy – or was it Kip? – had decided a bonfire was in order.

Tessa could have left after Fizzy confronted her, but she'd studied at Moxham's knee. She wanted to cut a deal. Stupid, stupid, stupid.

I pictured Tessa crying, the first day I met her. Just a baby.

'And she deserved to die?'

'She's mercenary, that girl, doesn't care what I've been through, doesn't care about anyone except herself...'

'You tampered with the zip-line.'

Fizzy laid a hand on my arm. Her fingers were cold, nails bitten ragged, polish disintegrating.

'Know what's funny?' There was no amusement in her voice. 'I told her, weeks ago, to stop using that zip-line, it wasn't safe. But she's a lazy little bitch who doesn't want to walk down the hill.'

I felt sick. Anyone could have used that zip-line after Fizzy damaged it.

'You need to turn yourself in,' I said.

'You sound like Diara.'

'She's right.'

Fizzy's fingers raked across my skin as they curled into a claw. She leaned closer.

'They deserved it.' Her breath, in my face, was sour. 'They were bad people. You get that, don't you?'

I reared away from her, grasping my steak knife from the table. 'No.'

I was alone with a killer. Where did I fall on Fizzy's moral scale? Good or bad?

'Going to stab me?' Fizzy asked, sounding preoccupied. 'A life for a life.' She heaved out a sigh. 'Don't worry, I'm already in hell. I got what I wanted, but the Grim Reaper took from me too.'

Her expression was so hollow, I had an eerie feeling she really had died on the beach and this was her corpse talking to me.

'Go to the police, if you tell the truth—'

She swept my words aside, shaking her head. When she moved, I flinched, raising my knife, but she was only pushing back her chair to stand up.

'I just wanted to say sorry.' She said it primly, like she was apologising for a faux pas at the dinner table.

'Wait...' Whatever I'd wanted from Fizzy and Kip, I hadn't got it. This island still contained so many secrets.

I tried to stand up too, forgetting about my ankle.

'What about Meredith?' My grip on the knife slackened. I teetered against the table. 'What happened? Did he kill her?'

'No.' Fizzy choked on the word. 'He's too weak.'

'He's not—'

'Doesn't have the mental clarity.'

'So, what happened to her?'

Fizzy hesitated, then took a step away from me.

'Please, tell me.'

'I don't know for sure. But it's there in the paperwork. You can find everything in the boring stuff no one bothers to read. Devil's in the details.'

It made me think of Moxham. *Got the devil on my back.* Her words were another riddle.

There was a rattling sound. I jumped, my bad ankle jolting against the table leg.

The door opened. A dark figure stepped into the frame, light spilling out behind him.

'Yes, yes, I'm coming,' Fizzy said, before Kip could speak.

I had more questions I wanted to ask, but I knew I wouldn't get anything else from her. I sagged back into my chair, overcome with exhaustion. She turned away. When she spoke, I couldn't tell if she was speaking to me or to Kip or to no one at all.

'This really is my favourite place in the world. I don't deserve it. I don't know what I deserve...' Her voice trailed into silence as the sea churned beneath us.

I sat in the darkness for a long time after they'd gone. Ethan brought me apple tart with whipped cream and then bustled away. I wanted to call after him, but my voice had disappeared. The cream dissolved into a white puddle.

My skin prickled with gooseflesh, but it didn't occur to me to go inside. What had Fizzy wanted from me? Forgiveness? Understanding? Could I understand her perspective? If Moxham and Tessa had done that to me, would I have killed them? The thought slipped down my throat like ice.

Out on the water, there was a light. It must be a boat crossing to Virgin Gorda.

I could leave. Finally, I could go home. If I ever figured out where home lay.

48

It was the end of the world, but I didn't care.

I was only at the party because I couldn't bear to be alone. 'Welcome, survivors' was daubed in 'blood' on a white sheet hung across the restaurant doors. Inside, red fabric, draped over the lights, gave everything a fallout-shelter vibe. Plastic skeletons, leftover from some past Halloween, squeaked and rattled from their places hanging off the beams.

Maria and Alex had masterminded the end-of-the-world party, even down to the detail of dragging canned food from the storeroom (I could only imagine Guillaume's disgust). I grabbed a tinned chipolata, which was jammed on a stick with a chunk of pineapple. It tasted like sawdust.

Everything around me had the sense of a hallucination. I palmed another two of my pain pills and swallowed them with a swig of my cocktail, a Painkiller. The result was a sensation like fingers reaching into my skull cavity and massaging my brain.

Last night, I'd gone back to the staff village. I'd wanted to talk to Diara, but she was nowhere to be seen. I hadn't slept, spending the night jumping at shadows.

Around me, the restaurant floor had been cleared of tables. People were dancing, but I couldn't concentrate on the beat of the music. Instead, I wedged myself into a chair, gazing out at Main Beach through the open shutters. A spectacular sunset threw reds and oranges across the sand. I wondered whether tonight would be the last time I'd see the sun set on Keeper Island.

I could be at the airport on Beef Island within a couple of hours. I could be in London by tomorrow. Was that what I wanted?

I wasn't dressed for a party, or for the weather, or for the end of the world. My oversized green hoodie, which I'd had since I was a teenager, was good to get lost in. God, I was sleepy. I could sleep right here.

My eyes were drifting shut when my phone buzzed.

'Helllooooooo.' I was drunker than I'd realised.

'Oh, my God!' Allie said.

Nausea, which had been swilling around my body all day, leapt in my belly.

'What?'

'I can't believe it,' Allie said.

I pressed the phone to my ear; it was too loud to hear. 'What? What's wrong?'

'I'm freaking out. Just got off the phone with the solicitor.'

At the other end, there was a whistling of wind, a snatch of sirens. Oh, fuck. What legal trouble had Allie got herself into? This had to be bad.

'Says she's getting everything finalised. Working late, 'cause it's urgent. Oh, my God, Lo, this is amazing.'

'What? I don't understand…'

I weaved through the crowd, not caring who I hit with my crutches.

'The flat,' she said. 'Thank you, thank you, thank you!'

Pushing at the door, I staggered outside, battling to get free of the white sheet. Faintly, on the other end of the line, I heard Flora echoing the words. *Thank you, thank you, thank you!* I imagined her pirouetting, pigtails spinning.

'The flat?'

'The car isn't exactly kid-friendly but… I mean, wow.'

'Allie…' I stumbled and sat down on the paving slabs, crutches clattering to the side, injured ankle throbbing. I wasn't certain I remembered how to stand anymore. 'I'm not following.'

It took several more minutes for me to extract the details from Allie. The flat – the overpriced one with great light and room for an art studio – it was hers now. She owned it outright. Kip's offer to the owner had been more than generous.

And the car. A bottle-green Aston Martin was parked on the street outside. This gift was for me; it even had custom number plates.

When had Kip done all this? The machinations must have taken days. While I was recuperating, Kip was scheming. He was buying me off.

Fuck. How was I going to tell my sister we had to give it all back?

'*No!*' A voice rose above the bass line of the music.

Around me, darkness had fallen. There was movement nearby, two figures, but I couldn't make them out. My hand had fallen away from my ear, but now I raised my phone again.

'Allie, I'll call you back.'

I imagined her bouncing on her toes. 'This is perfect, everything's amazing!'

'Call you back.' I ended the call.

Nearby, palm trees creaked and rattled in the breeze. The world was spinning.

'No, no, no!'

'It had to be done.'

'It didn't, I told—'

'It did.'

The voices washed over me. I still couldn't see them, but I knew who it was. Diara and Kip. I caught the gloss of his bald head in the moonlight, but she was obscured by the foliage that lined the path to the beach.

'Where is she?' Diara's voice was shrill, loud, her accent thickening.

'She's gone.'

Leaning hard on my crutches, I heaved myself to my feet. I limped several steps closer. Close enough that Kip's gaze skidded sideways. Diara remained oblivious to my presence.

'I know she gone.' Her hand chopped the air. 'Where d'you send her?'

'Venezuela.' He made a performance of checking his watch, a brief glow in the darkness. 'Flight will have left by now.'

When Diara tried to interrupt, he raised his voice in a blustery cadence, like this was a sales pitch. 'Up and coming sort of place. Lots of job opportunities. I'm investing in a couple of hotels there.'

'She was going to turn herself in. You said you'd give her a choice. But you want to control it all.'

'There's no choice. There's just reality.'

'You're punishing her.'

'She's getting a lovely new life.'

'She needs help—'

'I've arranged for help.'

'Arrange for it.' Diara bared her teeth. 'You arrange everyt'ing. Make me sick.'

'What's the alternative?' Kip's charm had worn thin; his eyes were bulging. 'Prison? And for you? Prison, as well. Accessory after the fact, my girl. Would we all be better off in the chokey?'

Kip turned to me, as if looking for an ally. Diara finally noticed me, as well. I saw the glitter of tears in her eyes. She shook her head, making her earrings jump. Red cardinals.

She cast Kip one final look of contempt and slipped away into the darkness.

*

The pills and the alcohol meant I slept like the dead that night. I awoke to Diara shaking my shoulder. When I let out a moan, she palmed a hand across my forehead.

'It's a hangover, I'm not dying.' My voice was raspy from my dry throat.

'OK, London, just checking. Don't want to lose another person.'

I heaved out a breath and sat up in bed. 'You ready to stop lying to me?' I was too tired for tact.

Diara's face was wet with tears. Catching my gaze, she rubbed her cheeks with her sleeve. 'Come on.' She nudged me. 'Let's go watch the sunrise.'

From the bush, a wild rooster crowed, signalling the right time for once in its life.

49

At Hidden Cove, I dug my toes into the sand, savouring the cold roughness of the underlayer. The bandage on my bad ankle was coming unwrapped. I toyed with one fraying end.

Diara was beside me, laid out like a corpse.

'You really didn't know Fizzy killed Moxham?' I asked.

'No.' Diara struggled upright. 'Not right away. Not for a long time. I thought there was somethin' off about Moxham's death. How could there not be? A man like that. But I didn't want to think she was involved.'

The sky above us was the ripe purple of a bruise, but there was a promise of light on the horizon. The sea appeared calm after so many days of calamity. Sheltered in this cove, cliffs rising up at either end, it was possible to pretend the rest of the island – the rest of the world – didn't exist.

'Kip really must love her like a daughter,' I said, 'to cover for her.'

'Love.' Diara spat the word. 'Everything he does, it's self-centred. He should have... looked after her better.'

Diara's lips twisted to reveal a hint of jealousy. What would she have done if Fizzy had come to her for help instead? I remembered the sight of blood running off Nathan's body, down the shower drain. You did whatever it took, for the ones you loved.

The silence between us stretched. The sky was lightening, pink at the horizon, the sunrise about to pop. Today, clear and cool, couldn't have been more different from the last time I'd been to Hidden Cove. Mist. Fizzy, a statue, supine on the sand.

'The pills,' I said. 'Did she really overdose or did Kip...?'

'The thing I've learned is.' Diara's voice was creaking. 'Murder isn't Kip's style. He knows how to destroy people other ways.'

Had he destroyed Meredith? Till there was no way out but suicide? What the hell did paperwork have to do with that?

Glare caught the corner of my eye as the sun burst over the horizon.

'Elizabeth always had depression, I knew that,' Diara said. 'I think when Fizzy spoke to Tessa's mother, she realised what she'd done.'

'She was that upset? Didn't sound that way yesterday.' I shuddered at the memory.

Diara's shoulders were curved inward, her gaze downcast, as if she couldn't bear to look at the sunrise.

'I have to... have to believe she was, she did care. She felt so sorry she tried to end it all. That night, after the overdose, when she woke up, she finally told me the truth.'

'That's when you switched sides, stopped helping me.' I produced a sour smile and Diara gave a dark laugh.

'Didn't know it would mean driving you into the arms of a lunatic.'

'We're even on that score, since you saved my life and everything.'

'No big thing.' Diara cut her eyes sideways at me. 'I just didn't want to deal with a new roommate.'

Around us, darkness was receding. Light reflected in the water, turning the lapping waves pink.

'I am leaving,' I said. 'Today.'

Diara jerked her head, a furrow appearing between her eyes. Before she could argue, I added:

'How can I stay? Seriously.' I told her about the flat in London, the sports car. 'He thinks he can buy me.'

Diara kicked a hollow in the sand with her heel. 'So, you leave and do what?'

'Start again.' I hated the way my voice cracked.

Always starting again, always hoping to become someone new.

'I don't want him to buy me.' I sniffed, squeezing away the tears.

'He can't, not if you don't let him.'

I started to argue, but the intensity of Diara's gaze stopped me. She gripped my shoulder, hard.

'London, he at your mercy,' she said. 'You can bide your time, squeeze him for all he's worth. Wait for the perfect opportunity for revenge.'

'Is that what you're doing?'

I shifted and she loosened her grip on me.

'I'm just tryin' to find a place to be happy. It might be his island, but it's my home.' She exhaled a long breath, eyes finding the sunrise at last. 'And I feel her here. The good parts of her, of us.'

I imagined Fizzy stepping off the plane in Venezuela, gliding wraithlike through the commotion of an anonymous arrivals hall. I hoped Kip wasn't full of shit, that there would be help for her there. Part of me wondered if he'd set up a maniac with a shiny new life. Would Fizzy kill again?

'I saw her, you know.' The memory jolted back to me. So much of the last week had felt unreal, but I remembered it now. I told Diara about seeing Fizzy, on the night Brady made me dig my own grave.

'Yeah, she was out there,' Diara said. 'We was at Kip's villa, all of us, packed in there, generators running. I thought she was upstairs sleeping, but she came in the front door, drenched and muddy, saying you was in trouble.'

'So, she saved me?'

She was the reason Diara headed out to find me. I sat back, rough sand digging into my palms, and mulled it over. I couldn't know for sure, but I think Fizzy went out into the bush planning to kill herself. She'd been doing something to a tree. I remembered that now. Tying a noose to hang herself. When she'd seen me, she'd made a choice. She'd chosen saving me over killing herself.

I voiced my theory and Diara's whole body crumpled. Ugly tears, a primal moan. I wrapped an arm around her, clutching her tight. She folded herself into me, as if her grief were making her physically smaller.

When I glanced up at the horizon, the sun was lifting in a pink haze. It was another everyday miracle in the most beautiful place on earth.

*

I planned to leave that day. And the next day. And the day after.

Two weeks passed and I was still here.

What was disconcerting was how normal everything felt. The sun rose. The sun set. Guests arrived, making demands like greedy toddlers, but you always knew they'd leave again. There were disasters, of course, but they could be fixed with a smile and a cocktail. My ankle healed. My bruises faded. The sun rose. The sun set.

*

The bonfire flashed, bright against the dark sky. *Pop*. A log disintegrated, sending up a shower of sparks. Reggie passed by, offering a bag of marshmallows. I jammed one onto a skewer and waved it at the fire.

'This marks a new era, a fresh start,' Kip had said this morning, during an all-staff meeting. He might be a killer – I still wasn't sure – but he was great at speeches, I'd give him that.

I hadn't yet adjusted to the fact that my office now included an array of screens. Moxham's legacy was that cameras had been installed everywhere. He'd get a chuckle out of that one. Safety was our watchword, according to Kip.

For most people, Keeper Island might not be a place they could call home. What I'd learned over the last month was that home wasn't a perfect place that dropped into your lap. You had to build it, brick by brick. You had to fight for it.

And if I had number forty-four on the Forbes Rich List by the balls? That was something, alright.

Diara appeared at my shoulder. 'Ready?' She was holding a cardboard box.

'As I'll ever be.'

She hesitated, then flung the box onto the bonfire. The olive-green notebook was the quickest thing to burn. The USB drives were slower. They glittered among the logs, warping until they resembled only charred lumps.

'Hey, what are you doing?' It was Tyson, bleary with booze.

'Cleaning house,' I said with a sweet smile. He gave a confused look and moved on.

I had eventually given a statement to the police. It was enough to nail Brady, who was staring down the barrel of twenty-five-to-life for my kidnap and Rory's murder. (Andrew had flipped on him too.) In one small way, Moxham's schemes had ended positively. Without them, that murder would never have come to light. At least now the red-headed boy's family could get justice.

In the end, the deaths of Moxham and Tessa were ruled accidental. Was it kinder to Tessa's mum that she never knew the truth? I wasn't sure.

My marshmallow had turned golden brown. 'Want it?'

'Why not?' Diara took the skewer. 'Hey' – her voice came out thick; she had a hand over her mouth as she munched on the marshmallow – 'yowheeboutdanooguy?'

I laughed. 'What?'

She swallowed, giving me a grin that was part marshmallow. 'You hear about the new guy?'

'Security guard? Starts tomorrow, right?'

Diara waggled her eyebrows. 'Got hold of his CV.' She waved her phone in the air.

'Let me see it then.' I was irritated Kip had hired him directly, without consulting me. I imagined the security guard would be a grizzled former policeman type who fancied a jaunt in the tropics. But the photo on Diara's phone showed a handsome, smiling Chinese man. His cheeks had a bronze glow, turning to shadow at his jaw as black stubble grew in.

The photo didn't show the wave tattoo crashing across his muscular chest. It didn't show him playing card tricks. It didn't show the way he'd kiss my neck and turn me to liquid.

He hadn't stopped looking. Of course he'd found me.

My first instinct was to leave, but I couldn't do that. No more running. No more hiding.

Could we be happy together here? That had been his dream for us; a world of our own, somewhere hot and beautiful. But could I forgive him? Could I forgive myself, for what I'd asked him to do?

Despite everything, Nathan felt like home.

I wanted that fresh start Kip had promised. This was my island now.

EPILOGUE

Six weeks previously

The phone was ringing and Shadow was going nuts.

'*Shush,*' she said out of the corner of her mouth. 'Hello?' She didn't recognise the number.

The Alsatian quieted, nosing between her legs.

'You're a difficult woman to find.' The voice on the other end was male.

'Sorry?'

'Reeling you in has taken some effort.' His accent was Australian, the smirk in his voice unmistakable.

'You have the wrong number.' She almost hung up, but the certainty in his tone stopped her.

'C'mon now, I don't wanna play games.'

'I don't know what you're talking about.'

She glanced around her living room, struck by a crazed notion that everything was fake. Her cosy chalet with its mountain views was a sound stage. Forcing a deep breath, she dug her fingers into Shadow's fur, scratching under his chin. This was her real life now. No one could take it from her.

'My question is,' he said, 'does your husband know you're still alive?'

'I don't have a husband.'

His laugh had no humour in it. 'If he does, he's an even better liar than I thought. If he doesn't... well, that makes you a fascinating individual, Meredith.'

She hadn't been Meredith for a decade. Meredith was a pathetic figure; cheated on, lied to, for years and years and years. All the shame, the humiliation. Her death had been the ultimate revenge on a husband who'd never loved her enough.

'Don't call me that.'

'How much is it worth?'

It was the sort of question Kip would have asked, delivered with one of those ravishing smiles. Her husband had never understood that not everything had a financial value.

Freedom, for instance, was priceless.

She wired a payment to the man on the phone, against her better instincts. What if she was on the hook forever? The man would return, asking for more. She'd already been blackmailed once before, in a shambling sort of way, by the official in Caracas who'd agreed to ID a bloated Jane Doe as her. Money could make these things go away.

Weeks passed and the Australian man didn't call again. Her relief was tempered with agitation, with a pulse of excitement. Now that it had happened once, it was only a matter of time before someone else found her.

She couldn't stay dead forever. One day, a new, stronger Meredith Clement would come back to life.

ACKNOWLEDGEMENTS

First of all, thank you (yes, you) for reading! If you'd like to keep reading, with free bonus material about these characters, please sign up to my e-newsletter at: nicolamartin.com

I owe a debt of gratitude to everyone involved in the editing and publishing of this book.

My literary agent, Sandra Sawicka, has a razor-sharp ability to identify what's working about a story (and what's not). Truly, this novel wouldn't exist without her.

Therese Keating put this book through boot camp, and I'm grateful for her witty and incisive comments. The whole team at Raven Books and Bloomsbury have been wonderful. Thank you to Faye Robinson, Emily Jones, Josephine Lane, Lin Vasey, Isobel Turton, Beth Maher. David Mann created a cover design that exceeded my wildest dreams.

I loved visiting the British Virgin Islands and getting to meet some of its residents. I recommend a visit. It's a lovely place to take a holiday, and it's highly unlikely you'll get murdered while you're there.

Richard Georges was my cultural sensitivity reader and I'm very grateful. Any mistakes that crept into the novel are my own.

'Let me check in with my YouTube buddies,' I'd say, of people I'd never met. Thanks to the BVI/USVI vloggers who were kind enough to share their lives with the world (and me), including Queen Sasha, Razor Empress, Charis Marie, Kariel Granger, Martina J, Andy Antonio.

I learned a lot about the dirty laundry of the hospitality trade from Imogen Edwards-Jones and her anonymous sources in the Babylon series of books, particularly *Beach Babylon*.

My writer friends, who gave invaluable feedback on parts of this novel as I was writing it, include Nadia Morris, Helen Fell, Joanne Stubbs, Ruby Vallis, Sara Nunn and Molly Walker. Tara Mahoney offered a last-minute sense-check.

My parents only want me to be happy, regardless of whether or not I've finished my next novel. My sister, Holly, is the voice in my ear saying: 'Could there be food in this scene? Could they be eating something delicious?'

Cheers, all.

A NOTE ON THE AUTHOR

NICOLA MARTIN studied at the University of East Anglia and the University of California, Berkeley. She lives in Bristol, where she works as a marketing manager and freelance writer. Her first novel, *Dead Ringer*, published by Saraband, won the Fiction Prize at the 2021 Lakeland Book of the Year Awards.

A NOTE ON THE TYPE

The text of this book is set in Fournier. Fournier is derived from the *romain du roi*, which was created towards the end of the seventeenth century from designs made by a committee of the Académie of Sciences for the exclusive use of the Imprimerie Royale. The original Fournier types were cut by the famous Paris founder Pierre Simon Fournier in about 1742. These types were some of the most influential designs of the eight and are counted among the earliest examples of the 'transitional' style of typeface. This Monotype version dates from 1924. Fournier is a light, clear face whose distinctive features are capital letters that are quite tall and bold in relation to the lower-case letters, and *decorative italics, which show the influence of the calligraphy of Fournier's time.*